GLAM PRIX RACERS

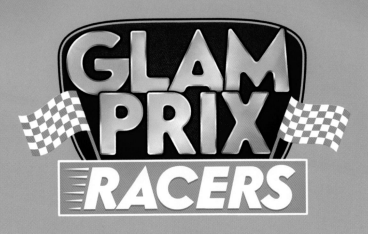

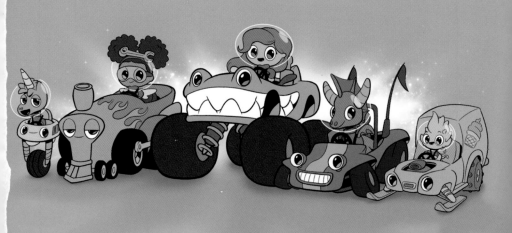

Also by Deanna Kent and Neil Hooson

Snazzy Cat Capers

Snazzy Cat Capers: The Fast and the Furriest

Snazzy Cat Capers: Meow or Never

For Sam, Max, Zach, Jake, Jackson, Ethan, Ella, Anna, Colton, Charlotte, Claire, Dean, Mackenzie, Parker, Tanner, Finn, Kristie, Mike, Rich, Kerri, Kim, Rob, Ophelia, Oscar, our parents & parental types, friends, librarians, and everyone who believes that sparkle and teamwork make the world more wonderful.

[Imprint]
MAKE YOUR MARK

A part of Macmillan Publishing Group, LLC

120 Broadway, New York, NY 10271

Library of Congress Cataloging-in-Publication Data

Names: Kent, Deanna, author. | Hooson, Neil, illustrator.
Title: Glam Prix racers / written by Deanna Kent ; illustrated by Neil Hooson.
Description: First edition. | New York : Imprint, 2021. | Series: Glam Prix racers | Audience: Ages 7—10. |
Audience: Grades 2—3. | Summary: Mio the mermaid, her monster truck Mudwick, and their team from Glittergear
Island compete for the magical Glam Prix Cup against the Cyclops Camper Crew and the Vroombots, who have diabolical plans.
Identifiers: LCCN 2020041006 | ISBN 9781250265388 (hardback)
Subjects: LCSH: Graphic novels. | CYAC: Graphic novels. | Automobile racing — Fiction. | Imaginary creatures — Fiction. |
Motor vehicles — Fiction. Classification: LCC PZ7.7.K454 Gl 2021 | DDC 741.5/973 — dc23
LC record available at https://lccn.loc.gov/2020041006

ISBN 978-1-250-26538-8 (hardcover) / ISBN 978-1-250-26539-5 (ebook)

Our books may be purchased in bulk for promotional, educational, or business use.
Please contact your local bookseller or the Macmillan Corporate and
Premium Sales Department at (800) 221-7945 ext. 5442 or by email
at MacmillanSpecialMarkets@macmillan.com.

Book design by Neil Hooson and Elynn Cohen

Illustrations by Neil Hooson

Imprint logo designed by Amanda Spielman

First edition, 2021

1 3 5 7 9 10 8 6 4 2

mackids.com

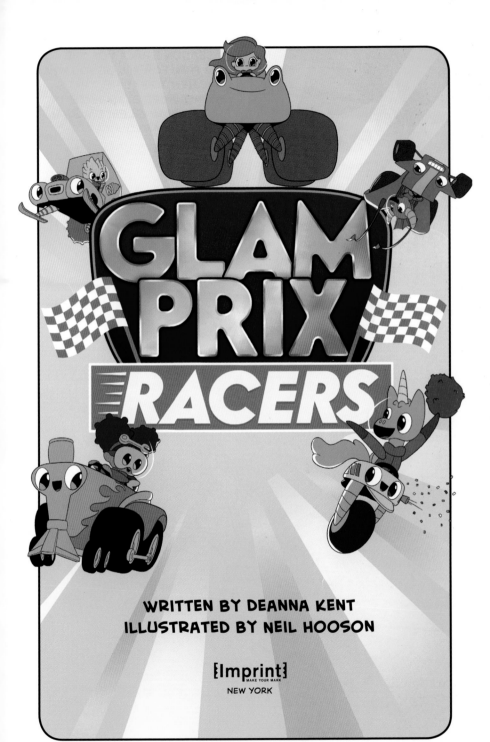

GLAM PRIX RACERS

WRITTEN BY DEANNA KENT
ILLUSTRATED BY NEIL HOOSON

{Imprint}
MAKE YOUR MARK
NEW YORK

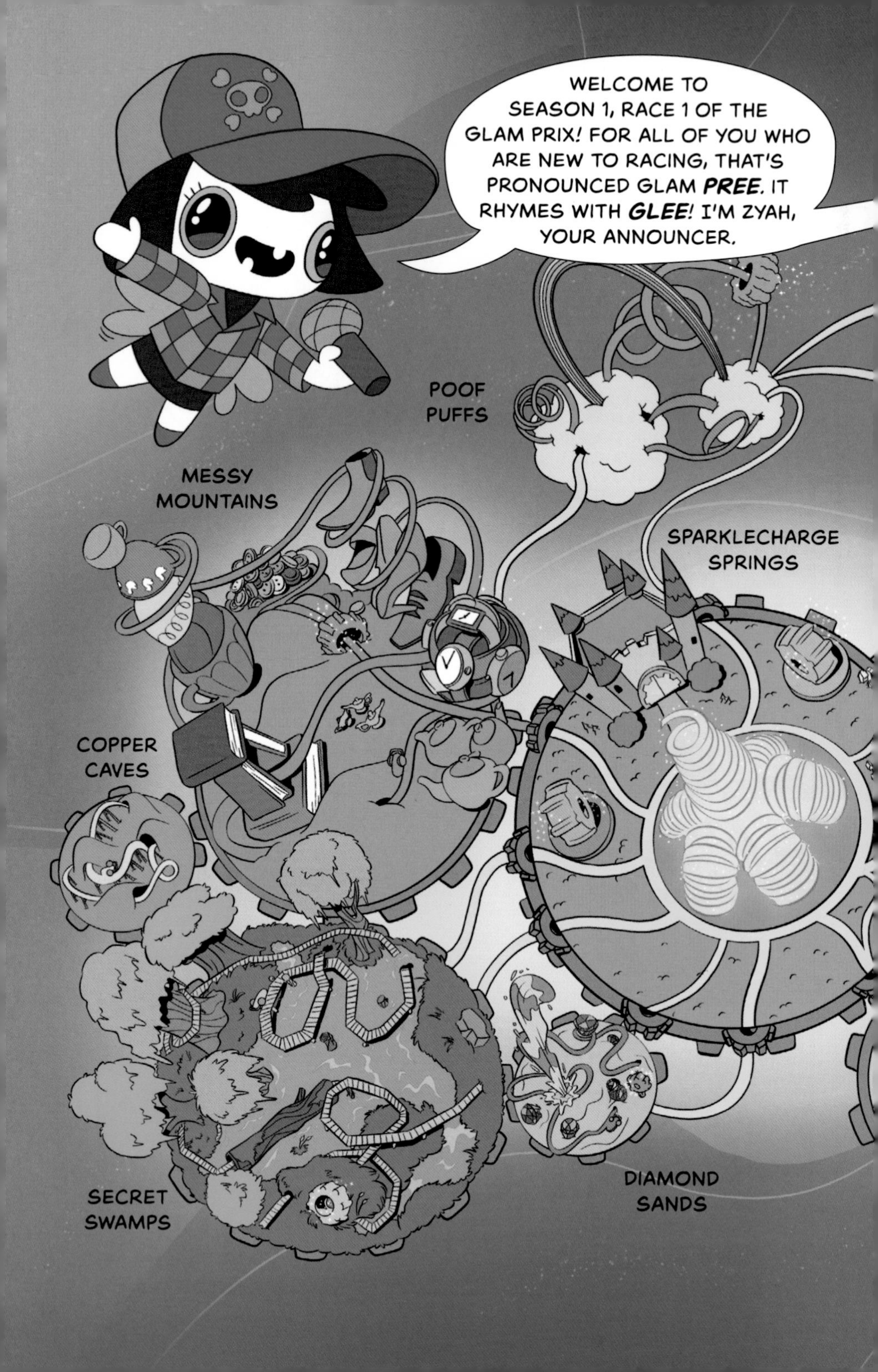
WELCOME TO SEASON 1, RACE 1 OF THE GLAM PRIX! FOR ALL OF YOU WHO ARE NEW TO RACING, THAT'S PRONOUNCED GLAM **PREE**. IT RHYMES WITH **GLEE**! I'M ZYAH, YOUR ANNOUNCER.
POOF PUFFS
MESSY MOUNTAINS
SPARKLECHARGE SPRINGS
COPPER CAVES
SECRET SWAMPS
DIAMOND SANDS

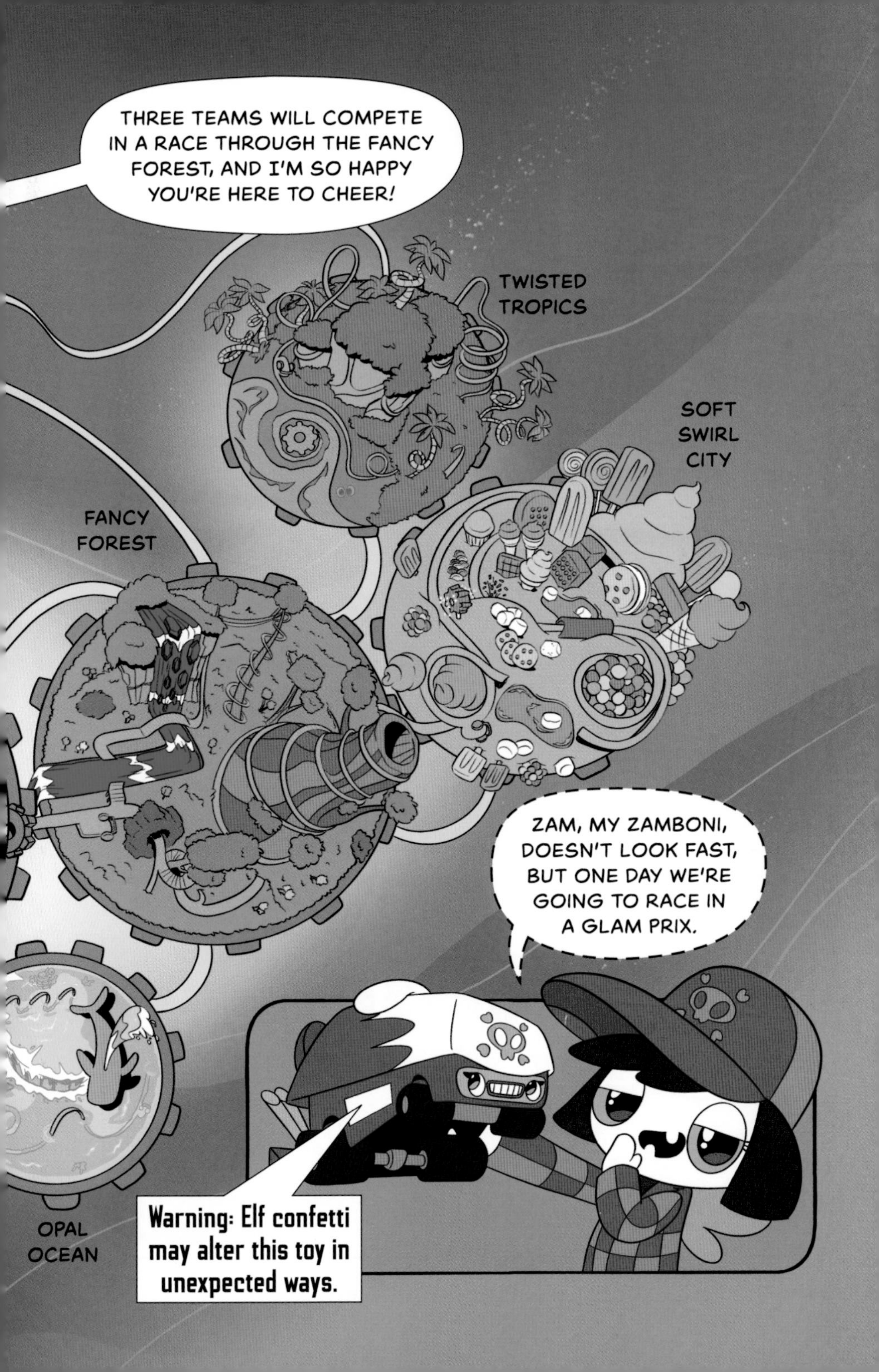
THREE TEAMS WILL COMPETE IN A RACE THROUGH THE FANCY FOREST, AND I'M SO HAPPY YOU'RE HERE TO CHEER!
TWISTED TROPICS
SOFT SWIRL CITY
FANCY FOREST
ZAM, MY ZAMBONI, DOESN'T LOOK FAST, BUT ONE DAY WE'RE GOING TO RACE IN A GLAM PRIX.
Warning: Elf confetti may alter this toy in unexpected ways.
OPAL OCEAN

MEET THE GLAM PRIX RACERS, A TERRIFIC TEAM OF TEN WHO WILL RACE OTHER CREWS TO TRY AND WIN THE GLAM PRIX CUP.

WILL THIS RACE CREW BE ABLE TO NAVIGATE THROUGH THE HIGHS AND LOWS OF THE FANCY FOREST . . . AND GET TO THE FINISH LINE BEFORE THEIR COMPETITORS?

MOTTO: FIRST TO THE FINISH LINE!

MIO & MUDWICK
HOME BASE: OPAL OCEAN

SPEED	
ENGINEERING SKILL	
TRICKS	
ENERGY	
CREATIVITY	

MOTTO: BUILD IT, BREAK IT, FIX IT, RACE IT!

FLIPP & FURIE
HOME BASE: FANCY FOREST

SPEED	
ENGINEERING SKILL	
TRICKS	
ENERGY	
CREATIVITY	

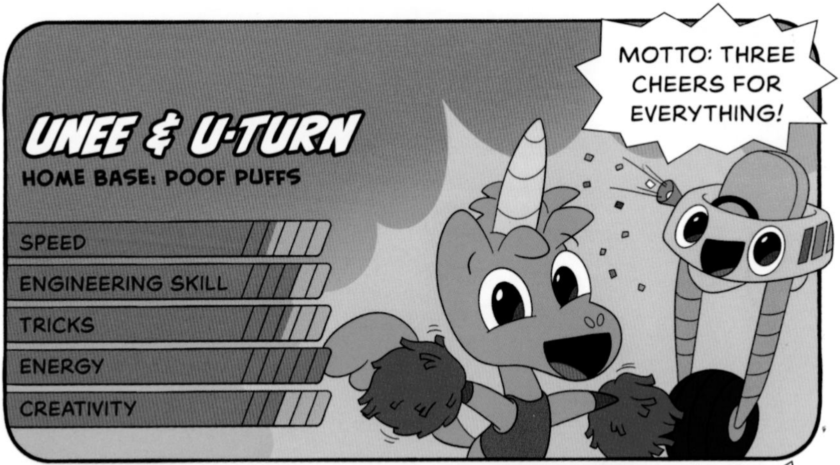
MOTTO: THREE CHEERS FOR EVERYTHING!
UNEE & U-TURN
HOME BASE: POOF PUFFS
SPEED
ENGINEERING SKILL
TRICKS
ENERGY
CREATIVITY

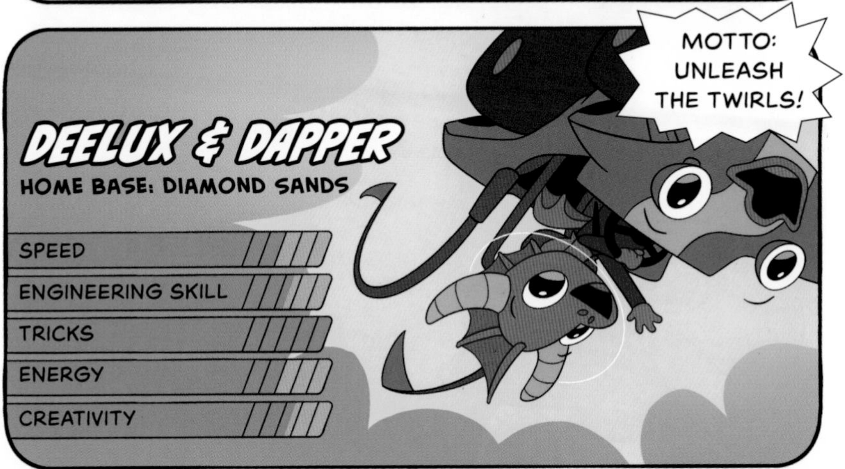
MOTTO: UNLEASH THE TWIRLS!
DEELUX & DAPPER
HOME BASE: DIAMOND SANDS
SPEED
ENGINEERING SKILL
TRICKS
ENERGY
CREATIVITY

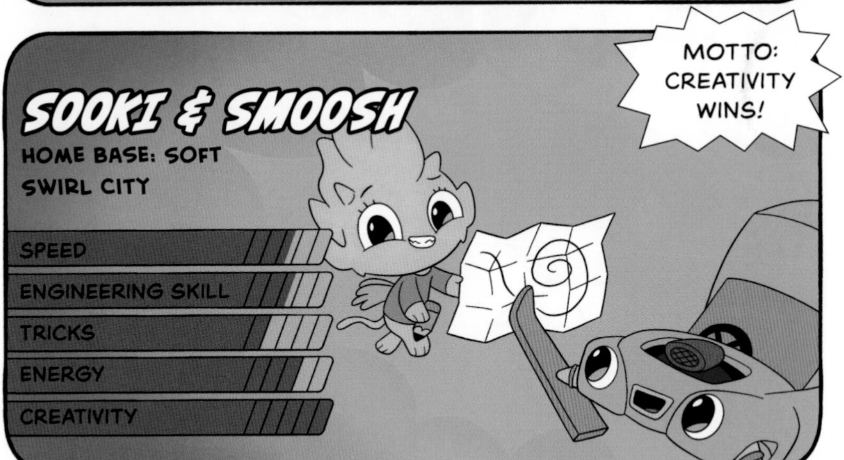
MOTTO: CREATIVITY WINS!
SOOKI & SMOOSH
HOME BASE: SOFT SWIRL CITY
SPEED
ENGINEERING SKILL
TRICKS
ENERGY
CREATIVITY

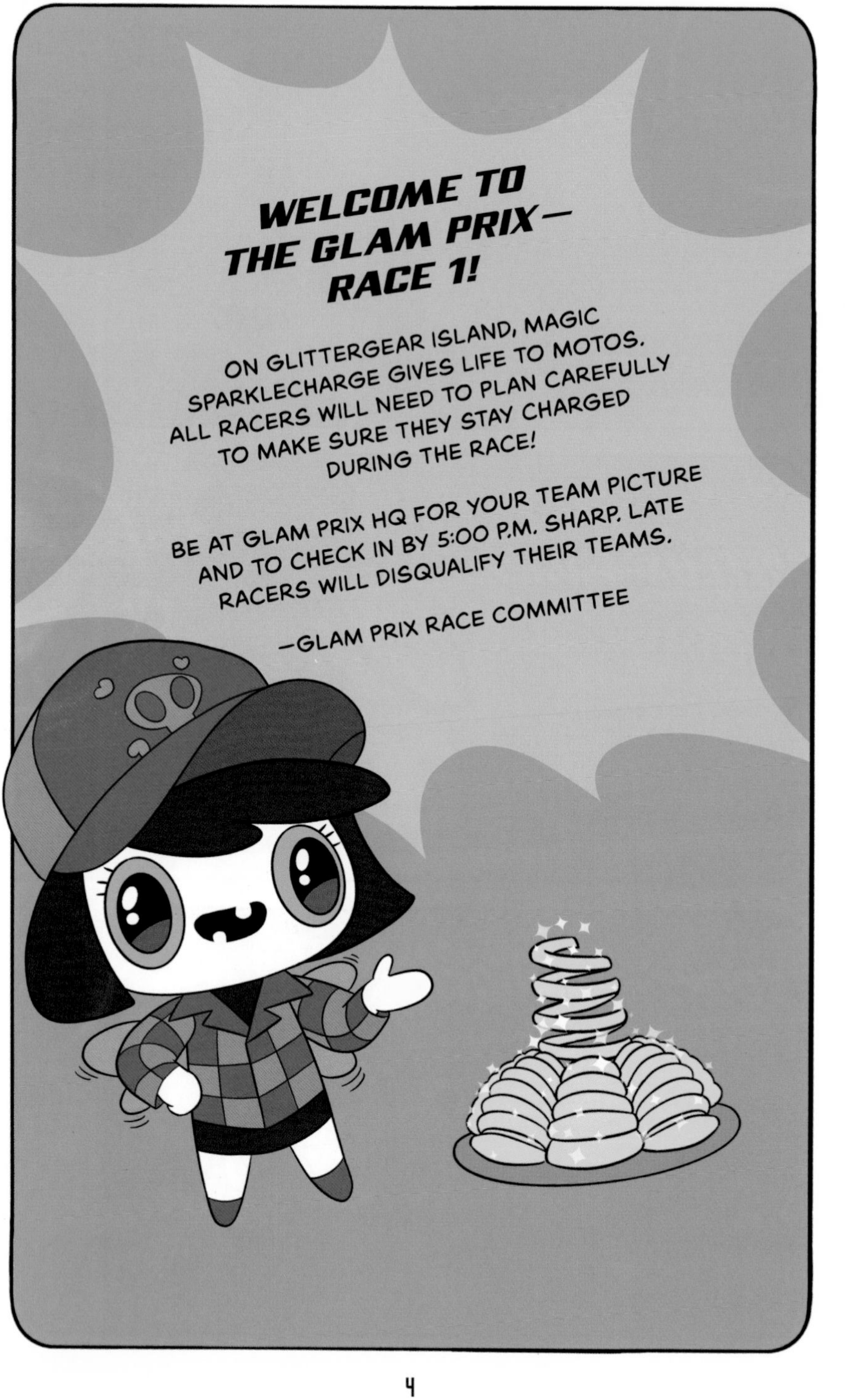
WELCOME TO THE GLAM PRIX—RACE 1!
ON GLITTERGEAR ISLAND, MAGIC SPARKLECHARGE GIVES LIFE TO MOTOS. ALL RACERS WILL NEED TO PLAN CAREFULLY TO MAKE SURE THEY STAY CHARGED DURING THE RACE!
BE AT GLAM PRIX HQ FOR YOUR TEAM PICTURE AND TO CHECK IN BY 5:00 P.M. SHARP. LATE RACERS WILL DISQUALIFY THEIR TEAMS.
—GLAM PRIX RACE COMMITTEE

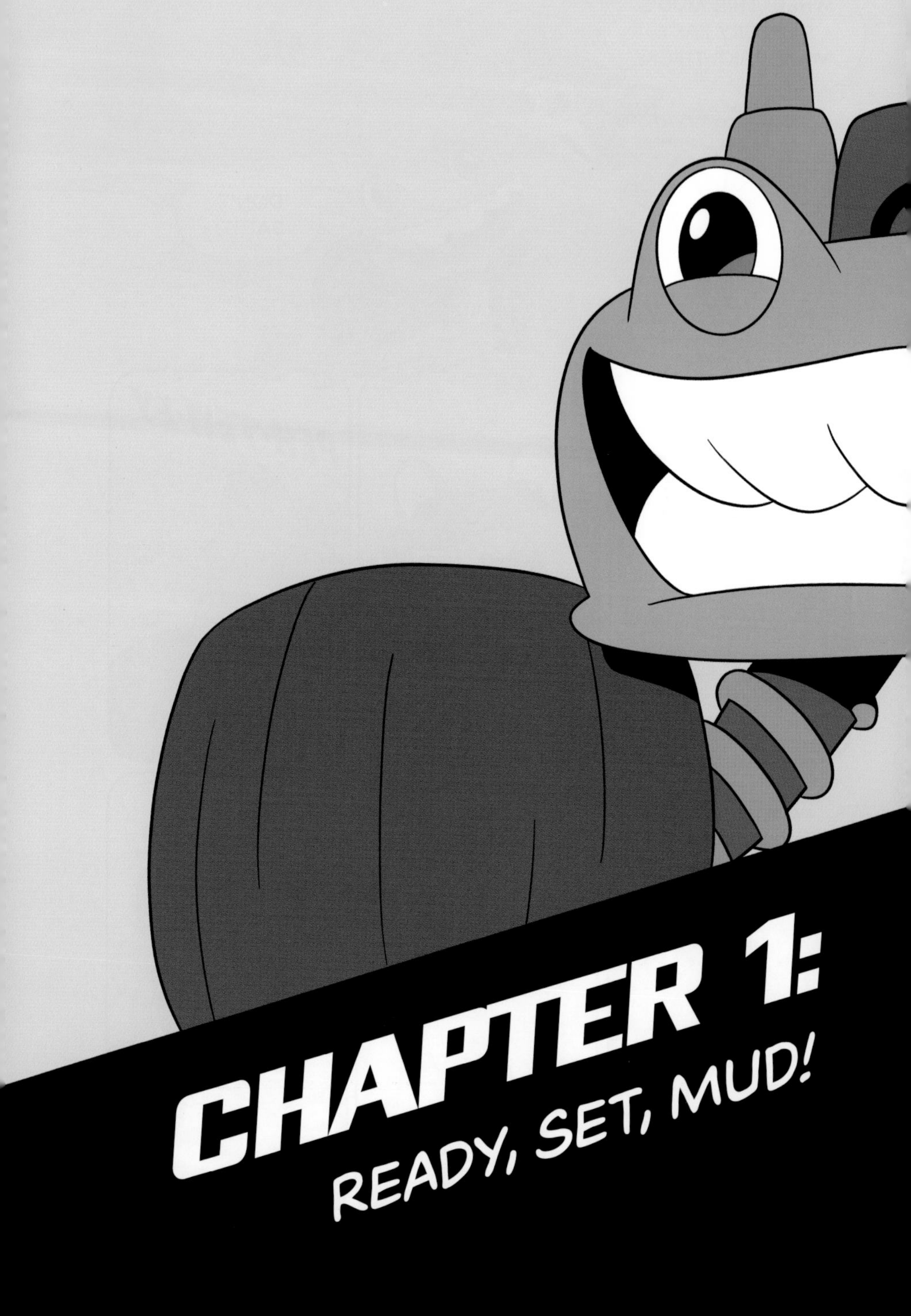

CHAPTER 1:
READY, SET, MUD!

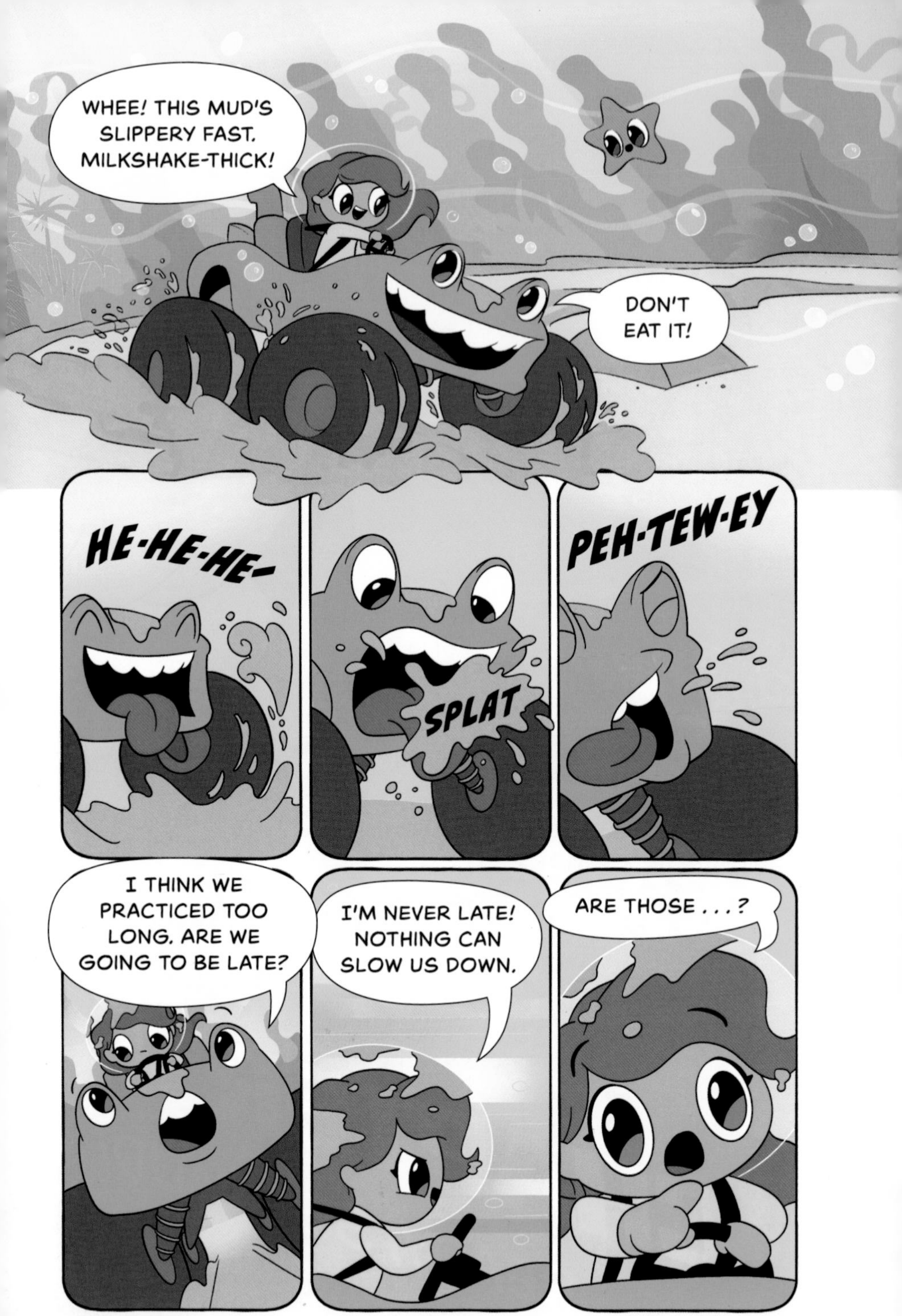
WHEE! THIS MUD'S SLIPPERY FAST. MILKSHAKE-THICK!
DON'T EAT IT!
HE-HE-HE-
SPLAT
PEH-TEW-EY
I THINK WE PRACTICED TOO LONG. ARE WE GOING TO BE LATE?
I'M NEVER LATE! NOTHING CAN SLOW US DOWN.
ARE THOSE . . . ?

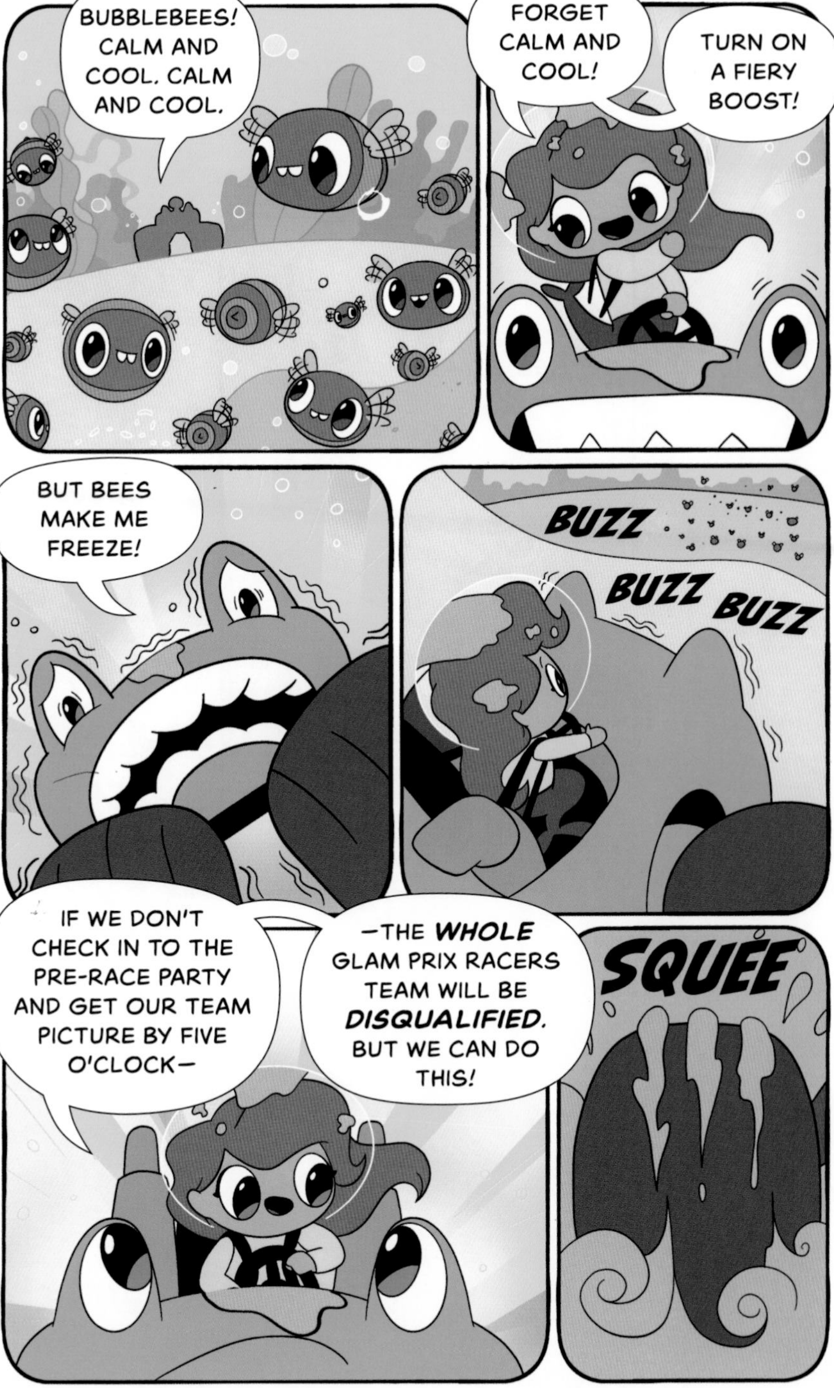
BUBBLEBEES! CALM AND COOL. CALM AND COOL.
FORGET CALM AND COOL!
TURN ON A FIERY BOOST!
BUT BEES MAKE ME FREEZE!
BUZZ
BUZZ
BUZZ
IF WE DON'T CHECK IN TO THE PRE-RACE PARTY AND GET OUR TEAM PICTURE BY FIVE O'CLOCK—
—THE *WHOLE* GLAM PRIX RACERS TEAM WILL BE ***DISQUALIFIED.*** BUT WE CAN DO THIS!
SQUEE

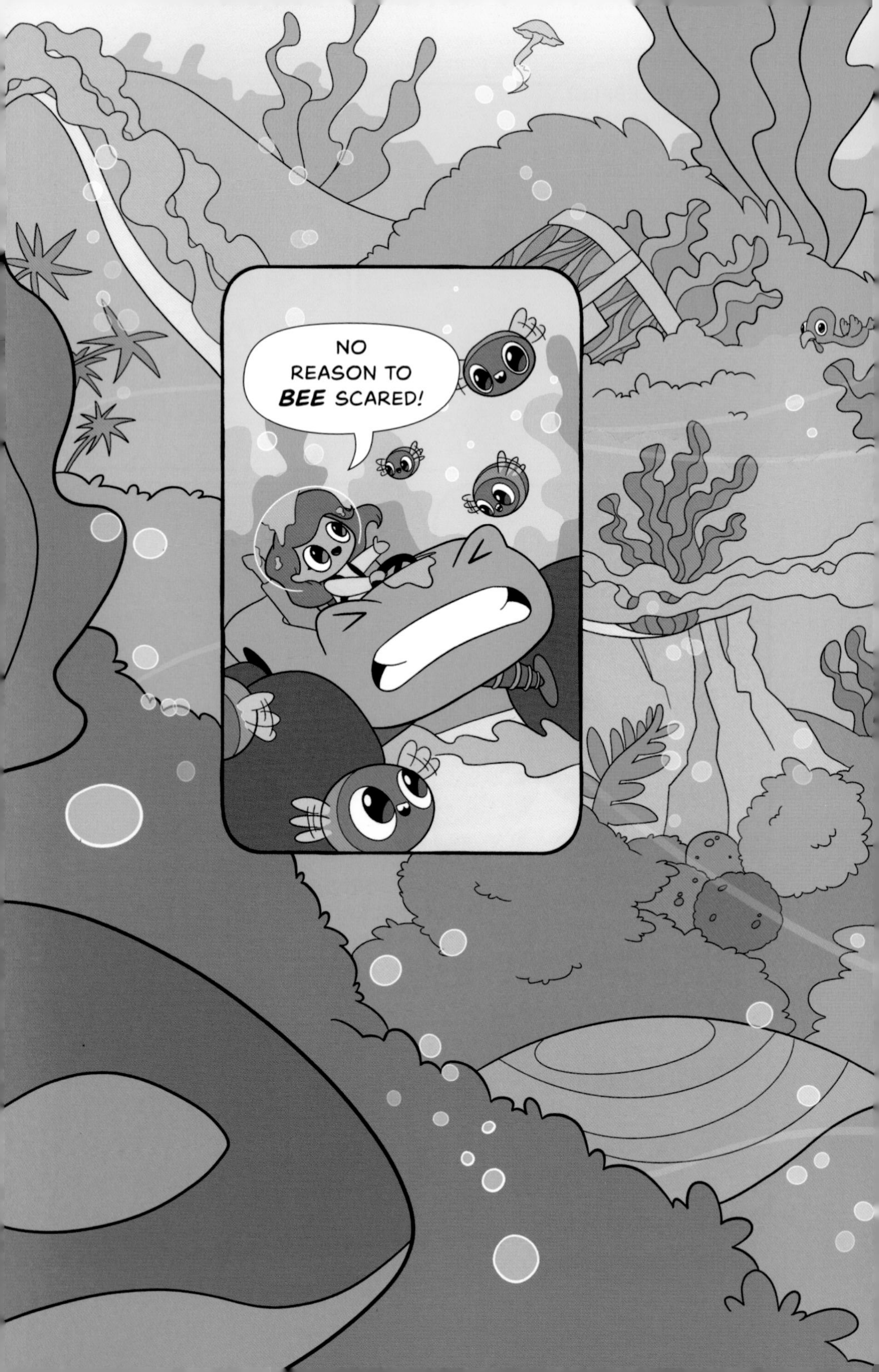
NO REASON TO **BEE** SCARED!

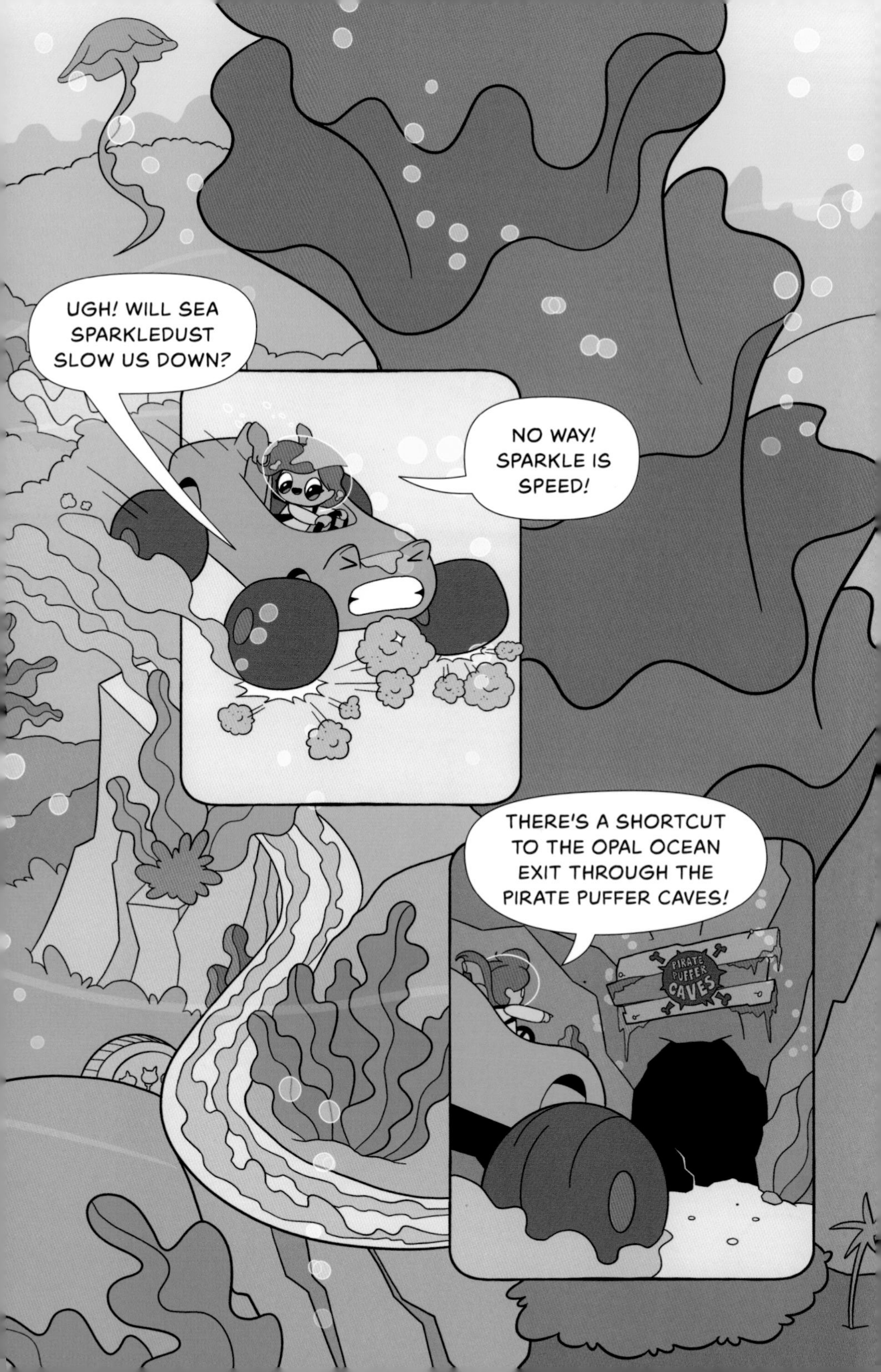
UGH! WILL SEA SPARKLEDUST SLOW US DOWN?
NO WAY! SPARKLE IS SPEED!
THERE'S A SHORTCUT TO THE OPAL OCEAN EXIT THROUGH THE PIRATE PUFFER CAVES!
PIRATE PUFFER CAVES

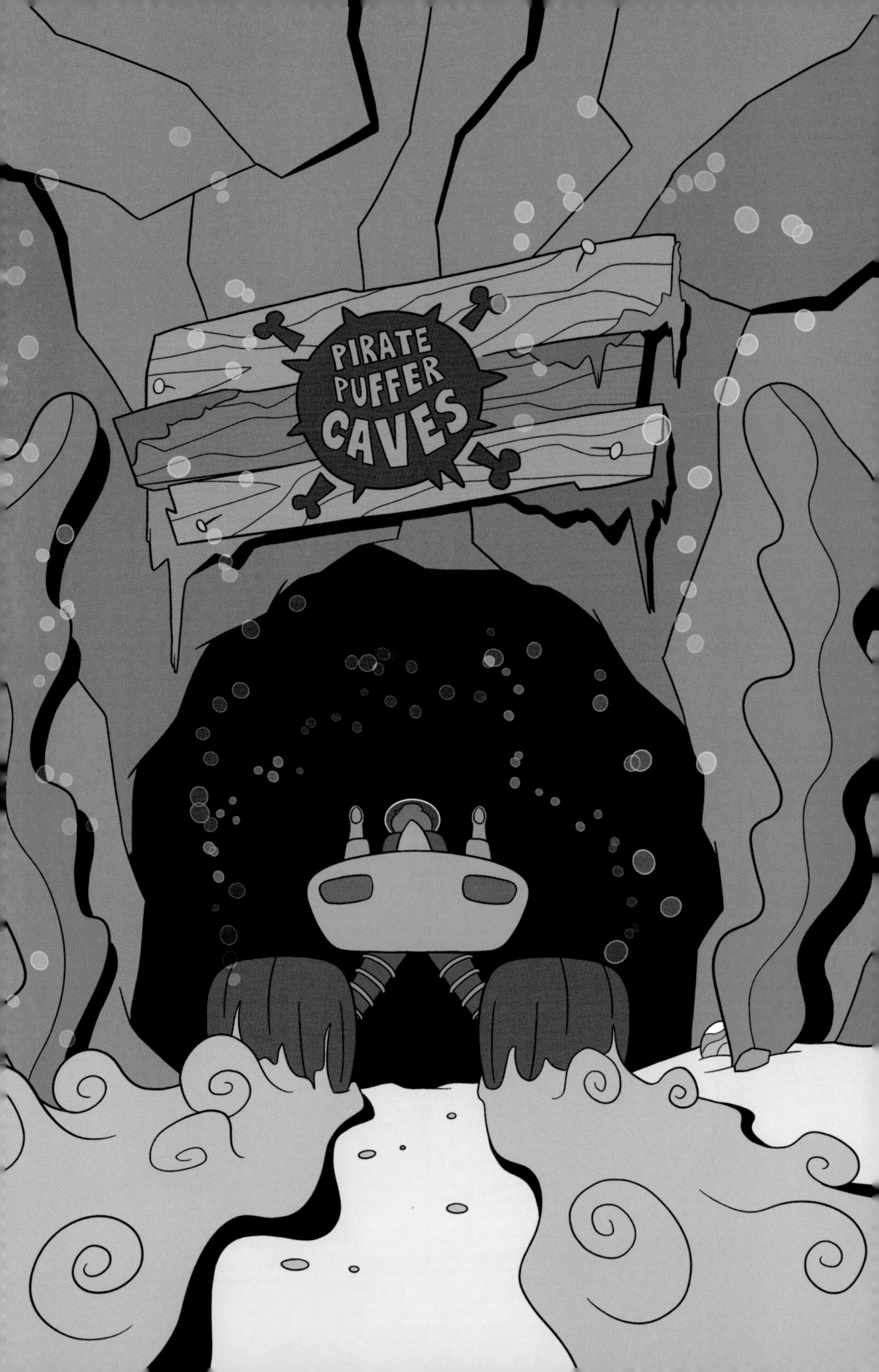
PIRATE
PUFFER
CAVES

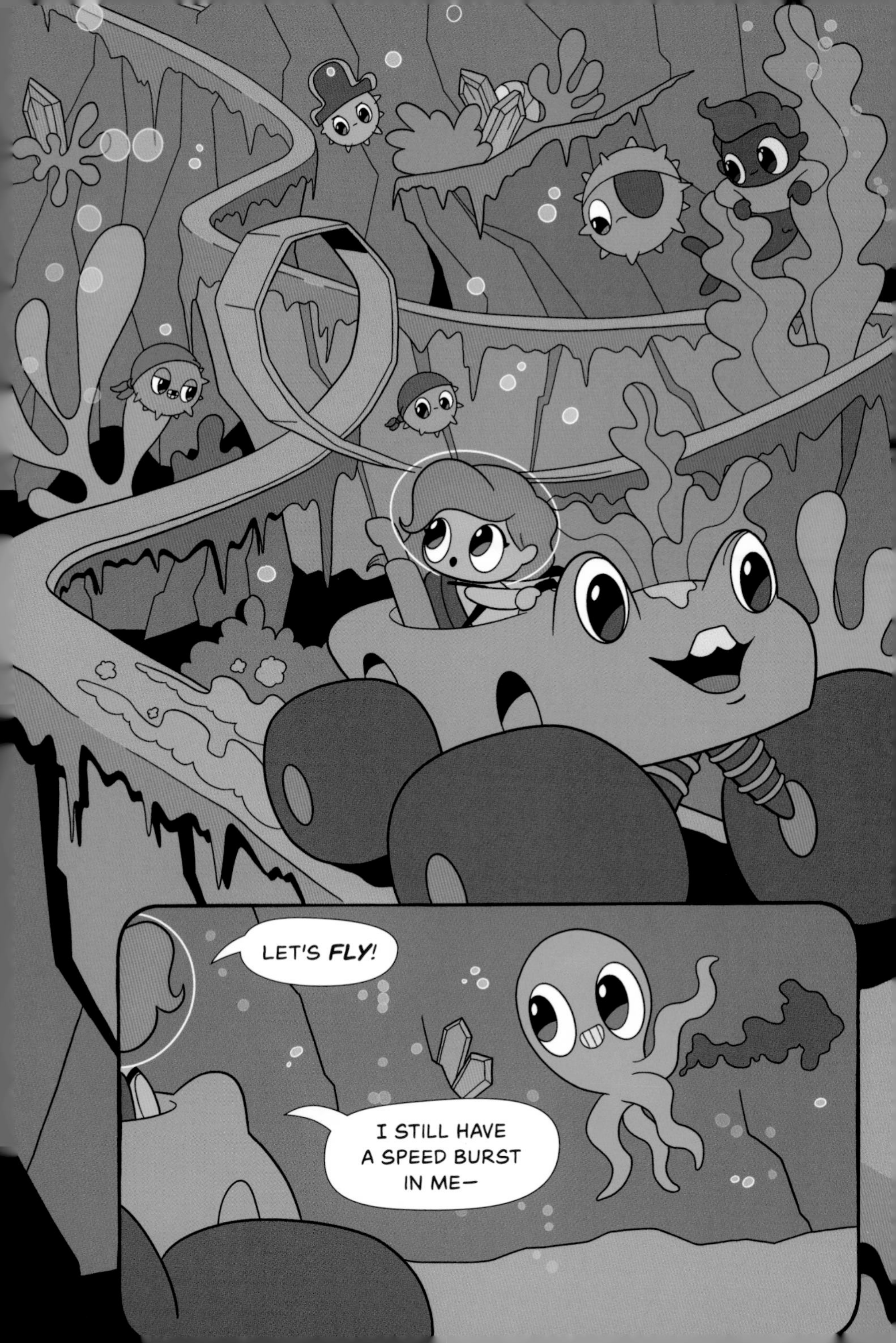
LET'S **FLY**!
I STILL HAVE A SPEED BURST IN ME—

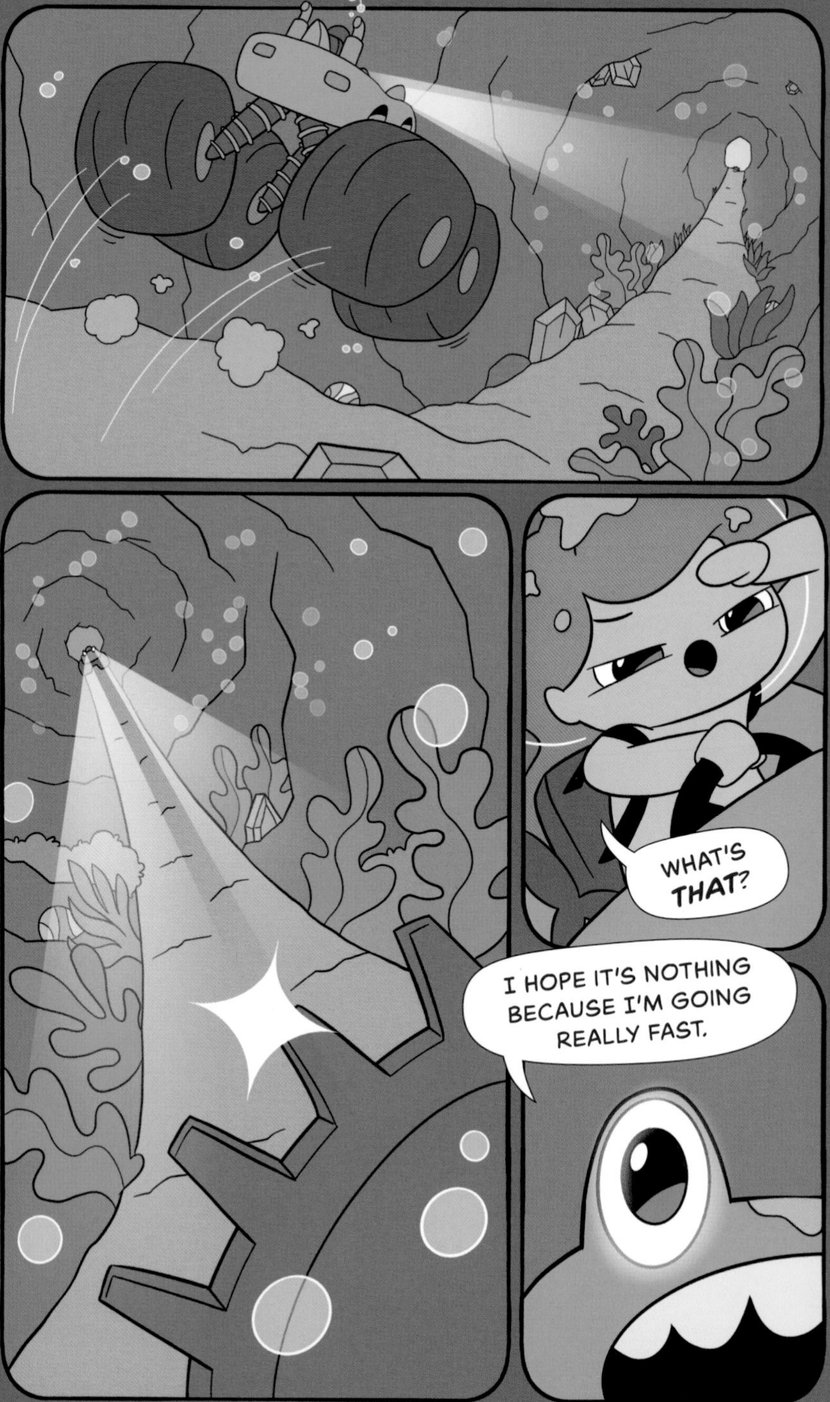
WHAT'S THAT?
I HOPE IT'S NOTHING BECAUSE I'M GOING REALLY FAST.

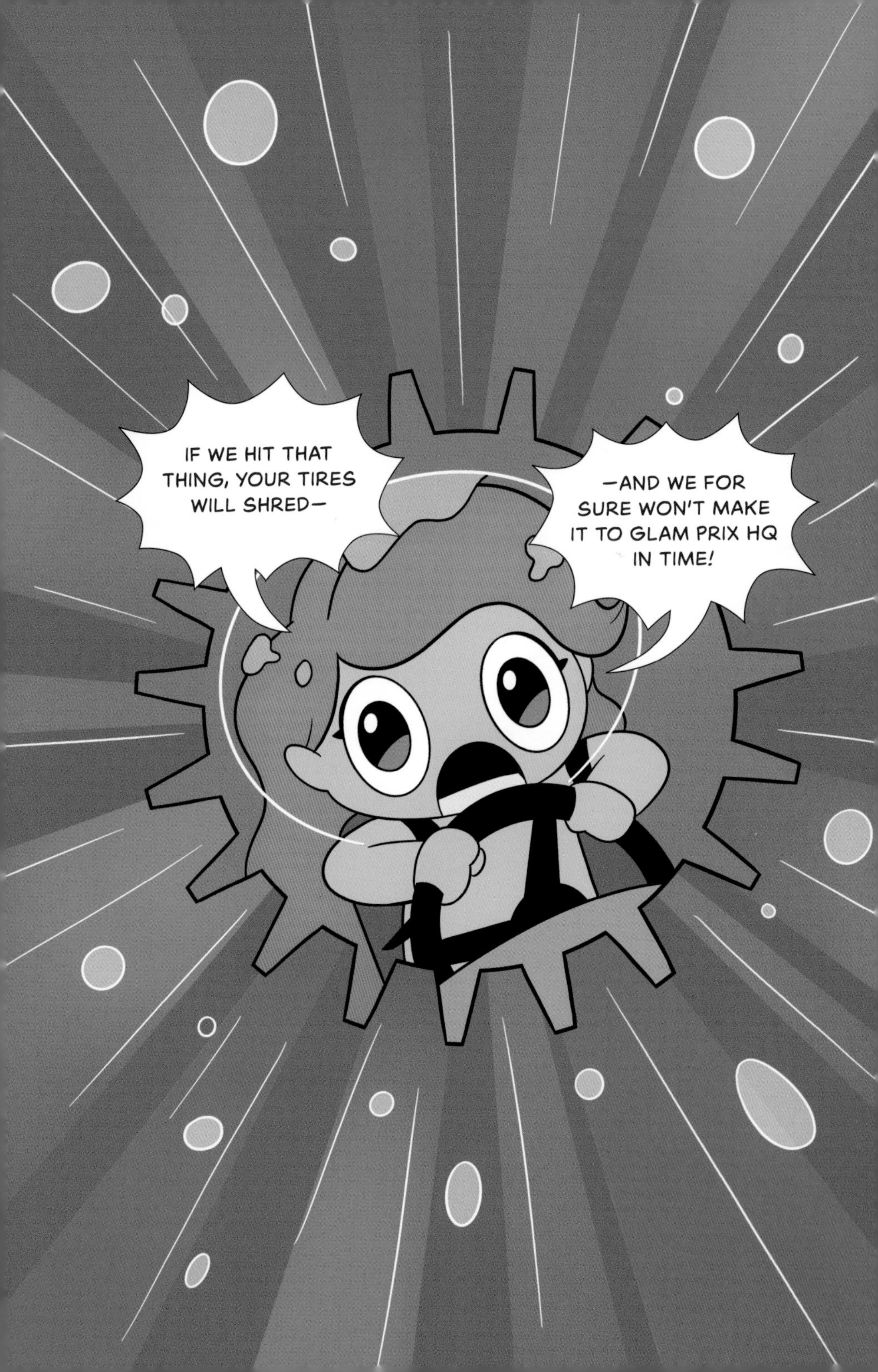
IF WE HIT THAT THING, YOUR TIRES WILL SHRED—
—AND WE FOR SURE WON'T MAKE IT TO GLAM PRIX HQ IN TIME!

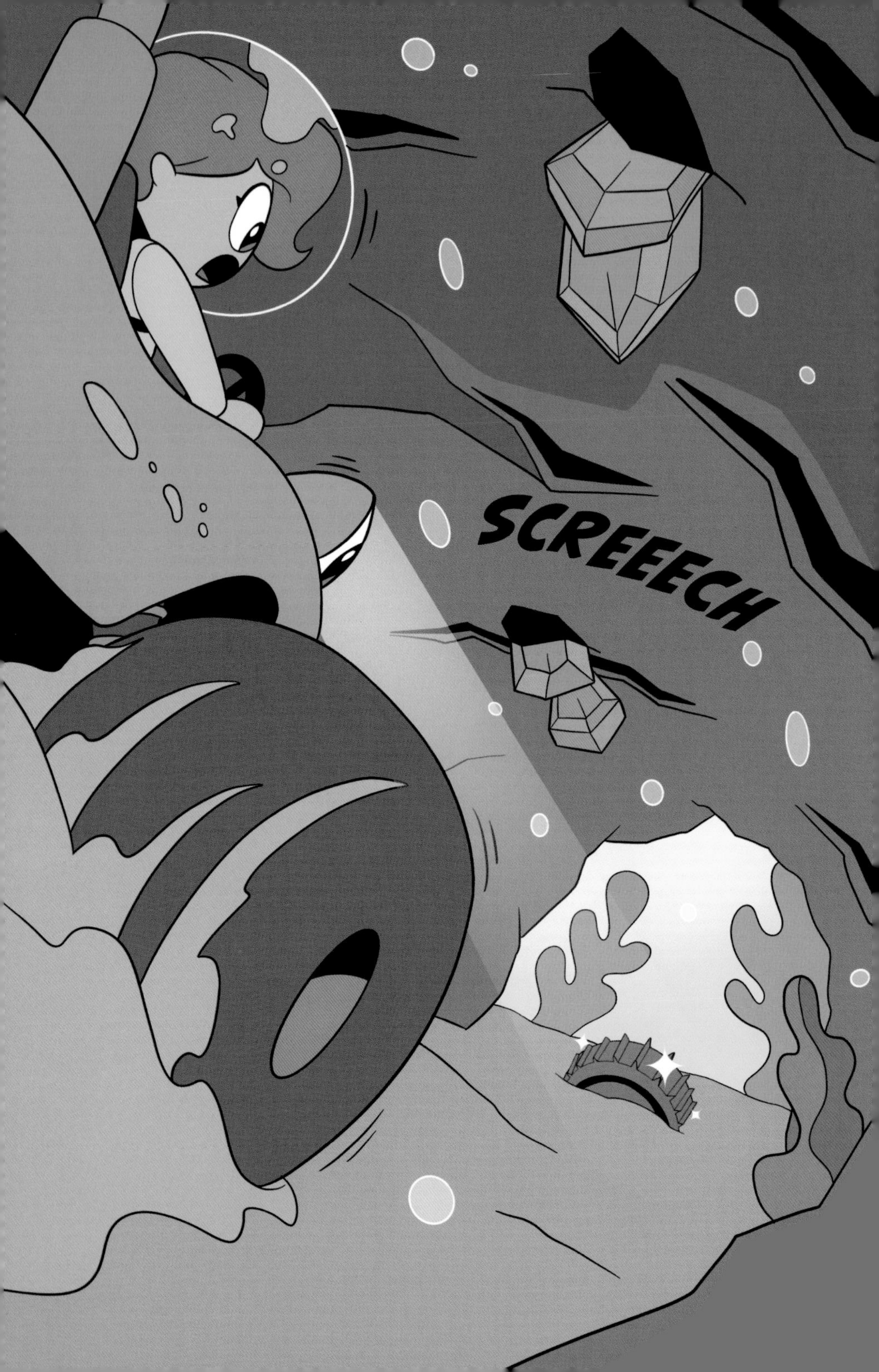
SCREEECH

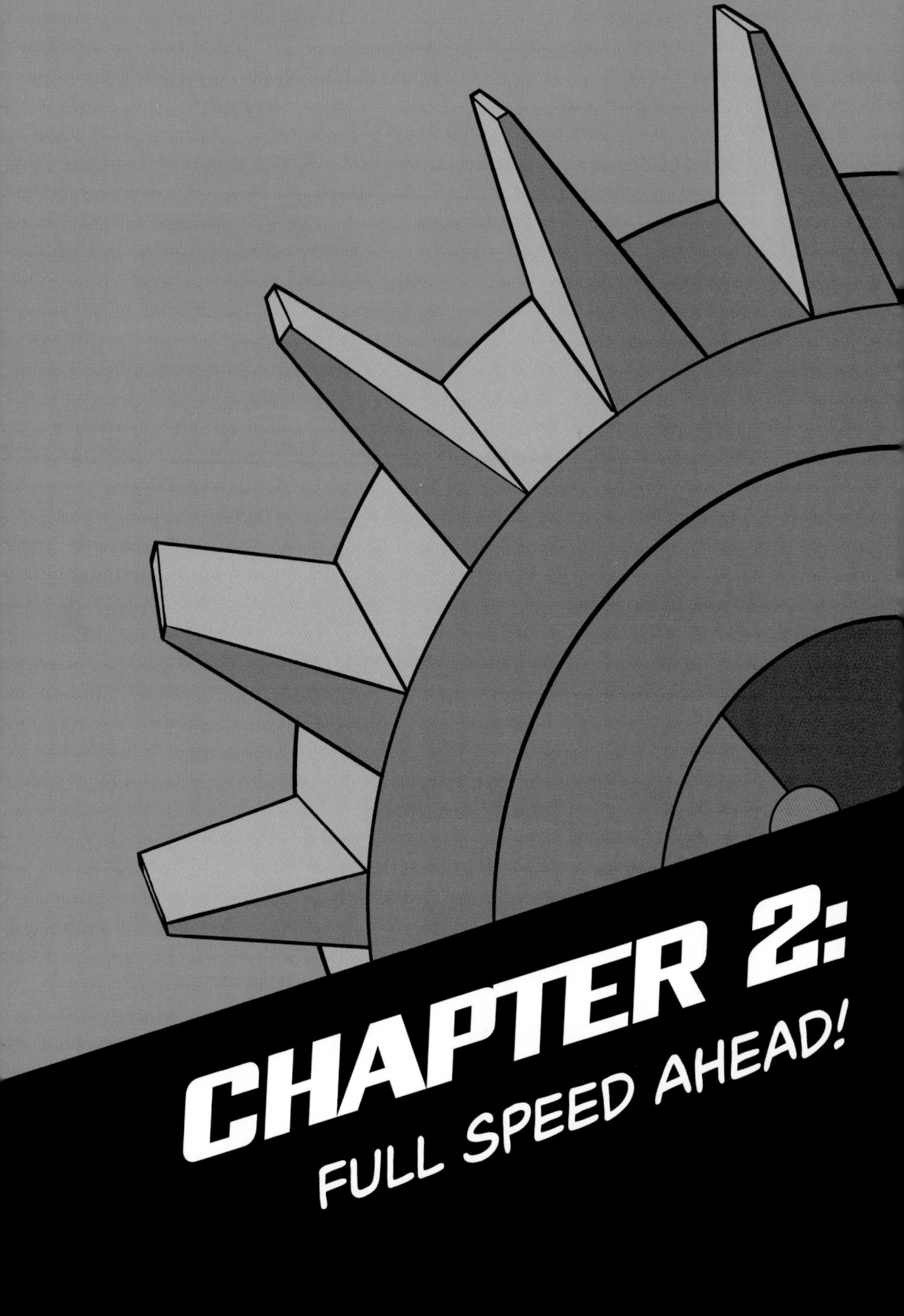

CHAPTER 2:
FULL SPEED AHEAD!

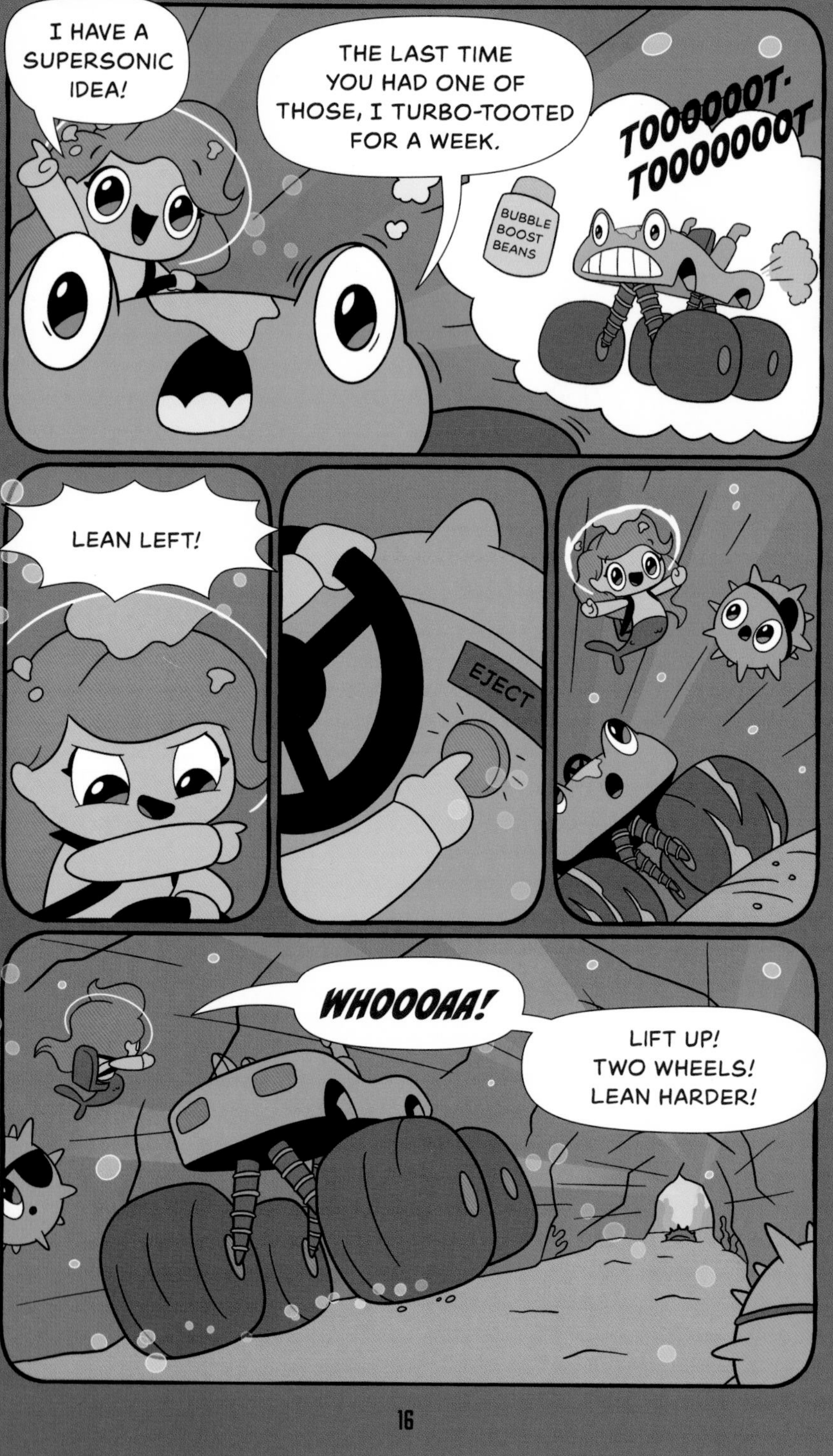
I HAVE A SUPERSONIC IDEA!
THE LAST TIME YOU HAD ONE OF THOSE, I TURBO-TOOTED FOR A WEEK.
TOOOOOOT-TOOOOOOOT
BUBBLE BOOST BEANS
LEAN LEFT!
EJECT
WHOOOAA!
LIFT UP! TWO WHEELS! LEAN HARDER!

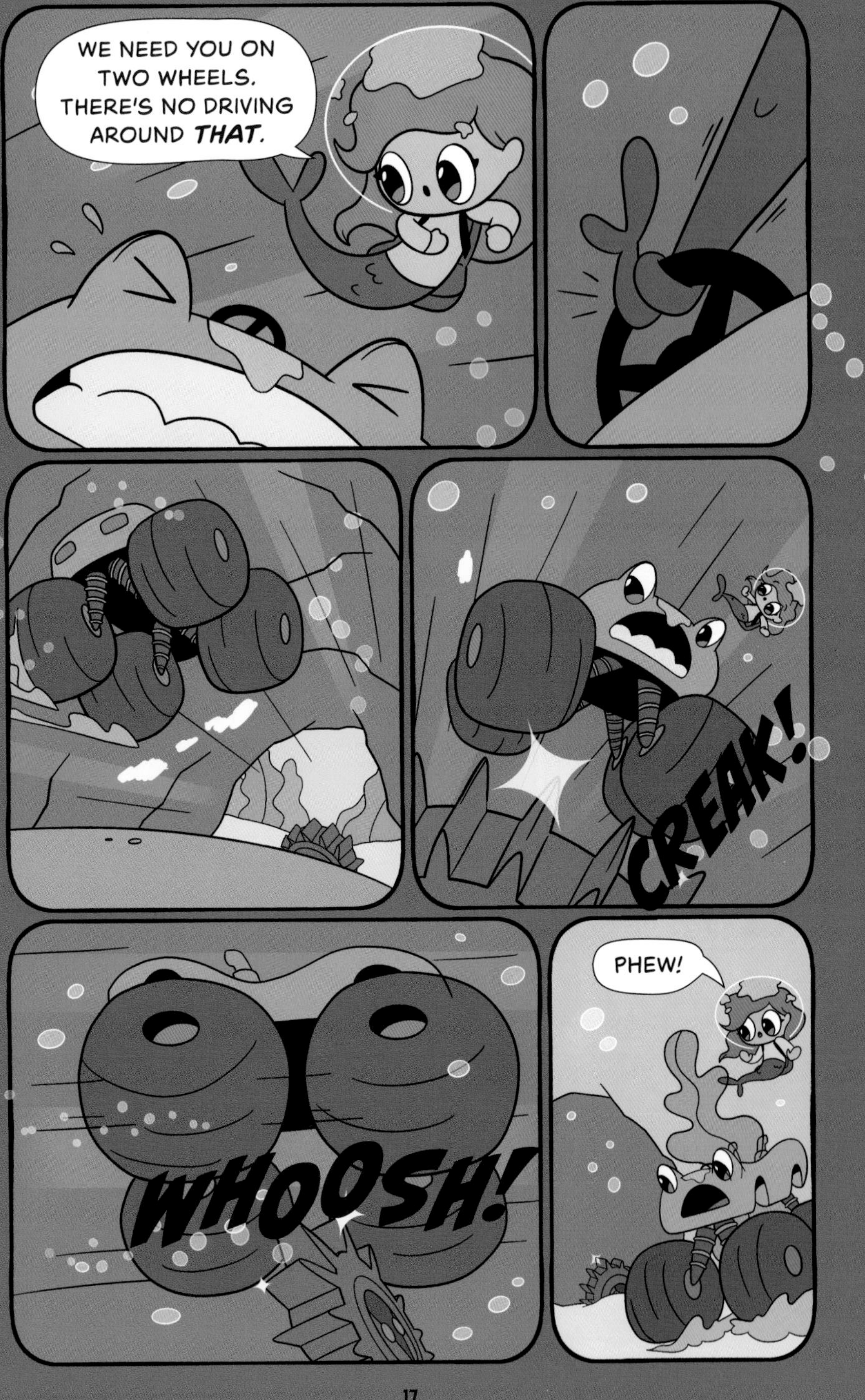
WE NEED YOU ON TWO WHEELS. THERE'S NO DRIVING AROUND THAT.
CREAK!
WHOOSH!
PHEW!

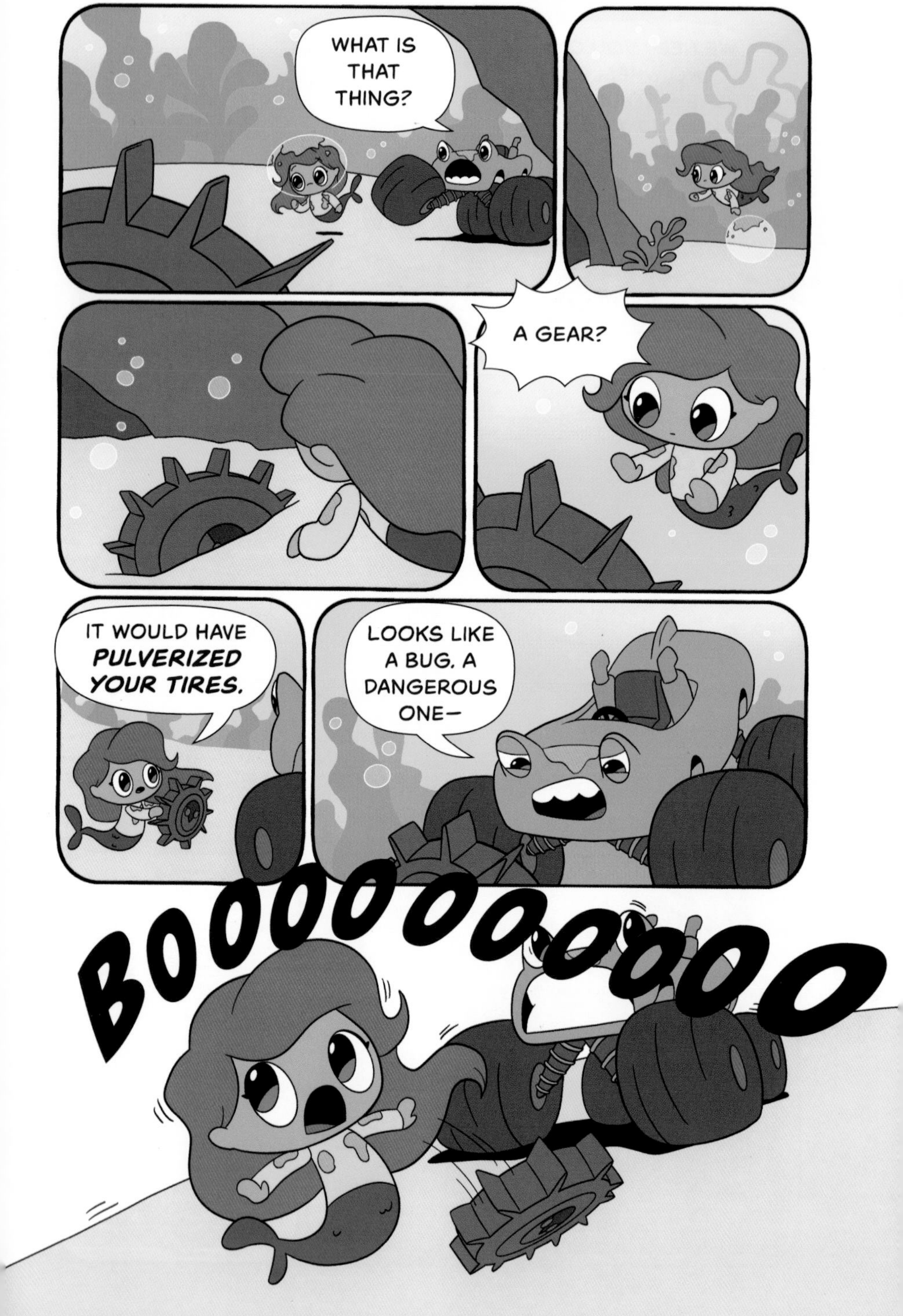
WHAT IS THAT THING?
A GEAR?
IT WOULD HAVE *PULVERIZED YOUR TIRES.*
LOOKS LIKE A BUG. A DANGEROUS ONE—
BOOOOOOOOOO

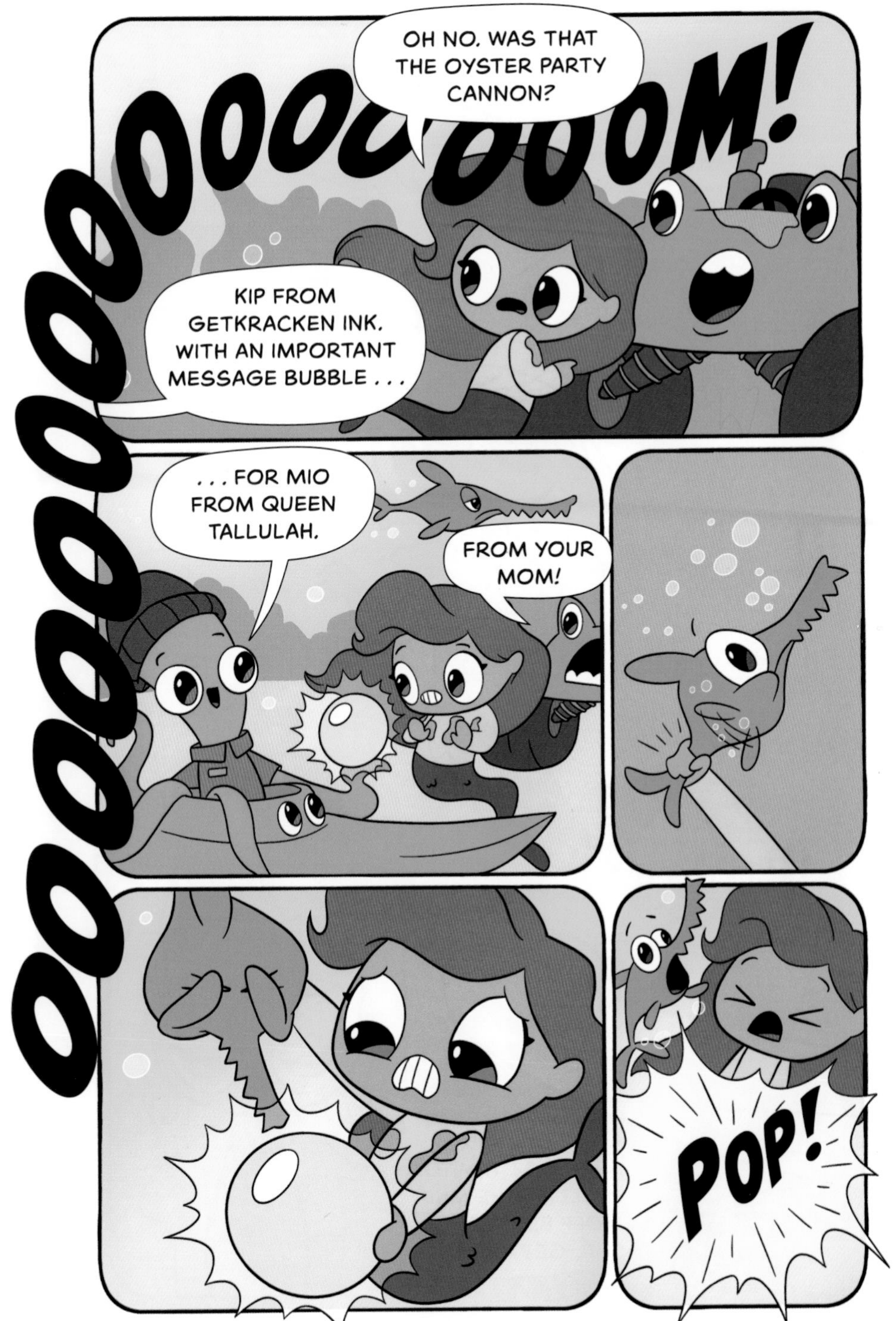
OOOOOOOOOOOOOOOM!
OH NO. WAS THAT THE OYSTER PARTY CANNON?
KIP FROM GETKRACKEN INK. WITH AN IMPORTANT MESSAGE BUBBLE . . .
. . . FOR MIO FROM QUEEN TALLULAH.
FROM YOUR MOM!
POP!

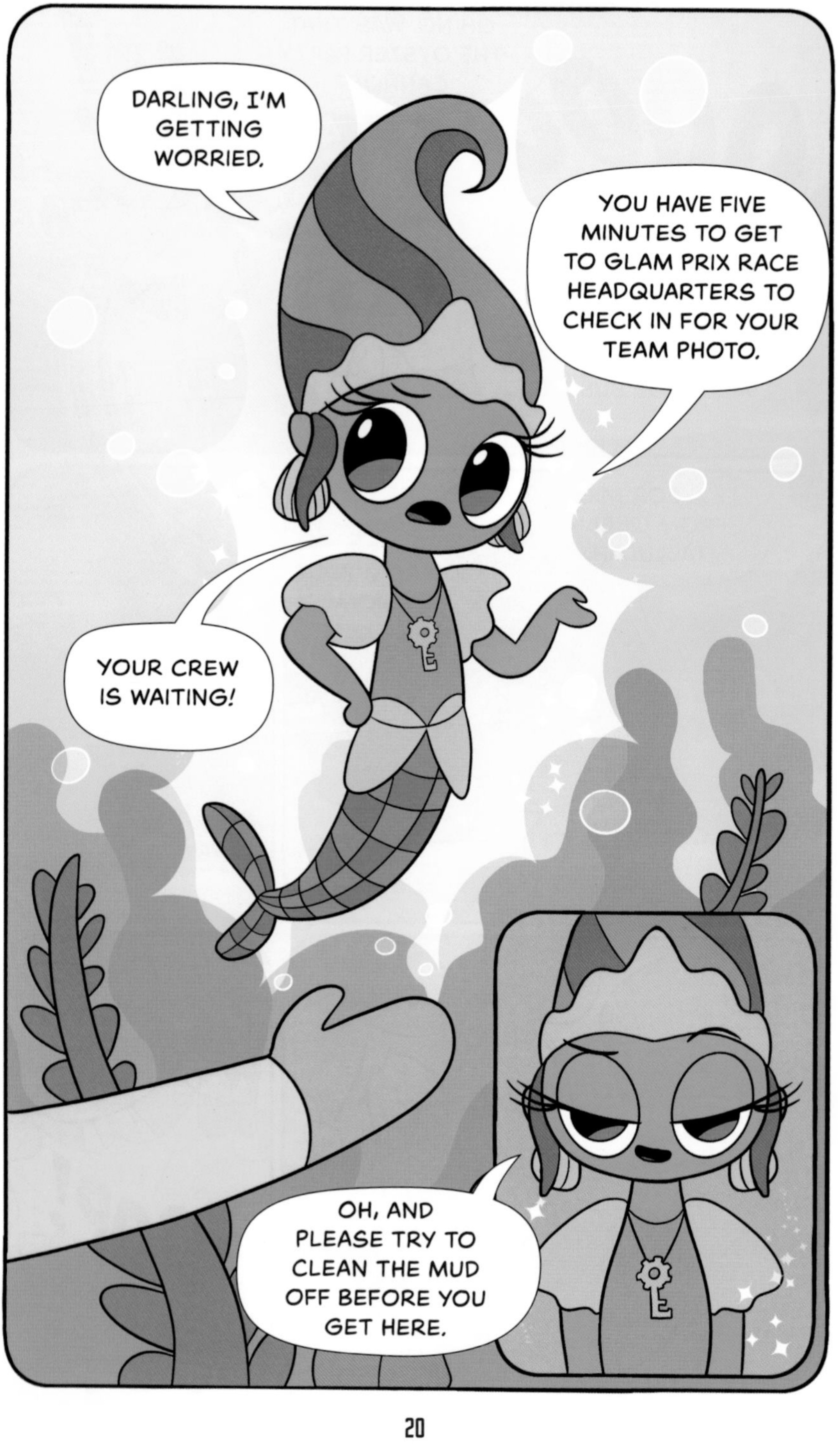
DARLING, I'M GETTING WORRIED.
YOU HAVE FIVE MINUTES TO GET TO GLAM PRIX RACE HEADQUARTERS TO CHECK IN FOR YOUR TEAM PHOTO.
YOUR CREW IS WAITING!
OH, AND PLEASE TRY TO CLEAN THE MUD OFF BEFORE YOU GET HERE.

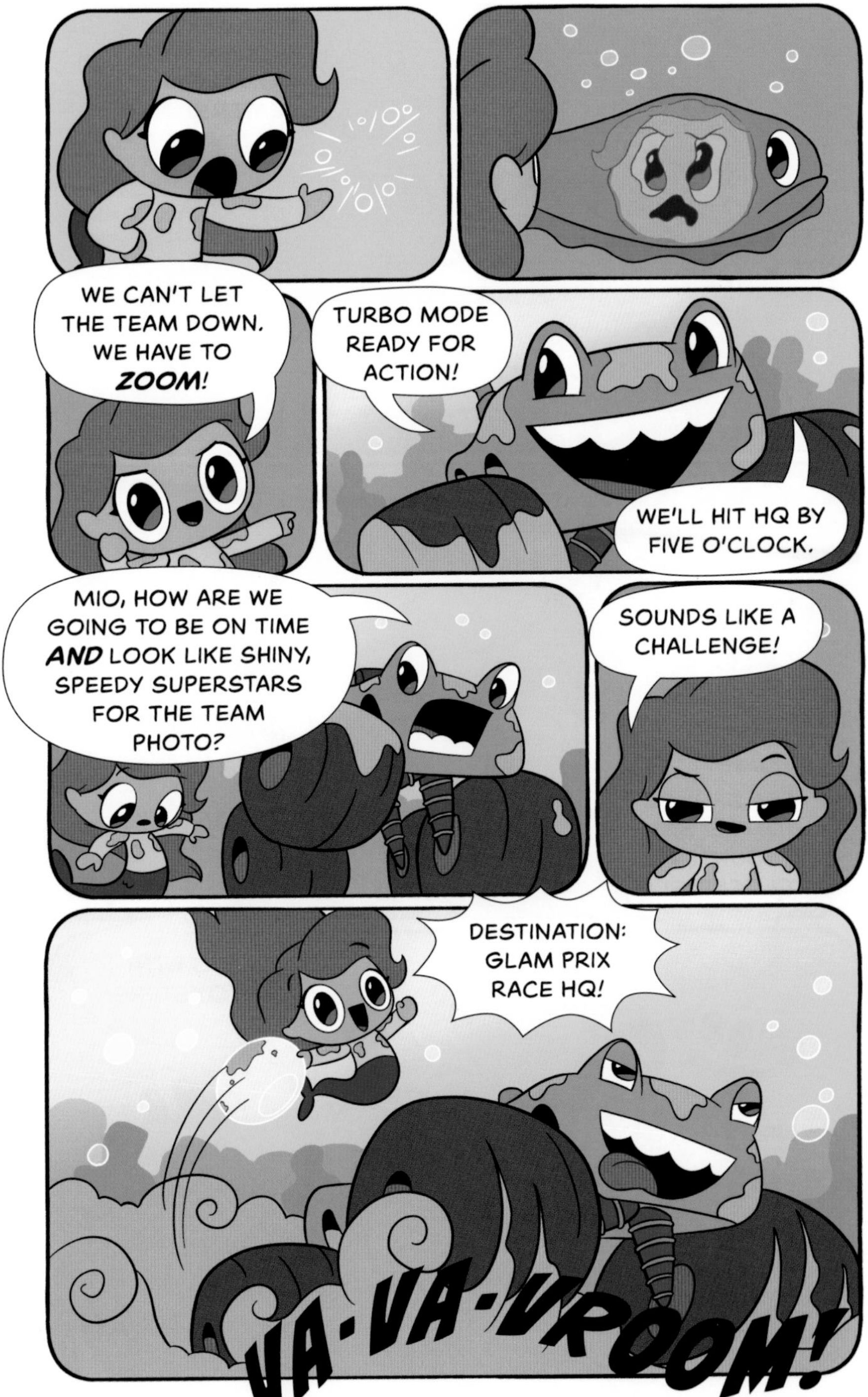
WE CAN'T LET THE TEAM DOWN. WE HAVE TO *ZOOM*!
TURBO MODE READY FOR ACTION!
WE'LL HIT HQ BY FIVE O'CLOCK.
MIO, HOW ARE WE GOING TO BE ON TIME *AND* LOOK LIKE SHINY, SPEEDY SUPERSTARS FOR THE TEAM PHOTO?
SOUNDS LIKE A CHALLENGE!
DESTINATION: GLAM PRIX RACE HQ!
VA-VA-VROOM!

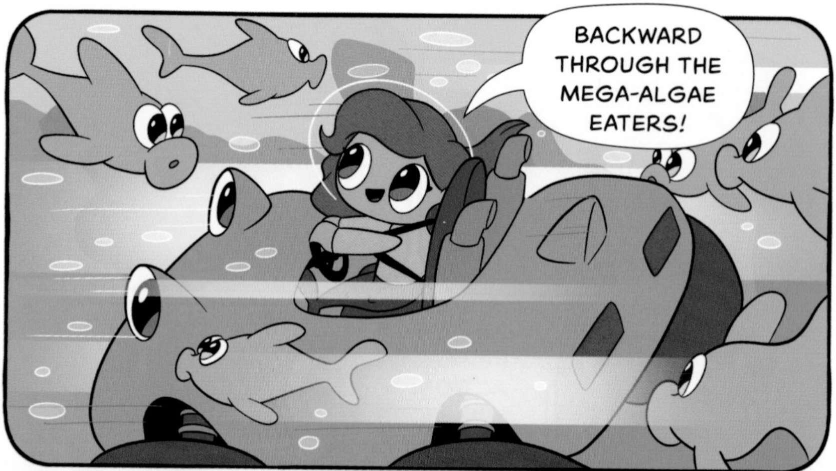
BACKWARD THROUGH THE MEGA-ALGAE EATERS!

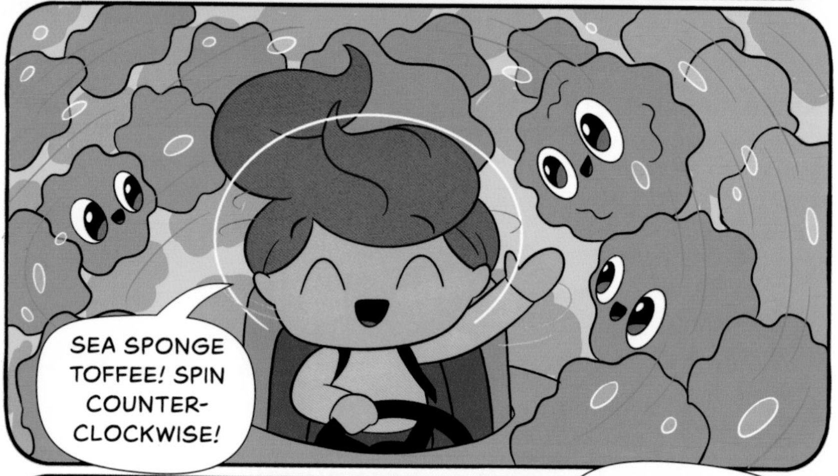
SEA SPONGE TOFFEE! SPIN COUNTER-CLOCKWISE!

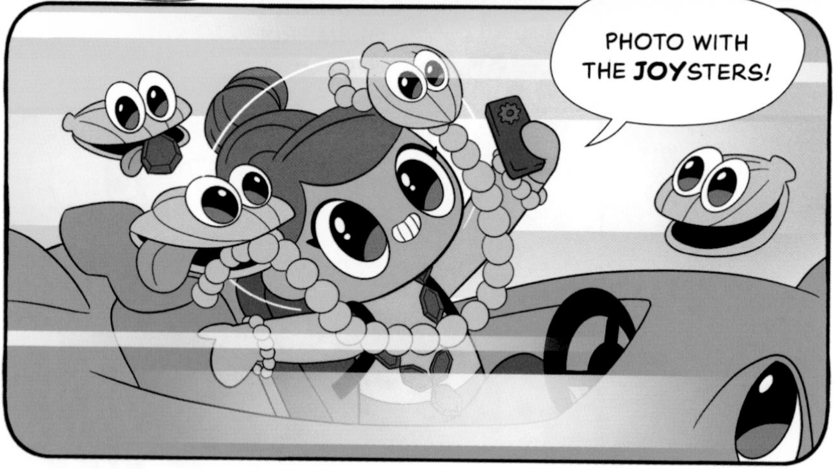
PHOTO WITH THE **JOY**STERS!

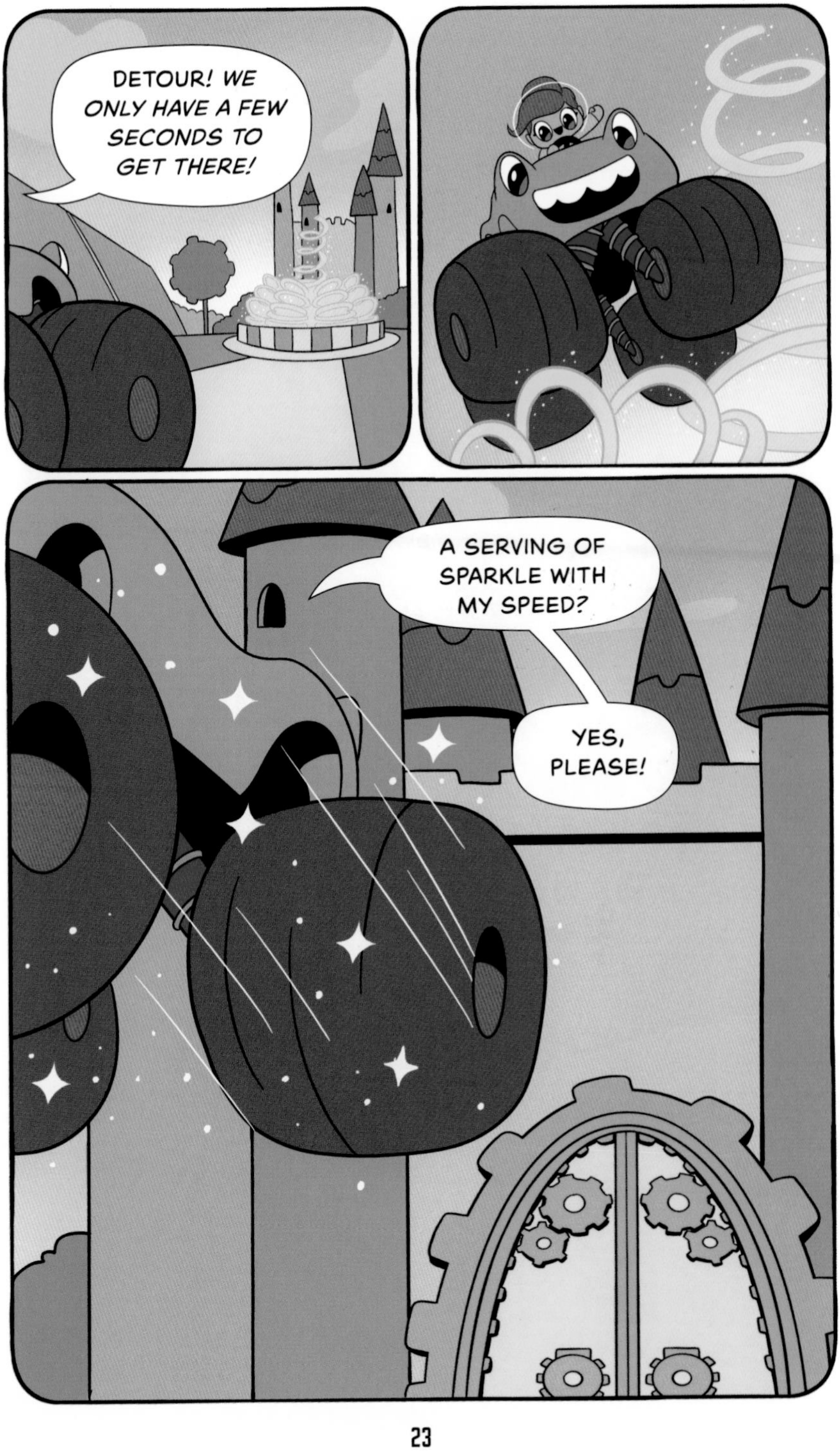
DETOUR! WE ONLY HAVE A FEW SECONDS TO GET THERE!
A SERVING OF SPARKLE WITH MY SPEED?
YES, PLEASE!

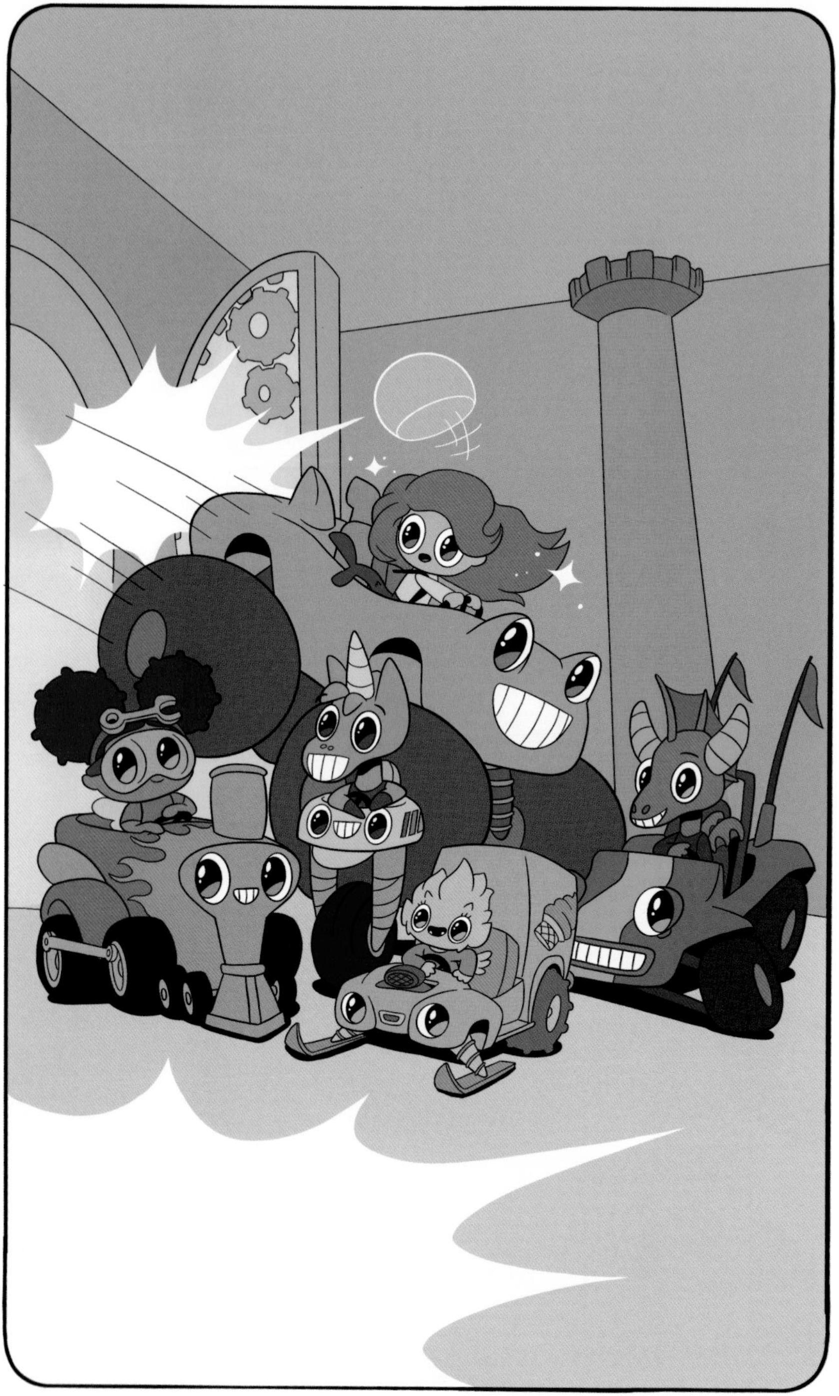

CHAPTER 3:
MEET THE TEAMS!

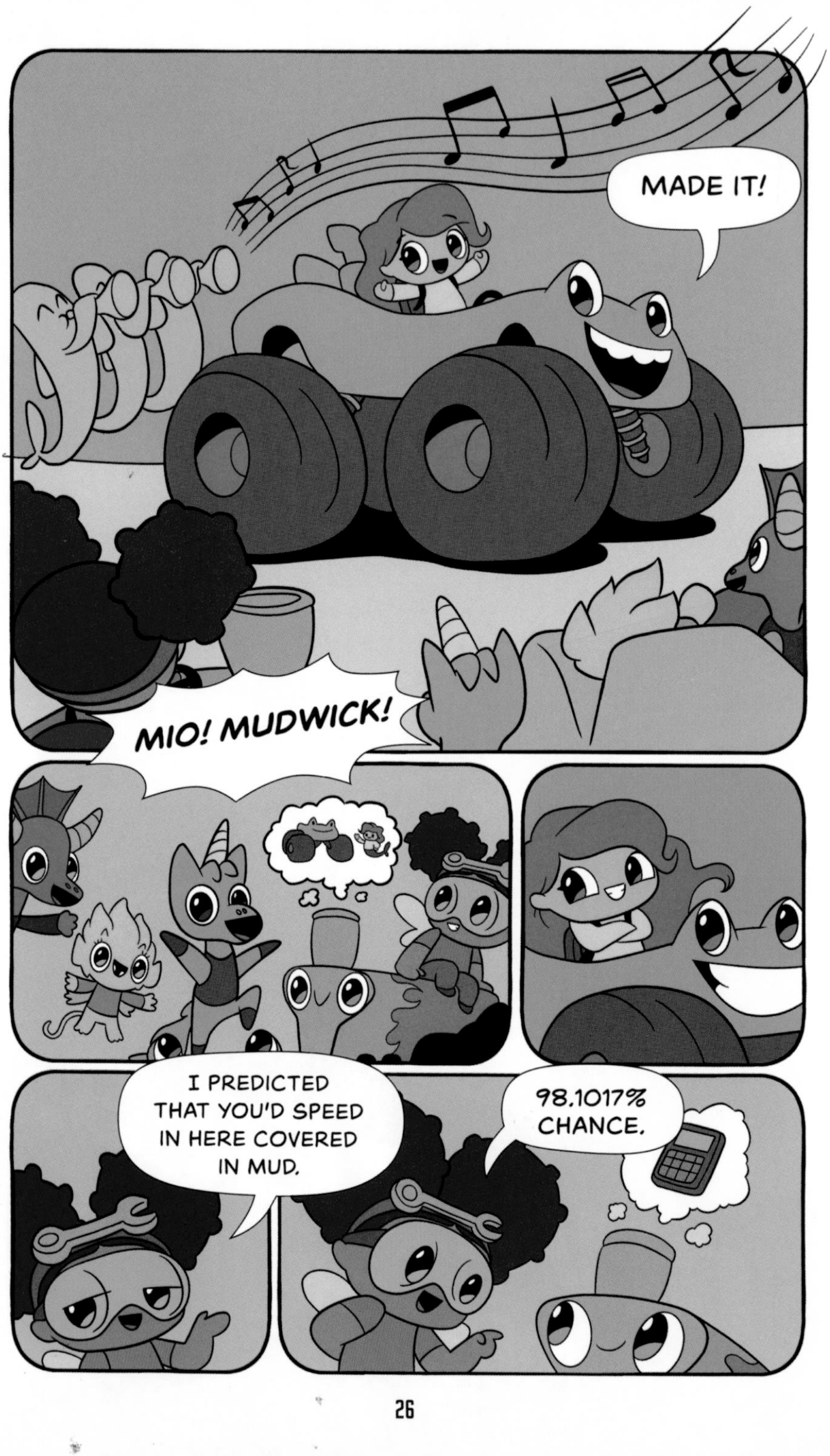
MADE IT!
MIO! MUDWICK!
I PREDICTED THAT YOU'D SPEED IN HERE COVERED IN MUD.
98.1017% CHANCE.

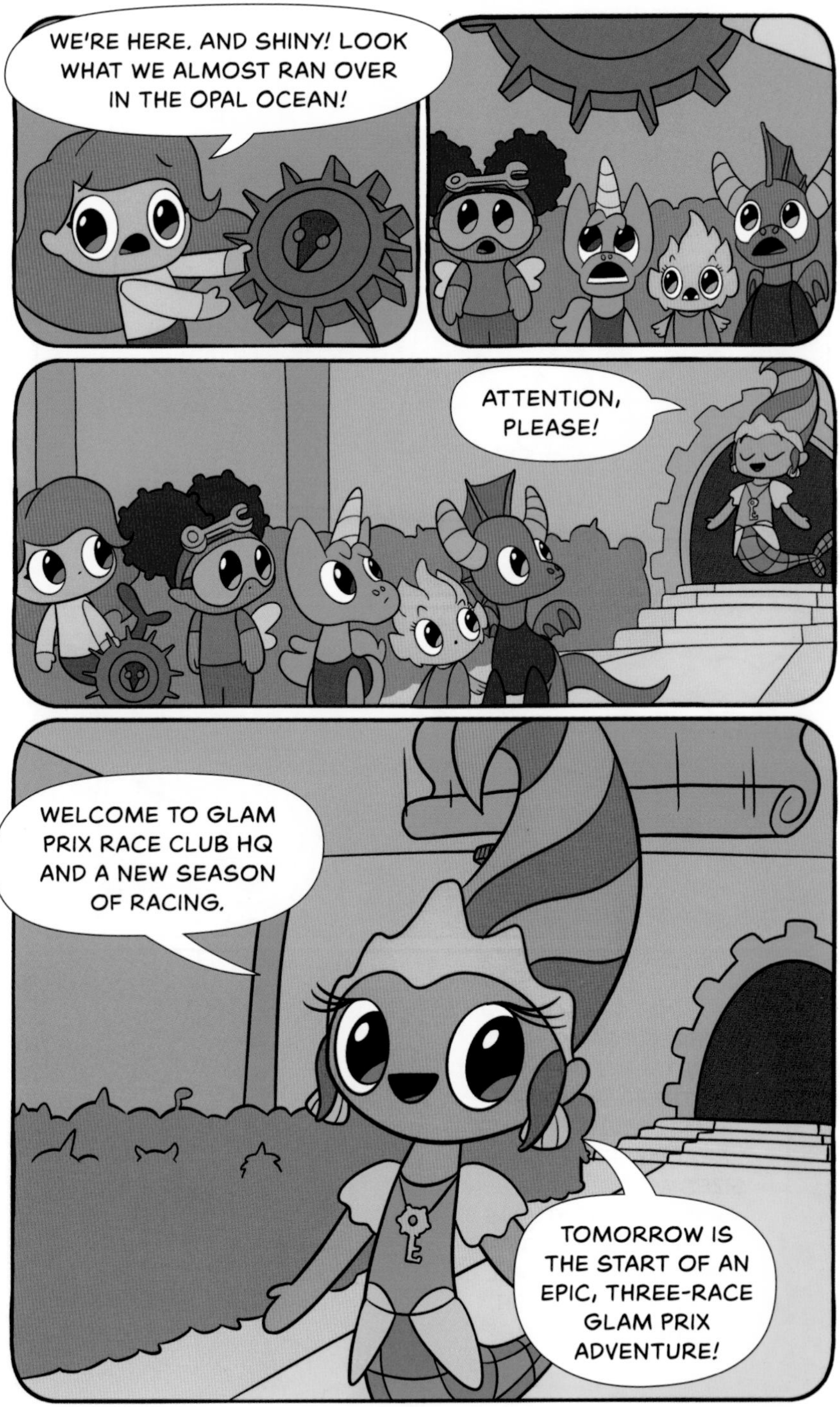
WE'RE HERE, AND SHINY! LOOK WHAT WE ALMOST RAN OVER IN THE OPAL OCEAN!
ATTENTION, PLEASE!
WELCOME TO GLAM PRIX RACE CLUB HQ AND A NEW SEASON OF RACING.
TOMORROW IS THE START OF AN EPIC, THREE-RACE GLAM PRIX ADVENTURE!

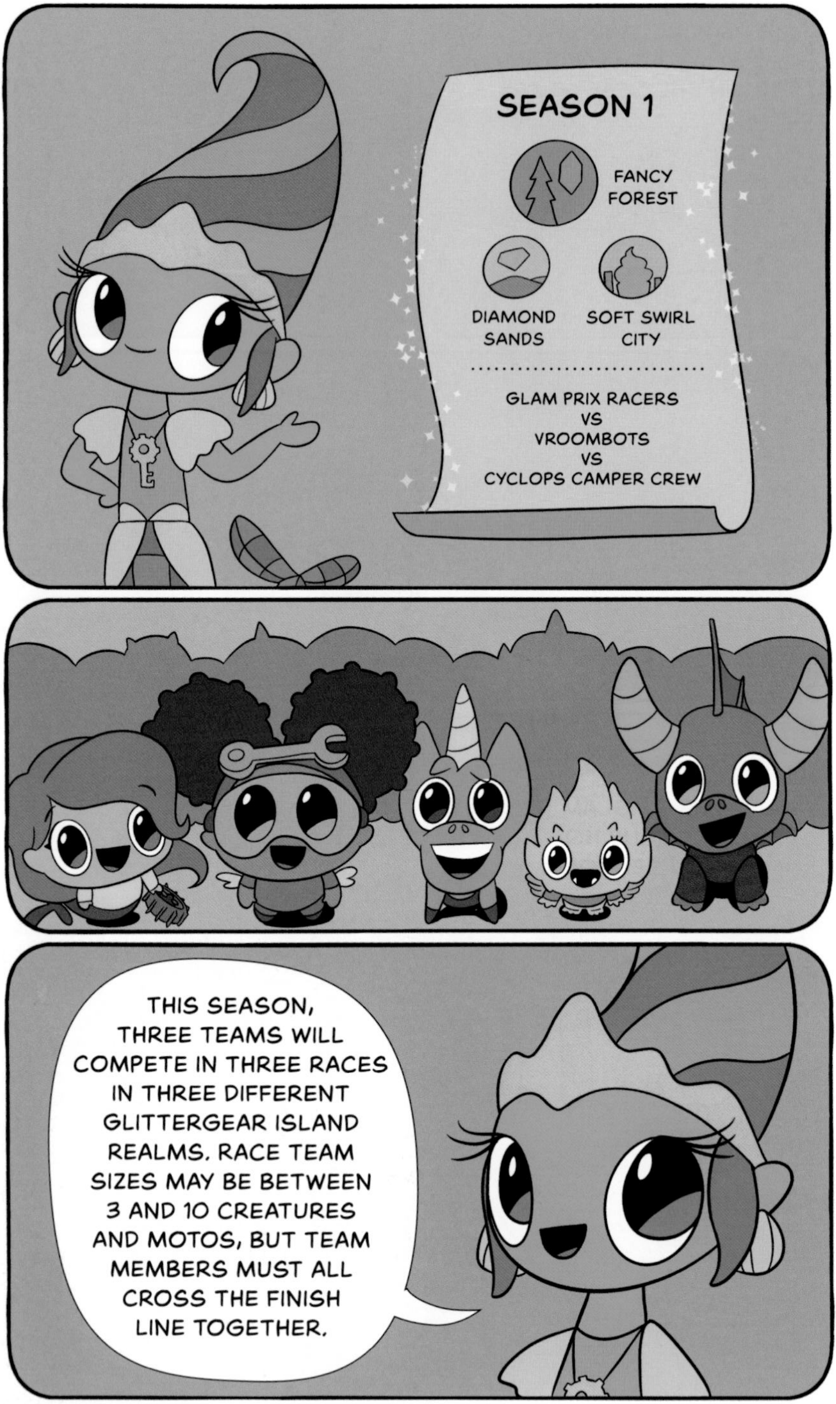
SEASON 1
FANCY FOREST
DIAMOND SANDS
SOFT SWIRL CITY
GLAM PRIX RACERS VS VROOMBOTS VS CYCLOPS CAMPER CREW
THIS SEASON, THREE TEAMS WILL COMPETE IN THREE RACES IN THREE DIFFERENT GLITTERGEAR ISLAND REALMS. RACE TEAM SIZES MAY BE BETWEEN 3 AND 10 CREATURES AND MOTOS, BUT TEAM MEMBERS MUST ALL CROSS THE FINISH LINE TOGETHER.

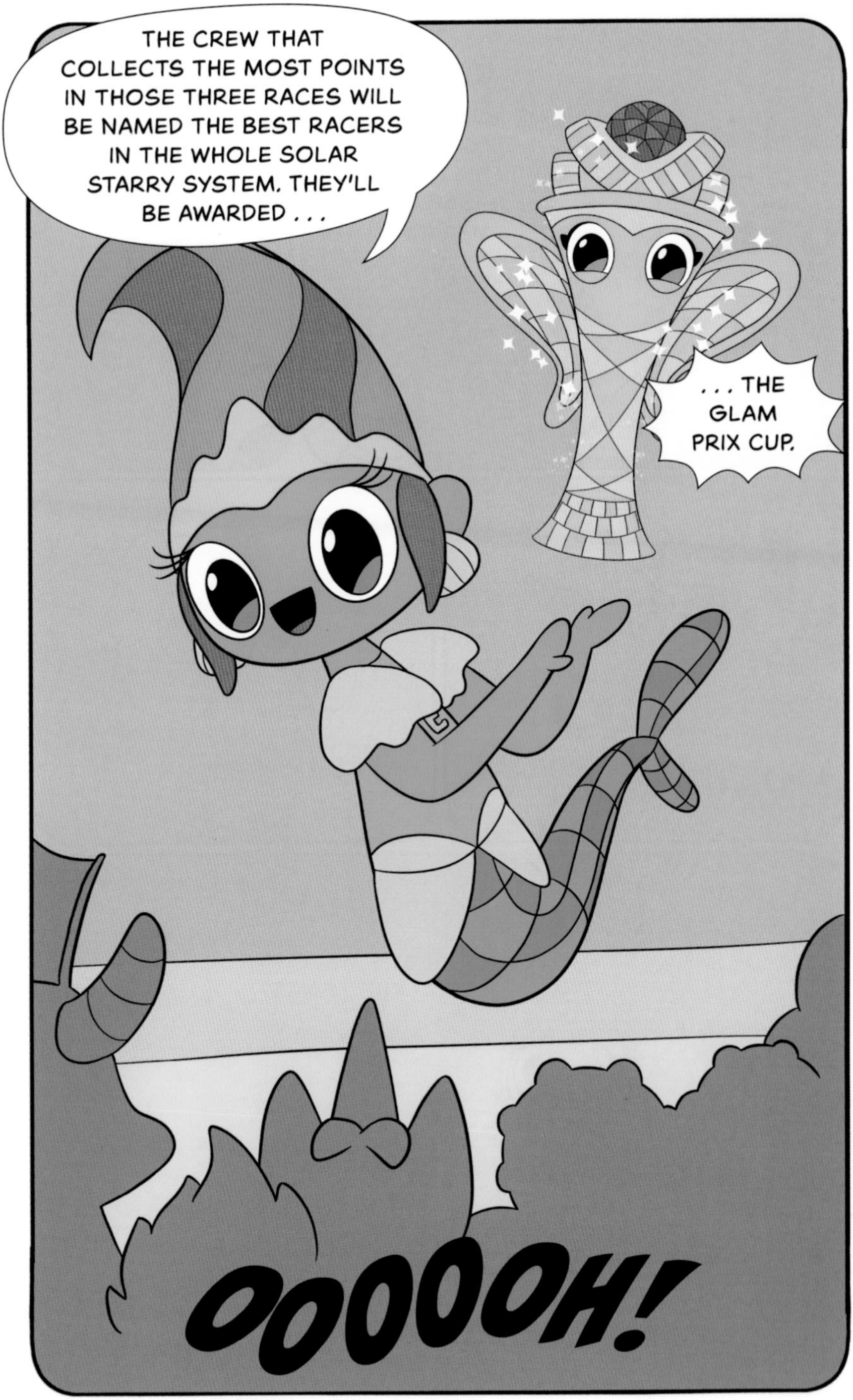
THE CREW THAT COLLECTS THE MOST POINTS IN THOSE THREE RACES WILL BE NAMED THE BEST RACERS IN THE WHOLE SOLAR STARRY SYSTEM. THEY'LL BE AWARDED . . .
. . . THE GLAM PRIX CUP.
OOOOOH!

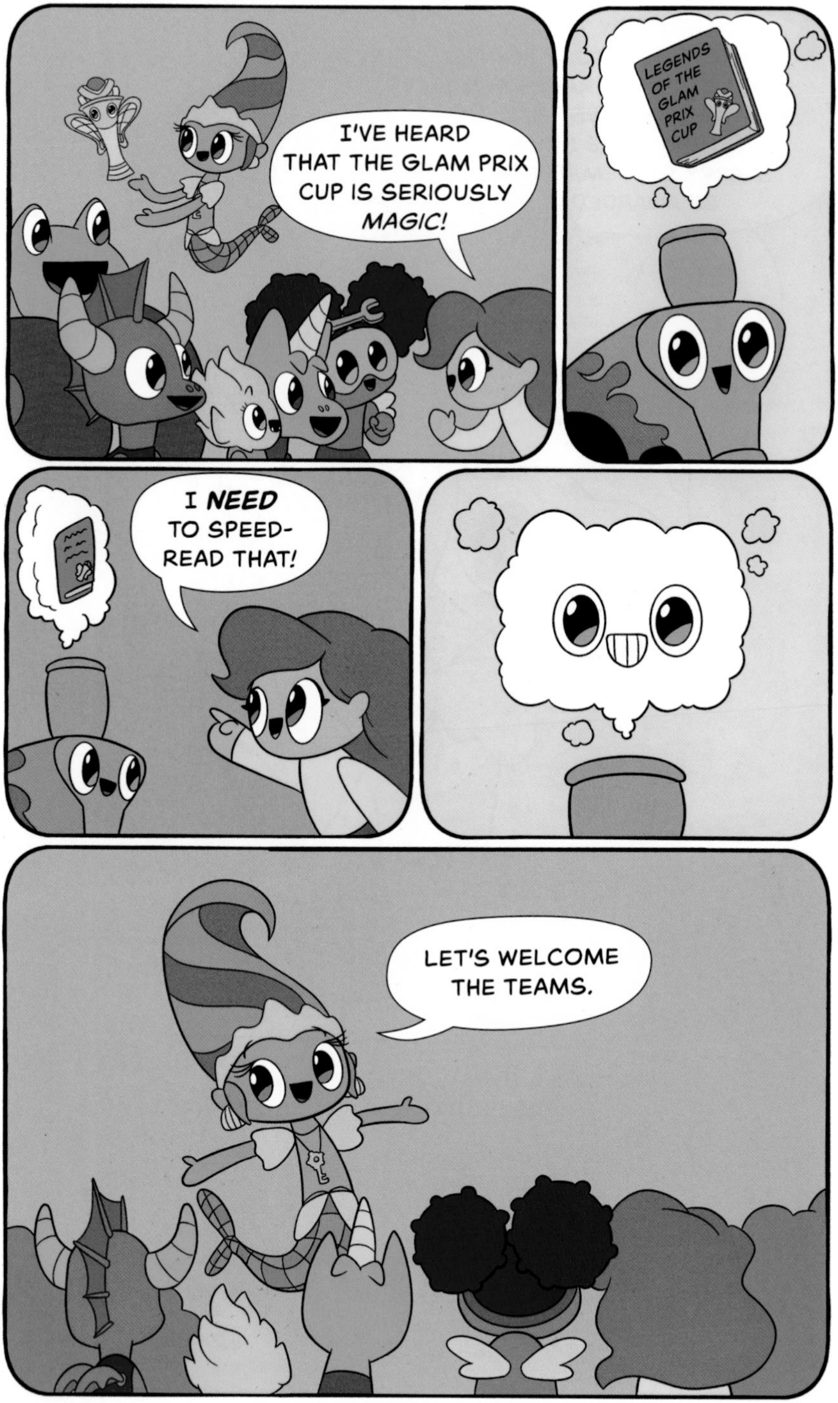
I'VE HEARD THAT THE GLAM PRIX CUP IS SERIOUSLY *MAGIC!*
LEGENDS OF THE GLAM PRIX CUP
I **NEED** TO SPEED-READ THAT!
LET'S WELCOME THE TEAMS.

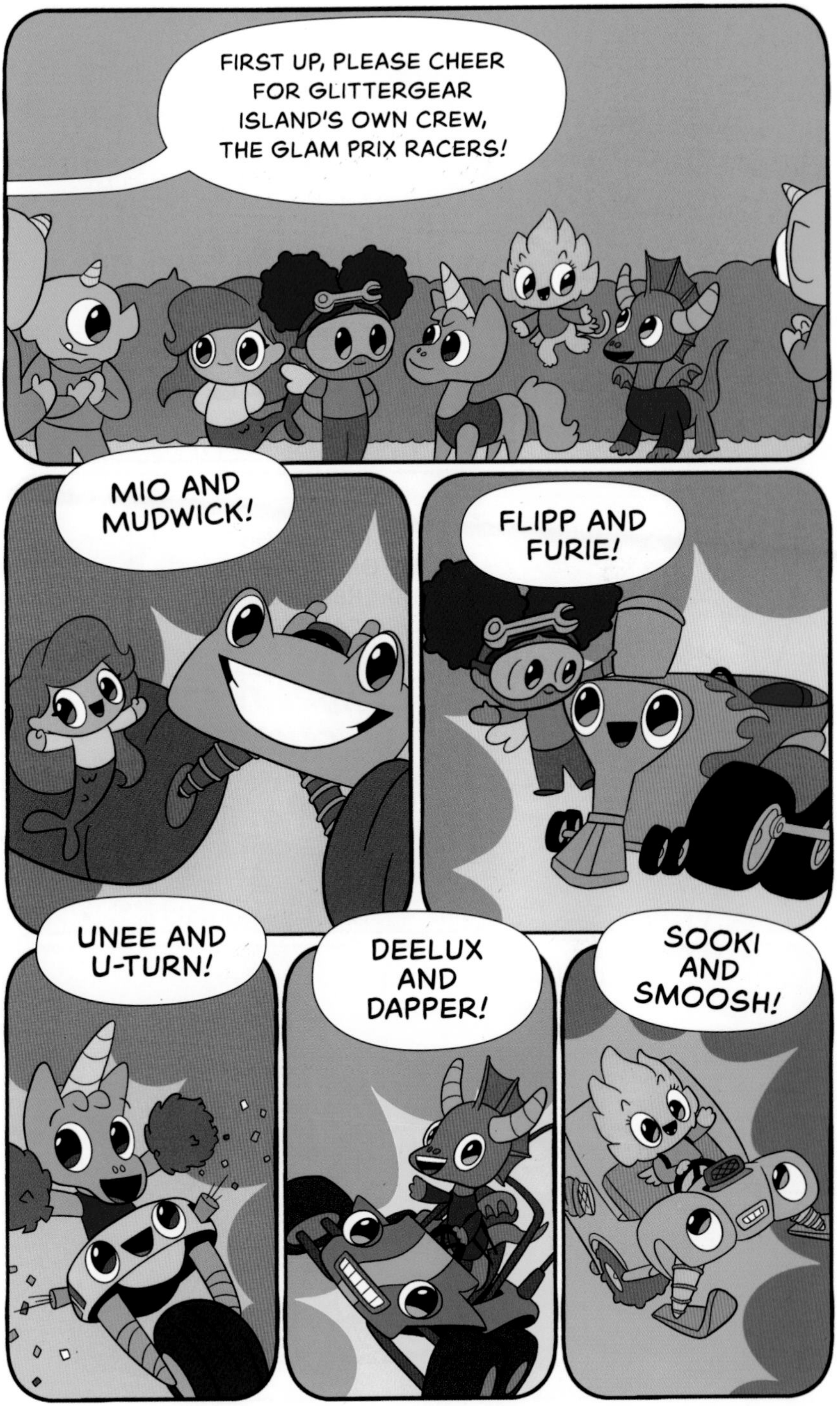
FIRST UP, PLEASE CHEER FOR GLITTERGEAR ISLAND'S OWN CREW, THE GLAM PRIX RACERS!
MIO AND MUDWICK!
FLIPP AND FURIE!
UNEE AND U-TURN!
DEELUX AND DAPPER!
SOOKI AND SMOOSH!

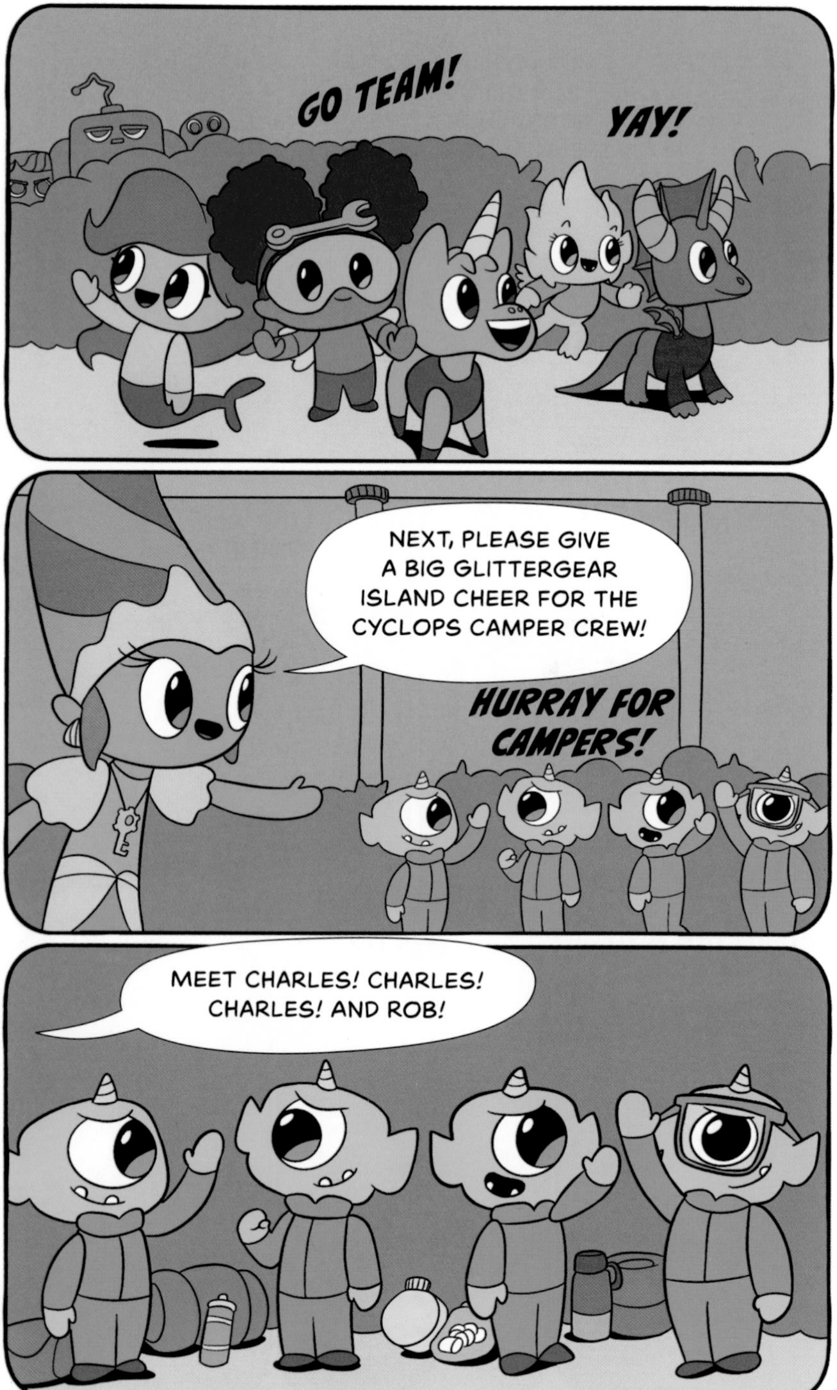
GO TEAM!
YAY!
NEXT, PLEASE GIVE A BIG GLITTERGEAR ISLAND CHEER FOR THE CYCLOPS CAMPER CREW!
HURRAY FOR CAMPERS!
MEET CHARLES! CHARLES! CHARLES! AND ROB!

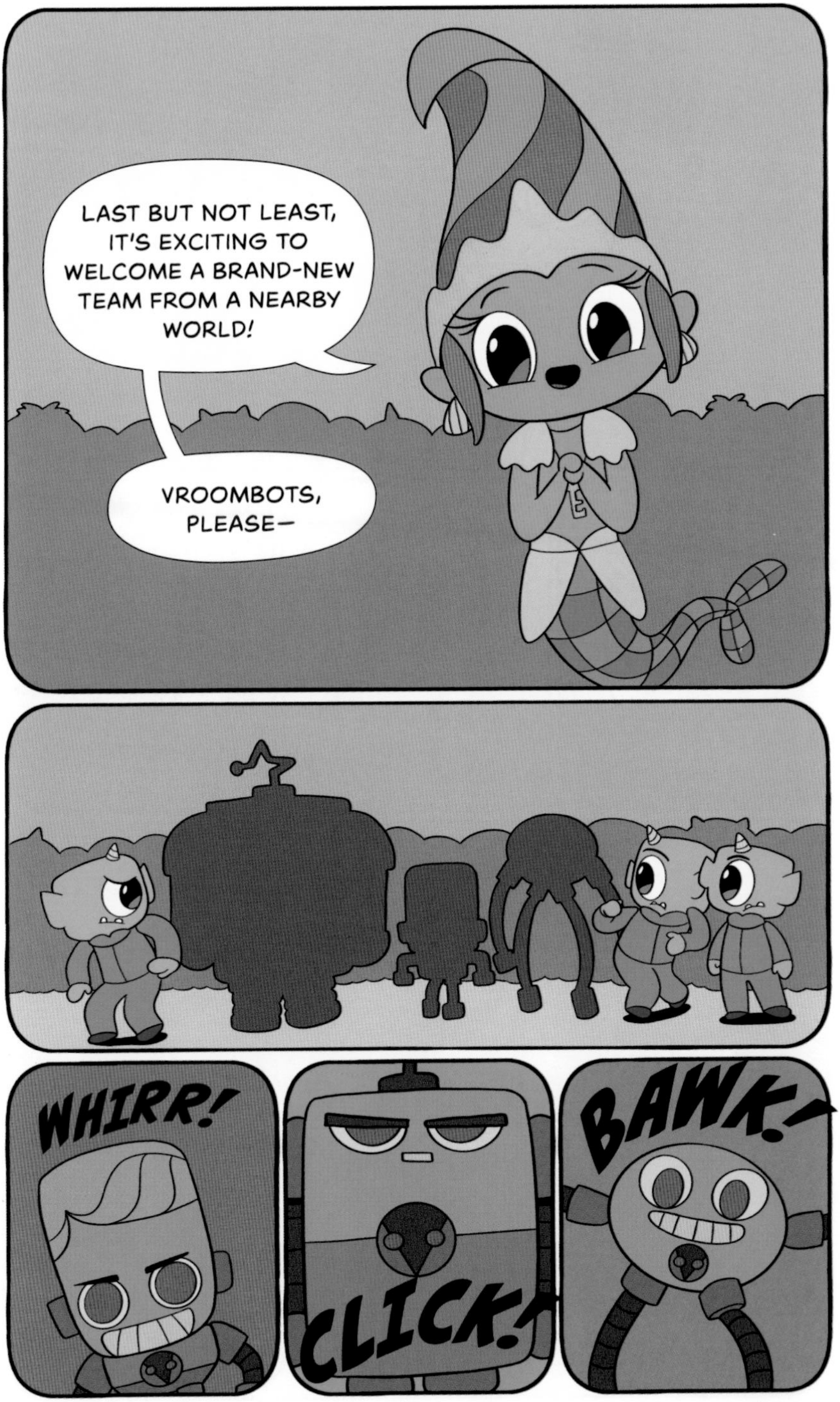
LAST BUT NOT LEAST, IT'S EXCITING TO WELCOME A BRAND-NEW TEAM FROM A NEARBY WORLD!
VROOMBOTS, PLEASE—
WHIRR!
CLICK!
BAWK!

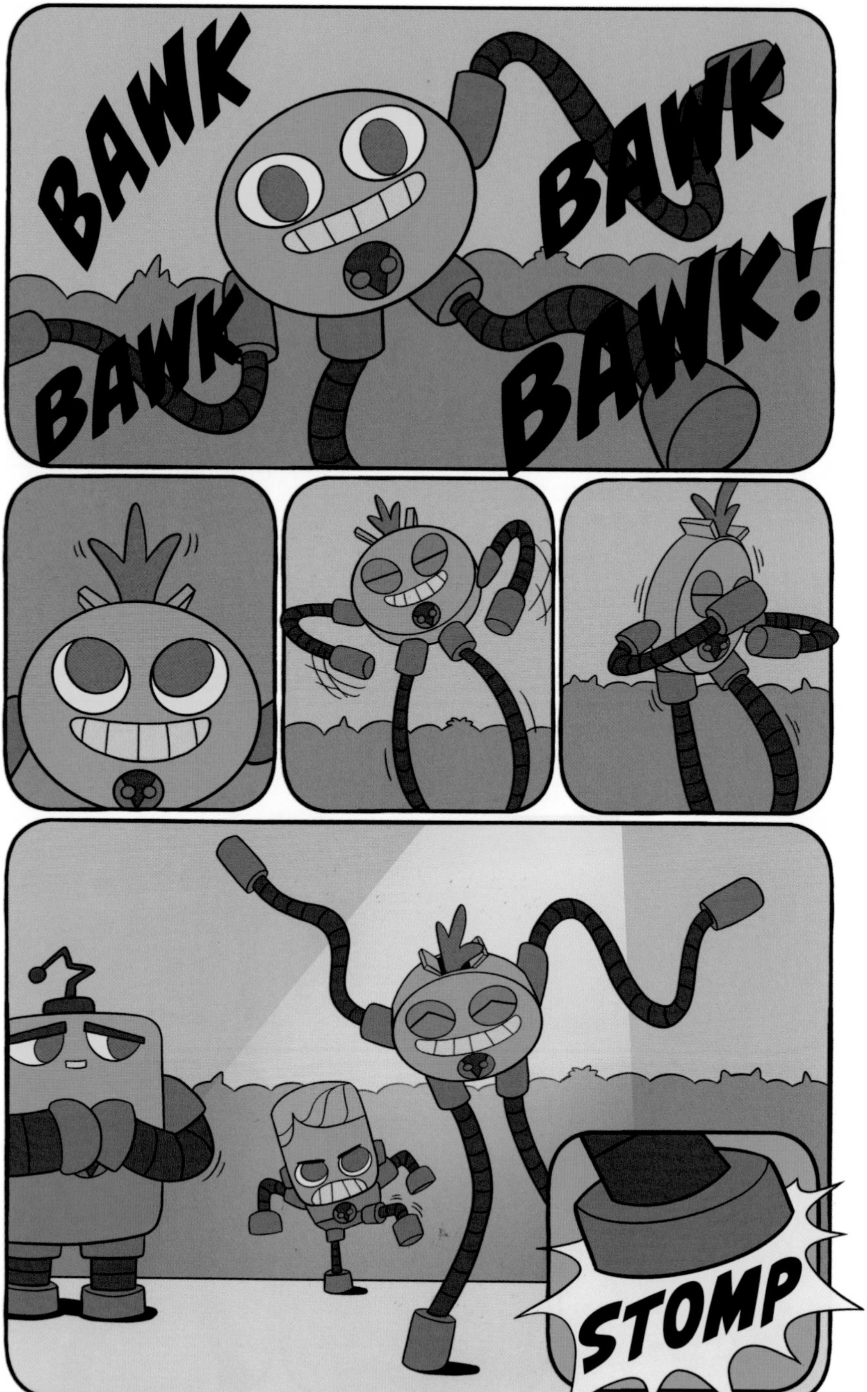
BAWK
BAWK
BAWK
BAWK!
STOMP

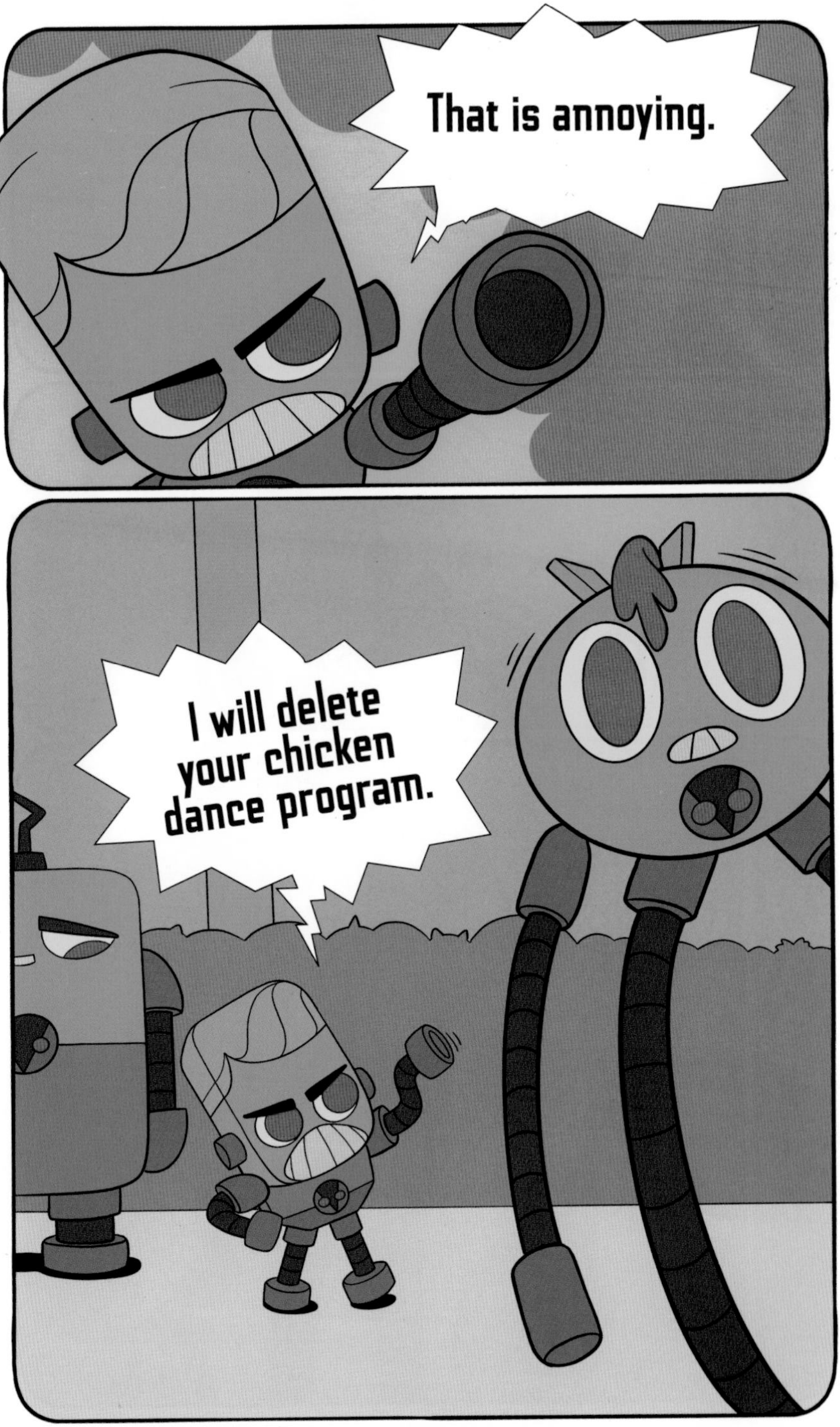
That is annoying.
I will delete your chicken dance program.

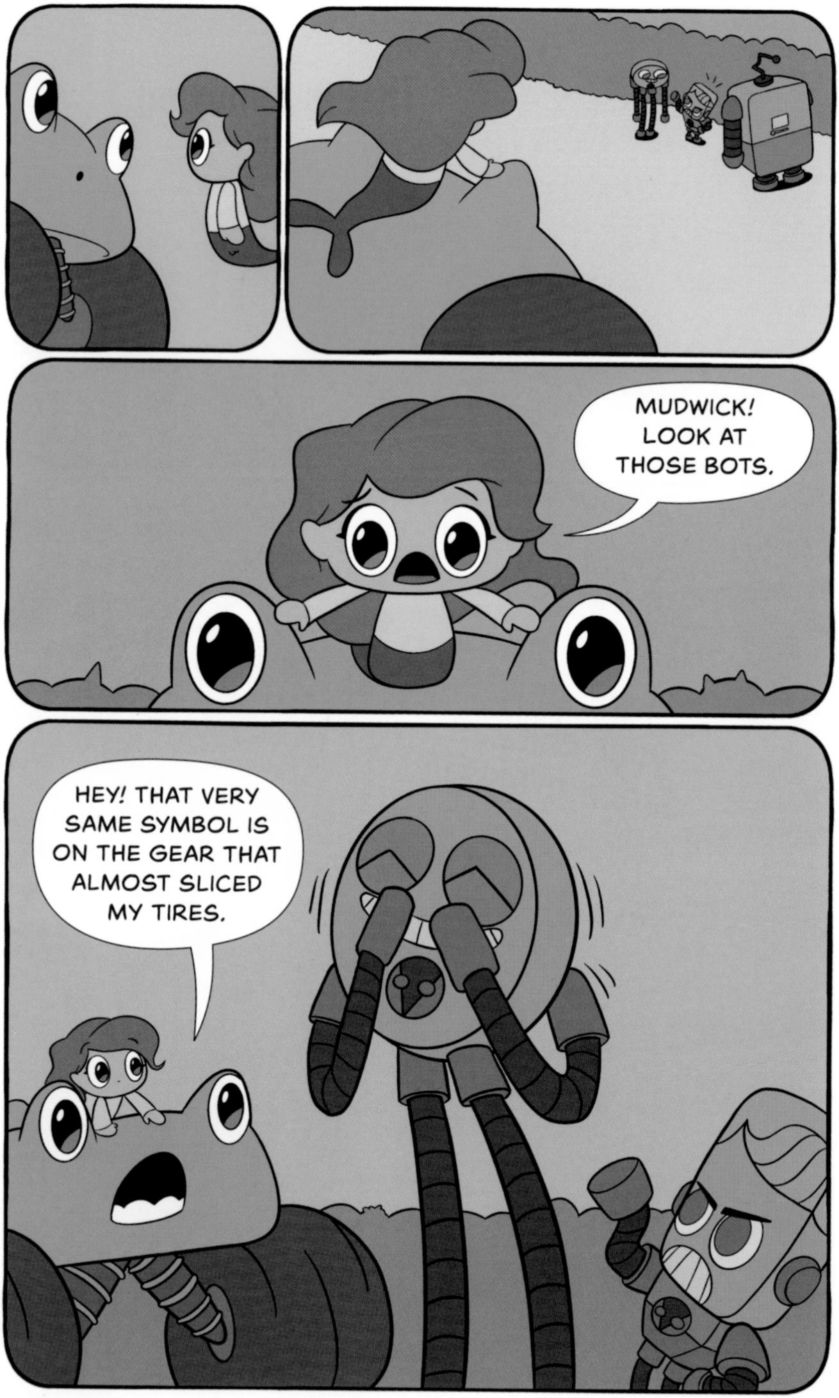
MUDWICK! LOOK AT THOSE BOTS.
HEY! THAT VERY SAME SYMBOL IS ON THE GEAR THAT ALMOST SLICED MY TIRES.

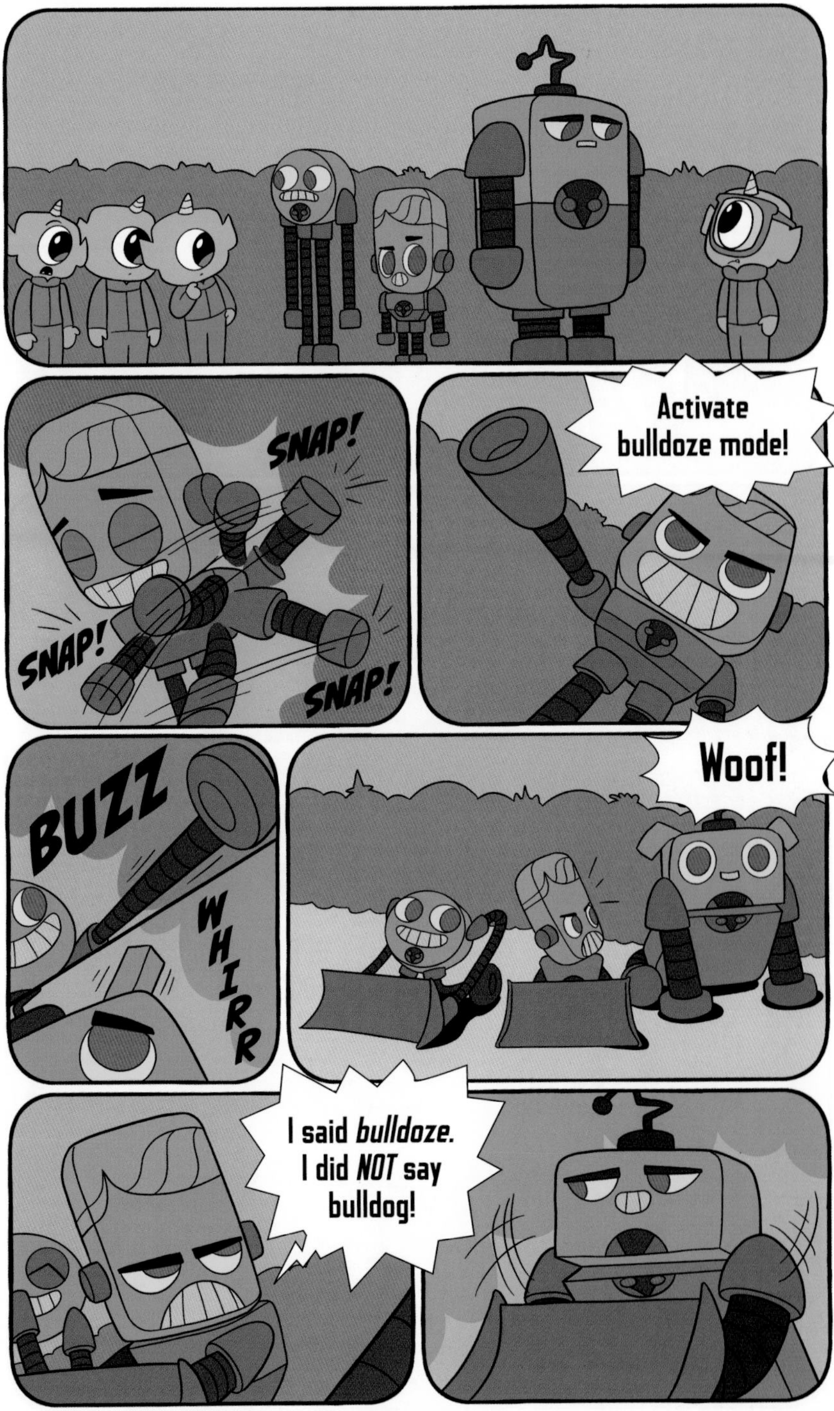
SNAP!
SNAP!
SNAP!
Activate bulldoze mode!
BUZZ
WHIRR
Woof!
I said *bulldoze.* I did *NOT* say bulldog!

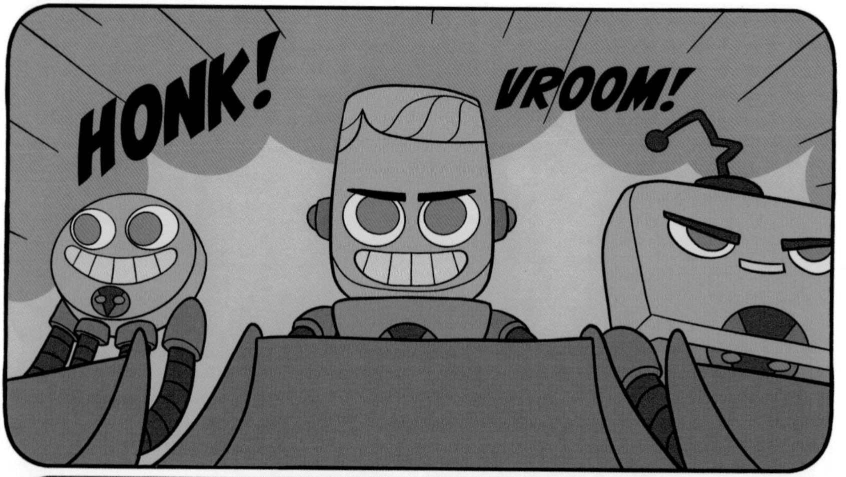
HONK!
VROOM!

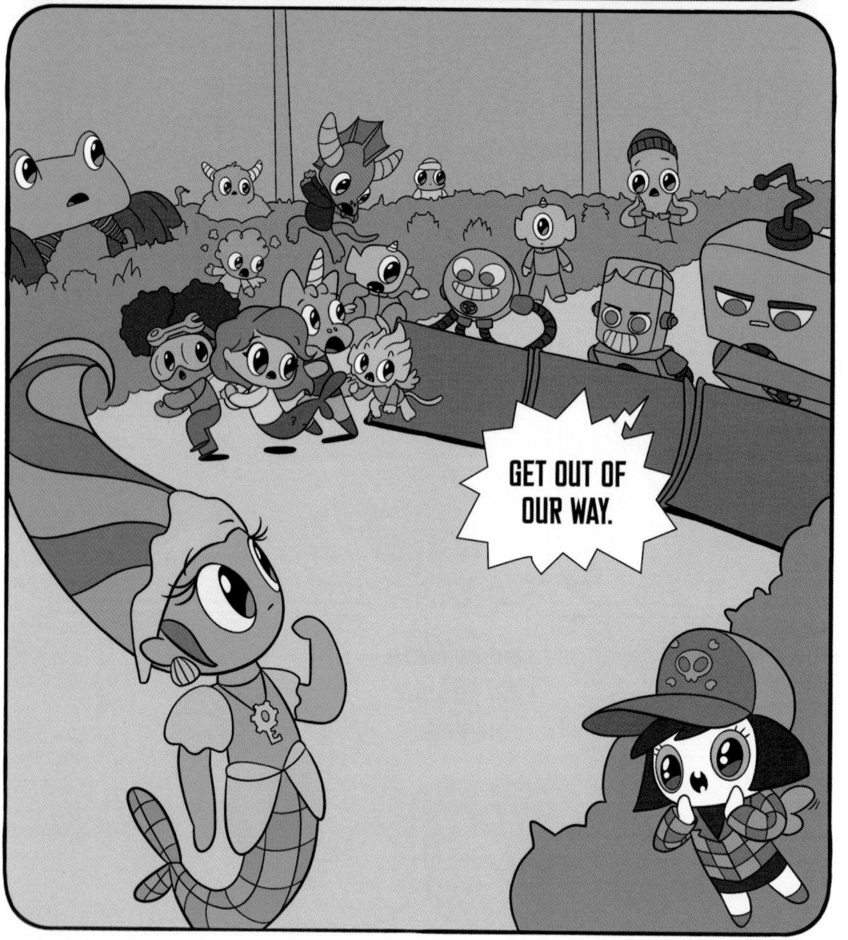
GET OUT OF OUR WAY.

CHAPTER 4:
WHO'S V-BEST?!

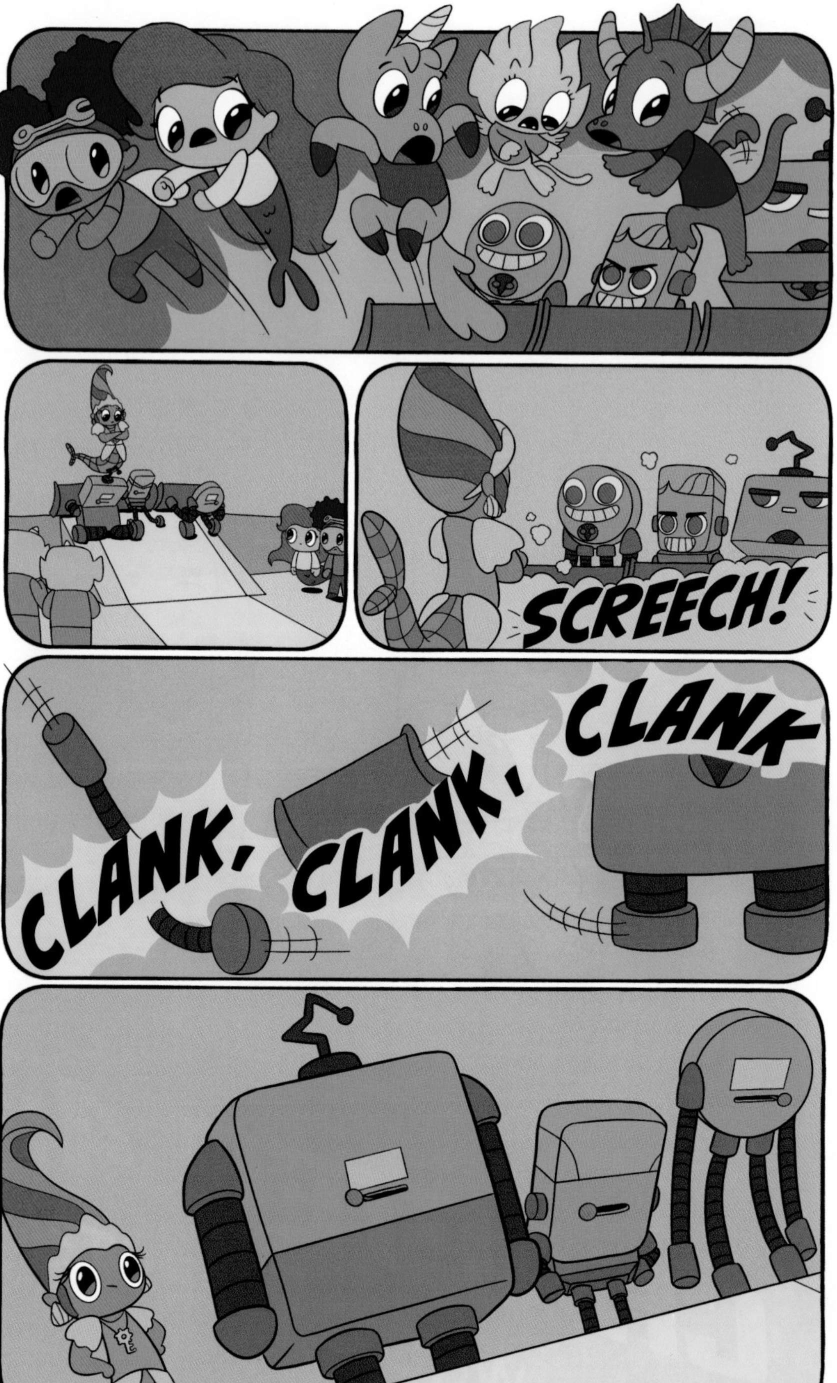
SCREECH!
CLANK, CLANK, CLANK

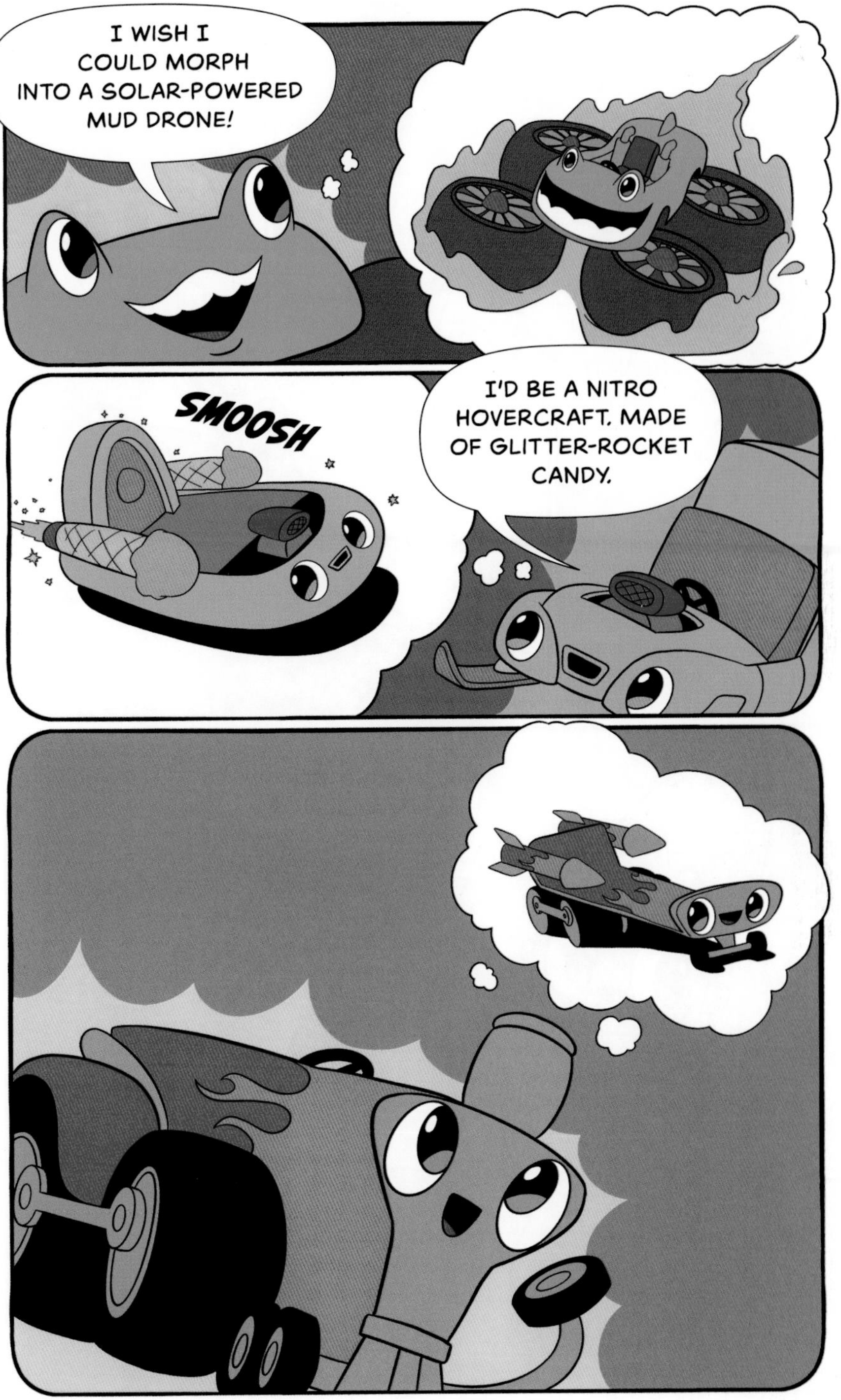
I WISH I COULD MORPH INTO A SOLAR-POWERED MUD DRONE!
SMOOSH
I'D BE A NITRO HOVERCRAFT. MADE OF GLITTER-ROCKET CANDY.

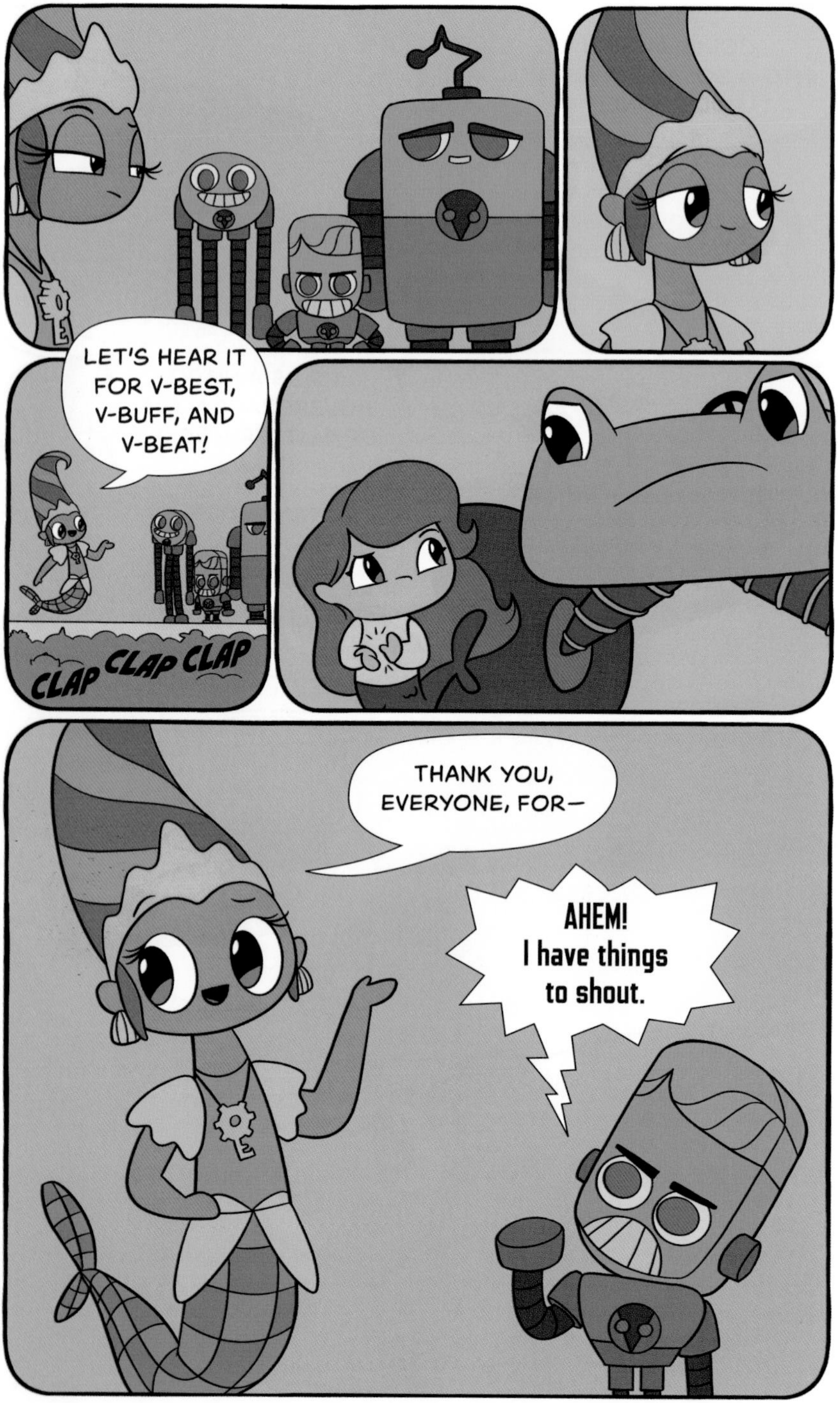
LET'S HEAR IT FOR V-BEST, V-BUFF, AND V-BEAT!
CLAP CLAP CLAP
THANK YOU, EVERYONE, FOR—
AHEM! I have things to shout.

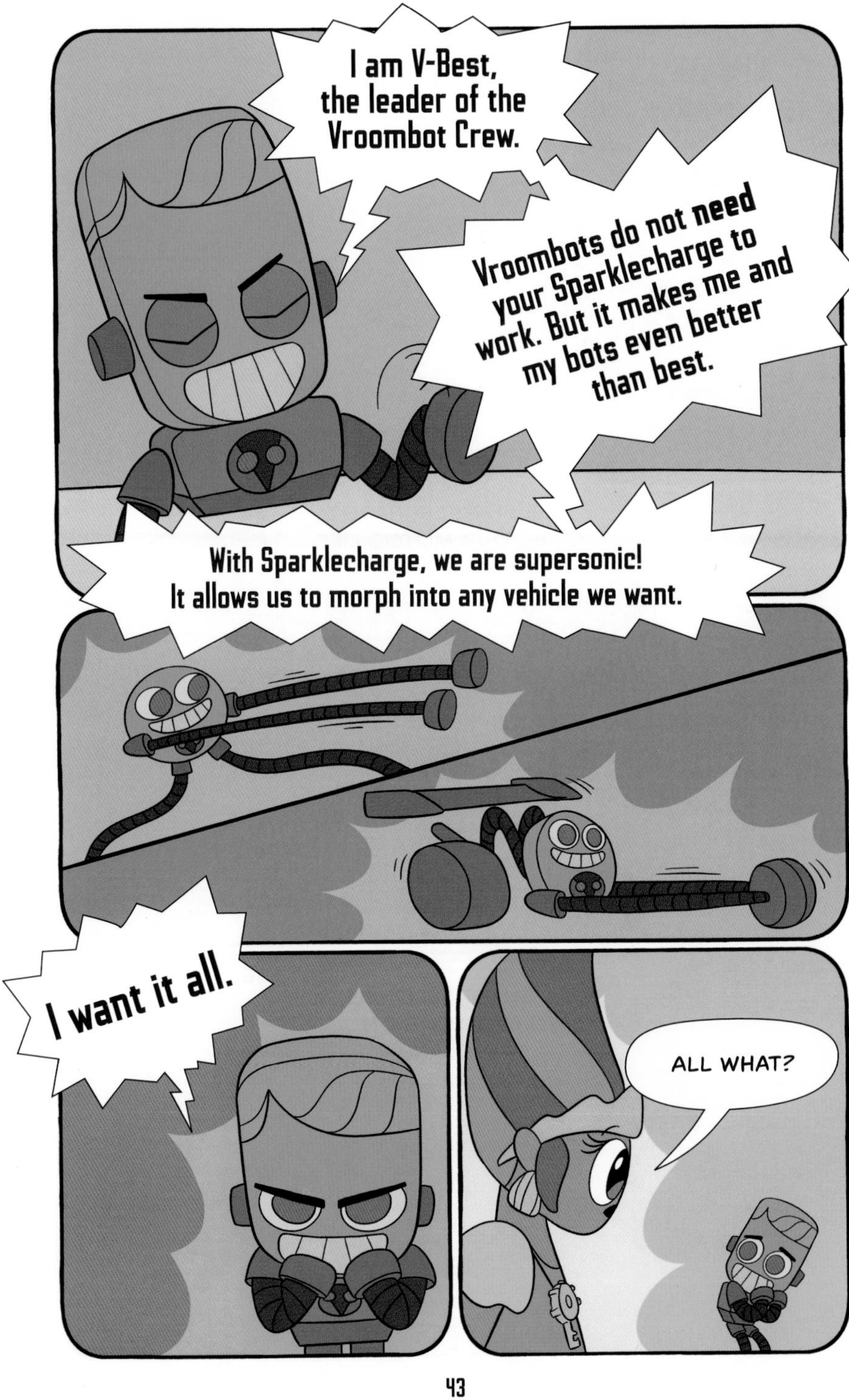
I am V-Best, the leader of the Vroombot Crew.
Vroombots do not **need** your Sparklecharge to work. But it makes me and my bots even better than best.
With Sparklecharge, we are supersonic! It allows us to morph into any vehicle we want.
I want it all.
ALL WHAT?

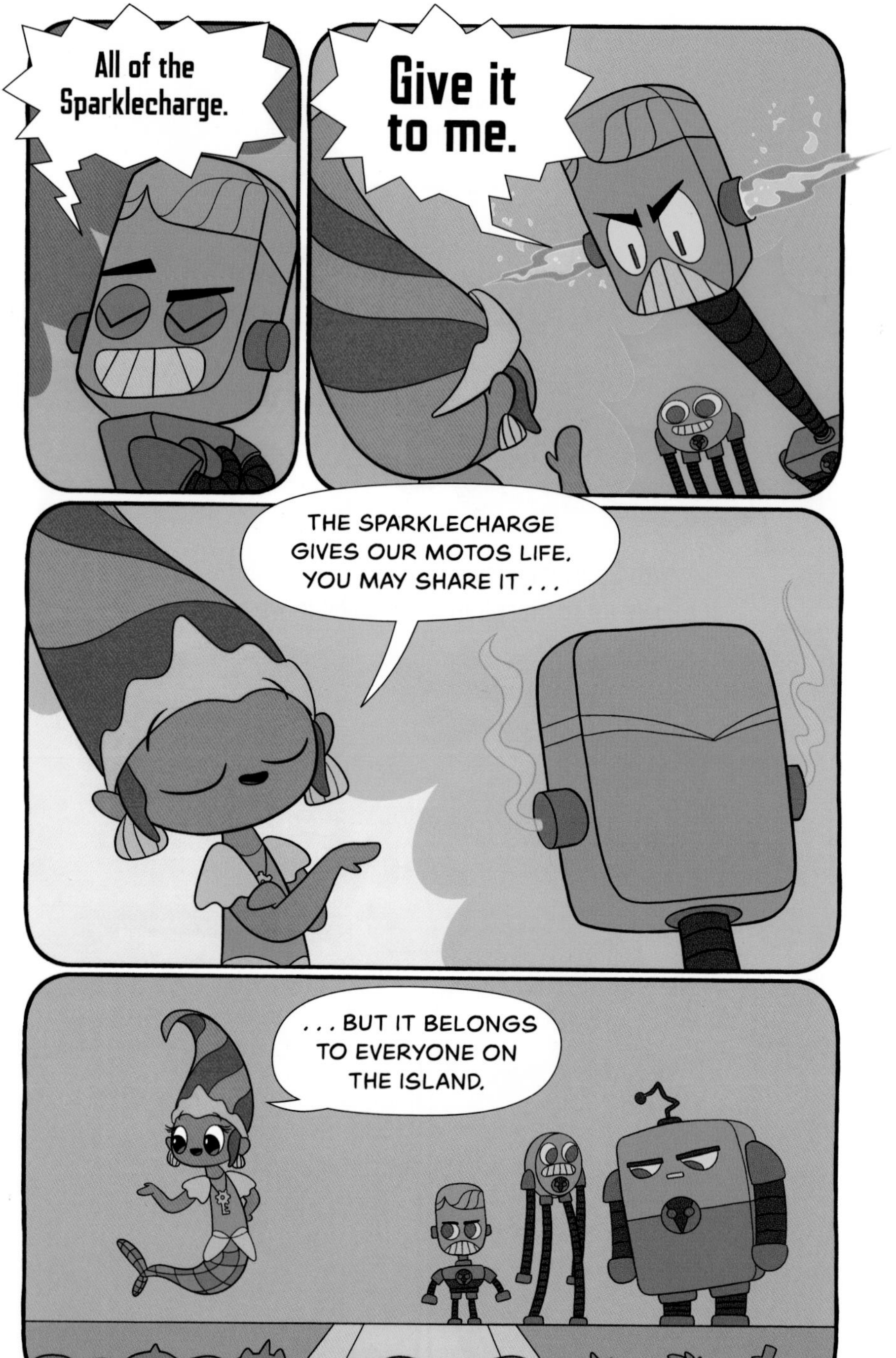
All of the Sparklecharge.
Give it to me.
THE SPARKLECHARGE GIVES OUR MOTOS LIFE. YOU MAY SHARE IT . . .
. . . BUT IT BELONGS TO EVERYONE ON THE ISLAND.

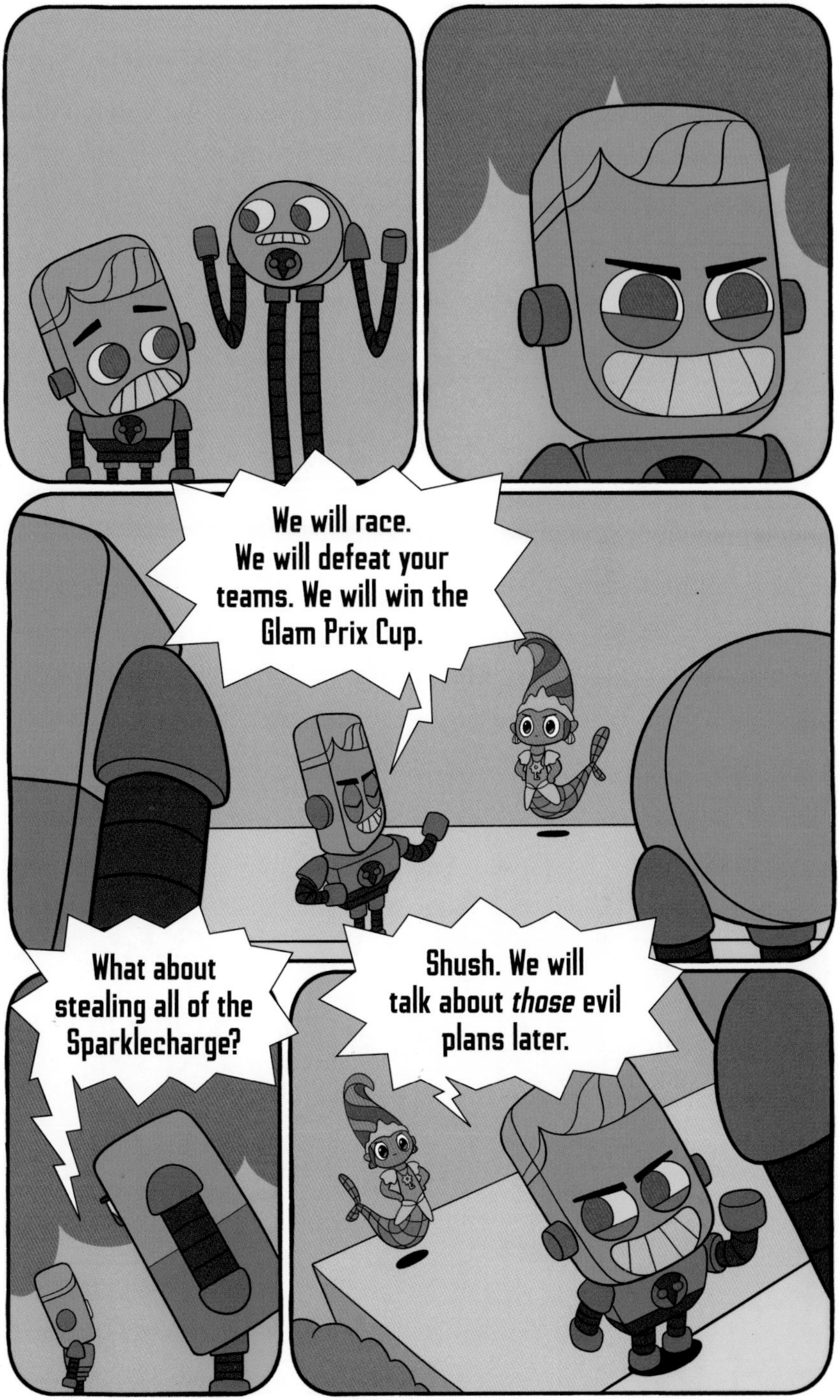
We will race. We will defeat your teams. We will win the Glam Prix Cup.
What about stealing all of the Sparklecharge?
Shush. We will talk about *those* evil plans later.

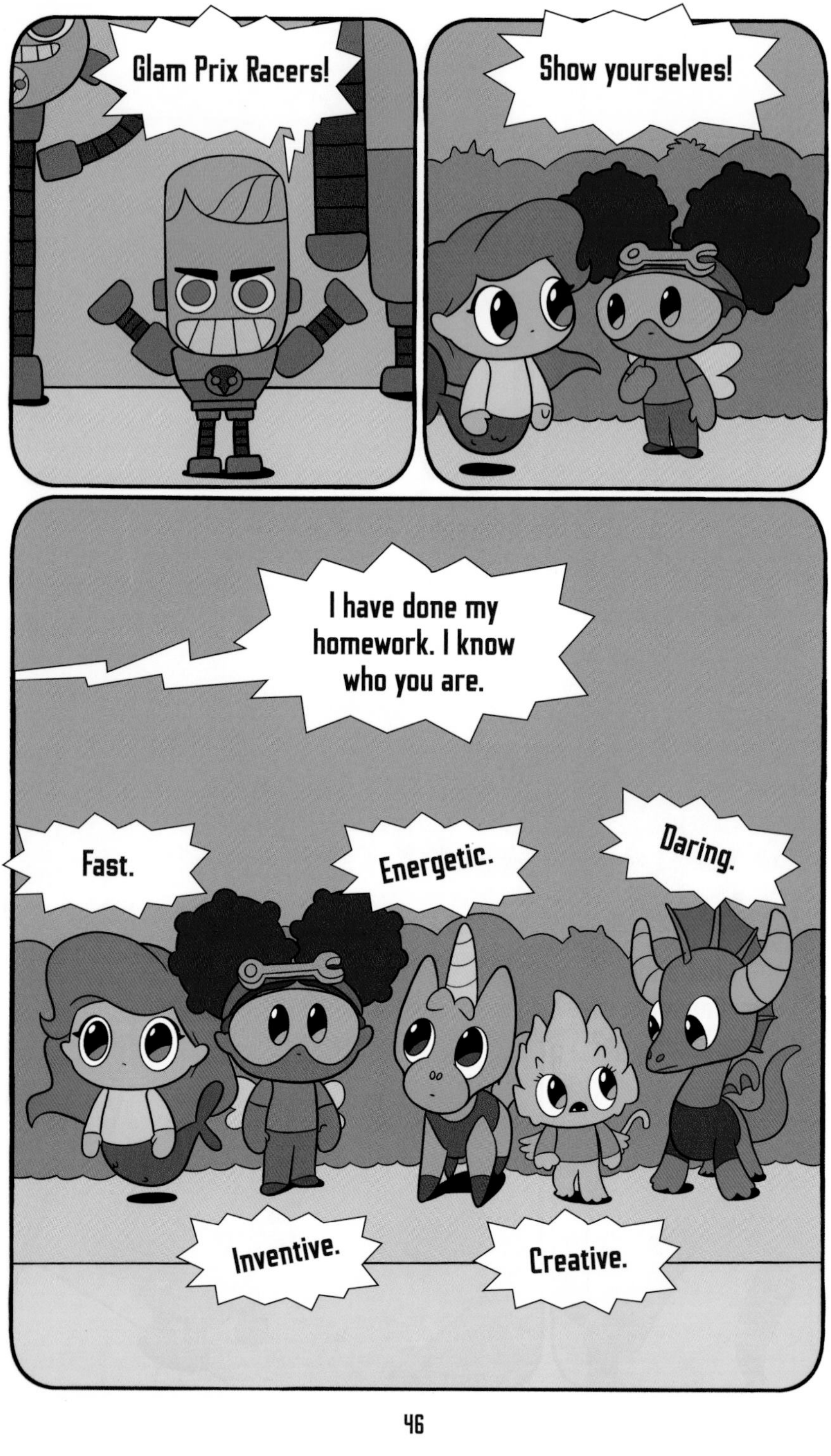
Glam Prix Racers!
Show yourselves!
I have done my homework. I know who you are.
Fast.
Energetic.
Daring.
Inventive.
Creative.

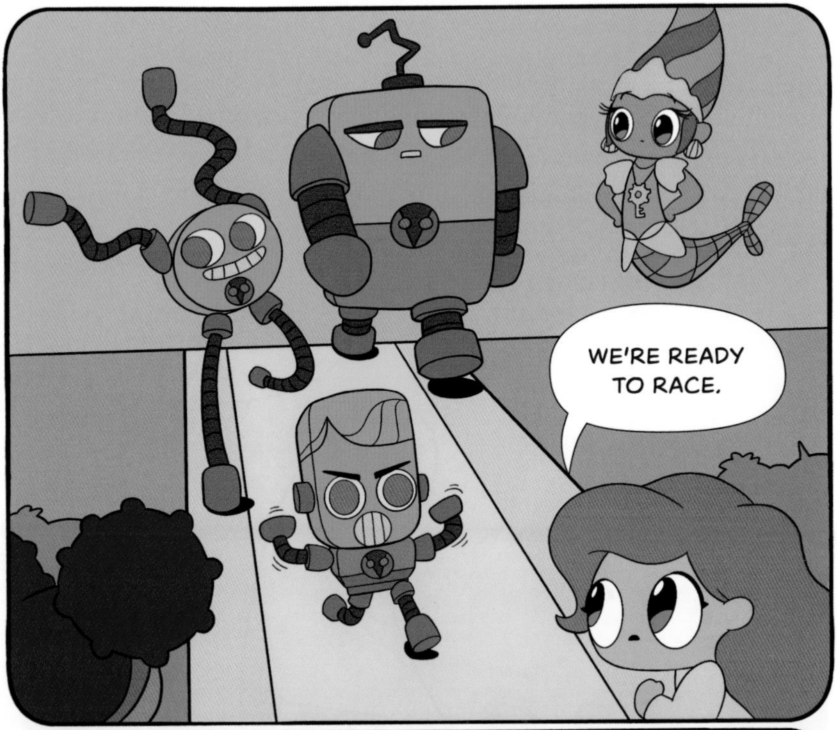
WE'RE READY TO RACE.

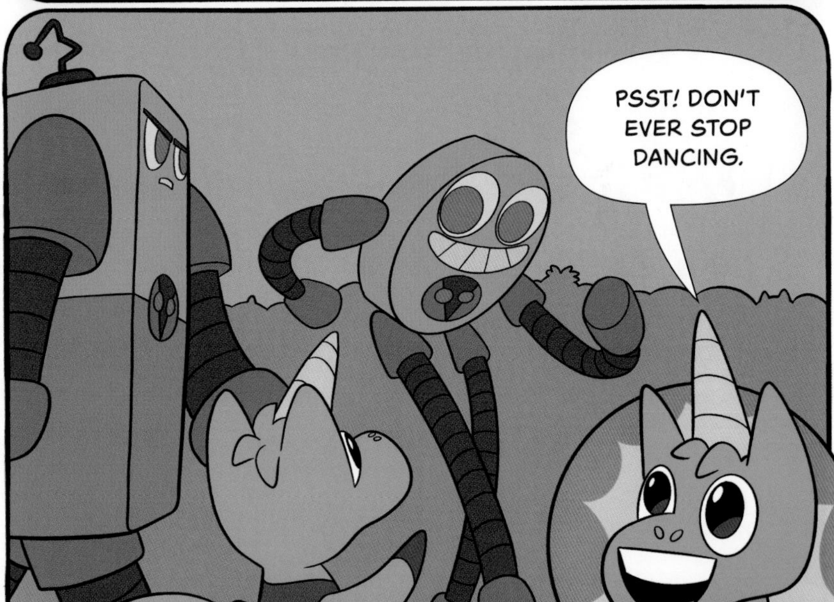
PSST! DON'T EVER STOP DANCING.

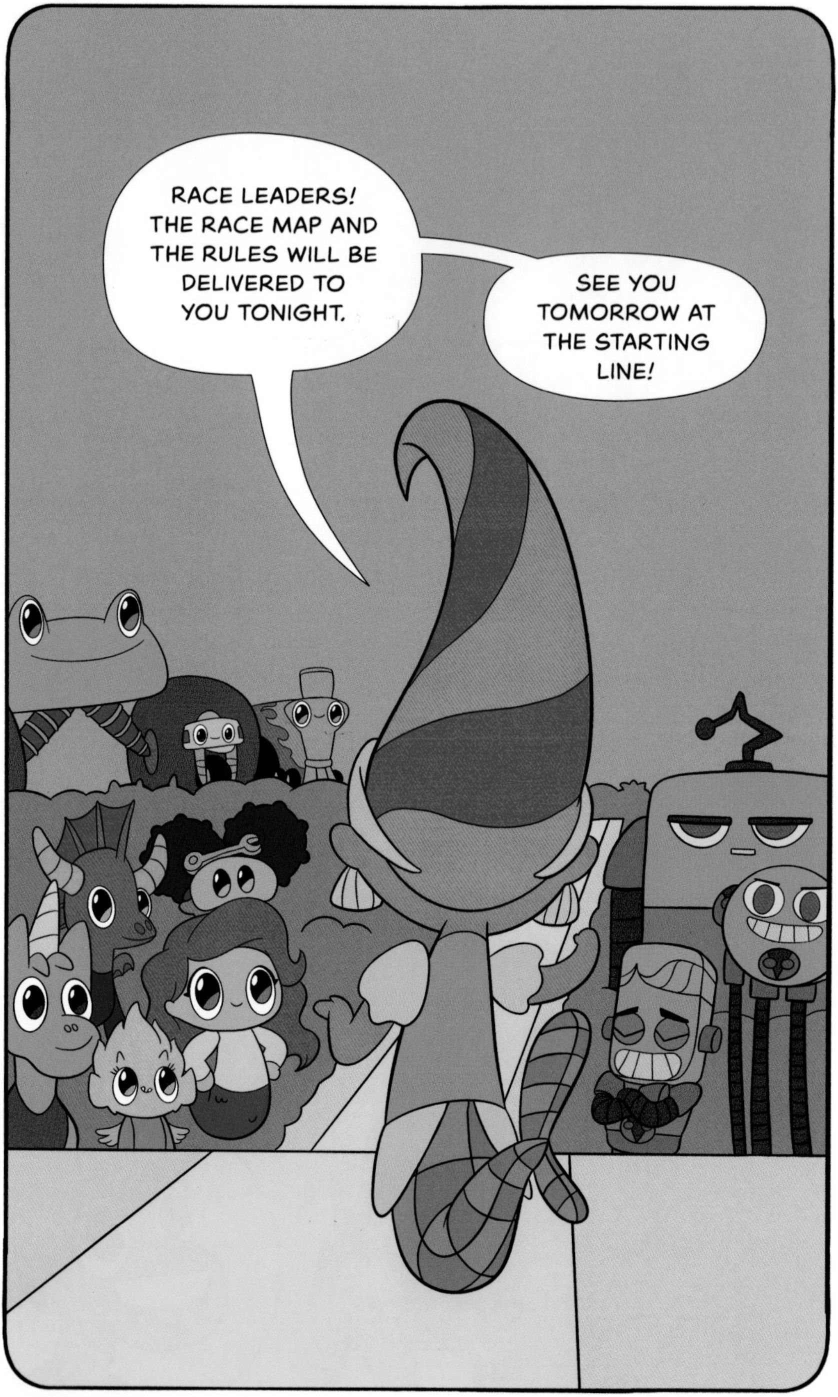
RACE LEADERS! THE RACE MAP AND THE RULES WILL BE DELIVERED TO YOU TONIGHT.
SEE YOU TOMORROW AT THE STARTING LINE!

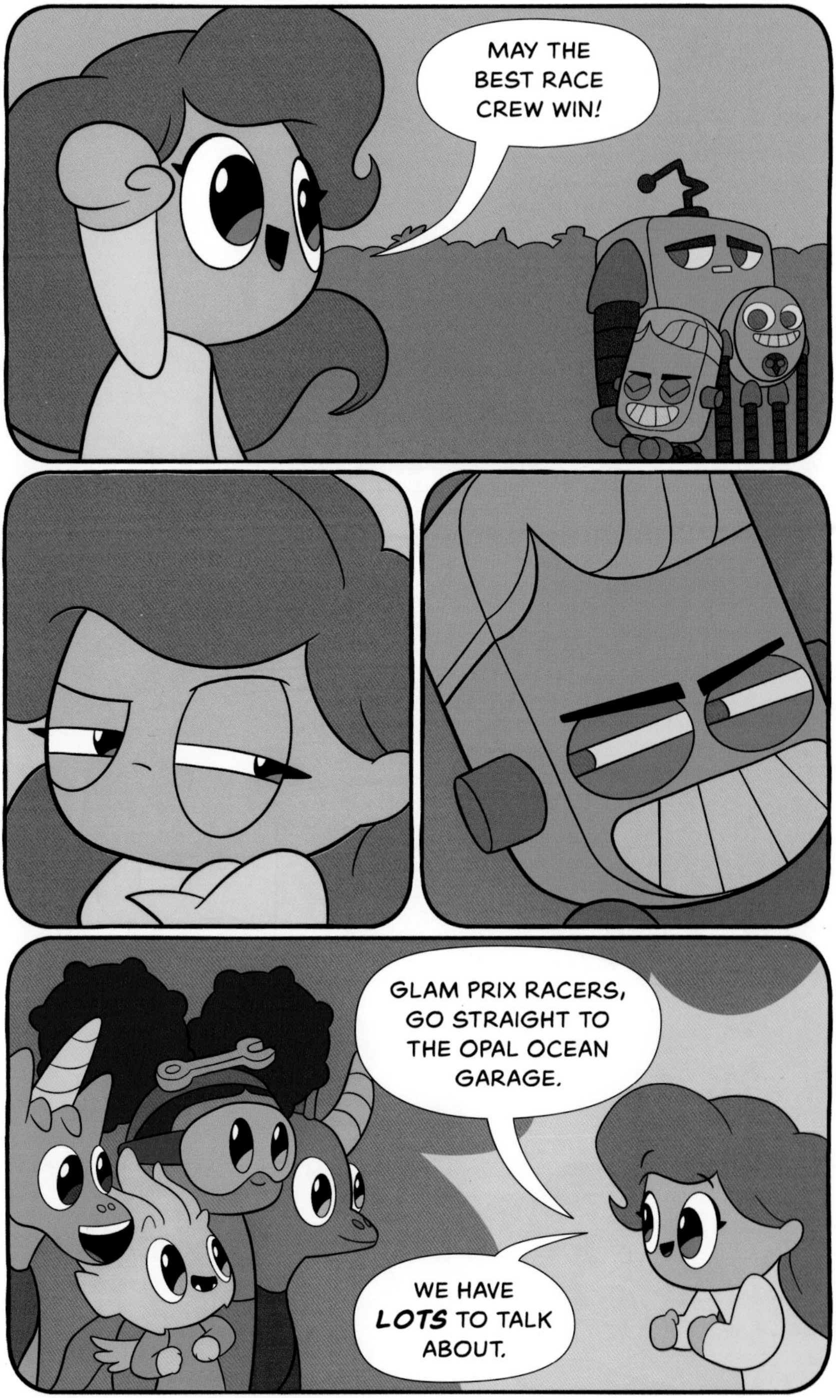
MAY THE BEST RACE CREW WIN!
GLAM PRIX RACERS, GO STRAIGHT TO THE OPAL OCEAN GARAGE.
WE HAVE ***LOTS*** TO TALK ABOUT.

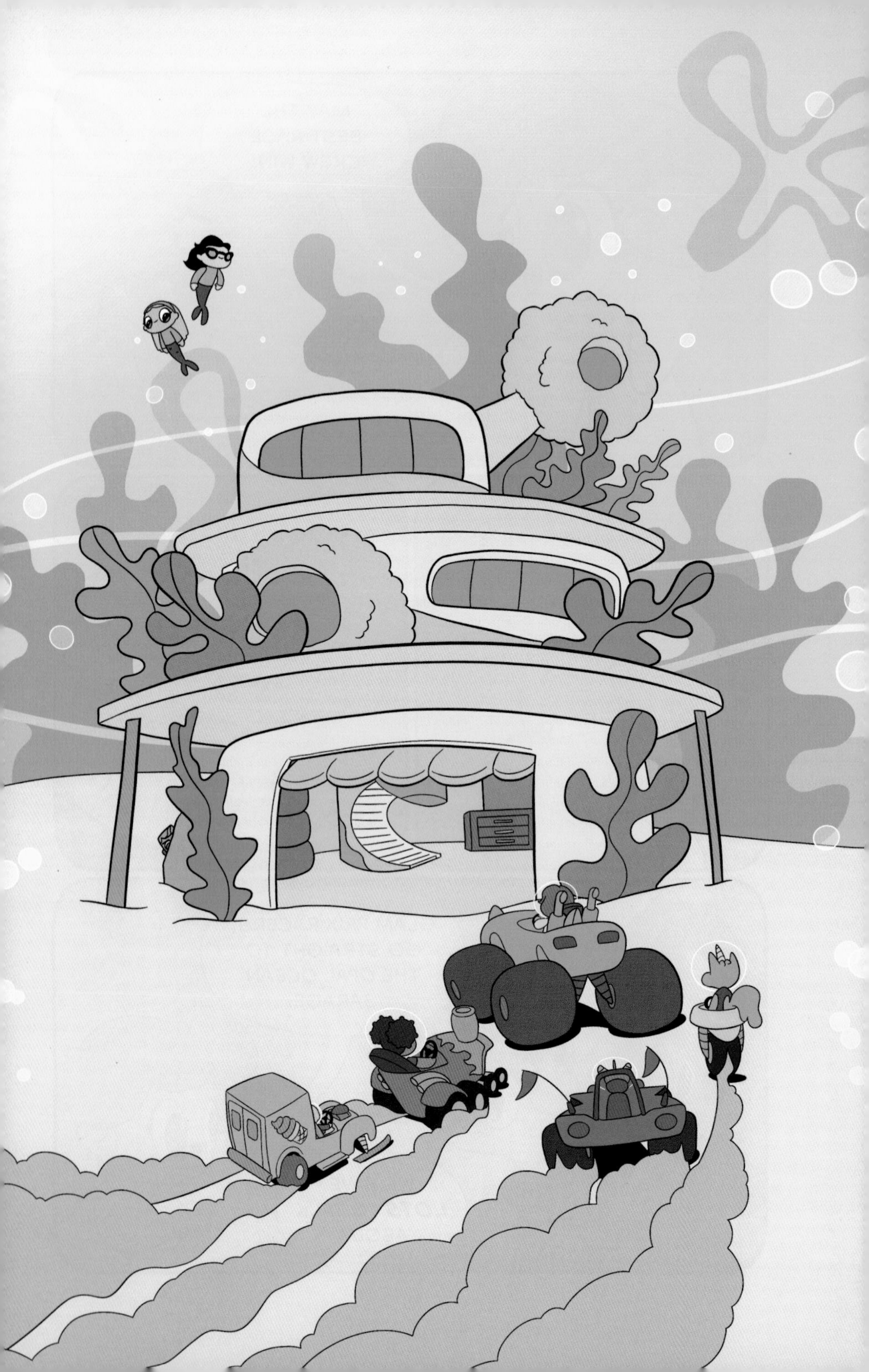

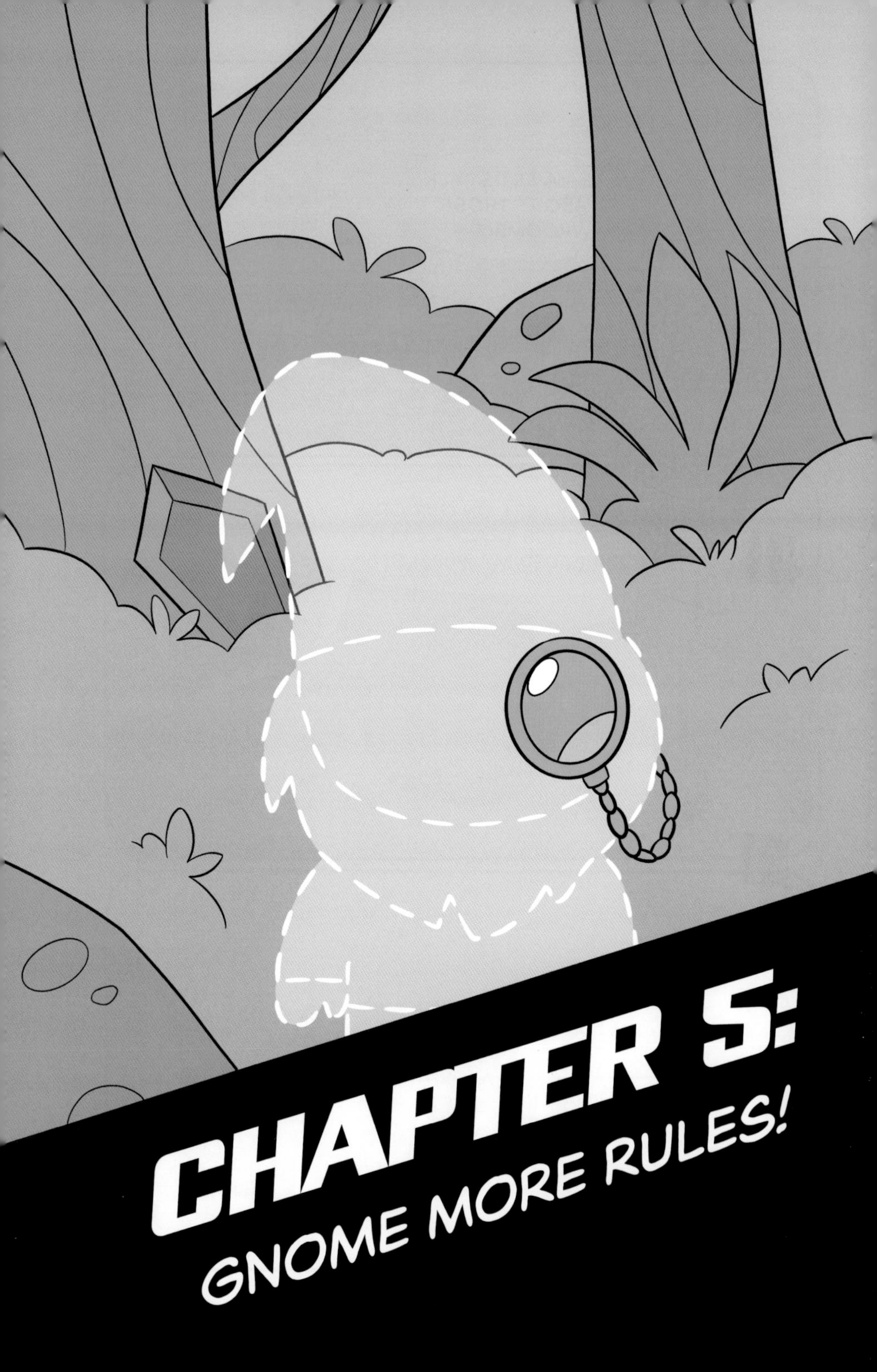

CHAPTER 5:
GNOME MORE RULES!

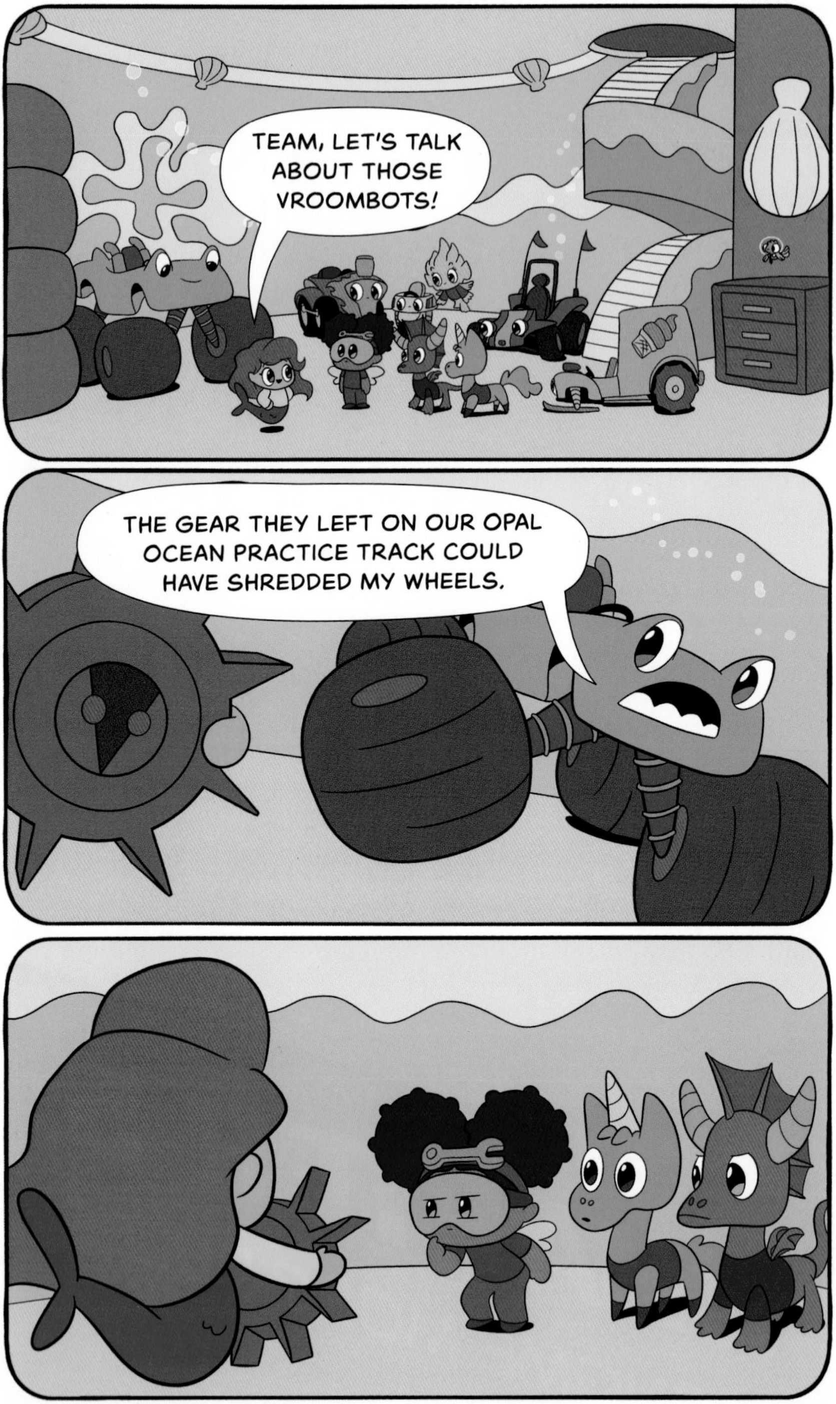
TEAM, LET'S TALK ABOUT THOSE VROOMBOTS!
THE GEAR THEY LEFT ON OUR OPAL OCEAN PRACTICE TRACK COULD HAVE SHREDDED MY WHEELS.

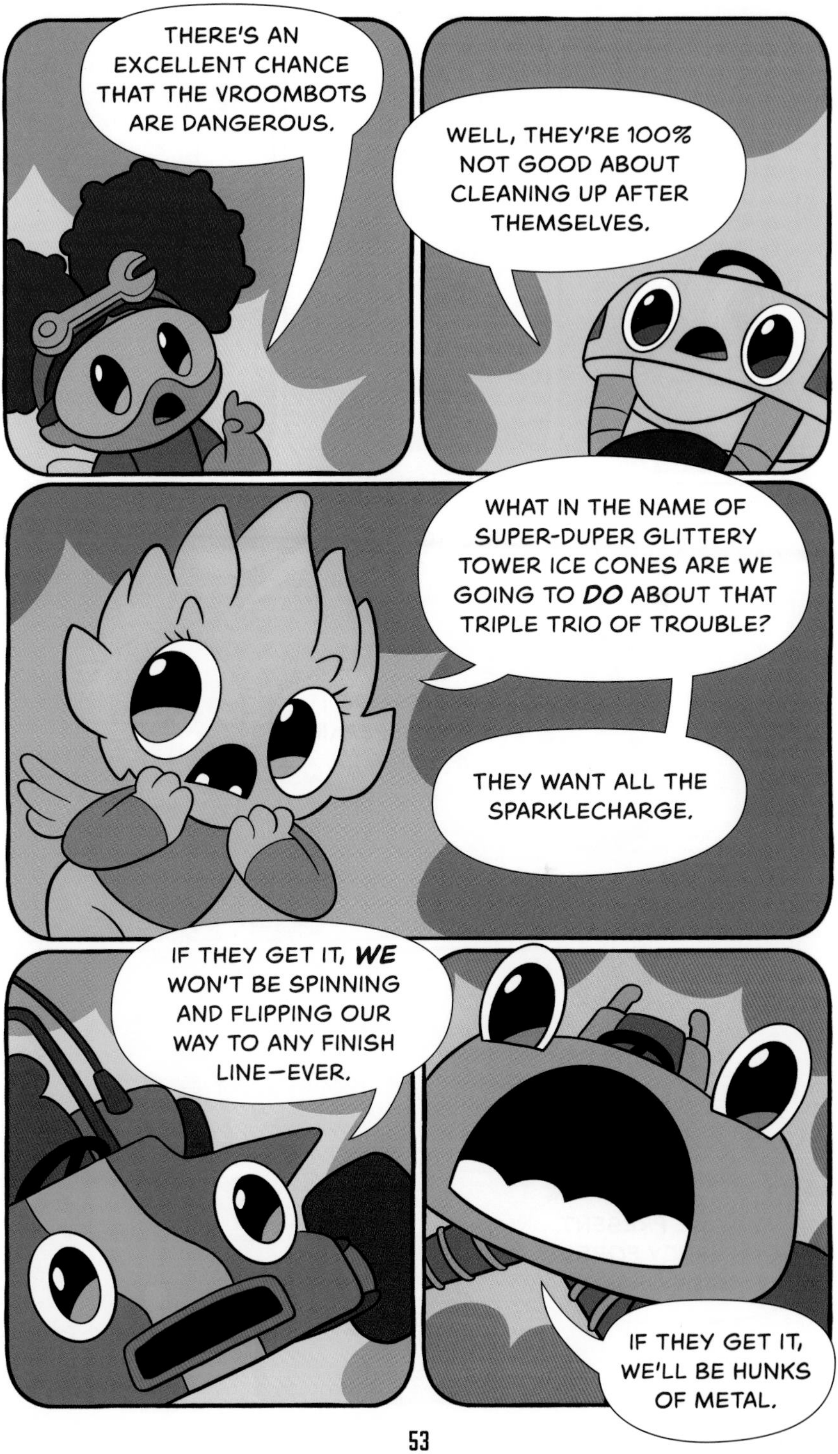
THERE'S AN EXCELLENT CHANCE THAT THE VROOMBOTS ARE DANGEROUS.
WELL, THEY'RE 100% NOT GOOD ABOUT CLEANING UP AFTER THEMSELVES.
WHAT IN THE NAME OF SUPER-DUPER GLITTERY TOWER ICE CONES ARE WE GOING TO ***DO*** ABOUT THAT TRIPLE TRIO OF TROUBLE?
THEY WANT ALL THE SPARKLECHARGE.
IF THEY GET IT, ***WE*** WON'T BE SPINNING AND FLIPPING OUR WAY TO ANY FINISH LINE—EVER.
IF THEY GET IT, WE'LL BE HUNKS OF METAL.

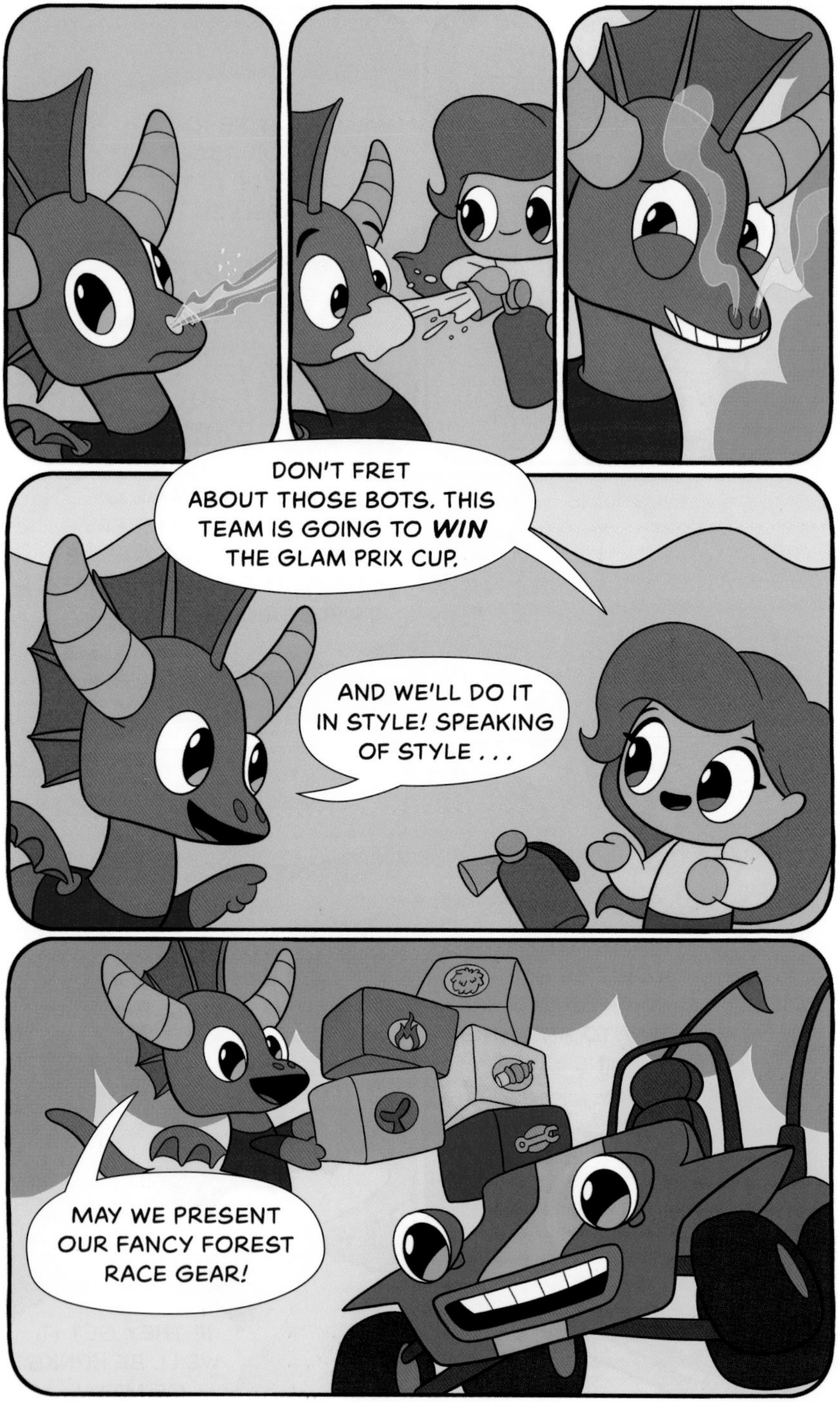
DON'T FRET ABOUT THOSE BOTS. THIS TEAM IS GOING TO **WIN** THE GLAM PRIX CUP.
AND WE'LL DO IT IN STYLE! SPEAKING OF STYLE . . .
MAY WE PRESENT OUR FANCY FOREST RACE GEAR!

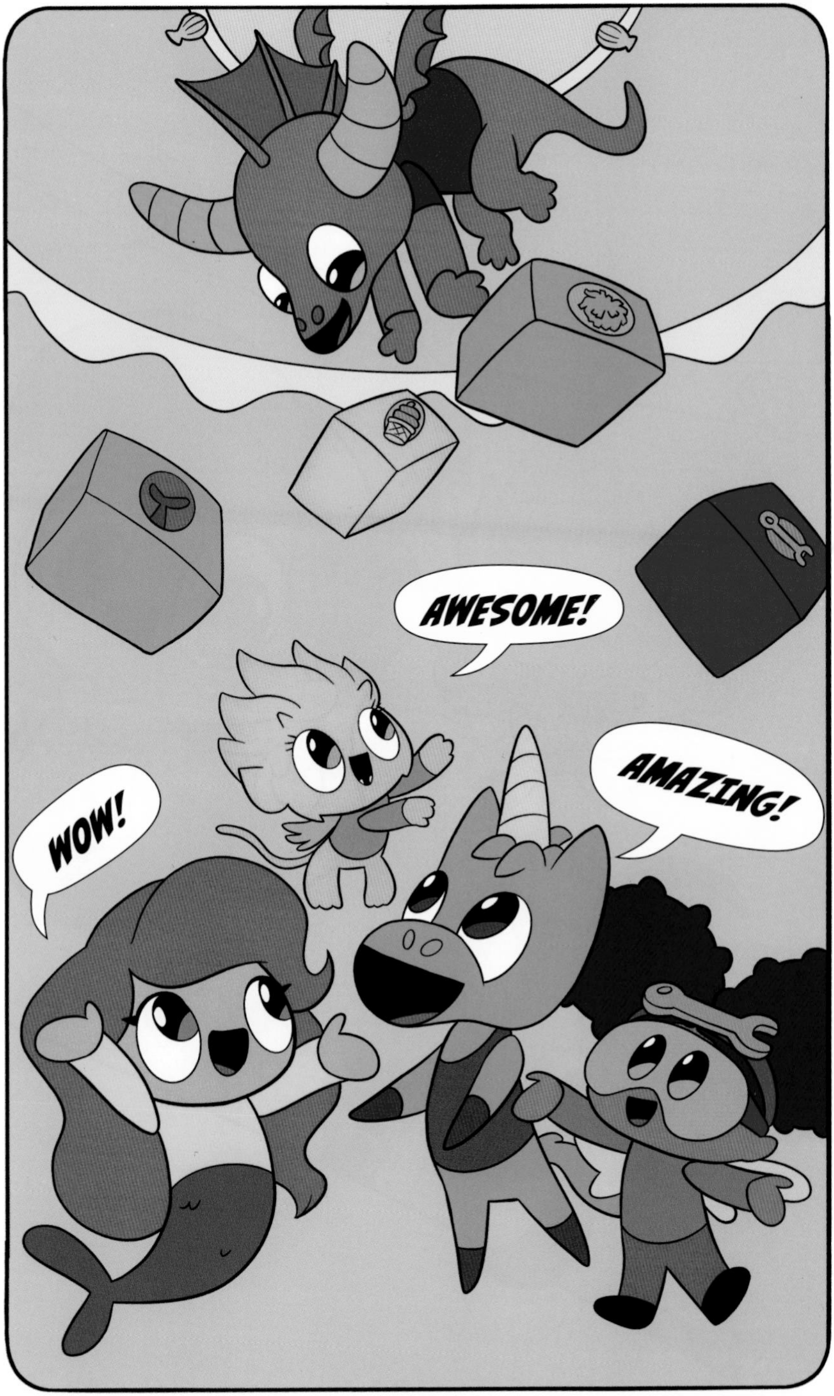
AWESOME!
WOW!
AMAZING!

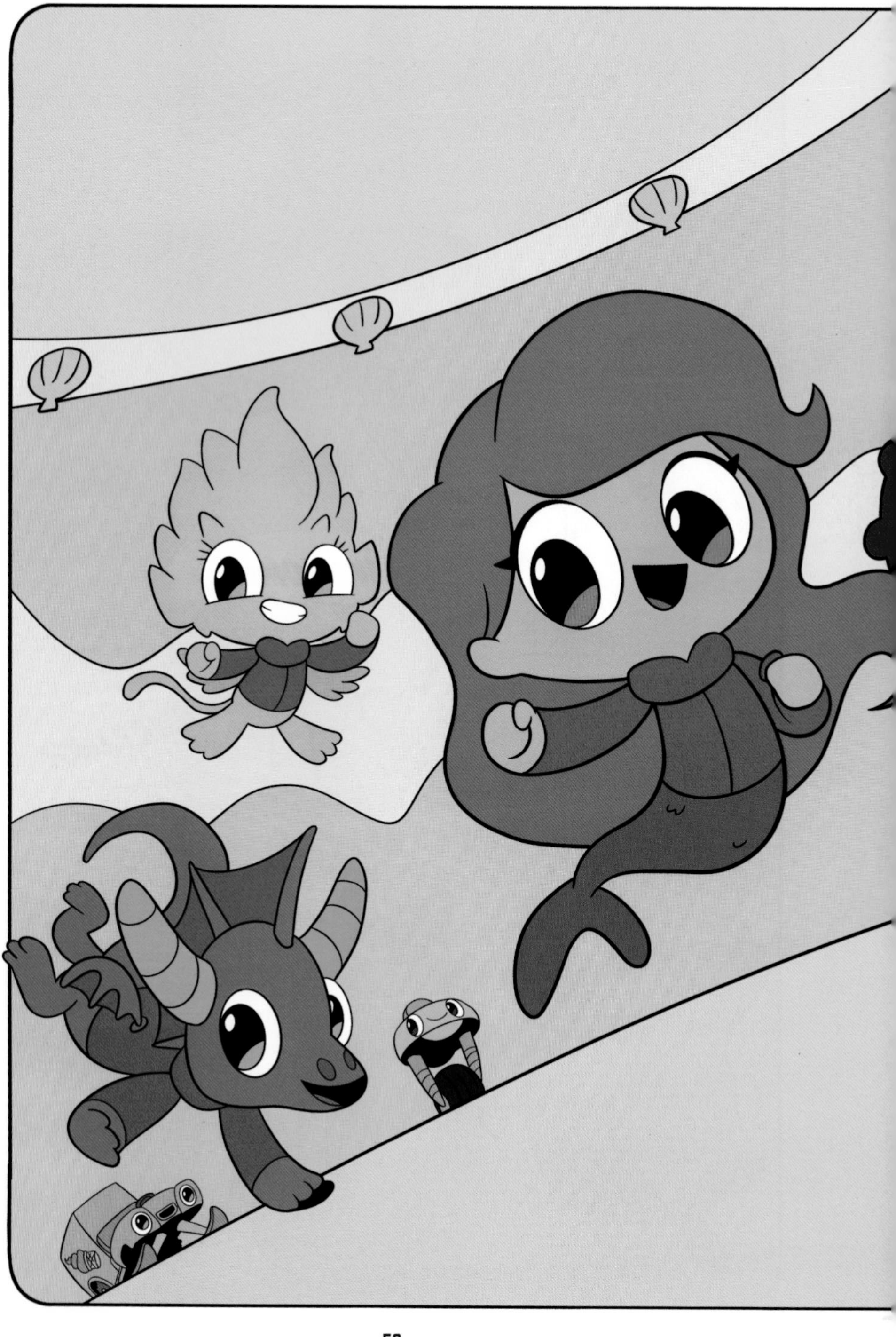

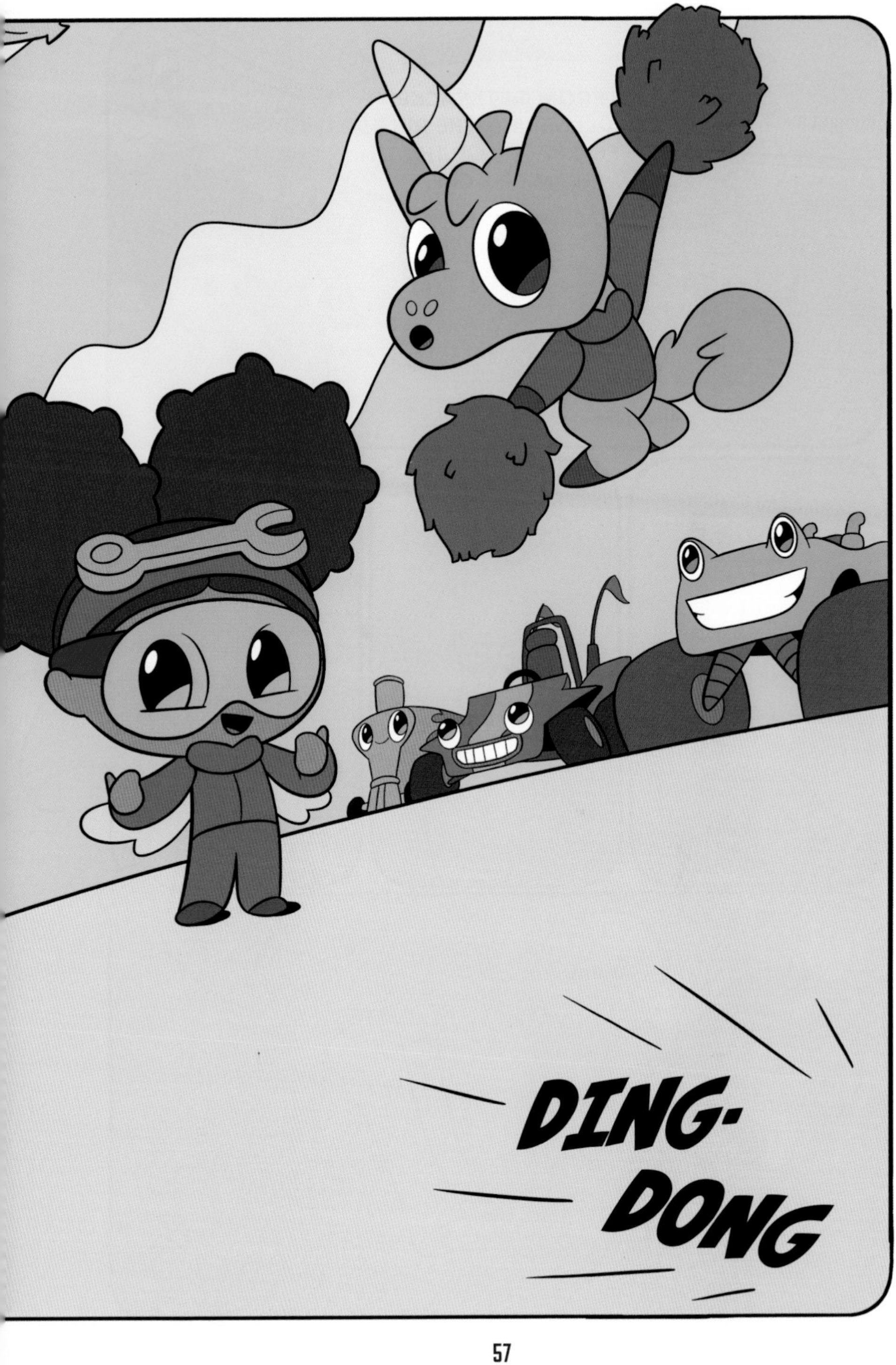
DING-
DONG

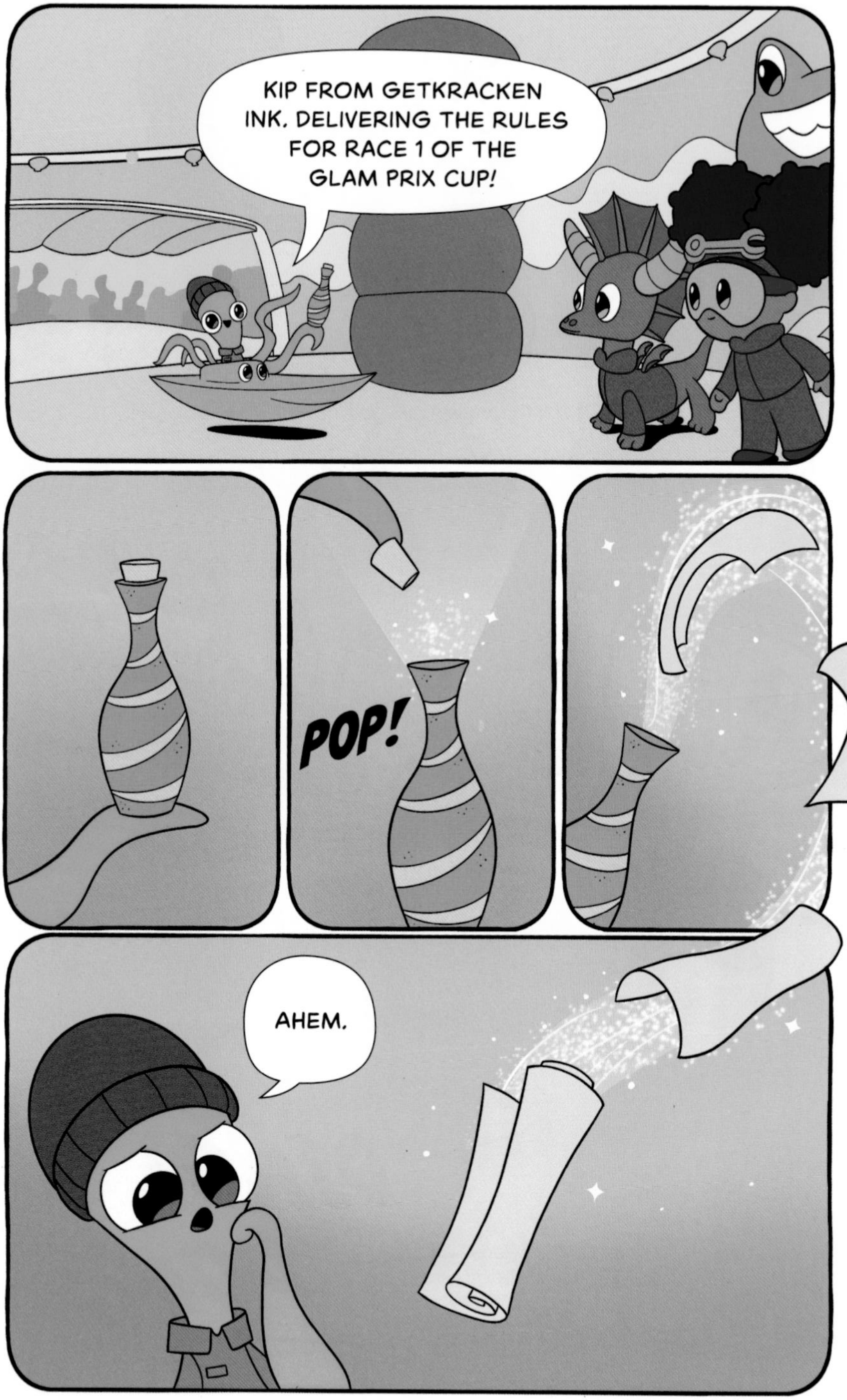
KIP FROM GETKRACKEN INK. DELIVERING THE RULES FOR RACE 1 OF THE GLAM PRIX CUP!
POP!
AHEM.

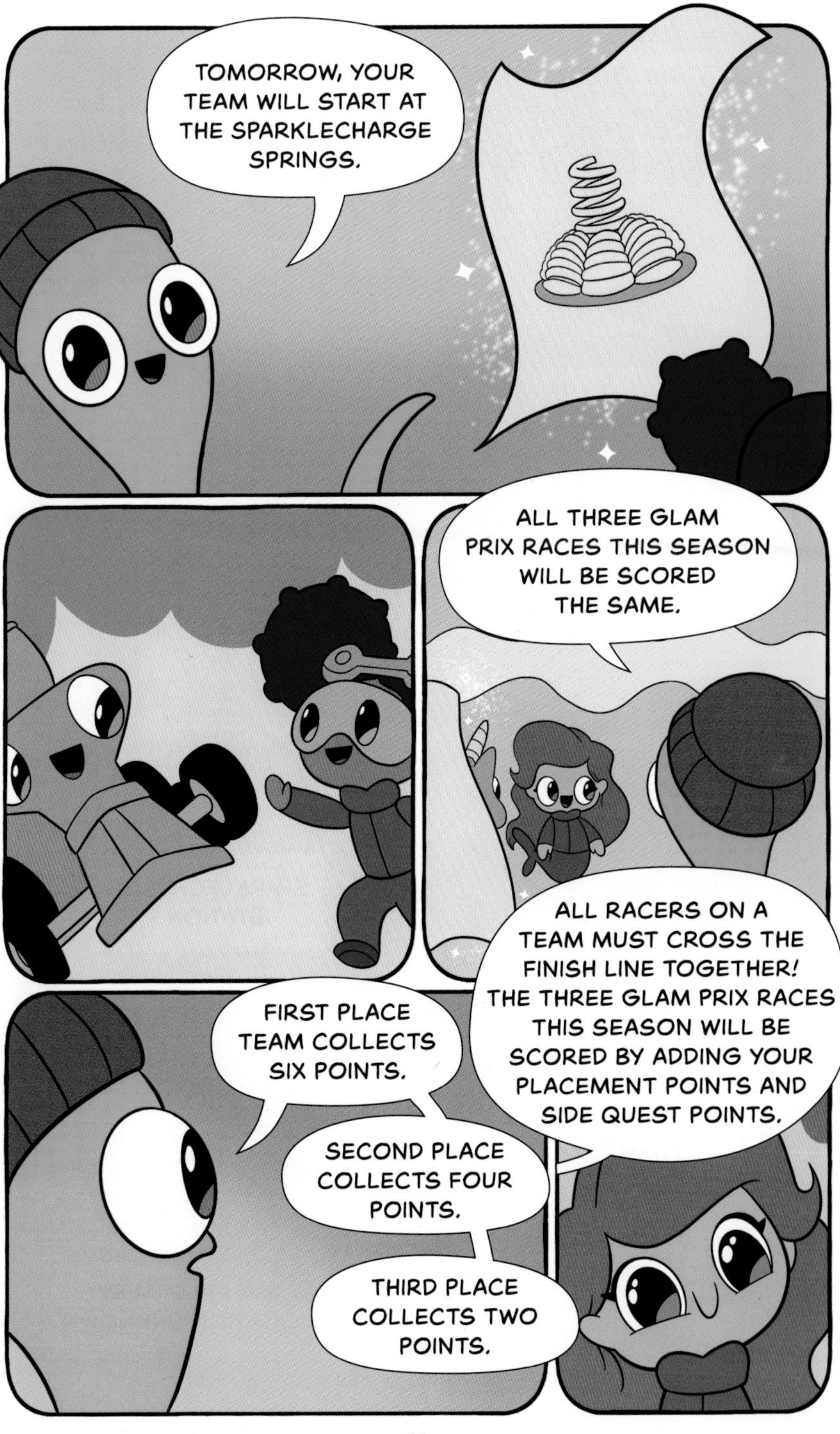
TOMORROW, YOUR TEAM WILL START AT THE SPARKLECHARGE SPRINGS.
ALL THREE GLAM PRIX RACES THIS SEASON WILL BE SCORED THE SAME.
ALL RACERS ON A TEAM MUST CROSS THE FINISH LINE TOGETHER! THE THREE GLAM PRIX RACES THIS SEASON WILL BE SCORED BY ADDING YOUR PLACEMENT POINTS AND SIDE QUEST POINTS.
FIRST PLACE TEAM COLLECTS SIX POINTS.
SECOND PLACE COLLECTS FOUR POINTS.
THIRD PLACE COLLECTS TWO POINTS.

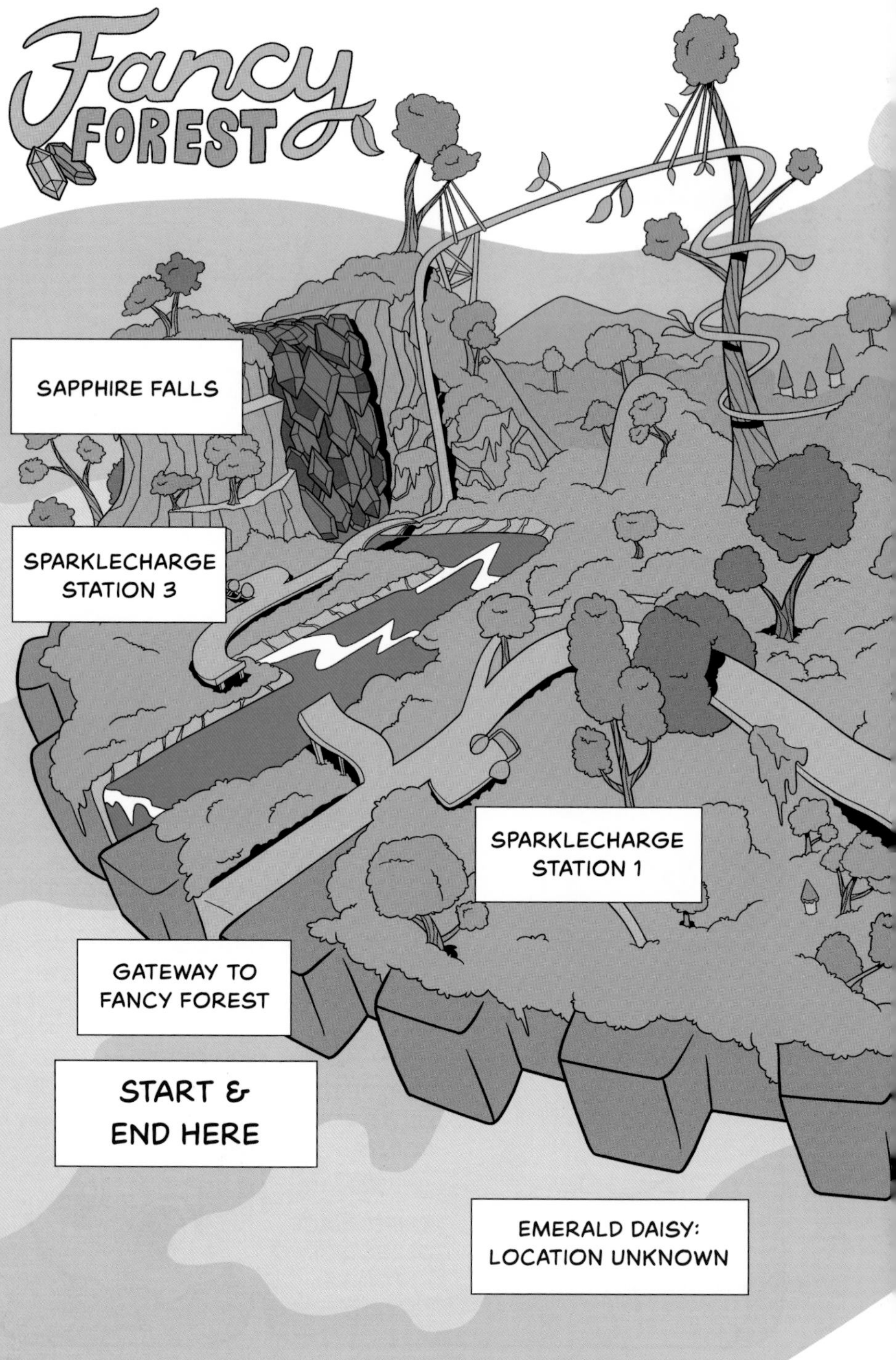
Fancy FOREST
SAPPHIRE FALLS
SPARKLECHARGE STATION 3
SPARKLECHARGE STATION 1
GATEWAY TO FANCY FOREST
START & END HERE
EMERALD DAISY: LOCATION UNKNOWN

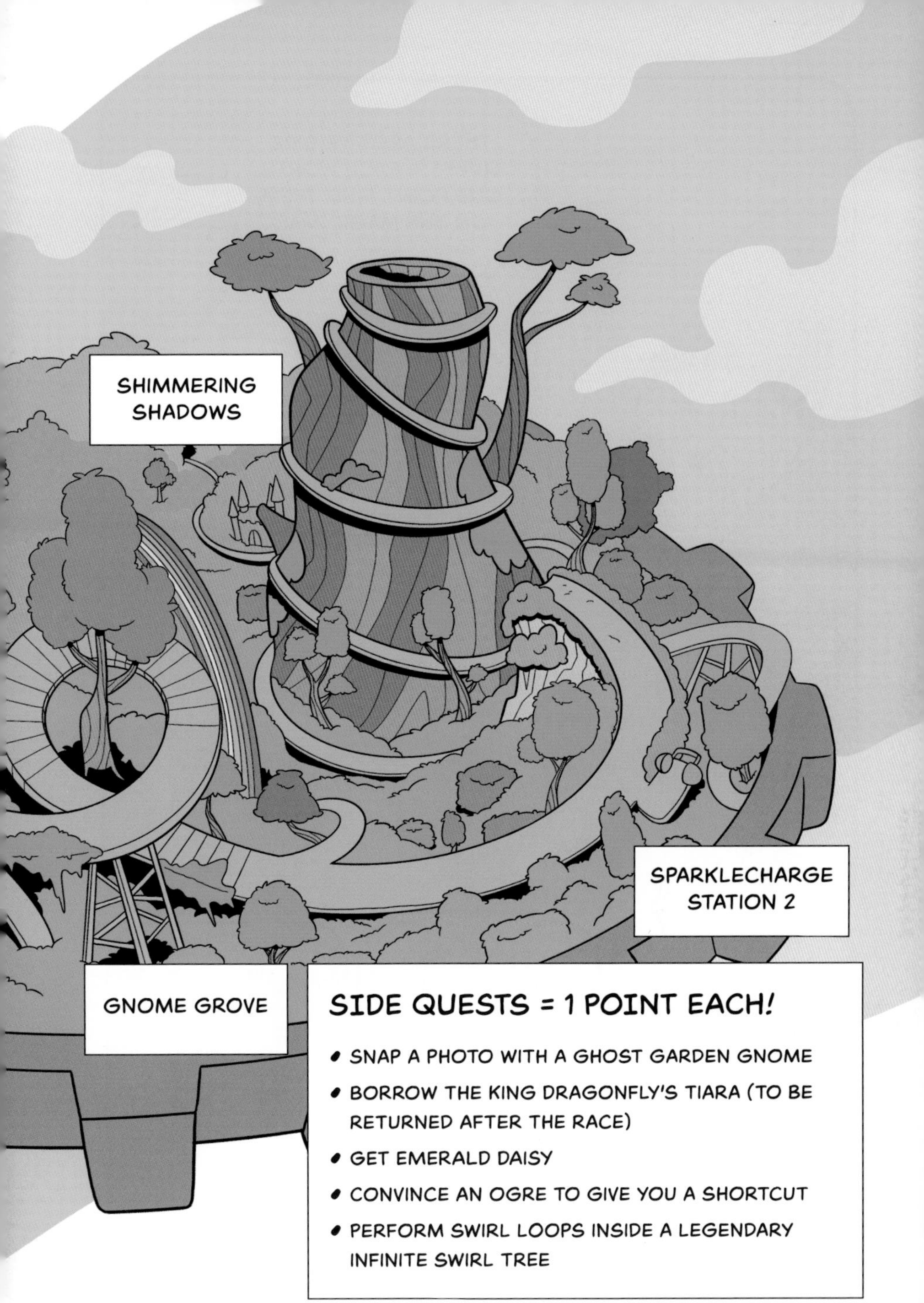
SHIMMERING SHADOWS
SPARKLECHARGE STATION 2
GNOME GROVE

SIDE QUESTS = 1 POINT EACH!

- SNAP A PHOTO WITH A GHOST GARDEN GNOME
- BORROW THE KING DRAGONFLY'S TIARA (TO BE RETURNED AFTER THE RACE)
- GET EMERALD DAISY
- CONVINCE AN OGRE TO GIVE YOU A SHORTCUT
- PERFORM SWIRL LOOPS INSIDE A LEGENDARY INFINITE SWIRL TREE

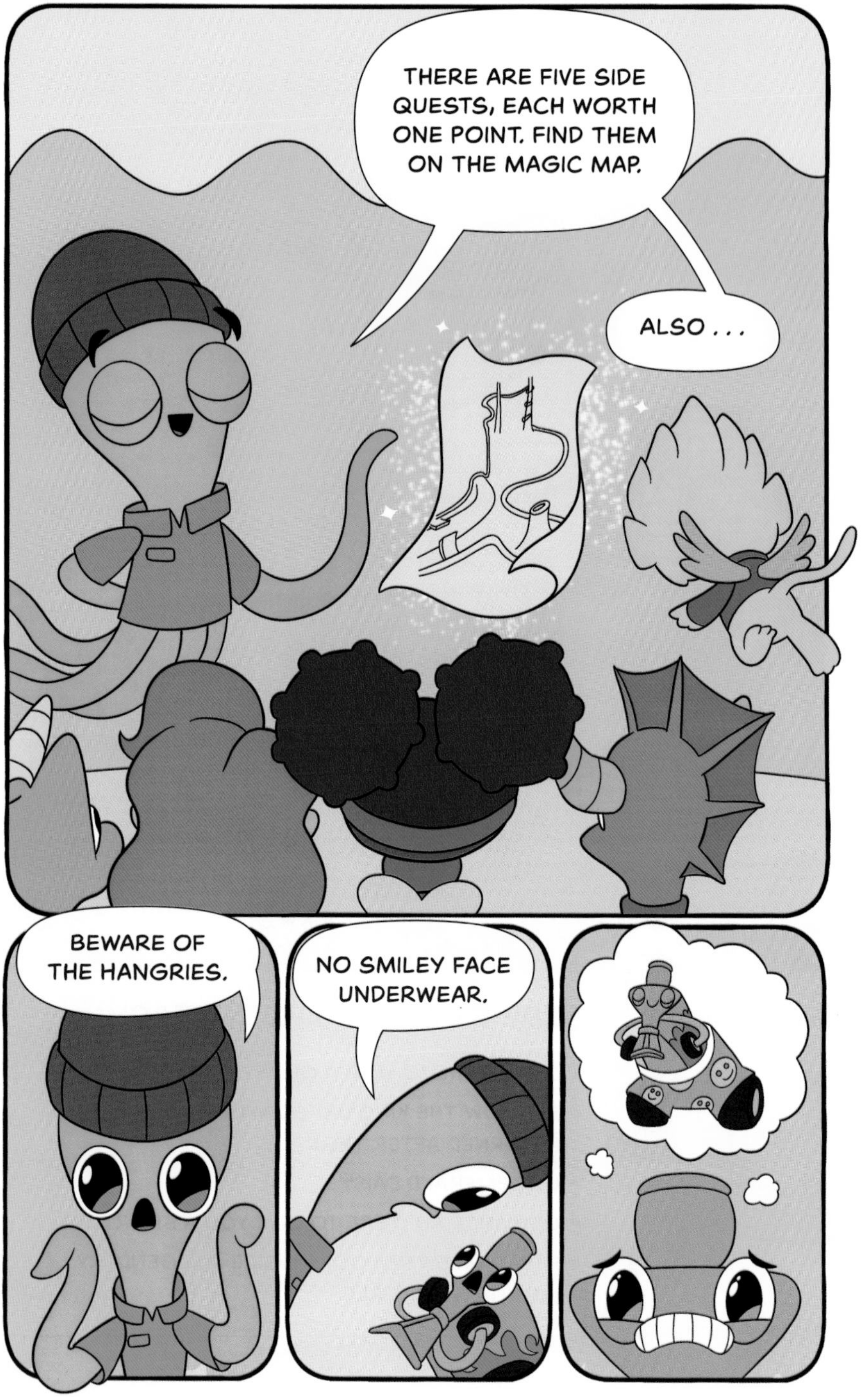
THERE ARE FIVE SIDE QUESTS, EACH WORTH ONE POINT. FIND THEM ON THE MAGIC MAP.
ALSO . . .
BEWARE OF THE HANGRIES.
NO SMILEY FACE UNDERWEAR.

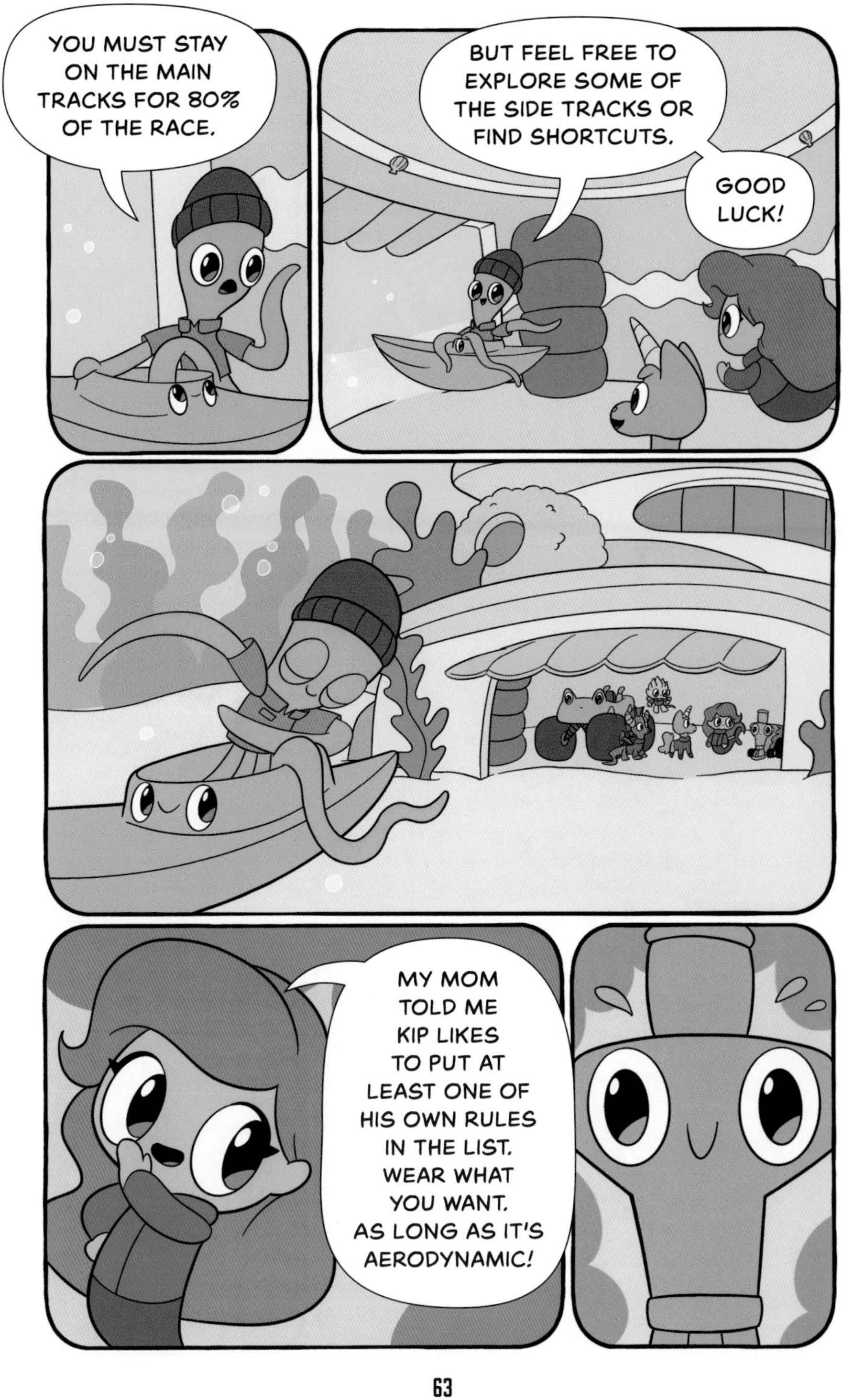
YOU MUST STAY ON THE MAIN TRACKS FOR 80% OF THE RACE.
BUT FEEL FREE TO EXPLORE SOME OF THE SIDE TRACKS OR FIND SHORTCUTS.
GOOD LUCK!
MY MOM TOLD ME KIP LIKES TO PUT AT LEAST ONE OF HIS OWN RULES IN THE LIST. WEAR WHAT YOU WANT. AS LONG AS IT'S AERODYNAMIC!

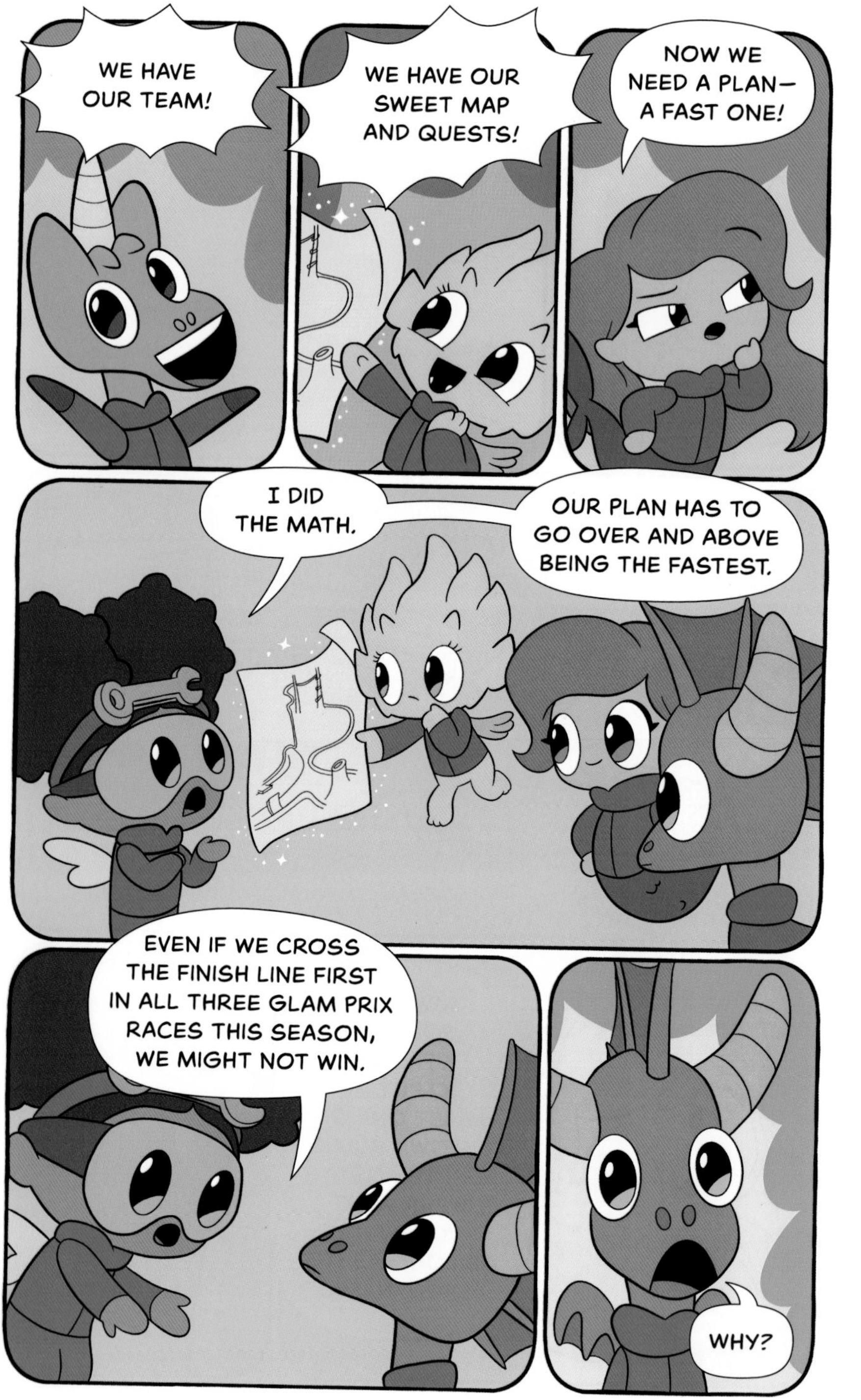
WE HAVE OUR TEAM!
WE HAVE OUR SWEET MAP AND QUESTS!
NOW WE NEED A PLAN— A FAST ONE!
I DID THE MATH.
OUR PLAN HAS TO GO OVER AND ABOVE BEING THE FASTEST.
EVEN IF WE CROSS THE FINISH LINE FIRST IN ALL THREE GLAM PRIX RACES THIS SEASON, WE MIGHT NOT WIN.
WHY?

IF A TEAM COMES IN SECOND PLACE FOR EVERY RACE BUT COLLECTS MORE OF THE SIDE QUESTS, THEY COULD EARN MORE POINTS—AND WIN THE GLAM PRIX CUP.

OKAY, SO LET'S GO FAST, WIN THIS RACE, **AND** GET AS MANY SIDE QUESTS AS POSSIBLE!

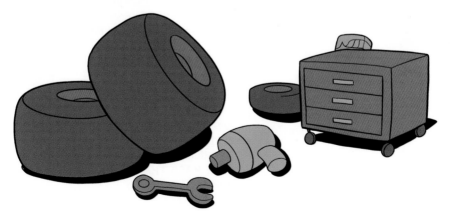

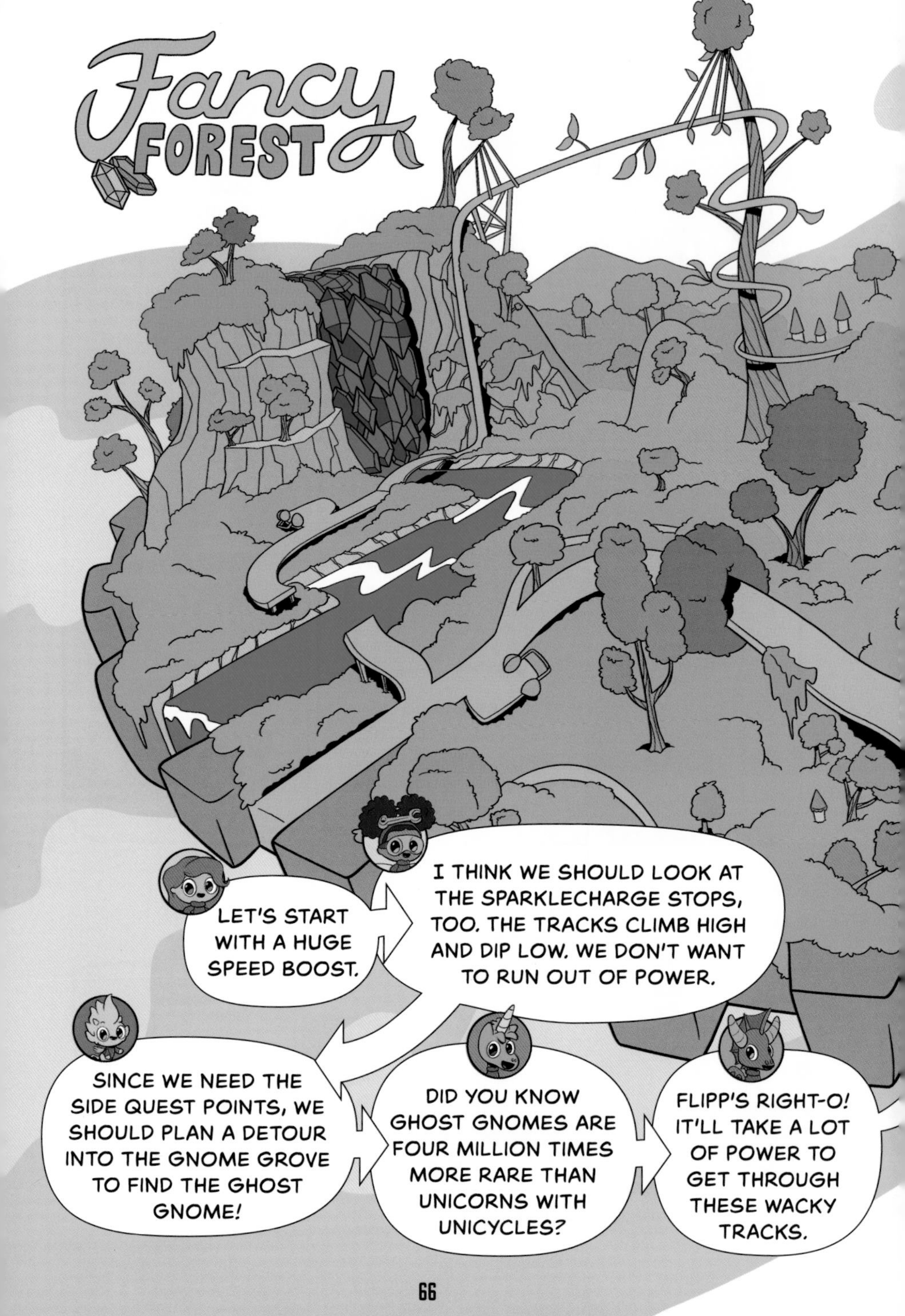
Fancy FOREST
LET'S START WITH A HUGE SPEED BOOST.
I THINK WE SHOULD LOOK AT THE SPARKLECHARGE STOPS, TOO. THE TRACKS CLIMB HIGH AND DIP LOW. WE DON'T WANT TO RUN OUT OF POWER.
SINCE WE NEED THE SIDE QUEST POINTS, WE SHOULD PLAN A DETOUR INTO THE GNOME GROVE TO FIND THE GHOST GNOME!
DID YOU KNOW GHOST GNOMES ARE FOUR MILLION TIMES MORE RARE THAN UNICORNS WITH UNICYCLES?
FLIPP'S RIGHT-O! IT'LL TAKE A LOT OF POWER TO GET THROUGH THESE WACKY TRACKS.

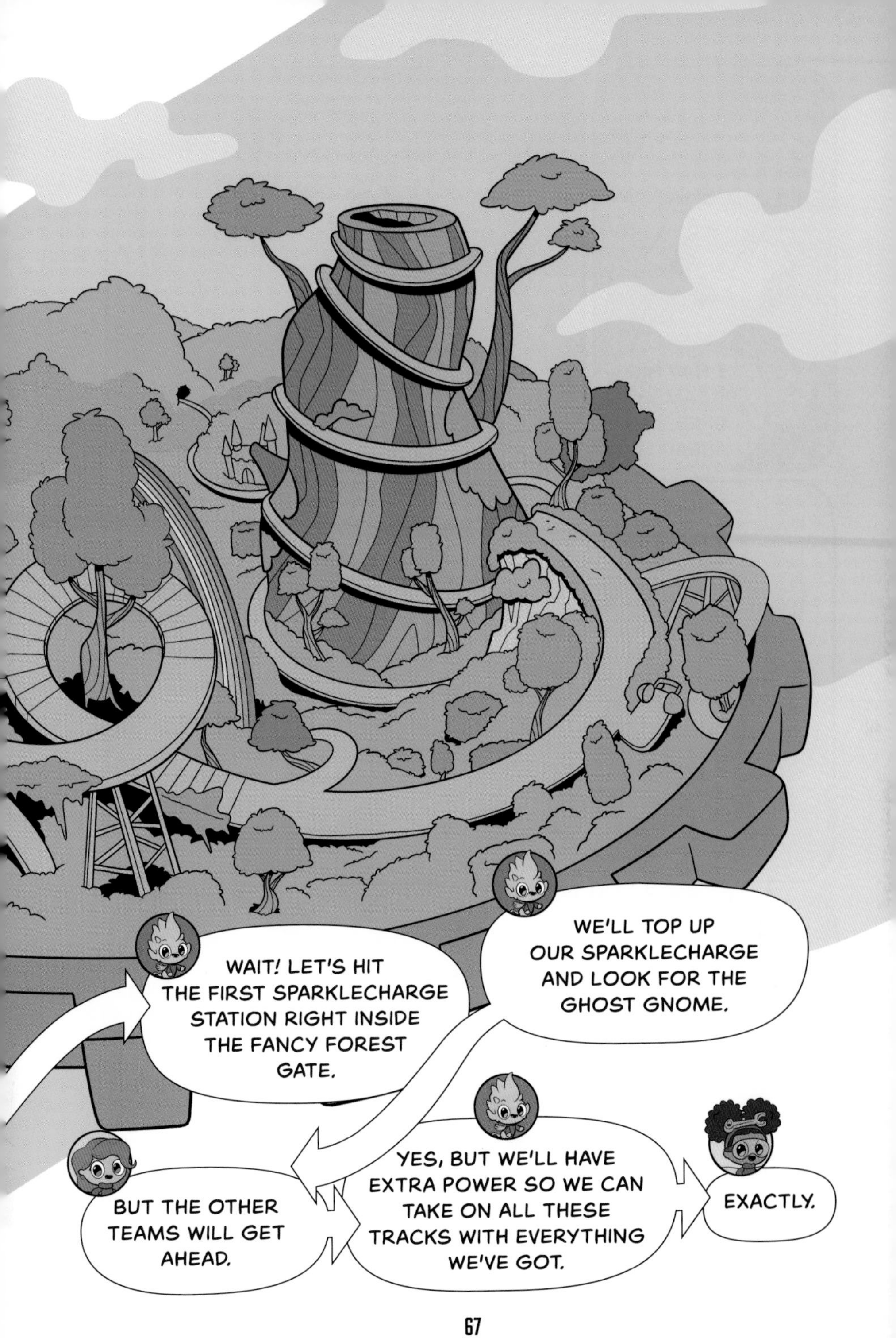
WAIT! LET'S HIT THE FIRST SPARKLECHARGE STATION RIGHT INSIDE THE FANCY FOREST GATE.
WE'LL TOP UP OUR SPARKLECHARGE AND LOOK FOR THE GHOST GNOME.
BUT THE OTHER TEAMS WILL GET AHEAD.
YES, BUT WE'LL HAVE EXTRA POWER SO WE CAN TAKE ON ALL THESE TRACKS WITH EVERYTHING WE'VE GOT.
EXACTLY.

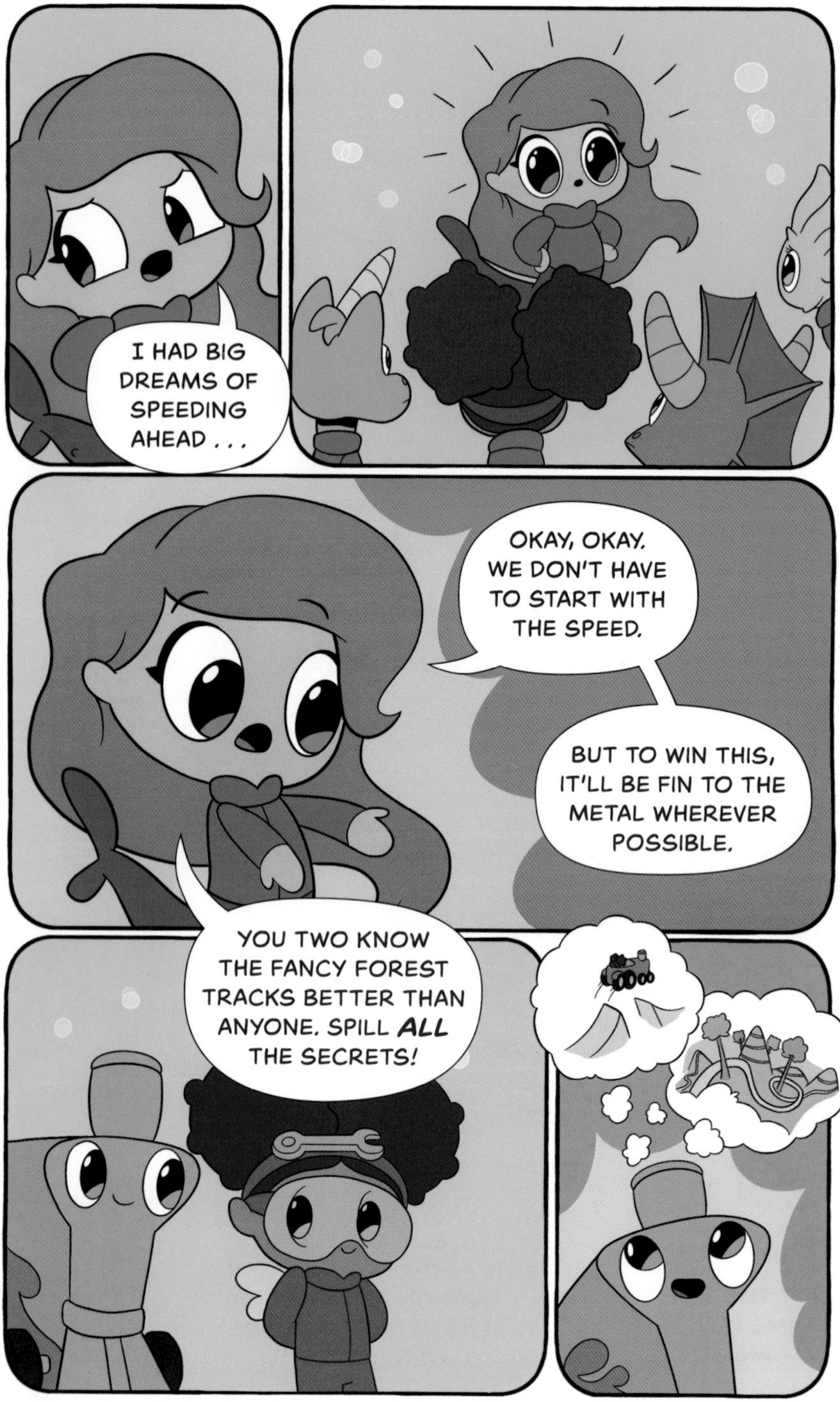
I HAD BIG DREAMS OF SPEEDING AHEAD . . .
OKAY, OKAY. WE DON'T HAVE TO START WITH THE SPEED.
BUT TO WIN THIS, IT'LL BE FIN TO THE METAL WHEREVER POSSIBLE.
YOU TWO KNOW THE FANCY FOREST TRACKS BETTER THAN ANYONE. SPILL ALL THE SECRETS!

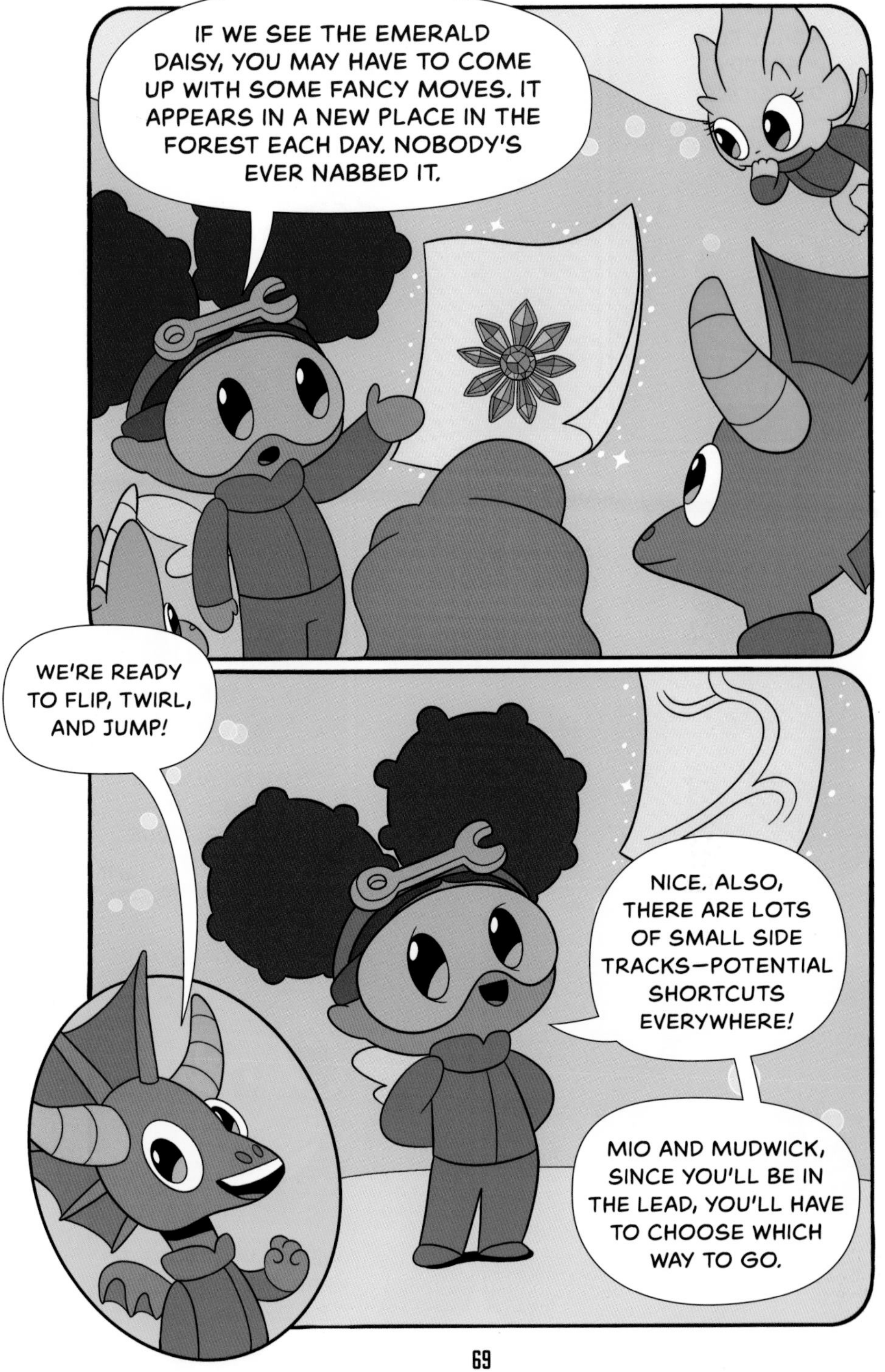
IF WE SEE THE EMERALD DAISY, YOU MAY HAVE TO COME UP WITH SOME FANCY MOVES. IT APPEARS IN A NEW PLACE IN THE FOREST EACH DAY. NOBODY'S EVER NABBED IT.
WE'RE READY TO FLIP, TWIRL, AND JUMP!
NICE. ALSO, THERE ARE LOTS OF SMALL SIDE TRACKS—POTENTIAL SHORTCUTS EVERYWHERE!
MIO AND MUDWICK, SINCE YOU'LL BE IN THE LEAD, YOU'LL HAVE TO CHOOSE WHICH WAY TO GO.

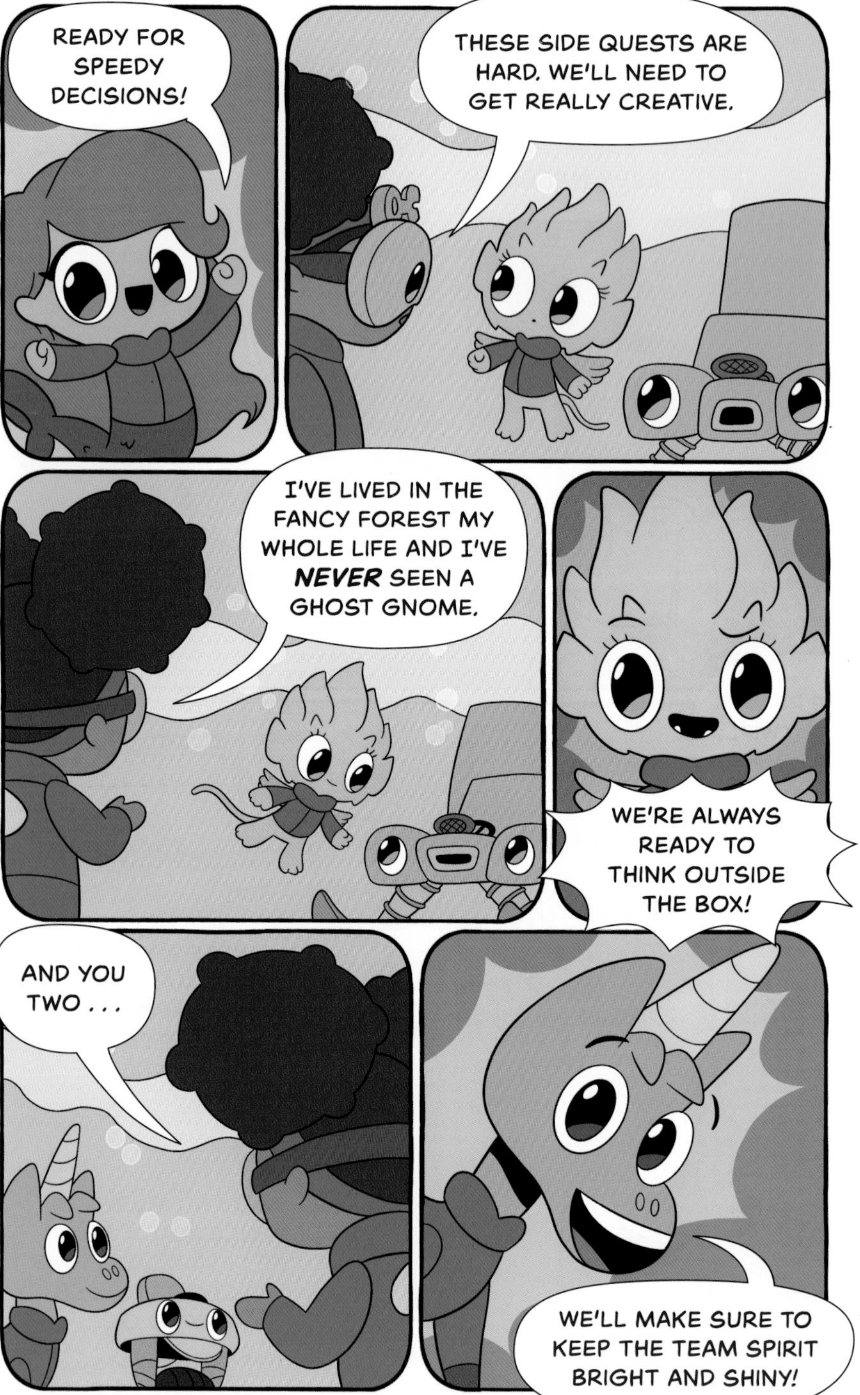
READY FOR SPEEDY DECISIONS!
THESE SIDE QUESTS ARE HARD. WE'LL NEED TO GET REALLY CREATIVE.
I'VE LIVED IN THE FANCY FOREST MY WHOLE LIFE AND I'VE ***NEVER*** SEEN A GHOST GNOME.
WE'RE ALWAYS READY TO THINK OUTSIDE THE BOX!
AND YOU TWO . . .
WE'LL MAKE SURE TO KEEP THE TEAM SPIRIT BRIGHT AND SHINY!

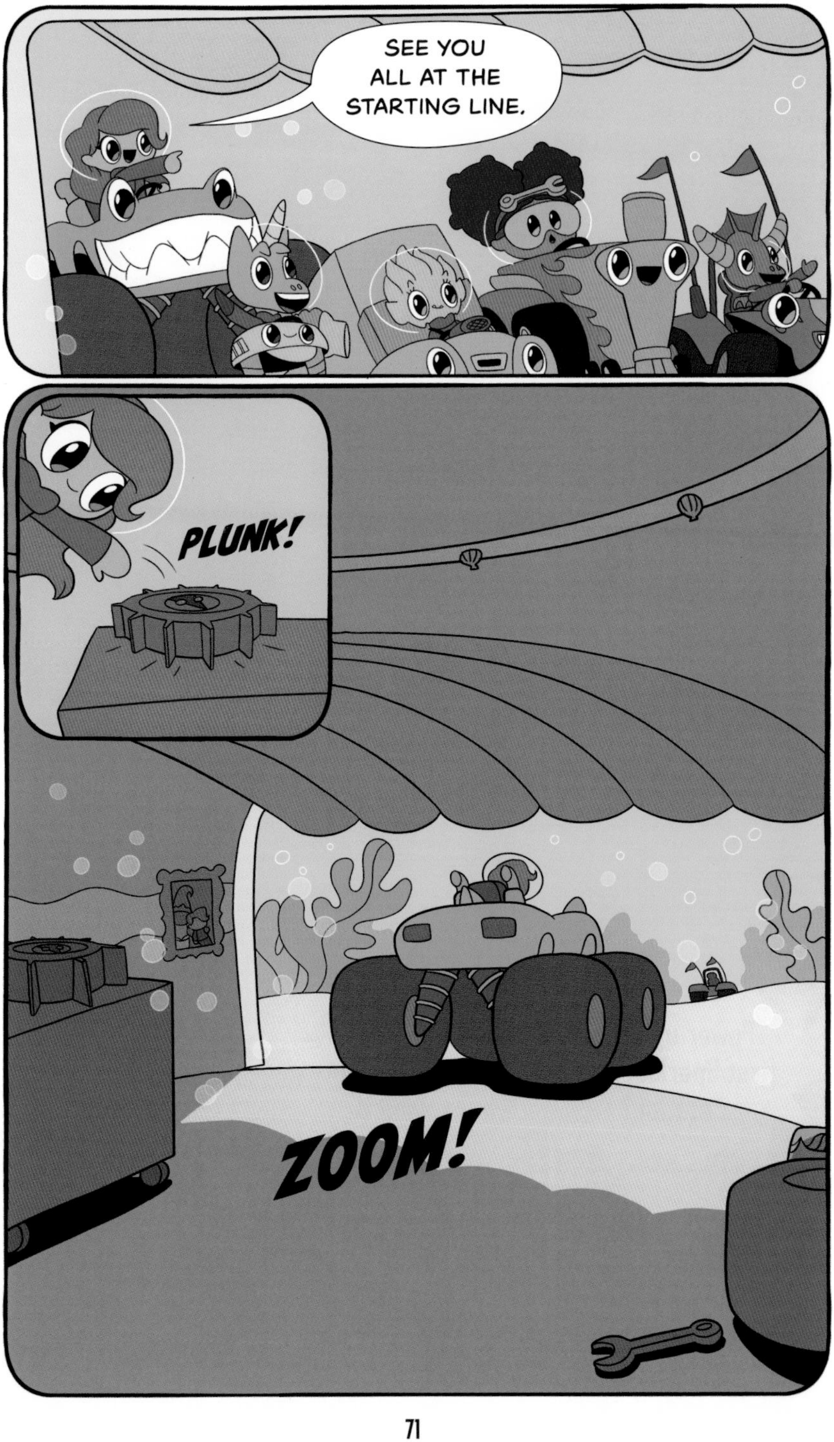
SEE YOU ALL AT THE STARTING LINE.
PLUNK!
ZOOM!

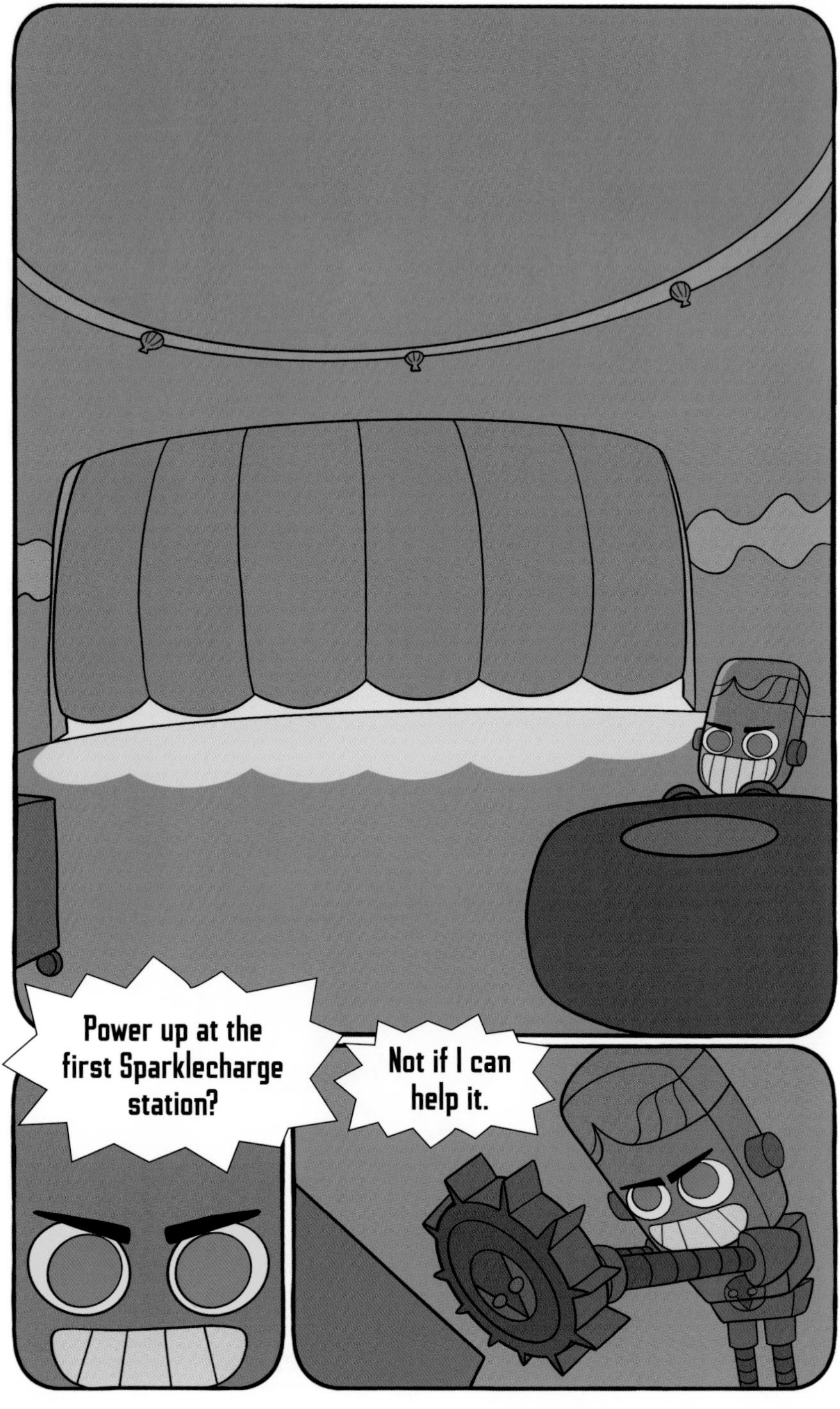
Power up at the first Sparklecharge station?
Not if I can help it.

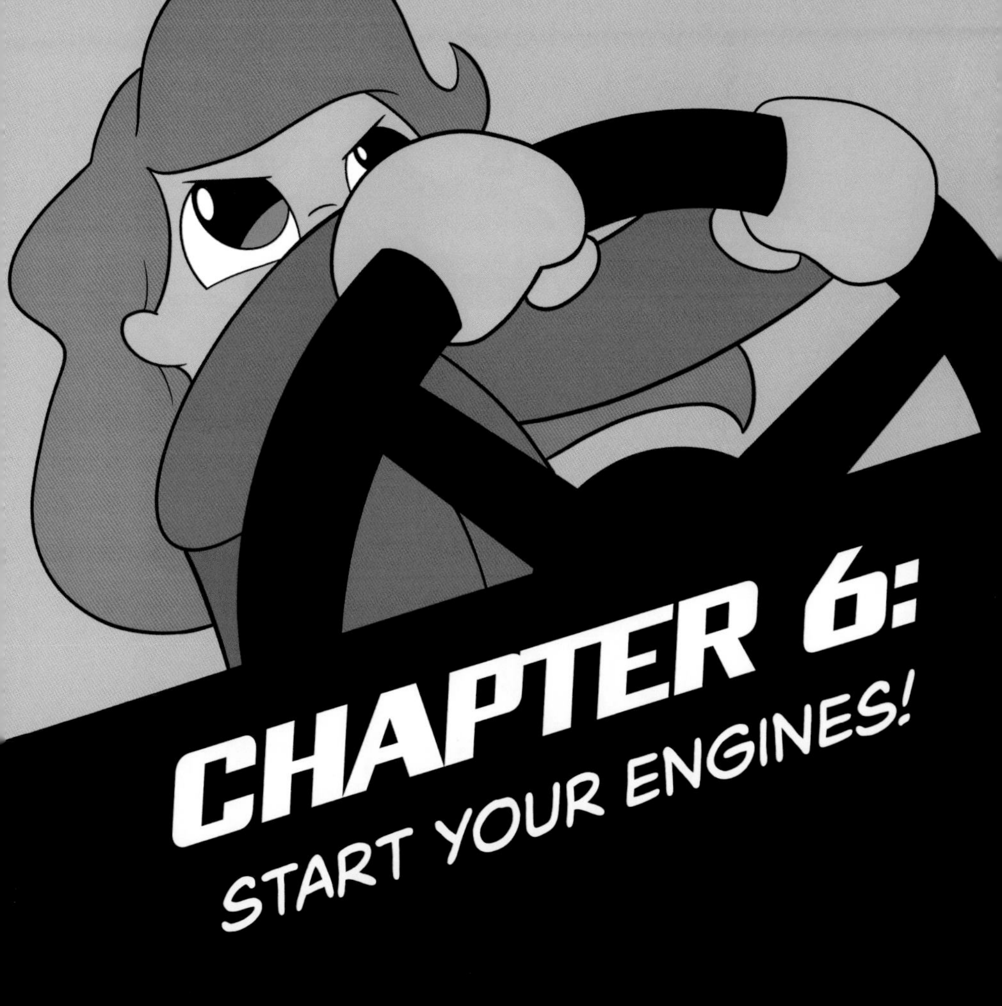

CHAPTER 6:
START YOUR ENGINES!

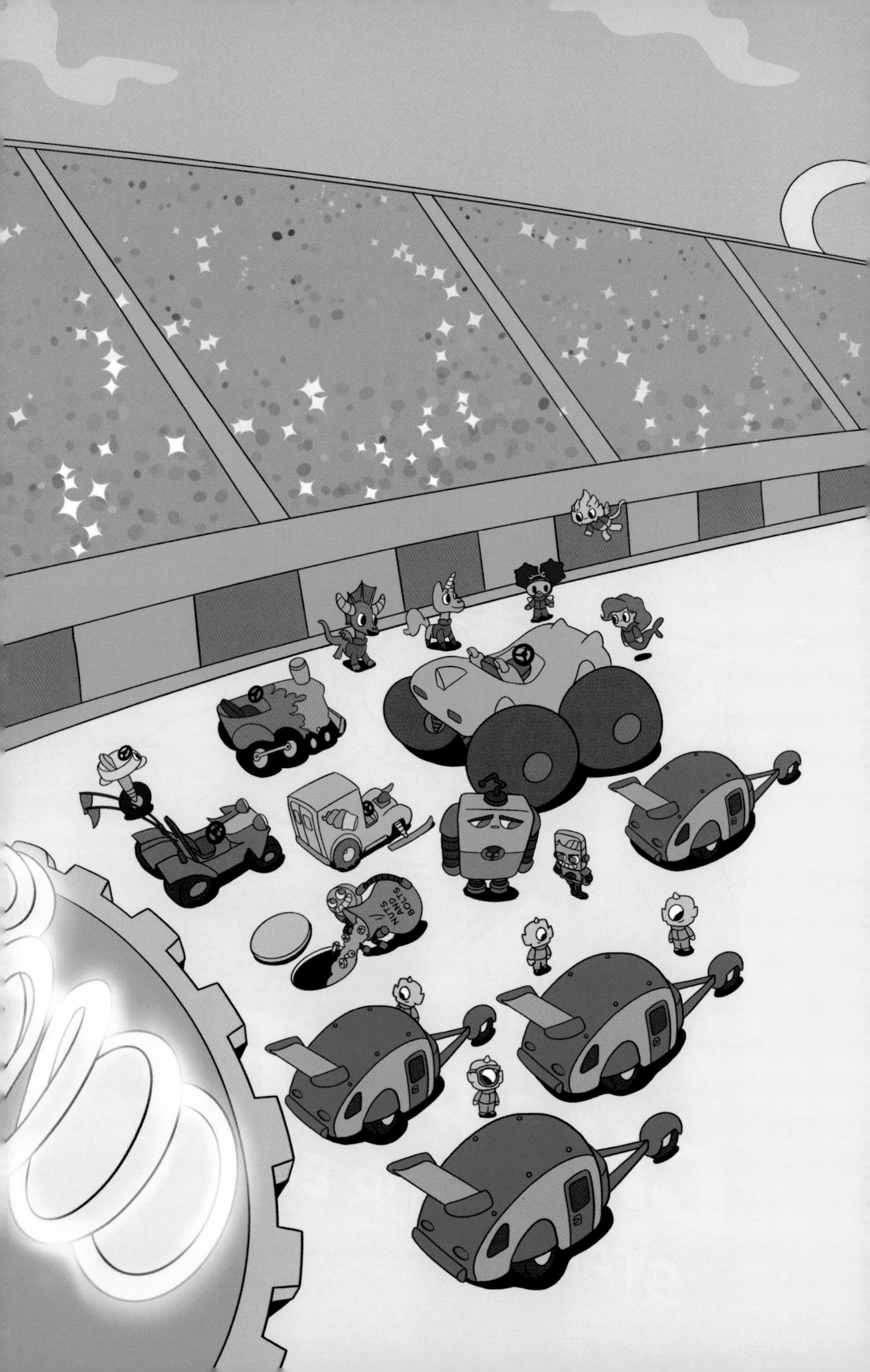
NUTS AND BOLTS

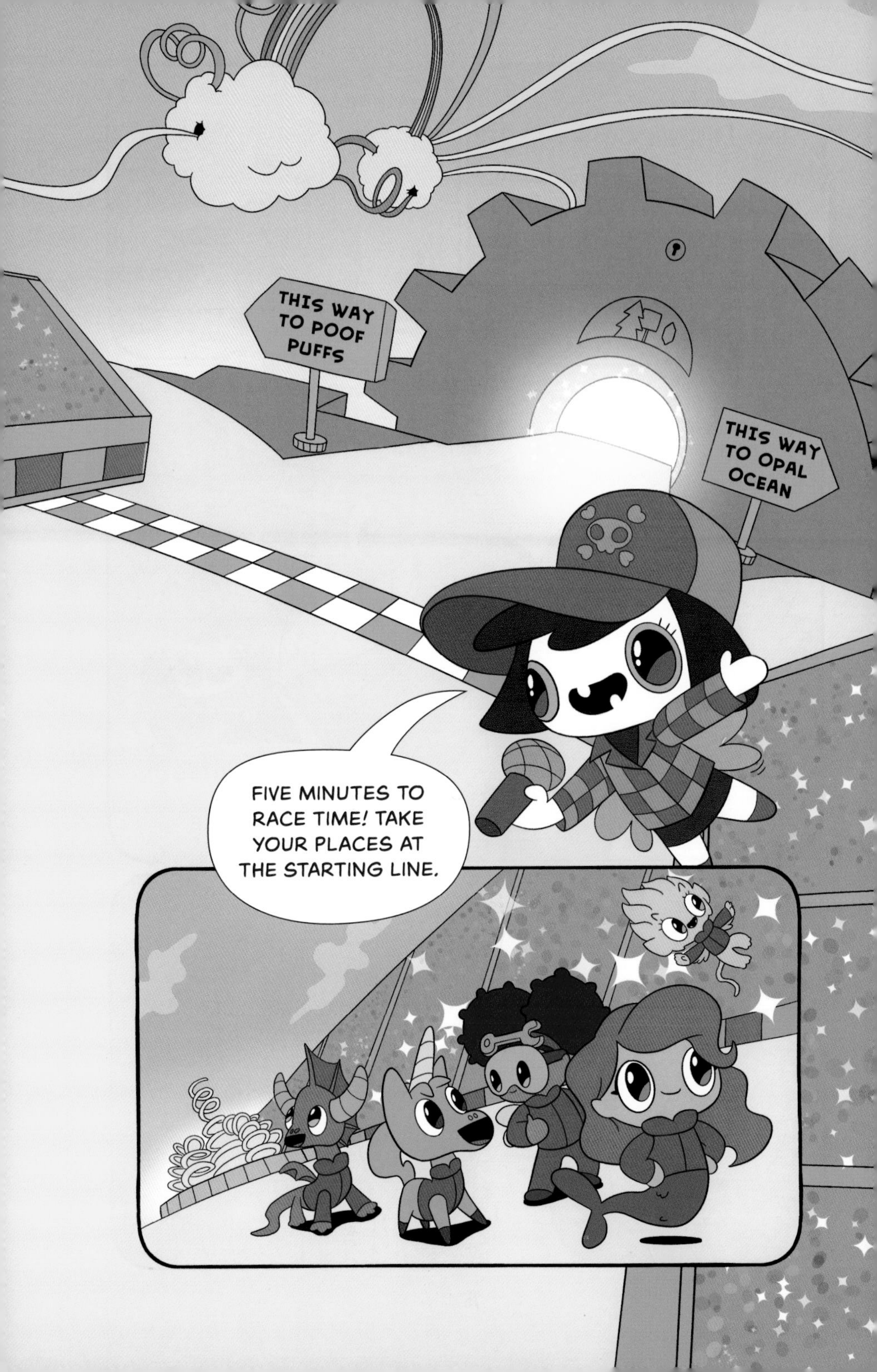
THIS WAY TO POOF PUFFS
THIS WAY TO OPAL OCEAN
FIVE MINUTES TO RACE TIME! TAKE YOUR PLACES AT THE STARTING LINE.

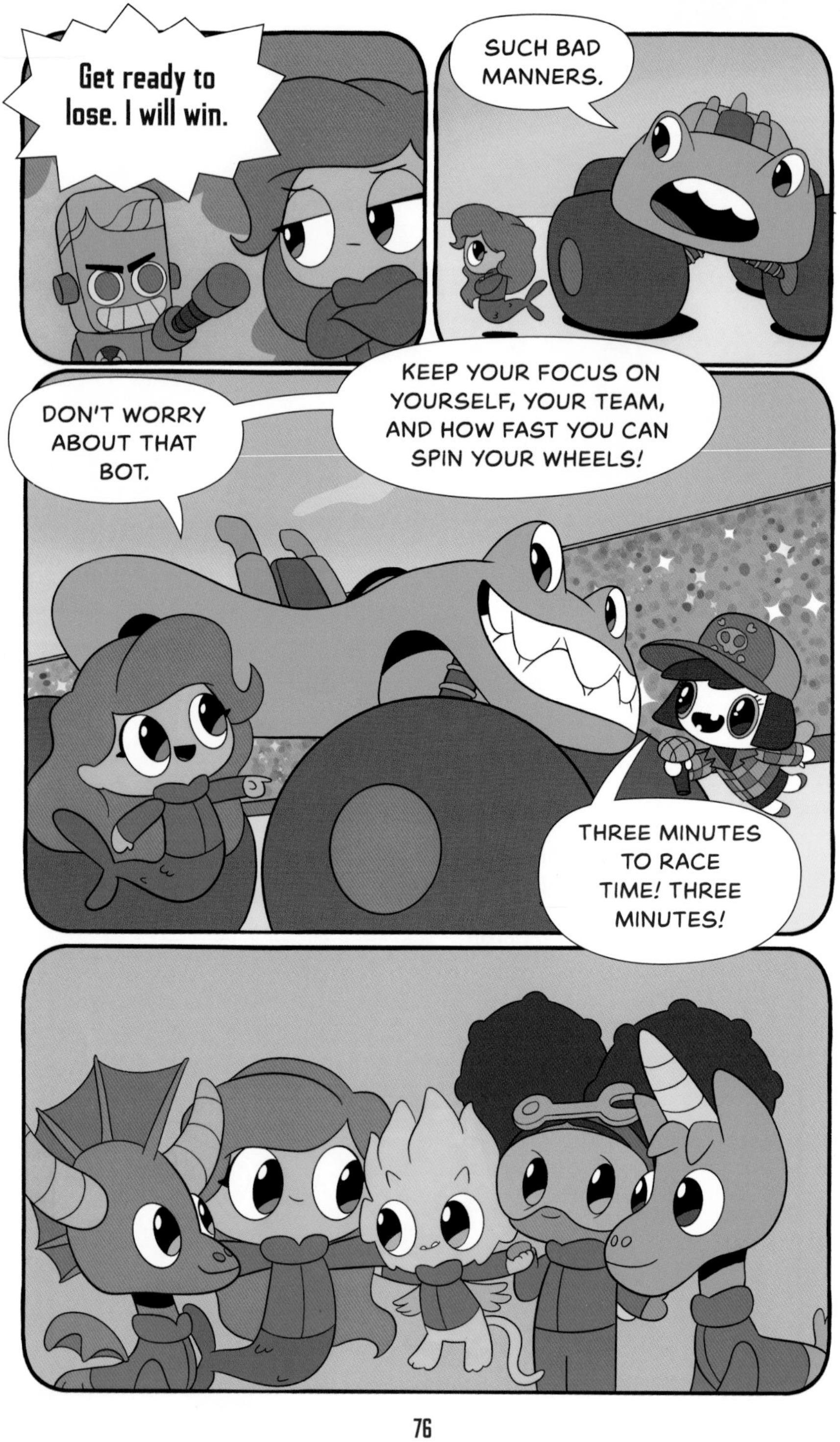
Get ready to lose. I will win.
SUCH BAD MANNERS.
DON'T WORRY ABOUT THAT BOT.
KEEP YOUR FOCUS ON YOURSELF, YOUR TEAM, AND HOW FAST YOU CAN SPIN YOUR WHEELS!
THREE MINUTES TO RACE TIME! THREE MINUTES!

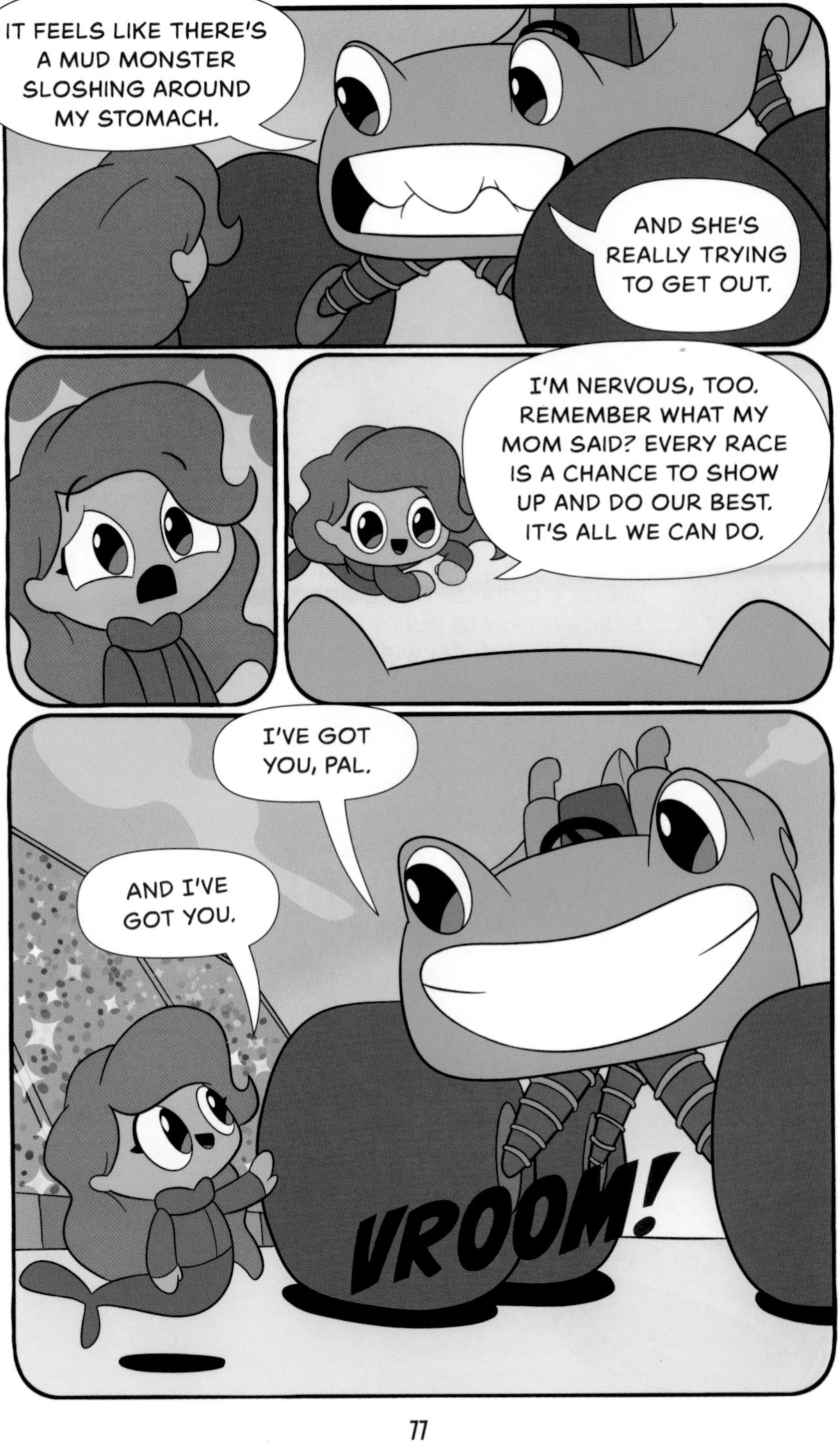
IT FEELS LIKE THERE'S A MUD MONSTER SLOSHING AROUND MY STOMACH.
AND SHE'S REALLY TRYING TO GET OUT.
I'M NERVOUS, TOO. REMEMBER WHAT MY MOM SAID? EVERY RACE IS A CHANCE TO SHOW UP AND DO OUR BEST. IT'S ALL WE CAN DO.
I'VE GOT YOU, PAL.
AND I'VE GOT YOU.
VROOM!

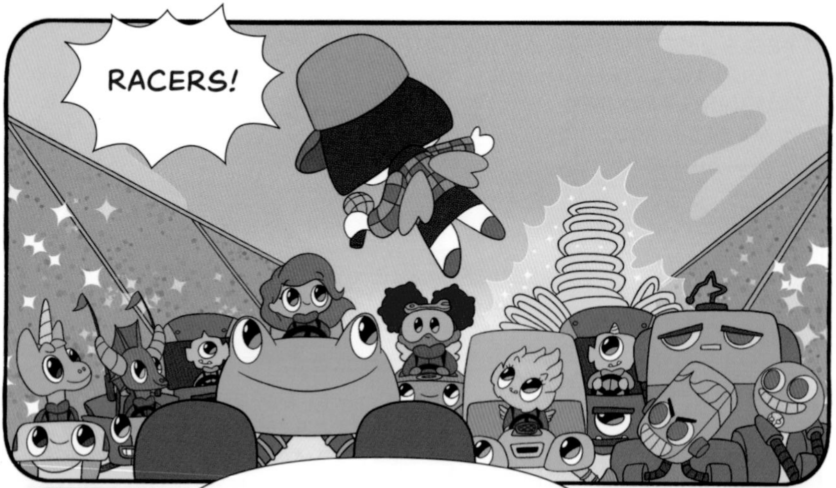
RACERS!

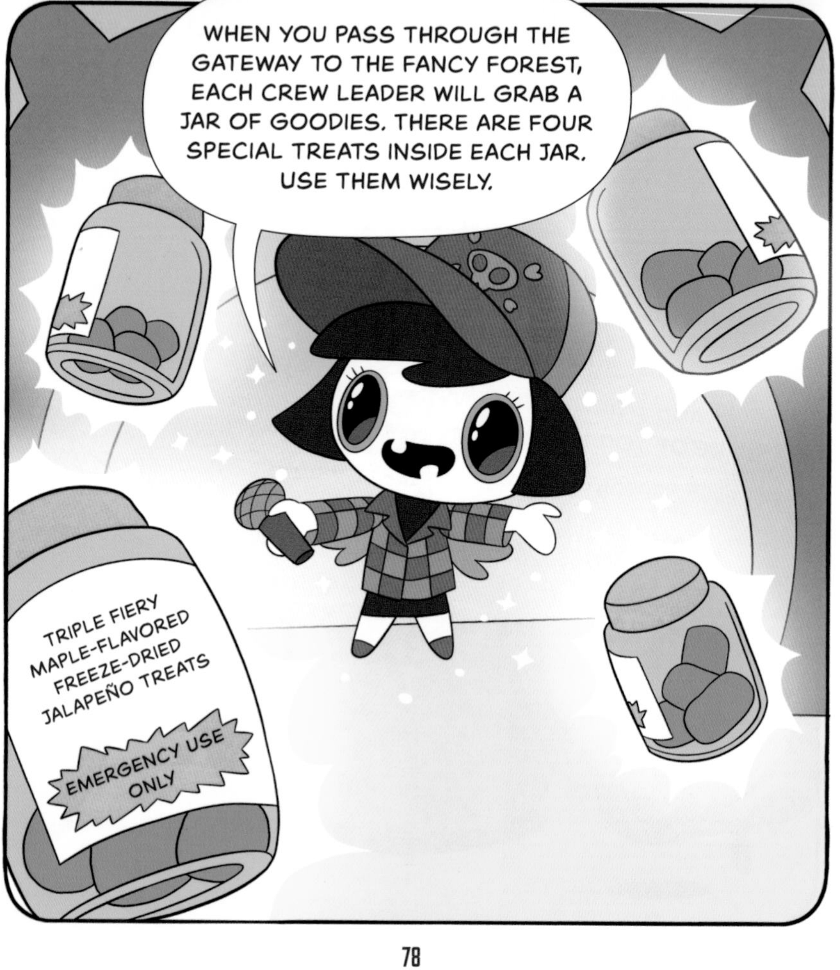
WHEN YOU PASS THROUGH THE GATEWAY TO THE FANCY FOREST, EACH CREW LEADER WILL GRAB A JAR OF GOODIES. THERE ARE FOUR SPECIAL TREATS INSIDE EACH JAR. USE THEM WISELY.
TRIPLE FIERY MAPLE-FLAVORED FREEZE-DRIED JALAPEÑO TREATS
EMERGENCY USE ONLY

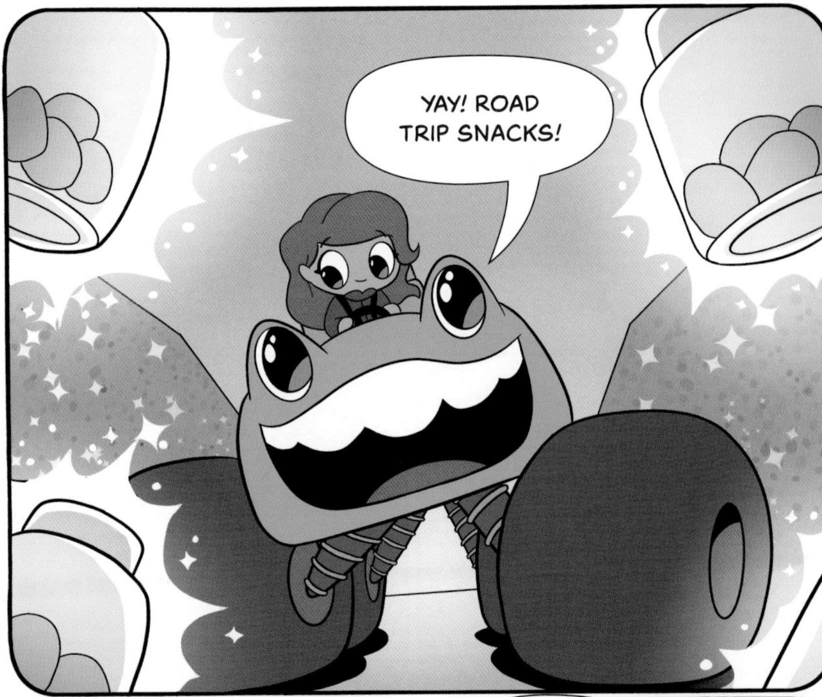
YAY! ROAD TRIP SNACKS!

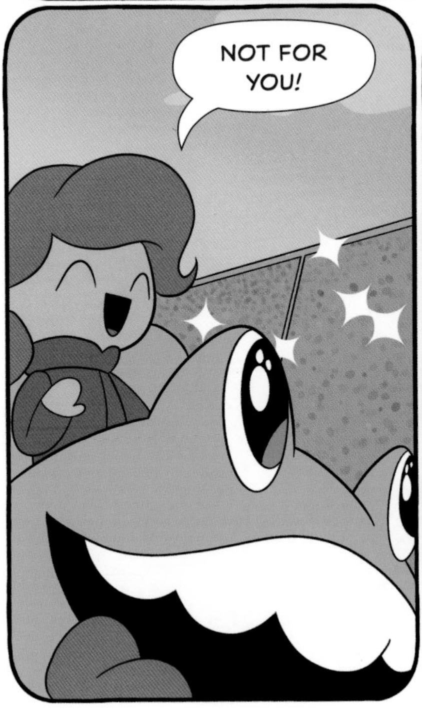
NOT FOR YOU!

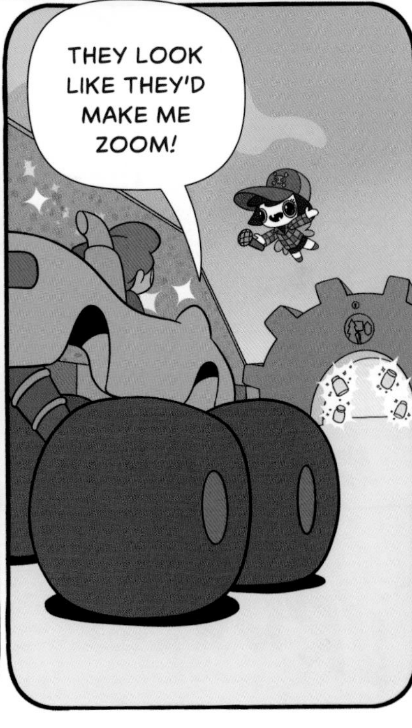
THEY LOOK LIKE THEY'D MAKE ME ZOOM!

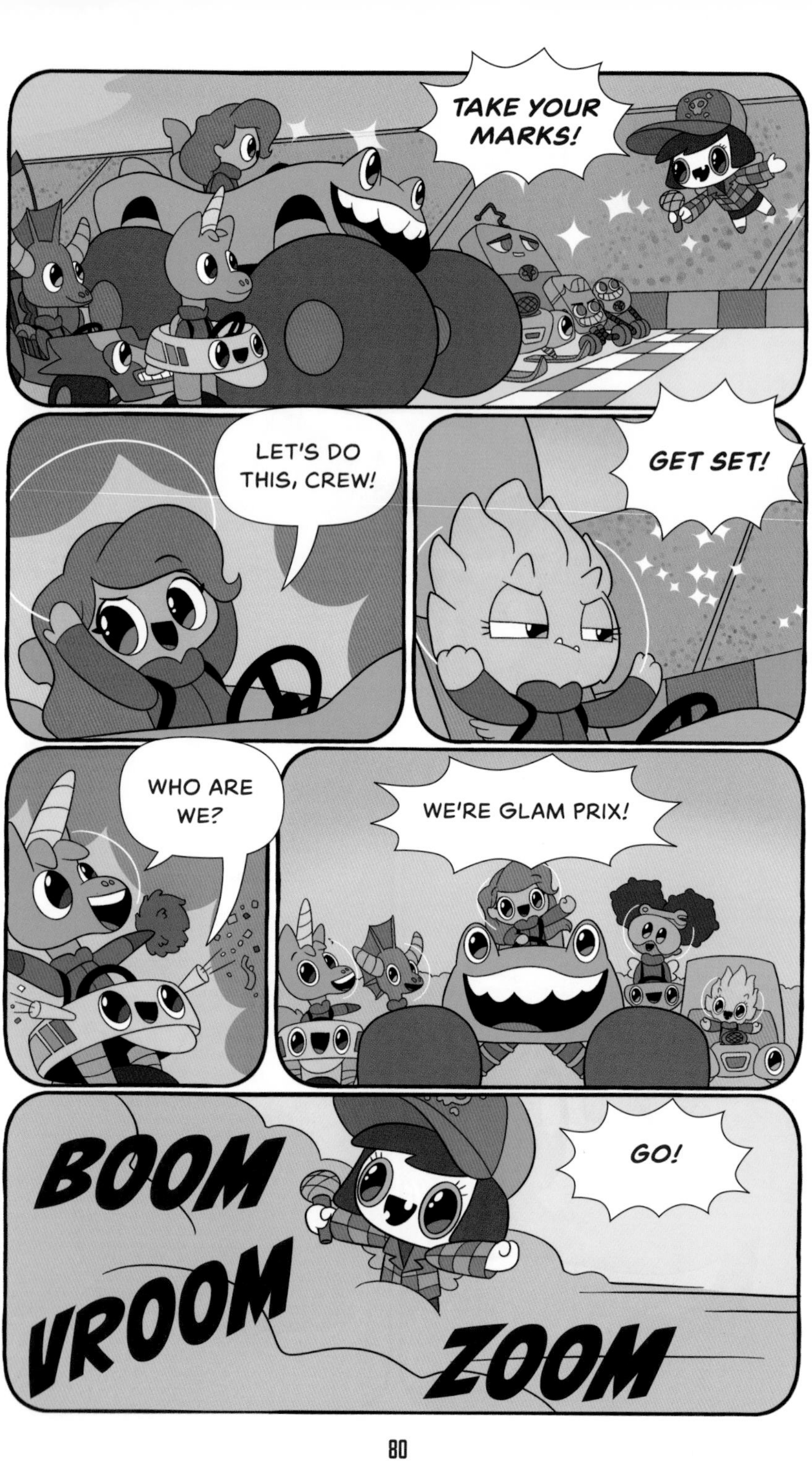
TAKE YOUR MARKS!
LET'S DO THIS, CREW!
GET SET!
WHO ARE WE?
WE'RE GLAM PRIX!
BOOM
VROOM
GO!
ZOOM

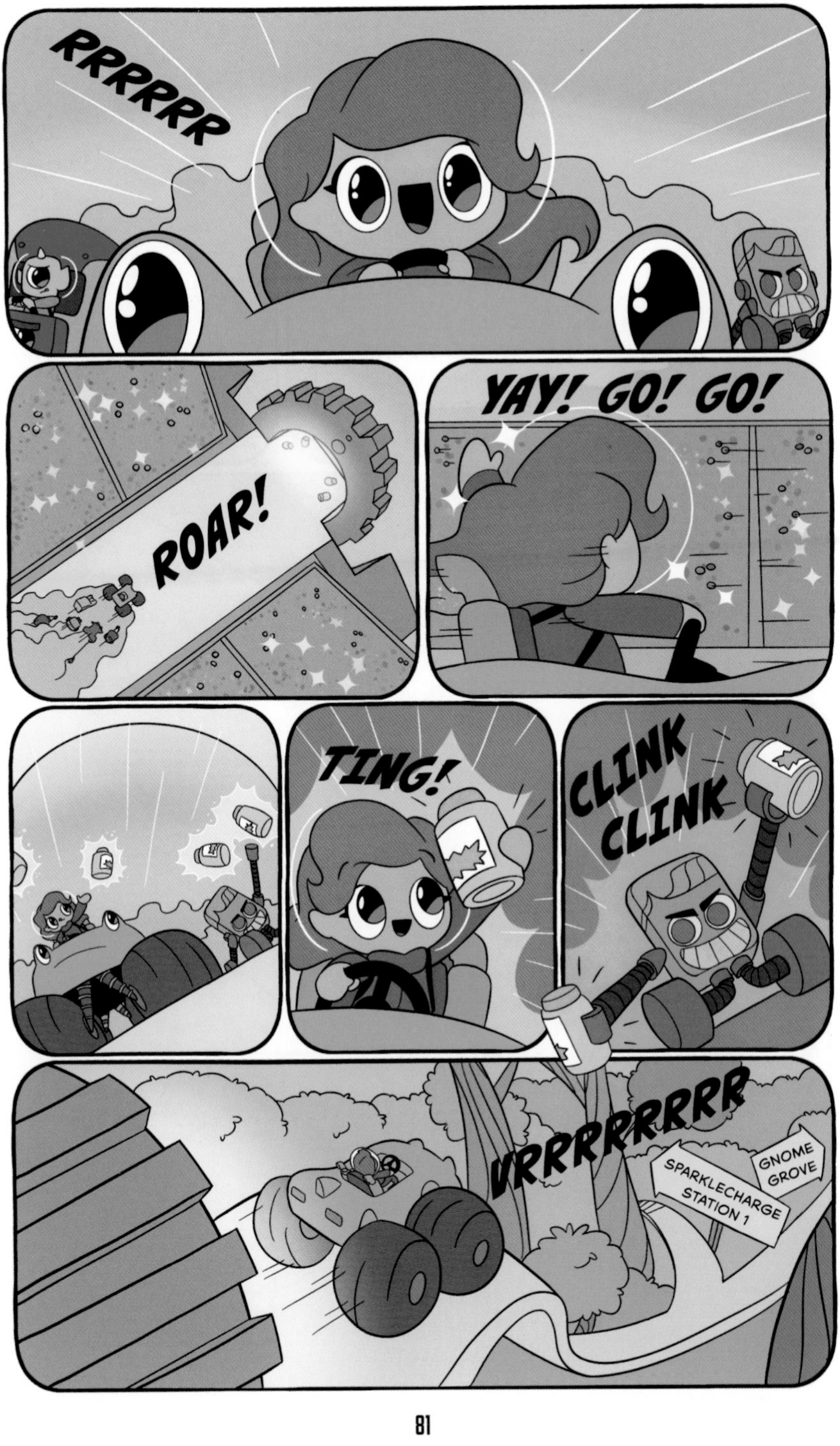
RRRRRR
ROAR!
YAY! GO! GO!
TING!
CLINK
CLINK
VRRRRRRRR
GNOME GROVE
SPARKLECHARGE STATION 1

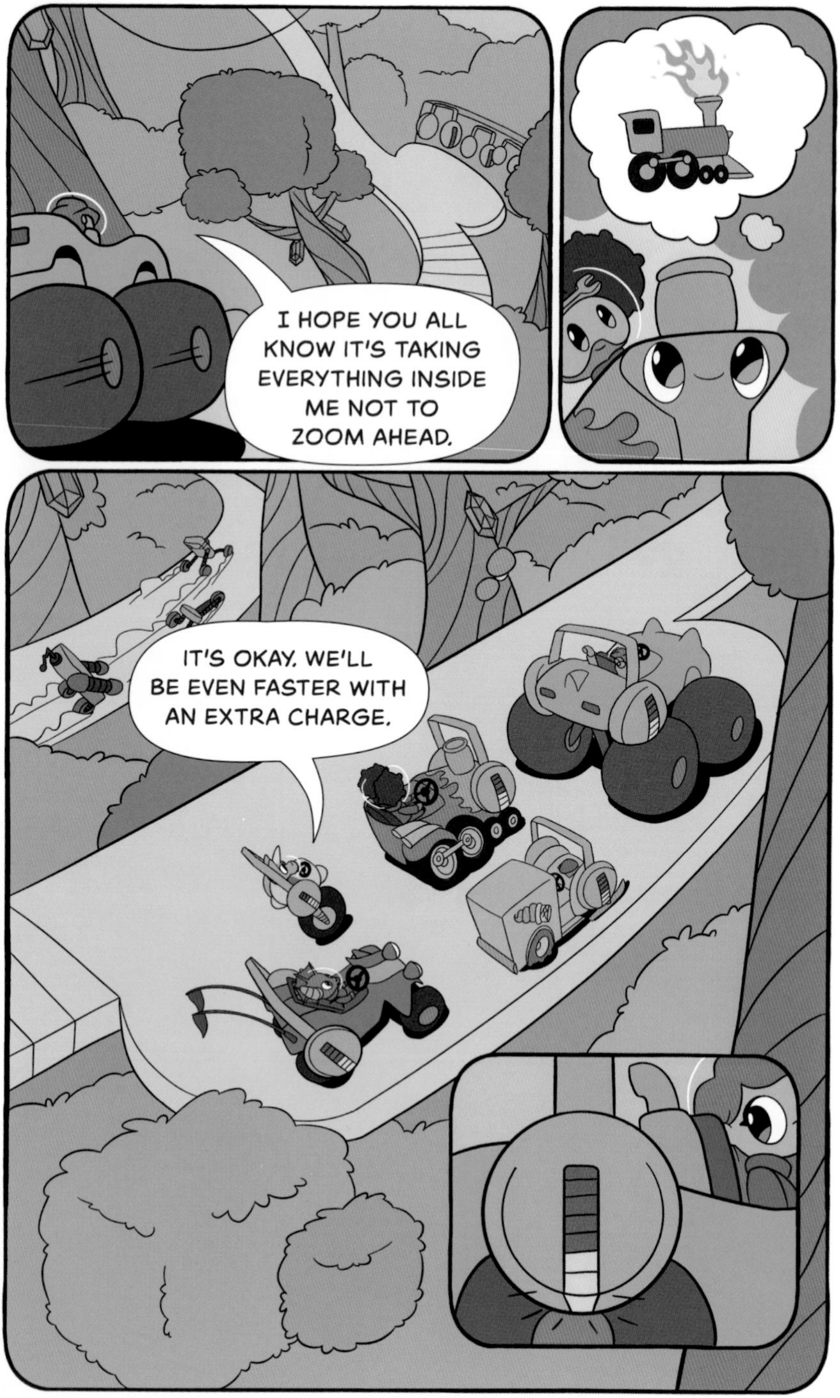
I HOPE YOU ALL KNOW IT'S TAKING EVERYTHING INSIDE ME NOT TO ZOOM AHEAD.
IT'S OKAY. WE'LL BE EVEN FASTER WITH AN EXTRA CHARGE.

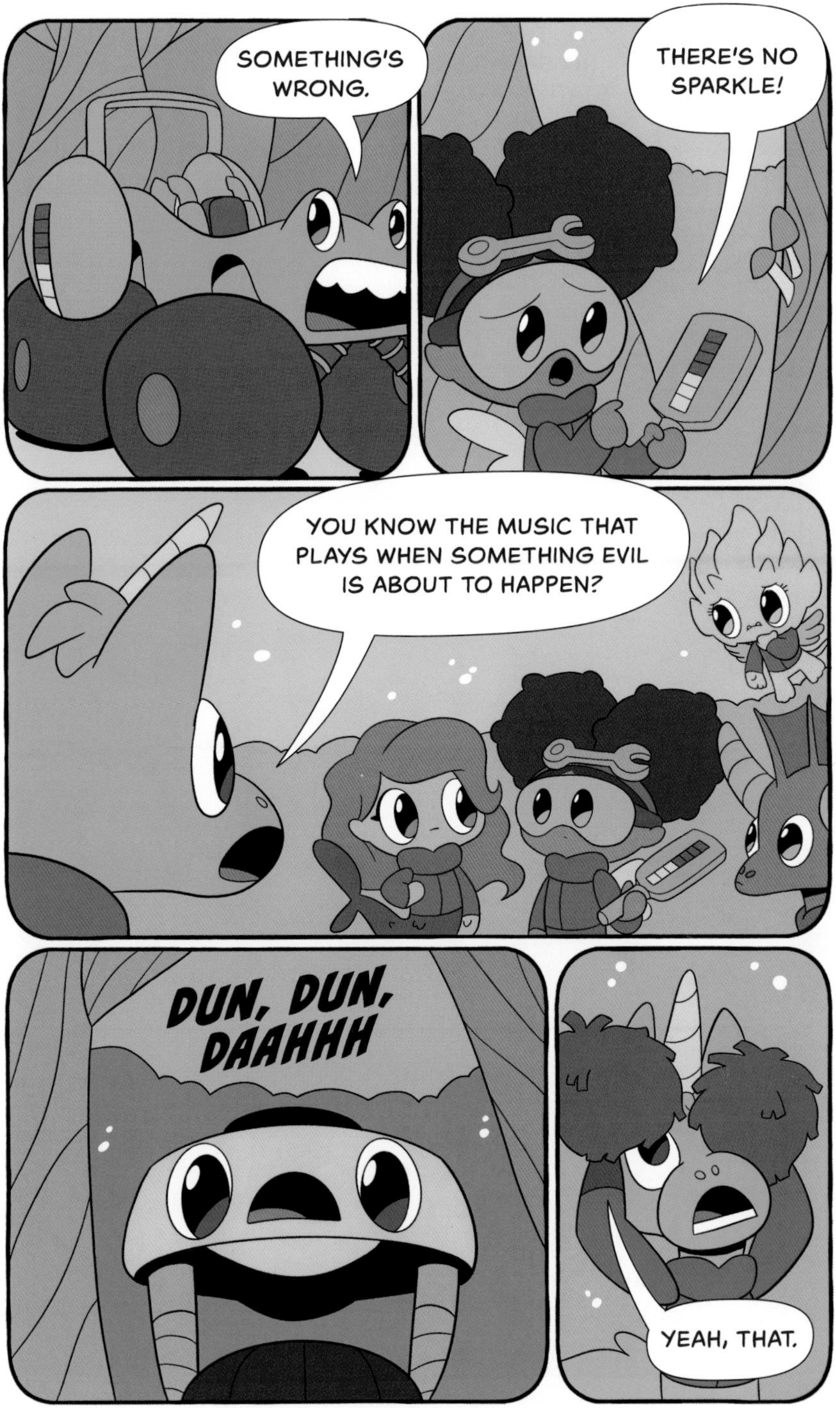
SOMETHING'S WRONG.
THERE'S NO SPARKLE!
YOU KNOW THE MUSIC THAT PLAYS WHEN SOMETHING EVIL IS ABOUT TO HAPPEN?
DUN, DUN, DAAHHH
YEAH, THAT.

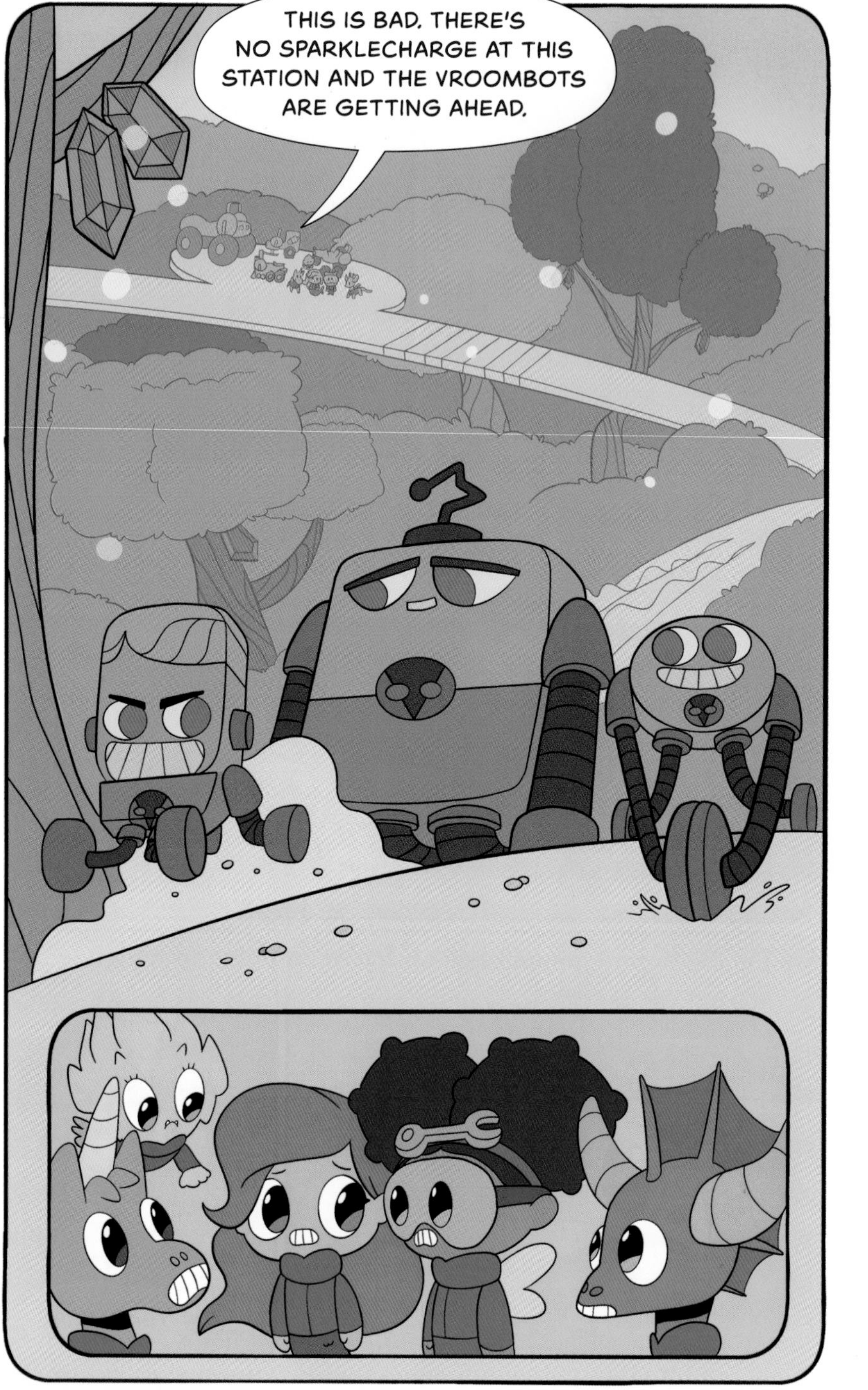
THIS IS BAD. THERE'S NO SPARKLECHARGE AT THIS STATION AND THE VROOMBOTS ARE GETTING AHEAD.

CHAPTER 7:
DIVIDE, CONQUER, AND SPARKLE!

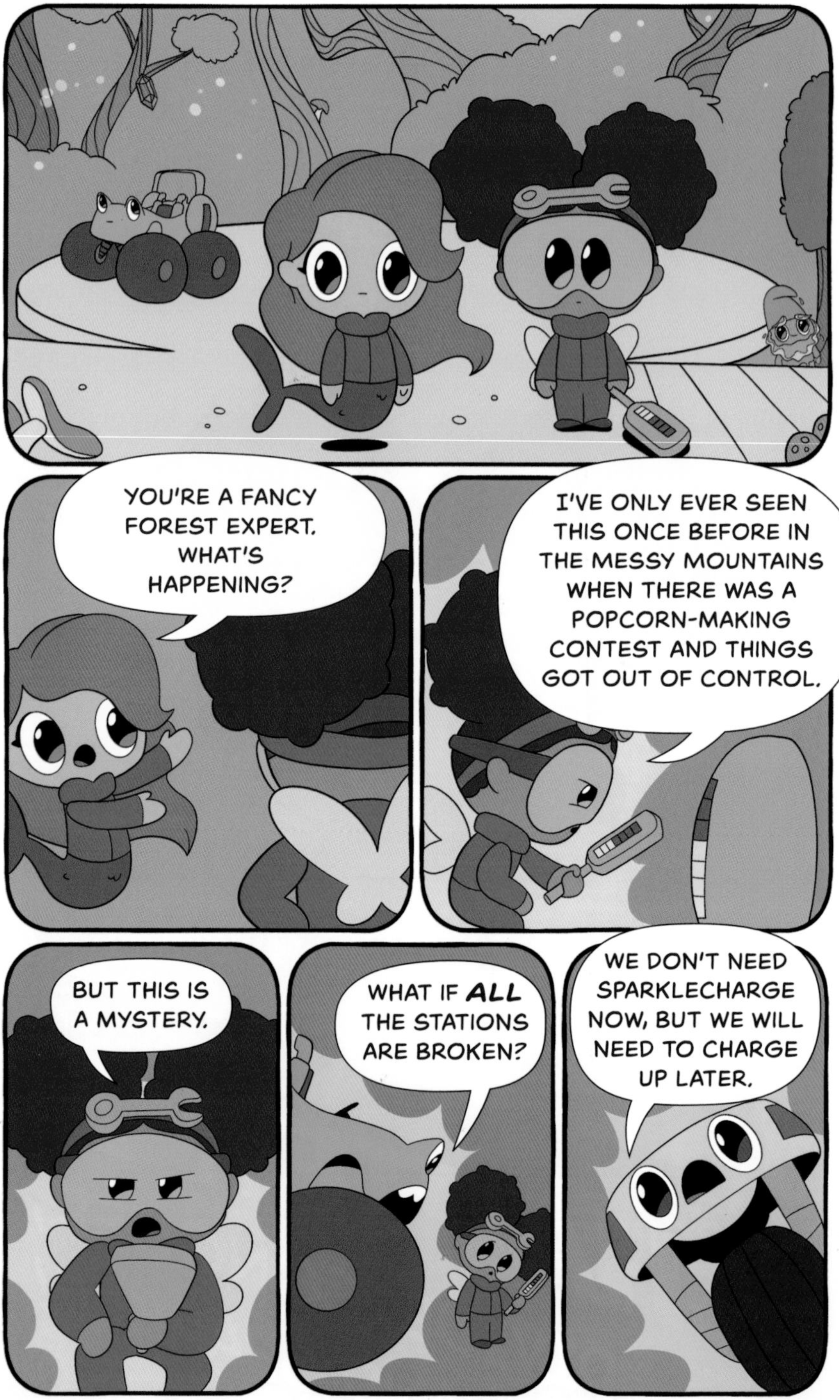
YOU'RE A FANCY FOREST EXPERT. WHAT'S HAPPENING?
I'VE ONLY EVER SEEN THIS ONCE BEFORE IN THE MESSY MOUNTAINS WHEN THERE WAS A POPCORN-MAKING CONTEST AND THINGS GOT OUT OF CONTROL.
BUT THIS IS A MYSTERY.
WHAT IF ***ALL*** THE STATIONS ARE BROKEN?
WE DON'T NEED SPARKLECHARGE NOW, BUT WE WILL NEED TO CHARGE UP LATER.

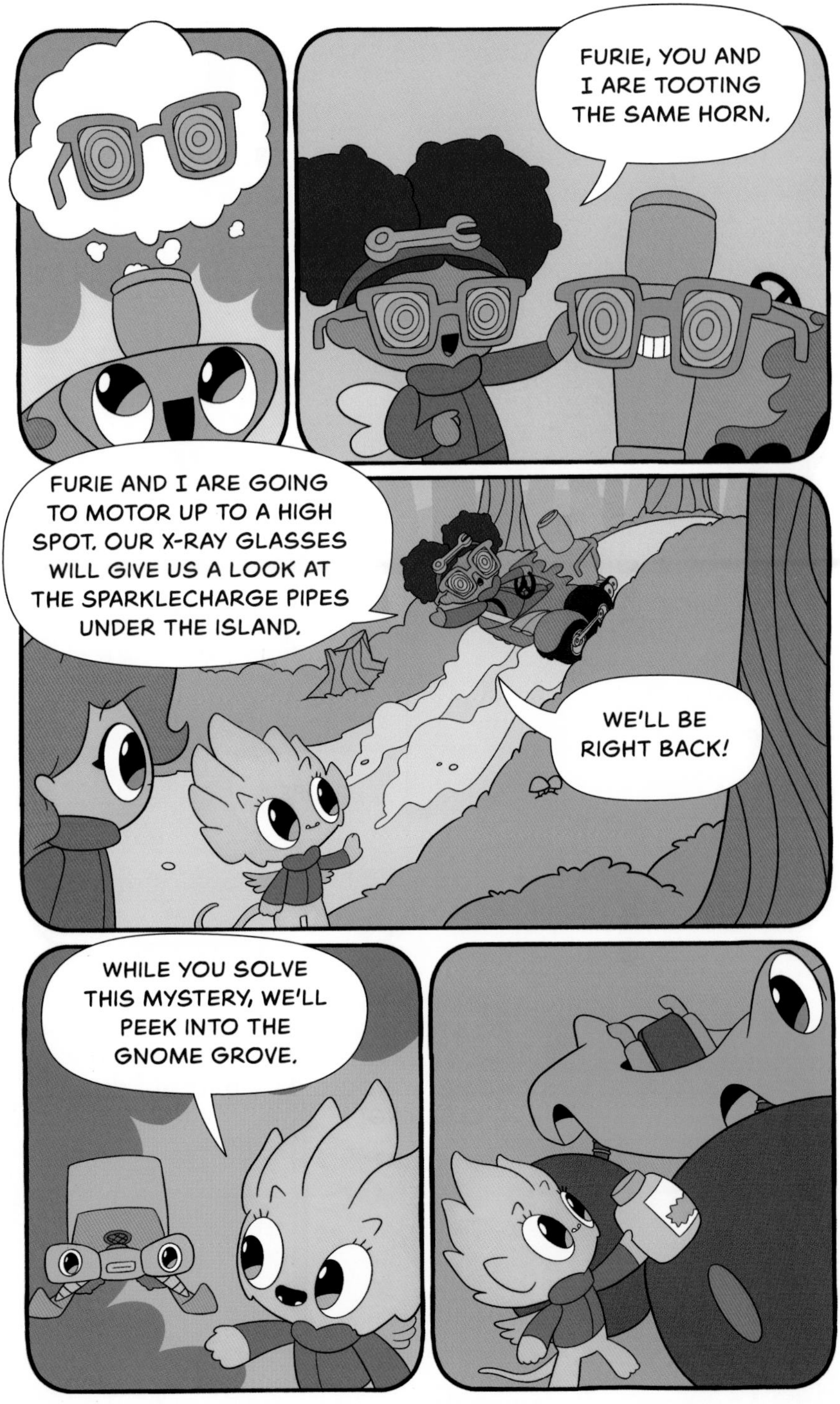
FURIE, YOU AND I ARE TOOTING THE SAME HORN.
FURIE AND I ARE GOING TO MOTOR UP TO A HIGH SPOT. OUR X-RAY GLASSES WILL GIVE US A LOOK AT THE SPARKLECHARGE PIPES UNDER THE ISLAND.
WE'LL BE RIGHT BACK!
WHILE YOU SOLVE THIS MYSTERY, WE'LL PEEK INTO THE GNOME GROVE.

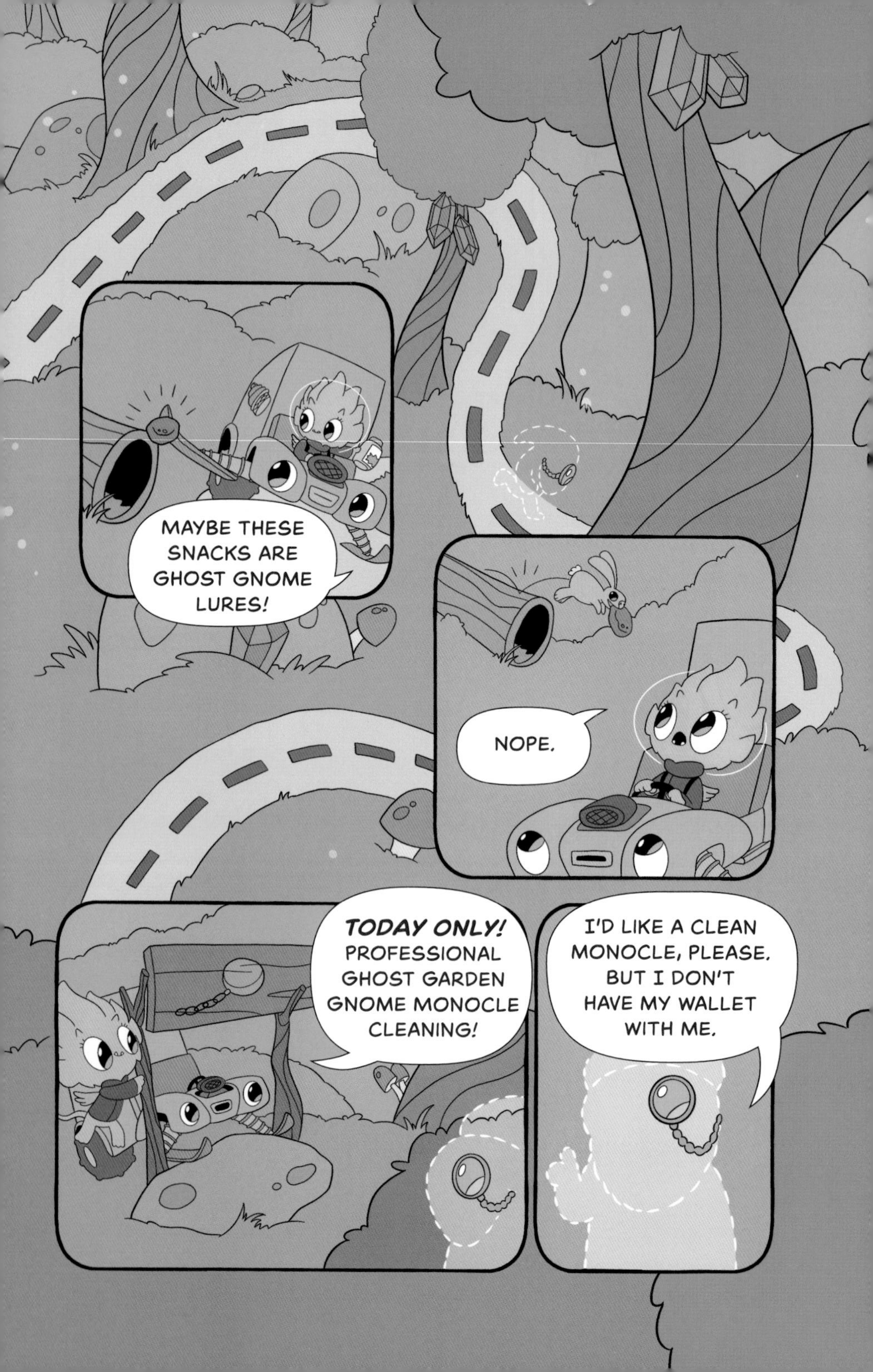
MAYBE THESE SNACKS ARE GHOST GNOME LURES!
NOPE.
TODAY ONLY! PROFESSIONAL GHOST GARDEN GNOME MONOCLE CLEANING!
I'D LIKE A CLEAN MONOCLE, PLEASE. BUT I DON'T HAVE MY WALLET WITH ME.

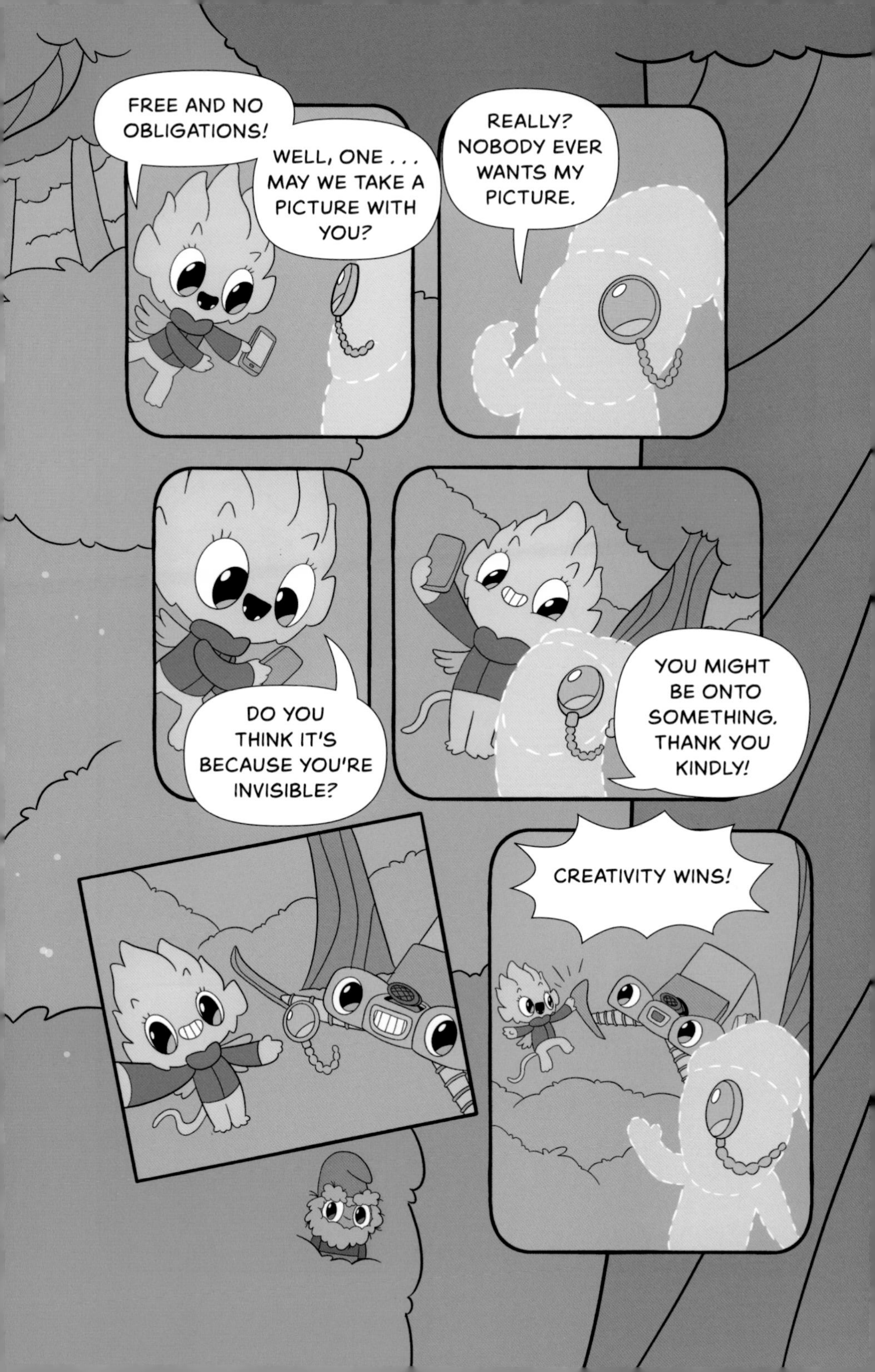
FREE AND NO OBLIGATIONS!
WELL, ONE . . . MAY WE TAKE A PICTURE WITH YOU?
REALLY? NOBODY EVER WANTS MY PICTURE.
DO YOU THINK IT'S BECAUSE YOU'RE INVISIBLE?
YOU MIGHT BE ONTO SOMETHING. THANK YOU KINDLY!
CREATIVITY WINS!

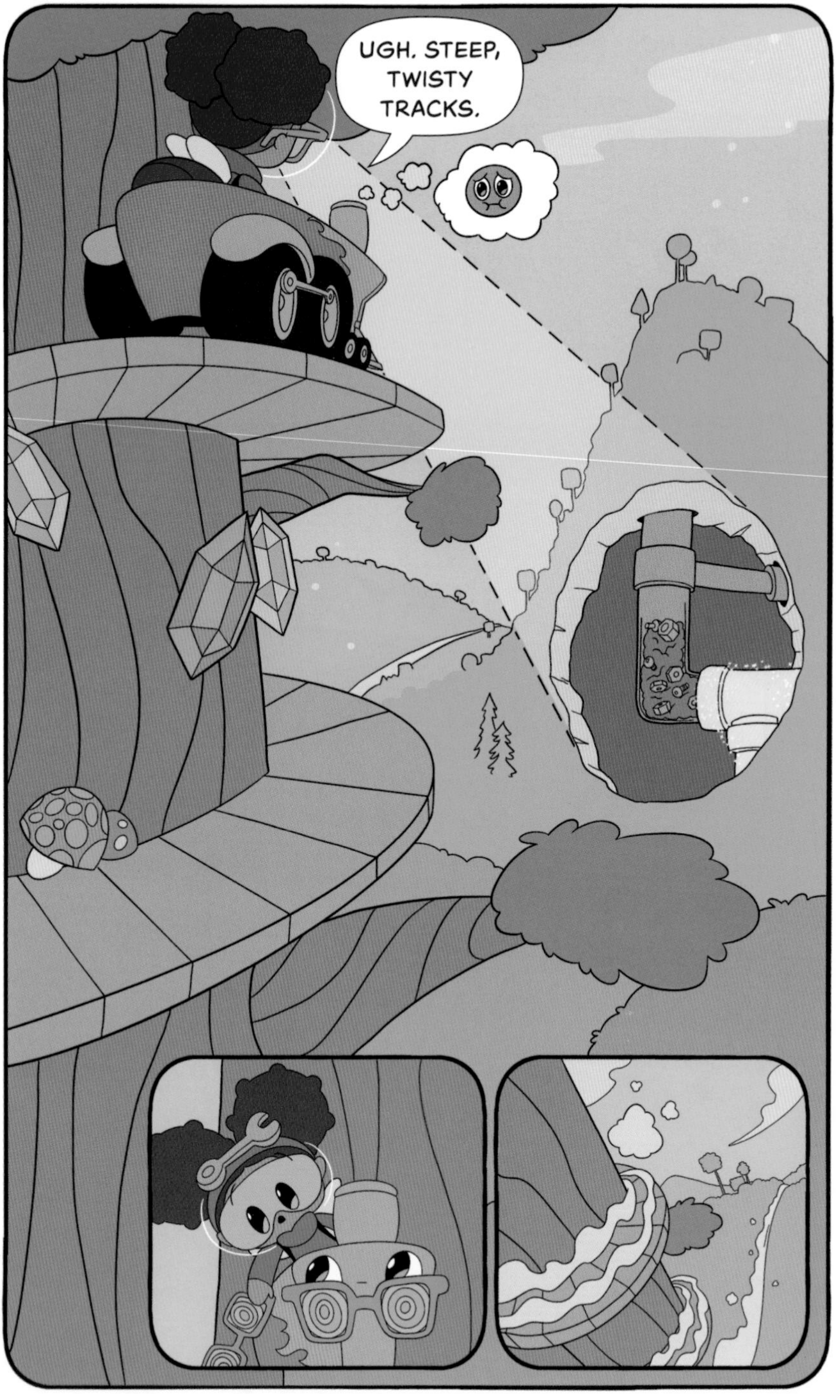
UGH. STEEP, TWISTY TRACKS.

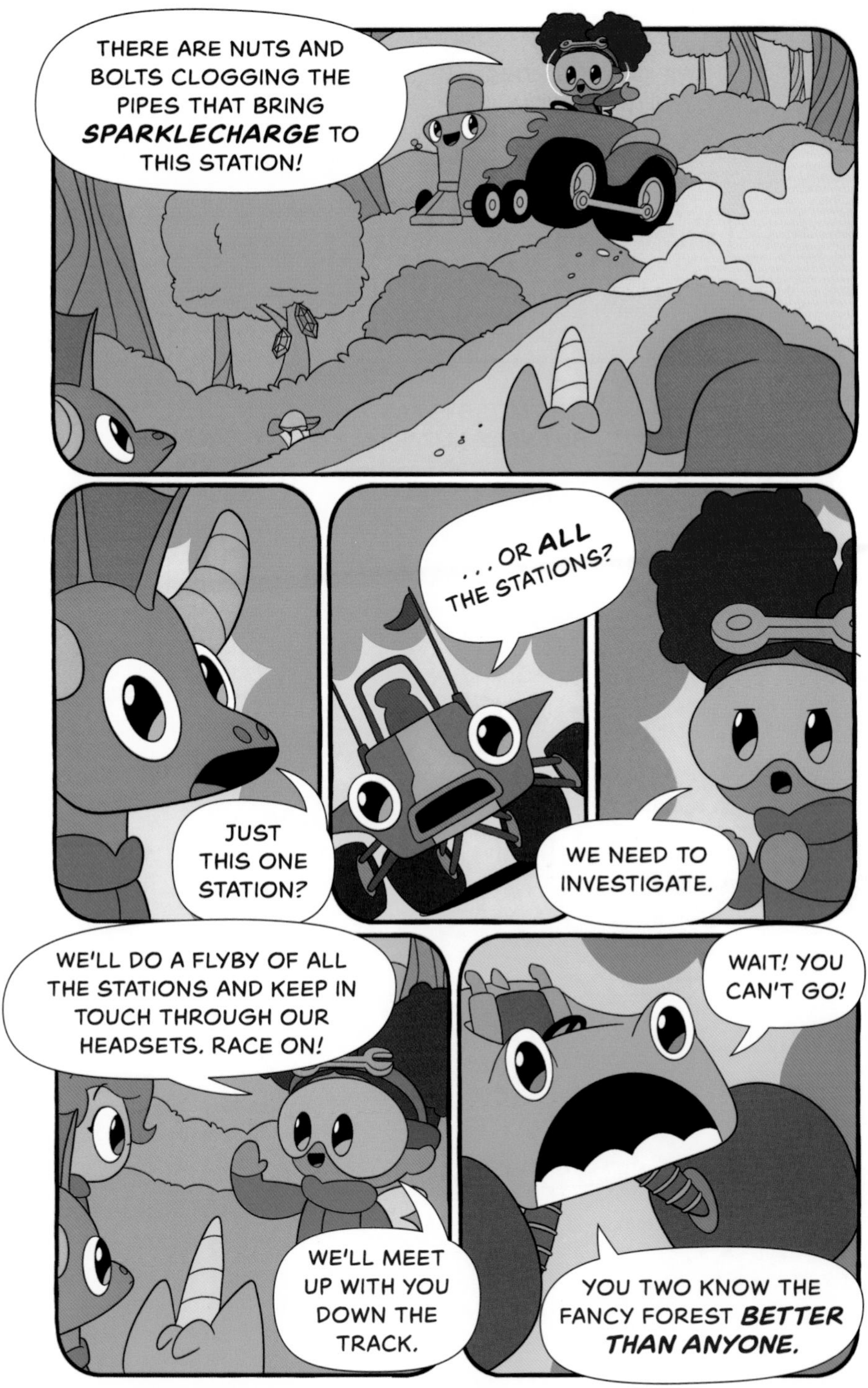
THERE ARE NUTS AND BOLTS CLOGGING THE PIPES THAT BRING SPARKLECHARGE TO THIS STATION!
JUST THIS ONE STATION?
. . . OR ALL THE STATIONS?
WE NEED TO INVESTIGATE.
WE'LL DO A FLYBY OF ALL THE STATIONS AND KEEP IN TOUCH THROUGH OUR HEADSETS. RACE ON!
WE'LL MEET UP WITH YOU DOWN THE TRACK.
WAIT! YOU CAN'T GO!
YOU TWO KNOW THE FANCY FOREST BETTER THAN ANYONE.

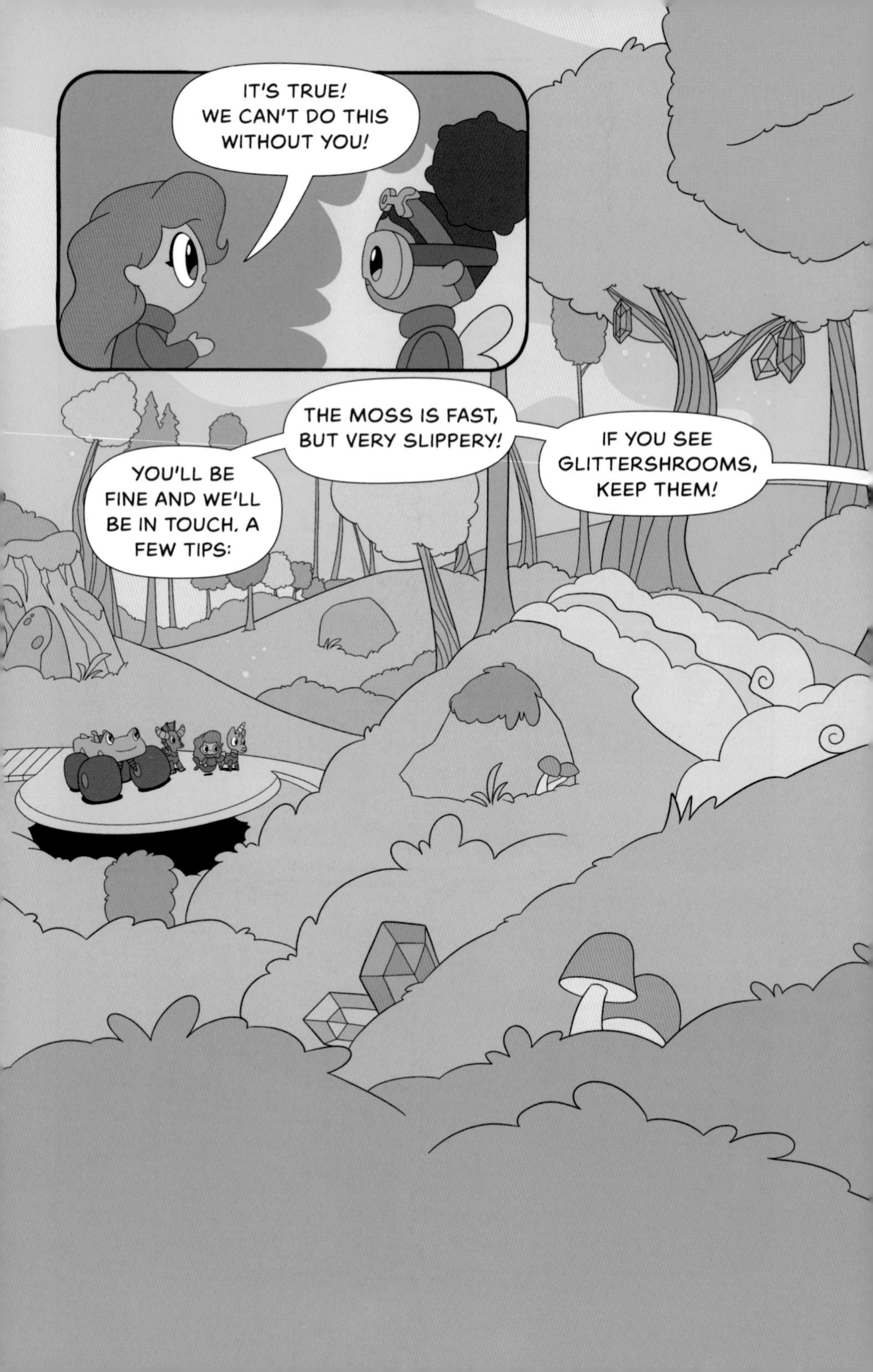
IT'S TRUE! WE CAN'T DO THIS WITHOUT YOU!
YOU'LL BE FINE AND WE'LL BE IN TOUCH. A FEW TIPS:
THE MOSS IS FAST, BUT VERY SLIPPERY!
IF YOU SEE GLITTERSHROOMS, KEEP THEM!

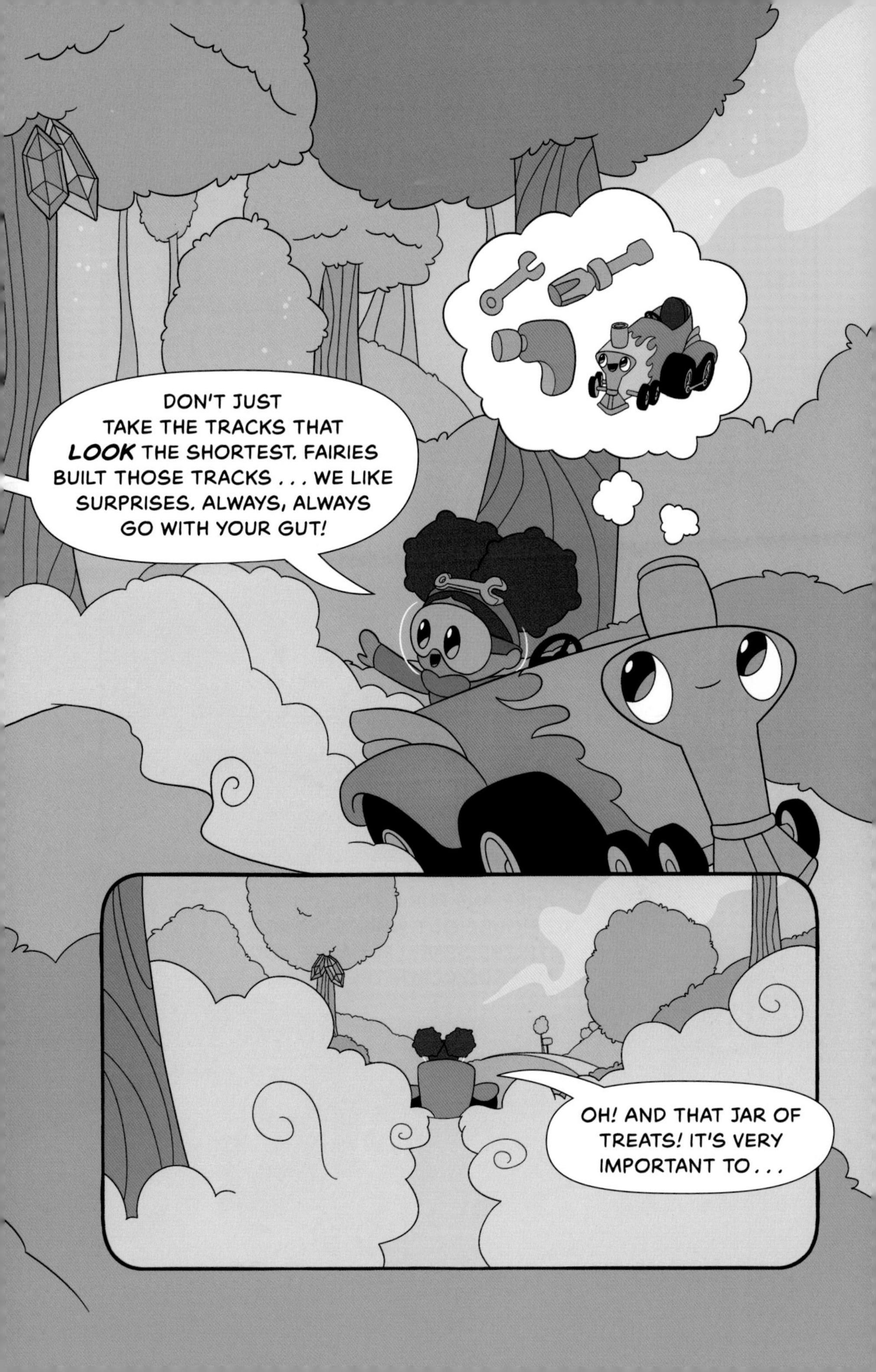
DON'T JUST TAKE THE TRACKS THAT ***LOOK*** THE SHORTEST. FAIRIES BUILT THOSE TRACKS . . . WE LIKE SURPRISES. ALWAYS, ALWAYS GO WITH YOUR GUT!
OH! AND THAT JAR OF TREATS! IT'S VERY IMPORTANT TO . . .

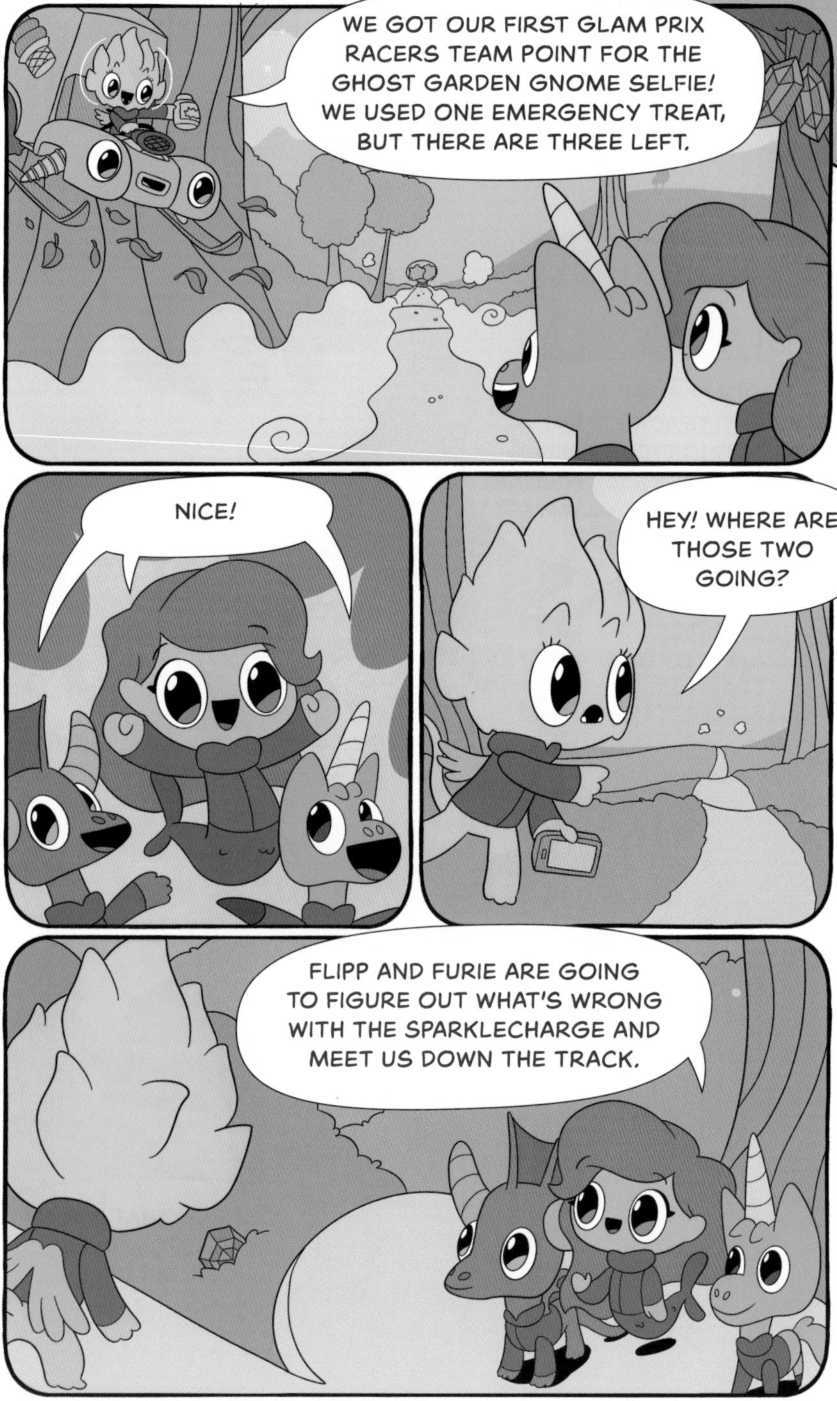
WE GOT OUR FIRST GLAM PRIX RACERS TEAM POINT FOR THE GHOST GARDEN GNOME SELFIE! WE USED ONE EMERGENCY TREAT, BUT THERE ARE THREE LEFT.
NICE!
HEY! WHERE ARE THOSE TWO GOING?
FLIPP AND FURIE ARE GOING TO FIGURE OUT WHAT'S WRONG WITH THE SPARKLECHARGE AND MEET US DOWN THE TRACK.

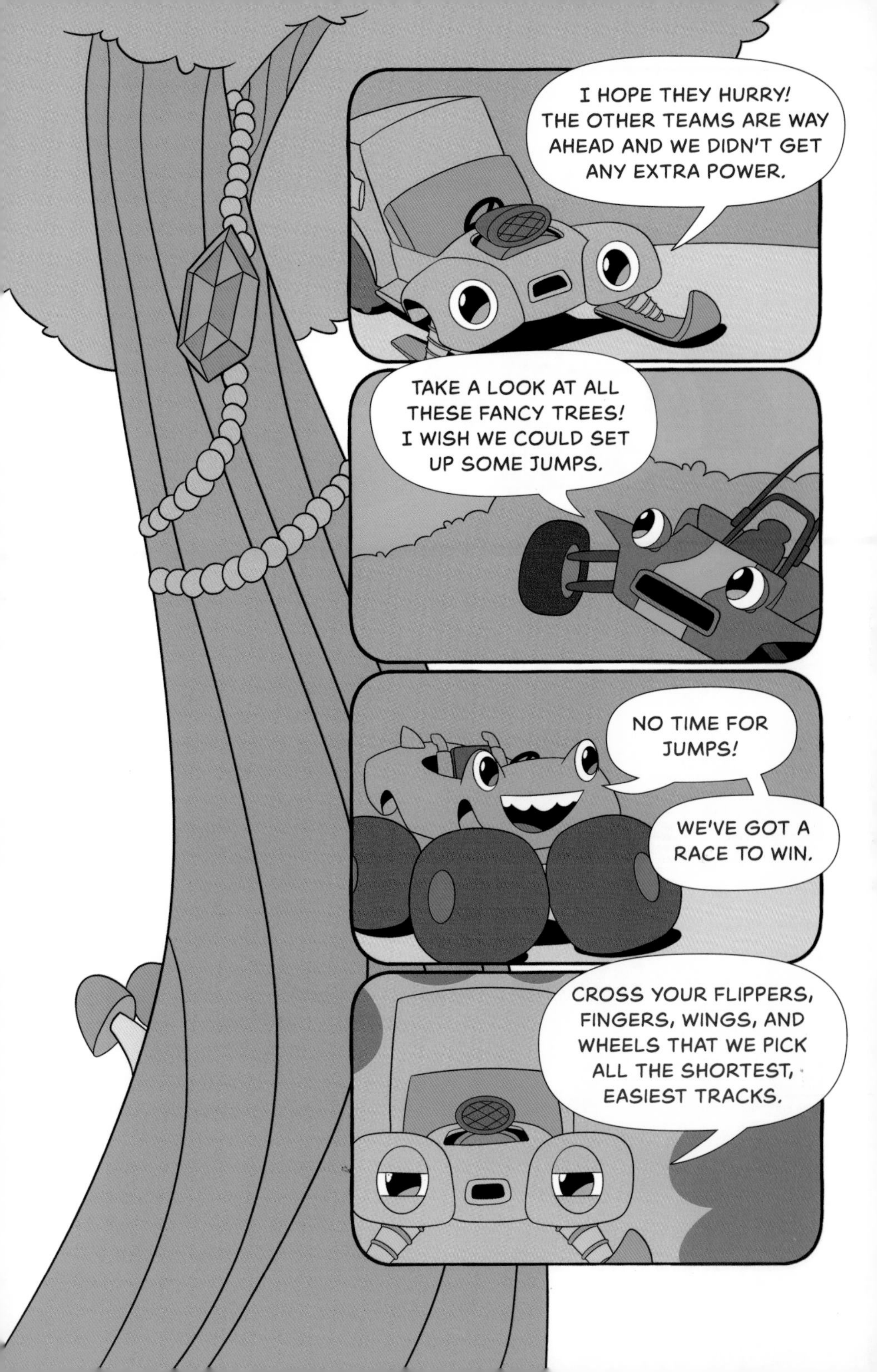
I HOPE THEY HURRY! THE OTHER TEAMS ARE WAY AHEAD AND WE DIDN'T GET ANY EXTRA POWER.
TAKE A LOOK AT ALL THESE FANCY TREES! I WISH WE COULD SET UP SOME JUMPS.
NO TIME FOR JUMPS!
WE'VE GOT A RACE TO WIN.
CROSS YOUR FLIPPERS, FINGERS, WINGS, AND WHEELS THAT WE PICK ALL THE SHORTEST, EASIEST TRACKS.

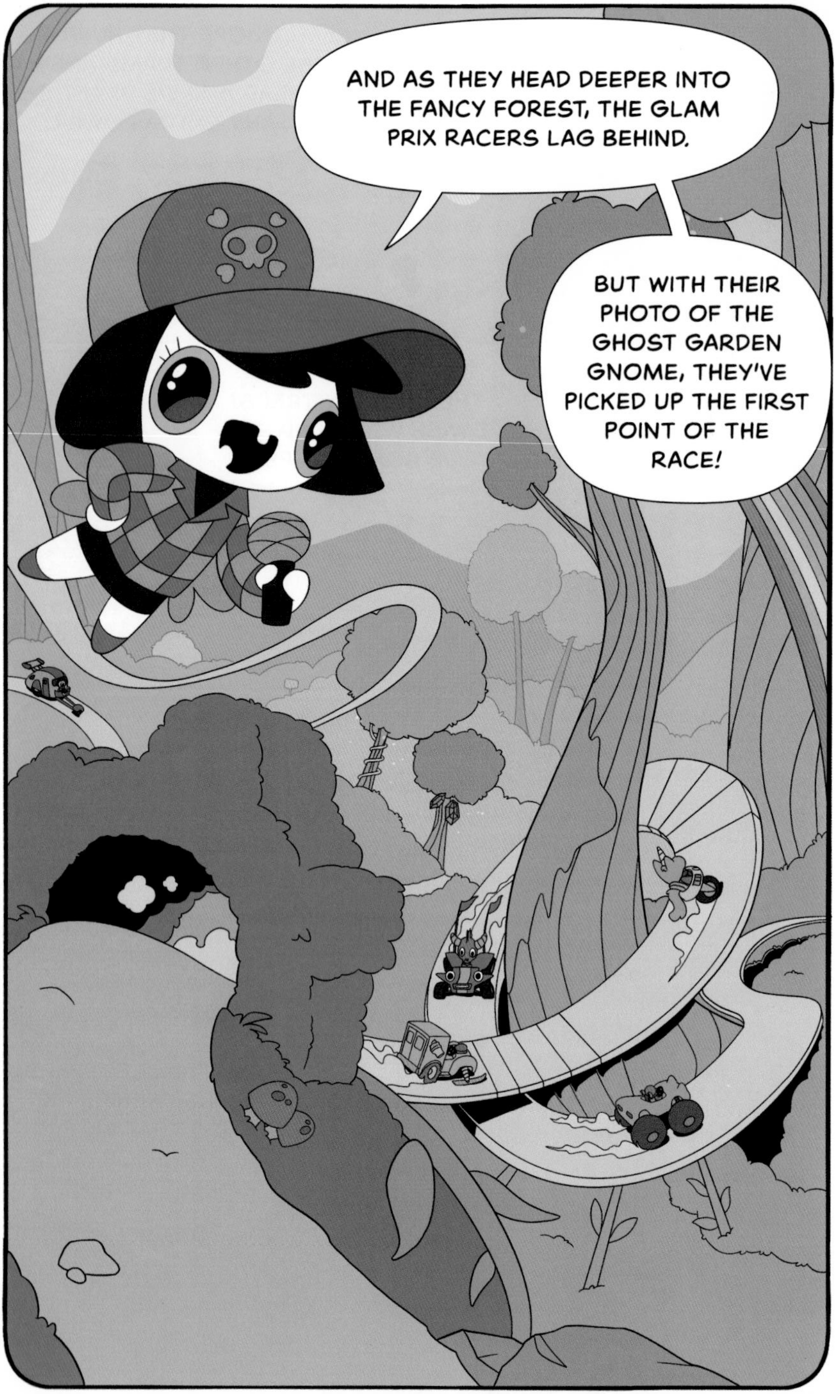
AND AS THEY HEAD DEEPER INTO THE FANCY FOREST, THE GLAM PRIX RACERS LAG BEHIND.
BUT WITH THEIR PHOTO OF THE GHOST GARDEN GNOME, THEY'VE PICKED UP THE FIRST POINT OF THE RACE!

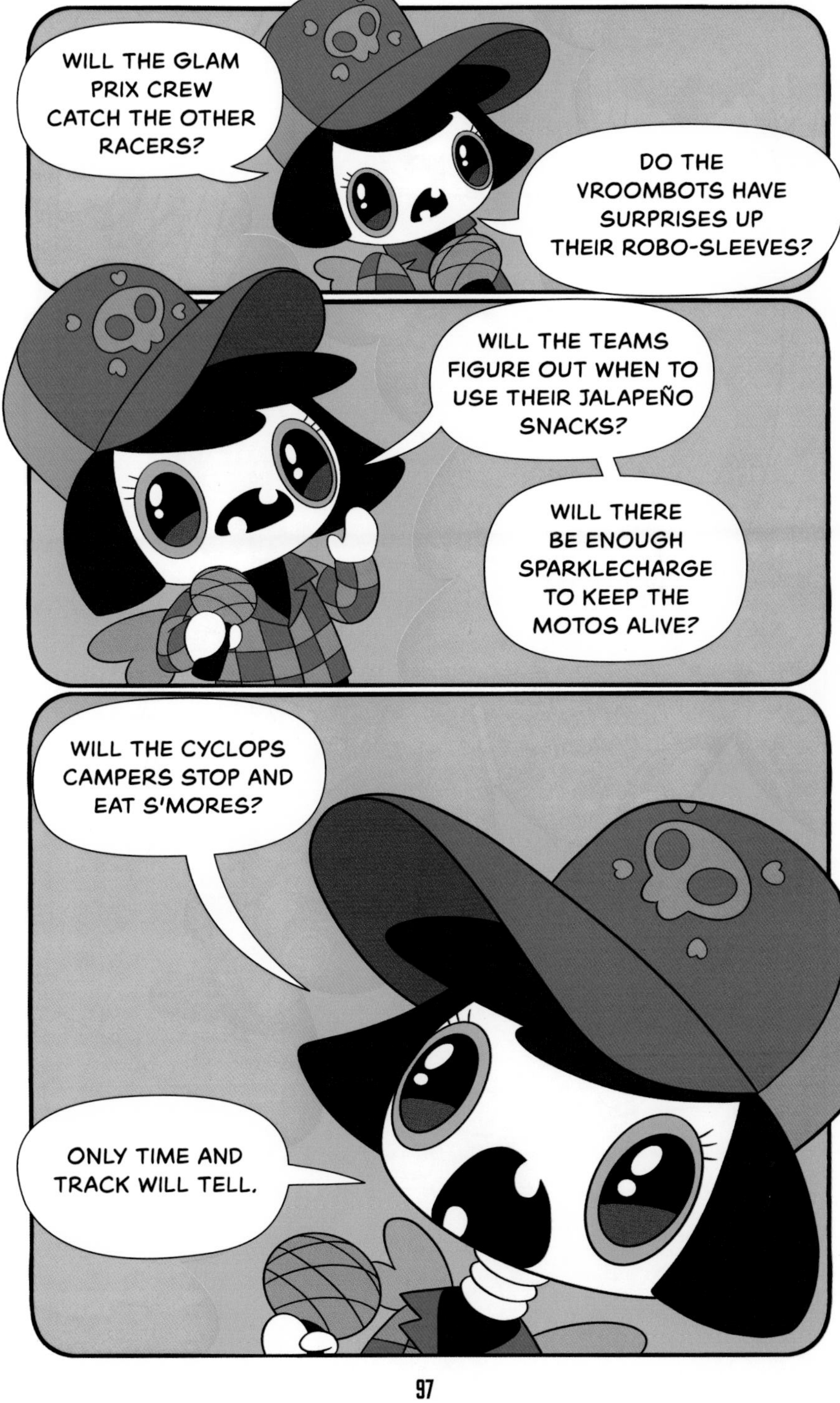
WILL THE GLAM PRIX CREW CATCH THE OTHER RACERS?
DO THE VROOMBOTS HAVE SURPRISES UP THEIR ROBO-SLEEVES?
WILL THE TEAMS FIGURE OUT WHEN TO USE THEIR JALAPEÑO SNACKS?
WILL THERE BE ENOUGH SPARKLECHARGE TO KEEP THE MOTOS ALIVE?
WILL THE CYCLOPS CAMPERS STOP AND EAT S'MORES?
ONLY TIME AND TRACK WILL TELL.

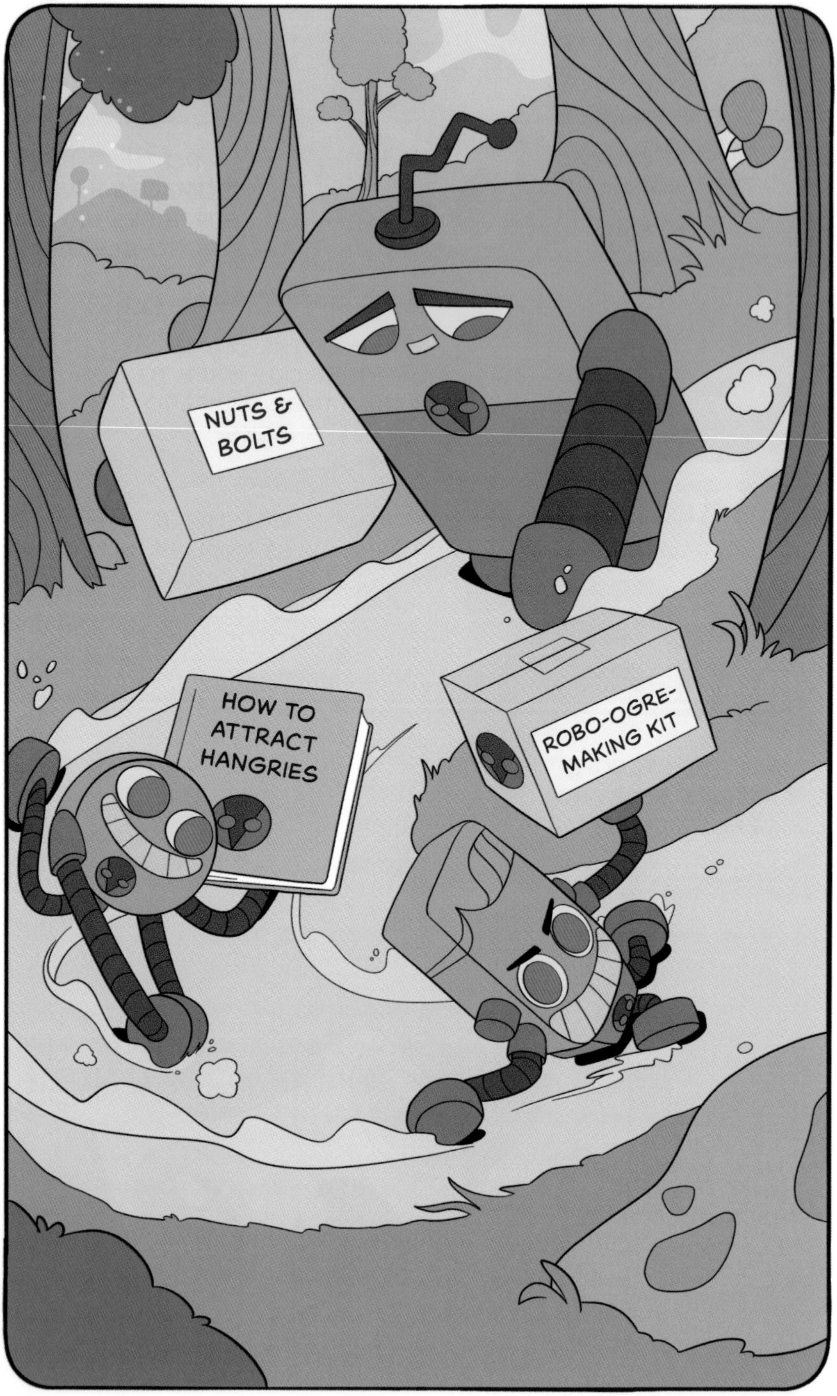
NUTS & BOLTS
HOW TO ATTRACT HANGRIES
ROBO-OGRE-MAKING KIT

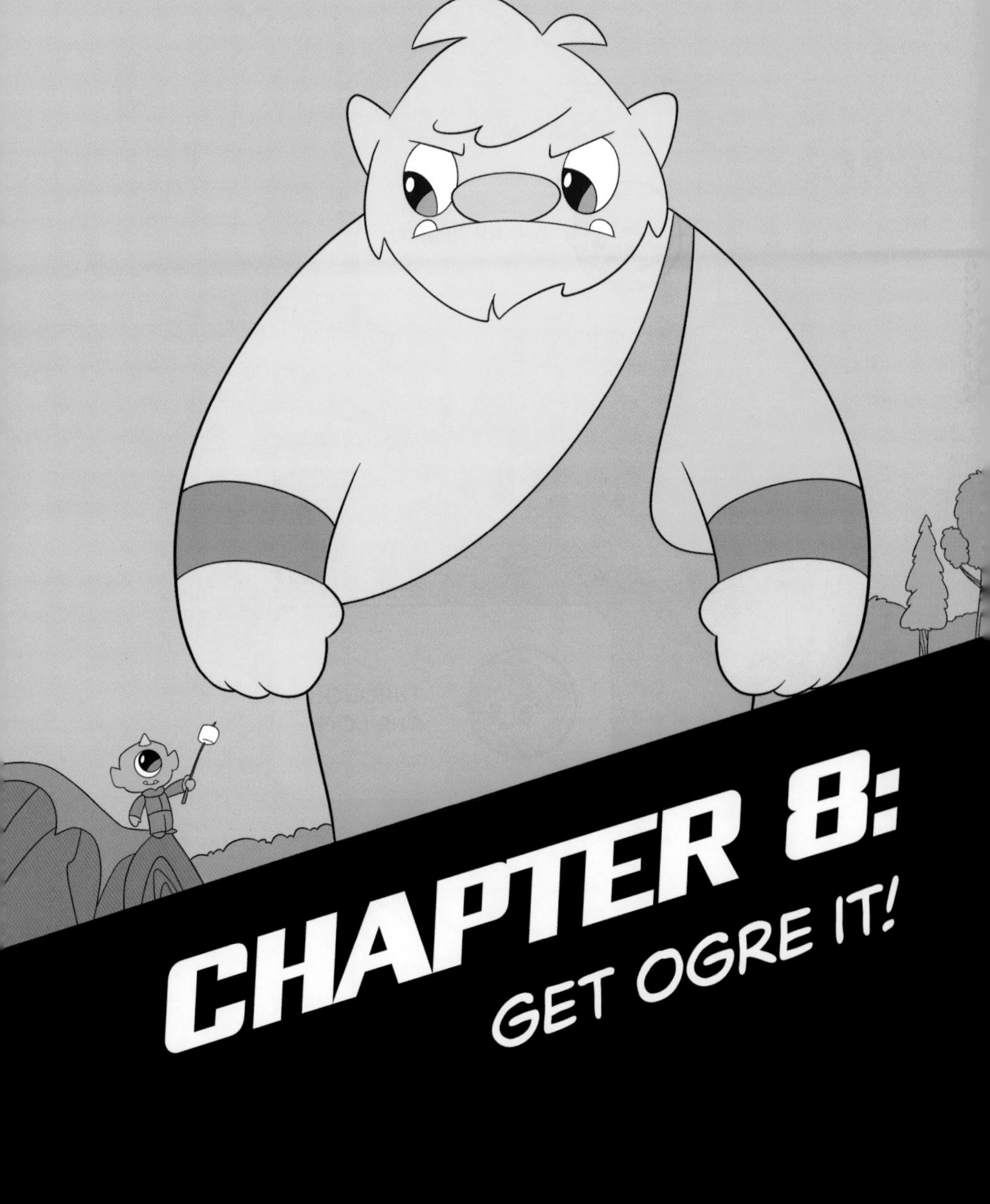

CHAPTER 8: GET OGRE IT!

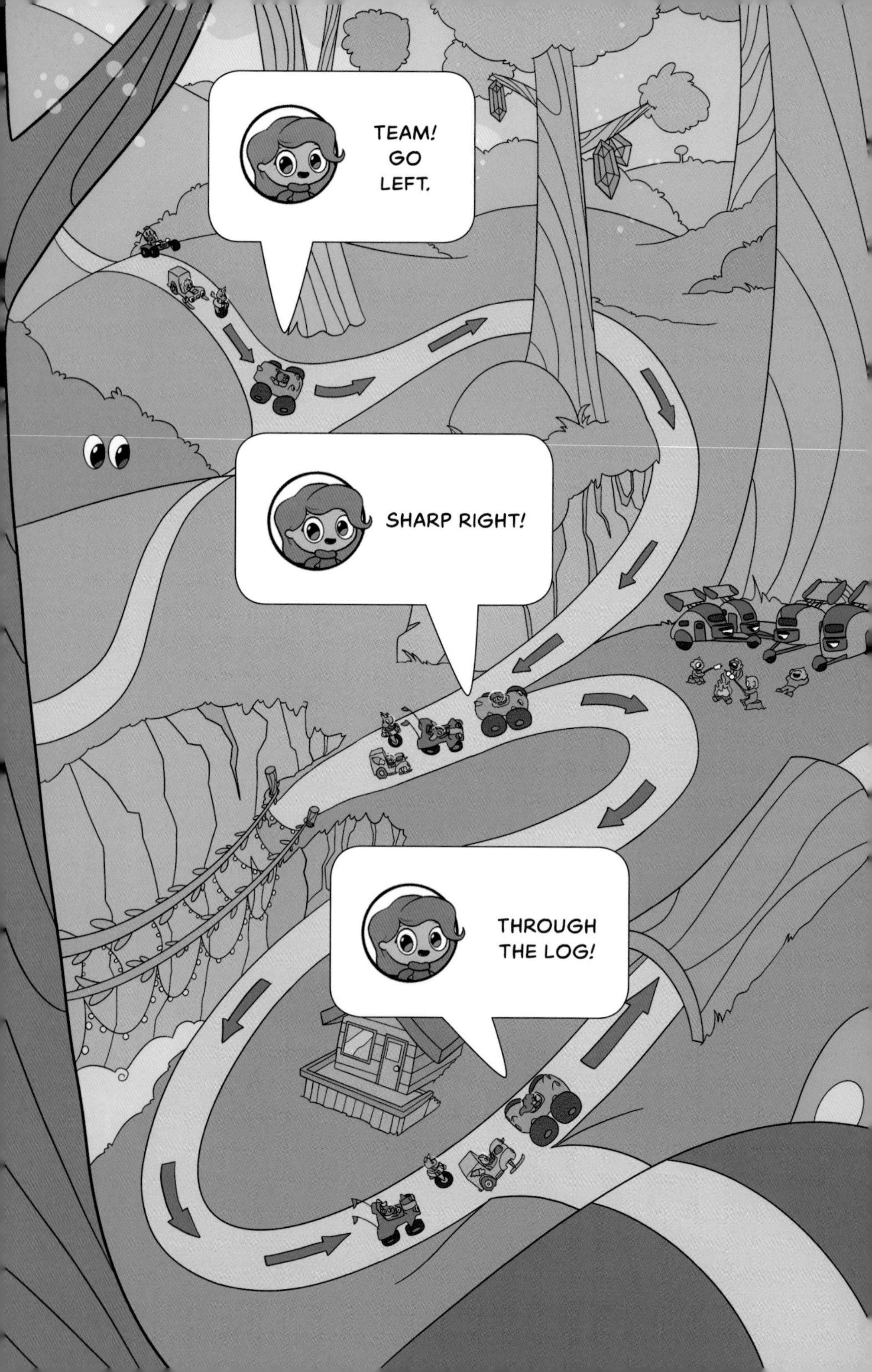
TEAM! GO LEFT.
SHARP RIGHT!
THROUGH THE LOG!

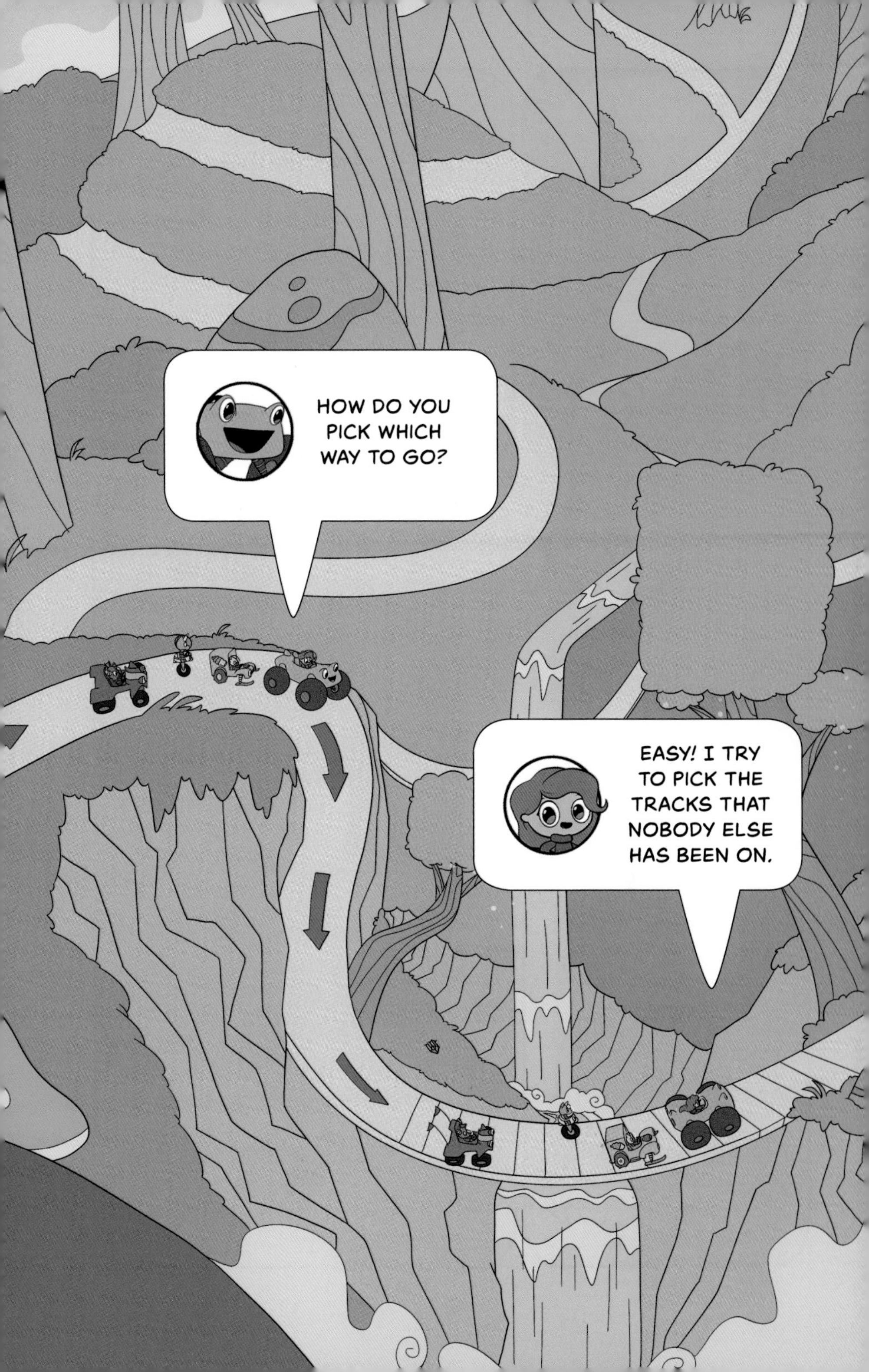
HOW DO YOU PICK WHICH WAY TO GO?
EASY! I TRY TO PICK THE TRACKS THAT NOBODY ELSE HAS BEEN ON.

THAT SEEMS RISKY!

IF WE TAKE THE SAME TRACKS AS EVERYONE, WE'LL STAY THE SAME PACE.

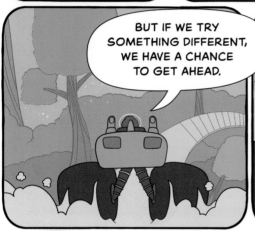

BUT IF WE TRY SOMETHING DIFFERENT, WE HAVE A CHANCE TO GET AHEAD.

SO THE TRACKS LESS TRAVELED WILL LEAD US TO GREATNESS— AND FIRST TO THE FINISH LINE?

THAT . . . OR TO VROOMBOTS AND DOOM.

I'M BETTING ON GREATNESS!

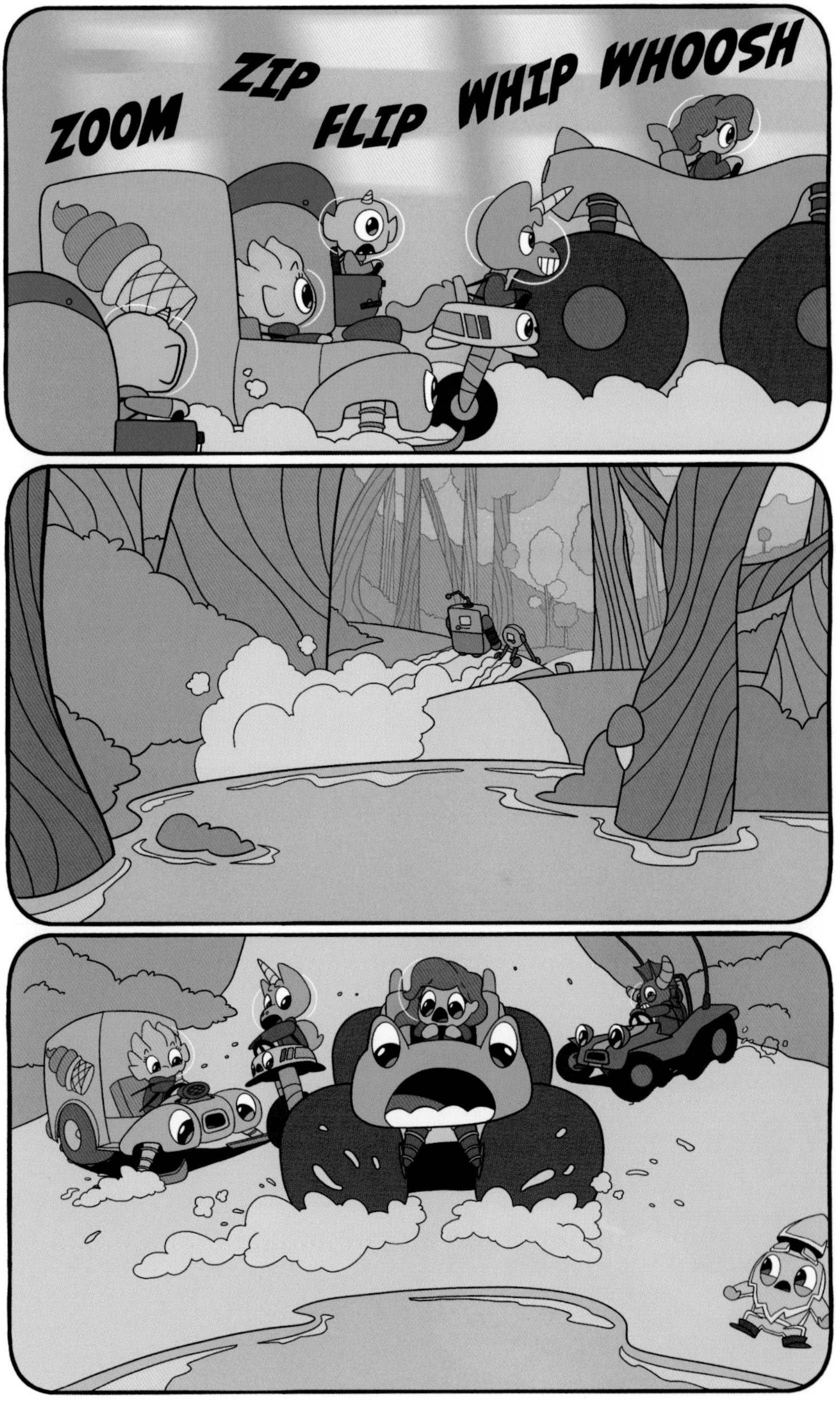
ZOOM
ZIP
FLIP
WHIP
WHOOSH

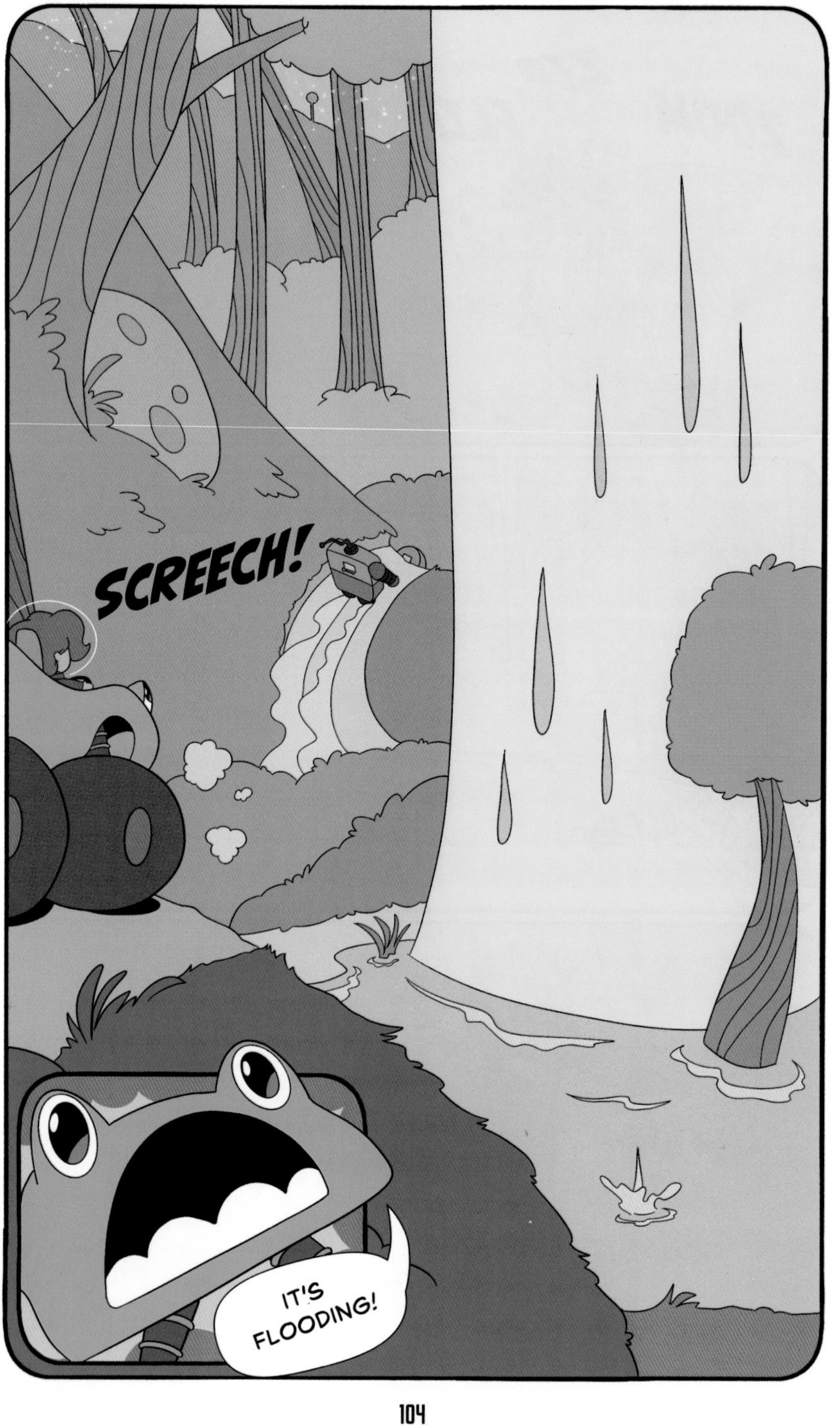
SCREECH!
IT'S FLOODING!

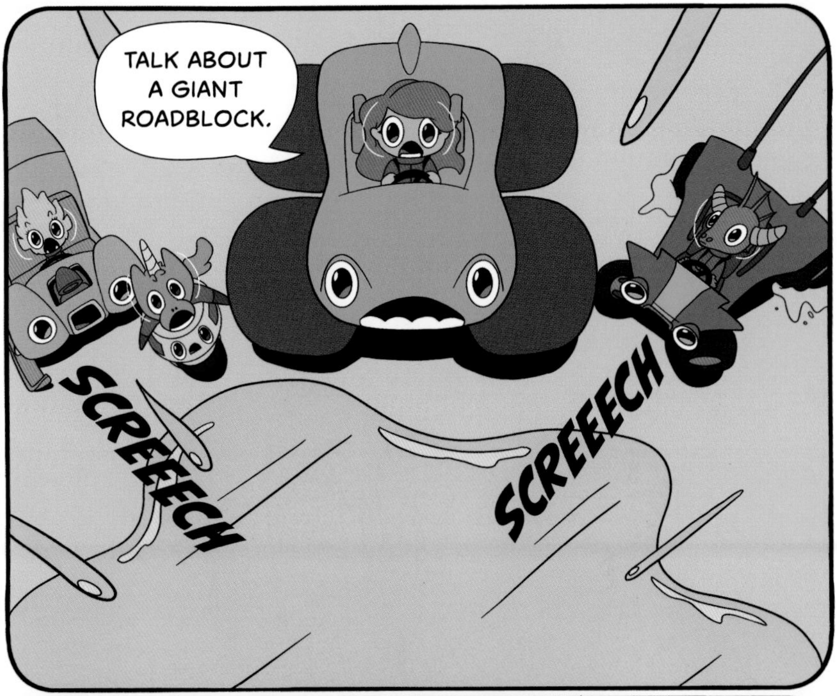
TALK ABOUT A GIANT ROADBLOCK.
SCREEECH
SCREEECH

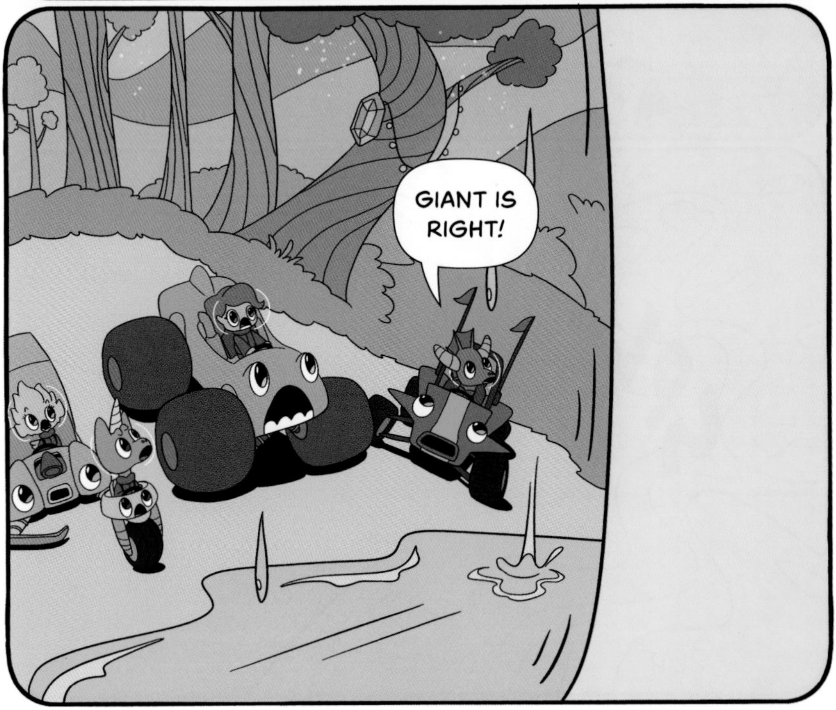
GIANT IS RIGHT!

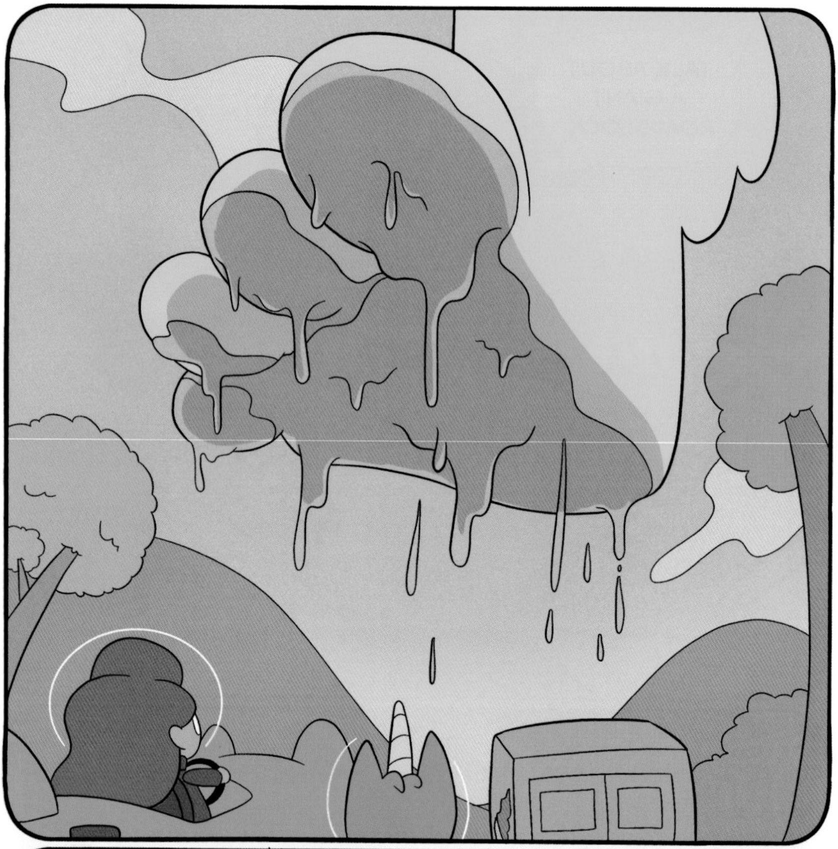

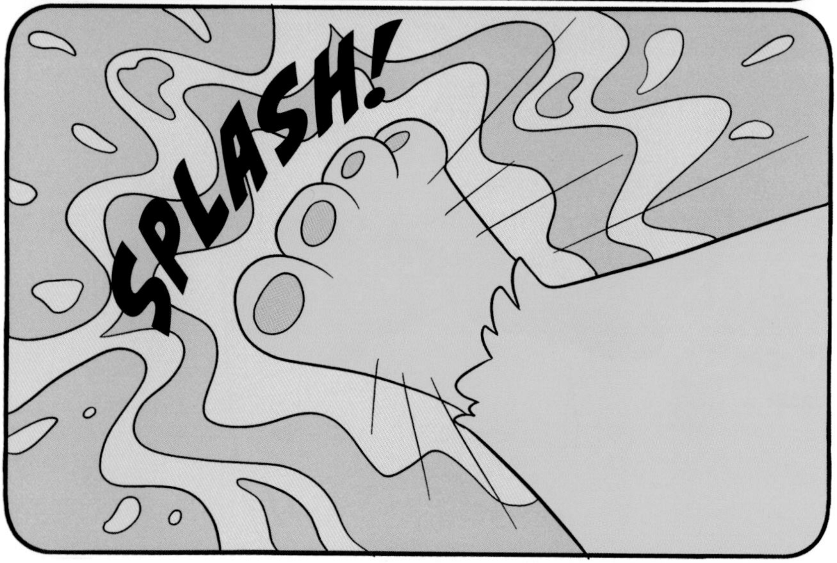
SPLASH!

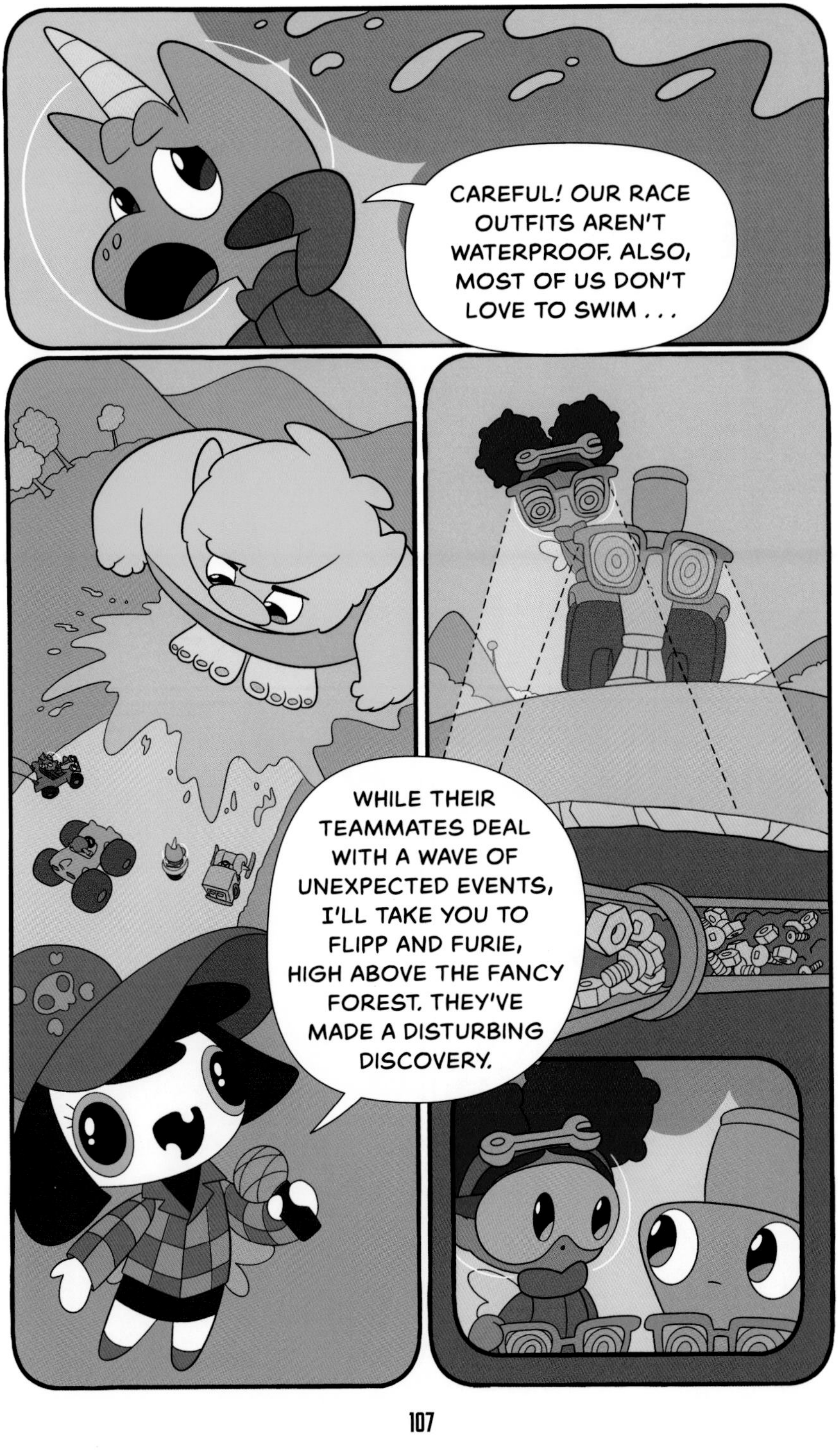

CAREFUL! OUR RACE OUTFITS AREN'T WATERPROOF. ALSO, MOST OF US DON'T LOVE TO SWIM . . .
WHILE THEIR TEAMMATES DEAL WITH A WAVE OF UNEXPECTED EVENTS, I'LL TAKE YOU TO FLIPP AND FURIE, HIGH ABOVE THE FANCY FOREST. THEY'VE MADE A DISTURBING DISCOVERY.

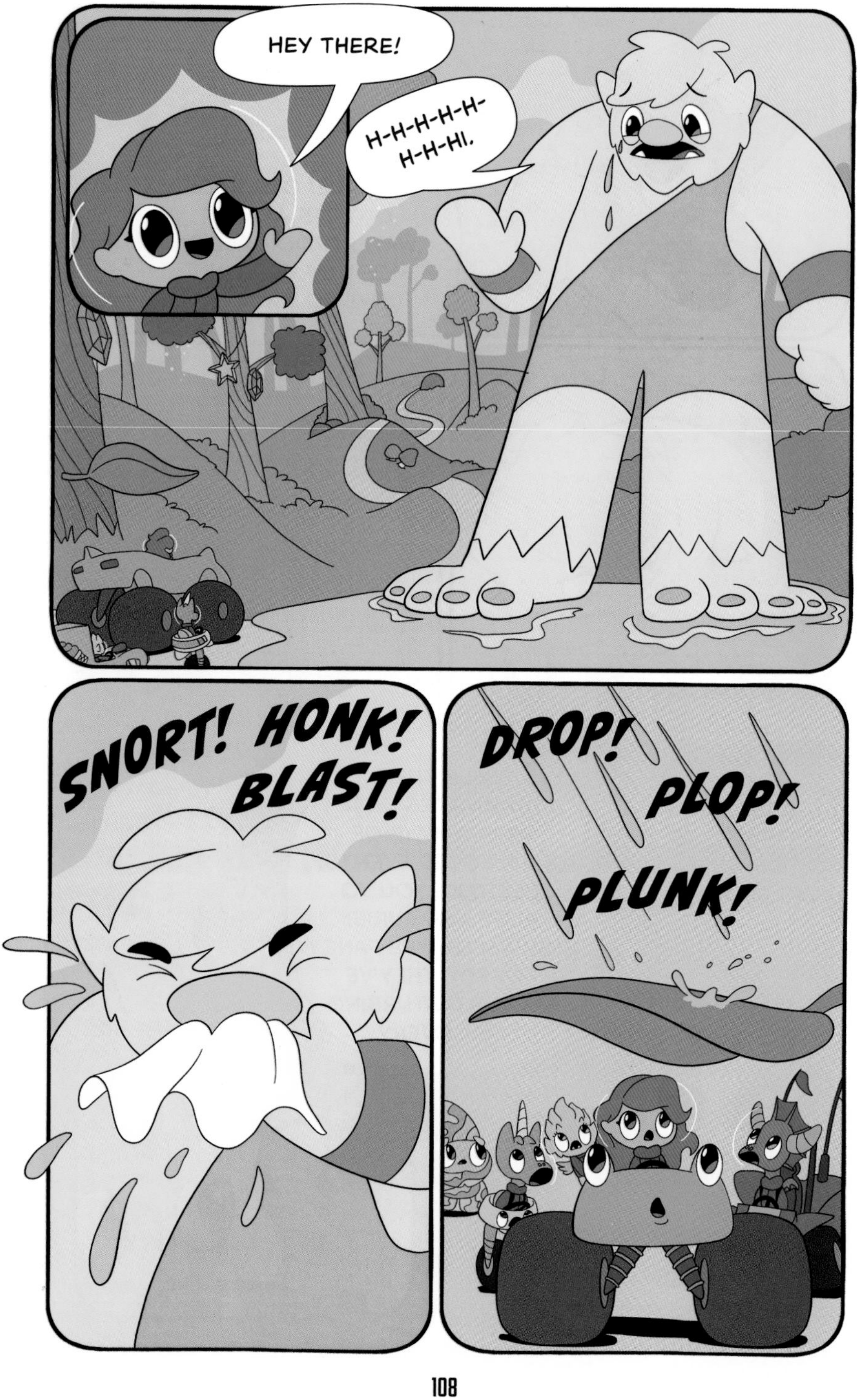
HEY THERE!
H-H-H-H-H-
H-H-HI.
SNORT! HONK!
BLAST!
DROP!
PLOP!
PLUNK!

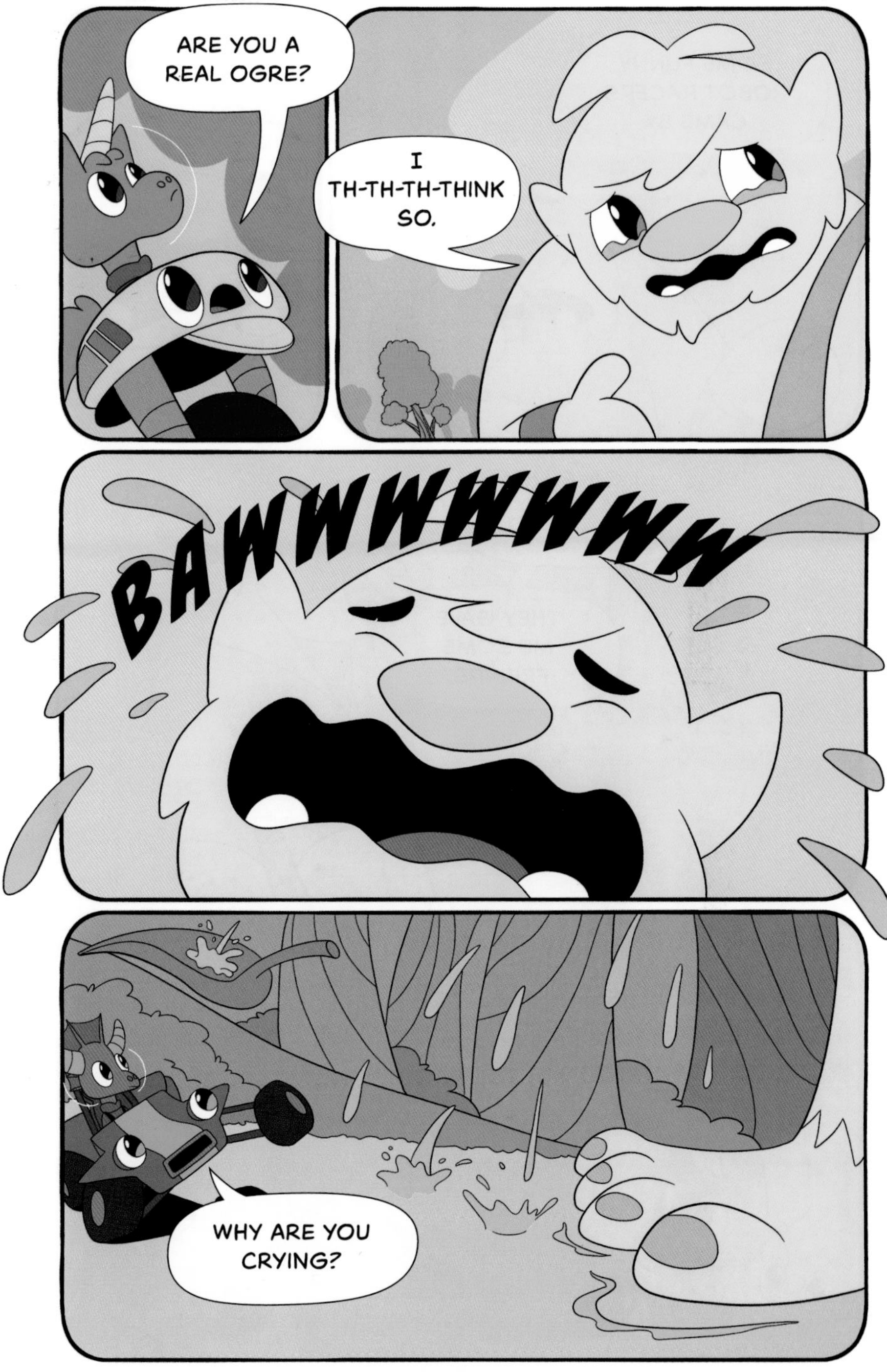
ARE YOU A REAL OGRE?
I TH-TH-TH-THINK SO.
BAWWWWWWWW
WHY ARE YOU CRYING?

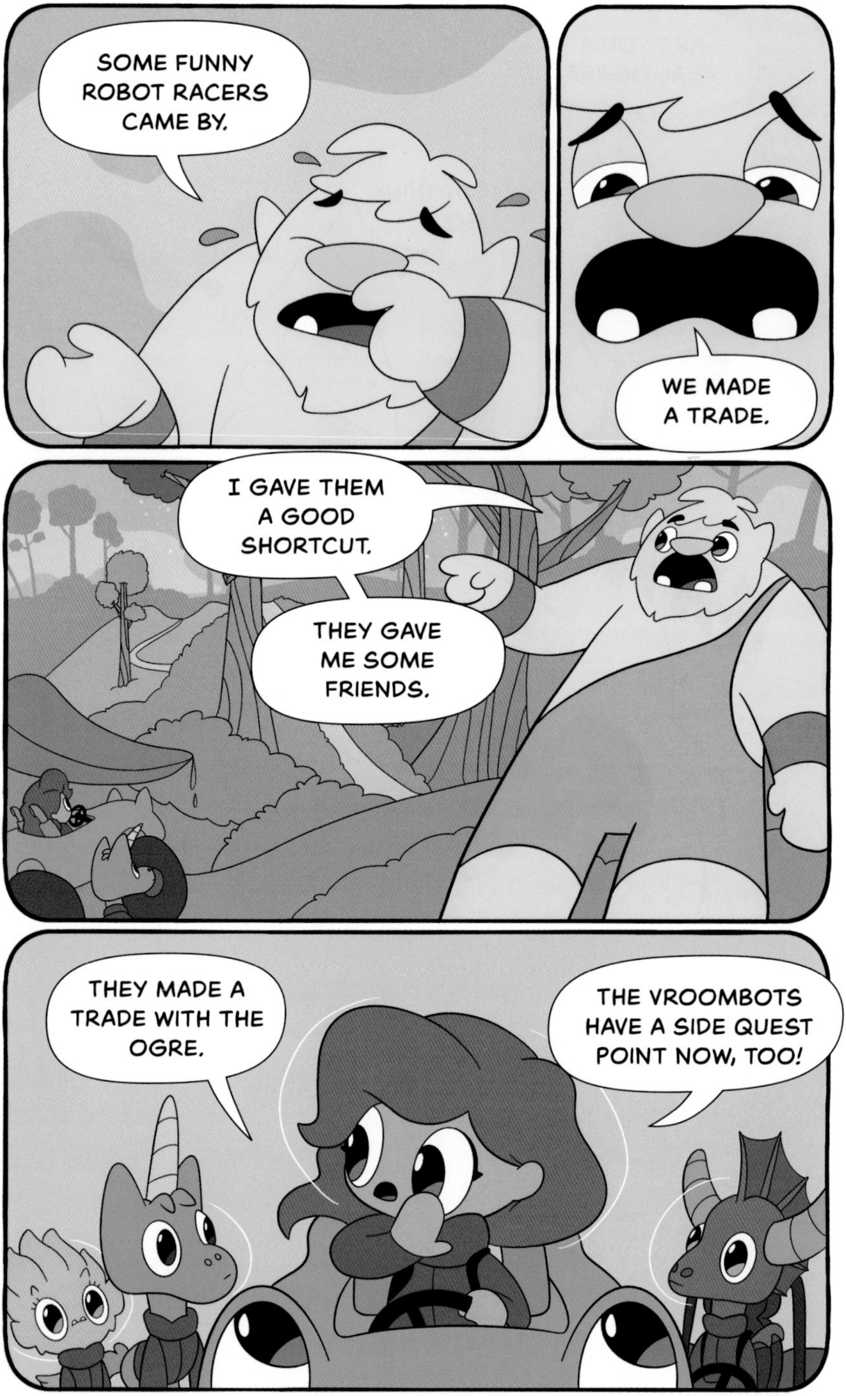
SOME FUNNY ROBOT RACERS CAME BY.
WE MADE A TRADE.
I GAVE THEM A GOOD SHORTCUT.
THEY GAVE ME SOME FRIENDS.
THEY MADE A TRADE WITH THE OGRE.
THE VROOMBOTS HAVE A SIDE QUEST POINT NOW, TOO!

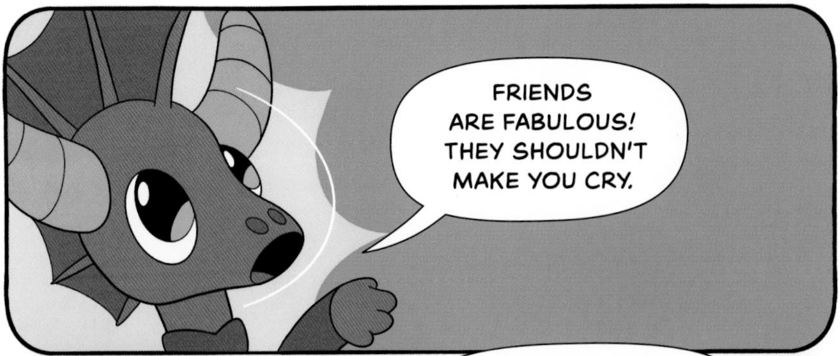
FRIENDS ARE FABULOUS! THEY SHOULDN'T MAKE YOU CRY.

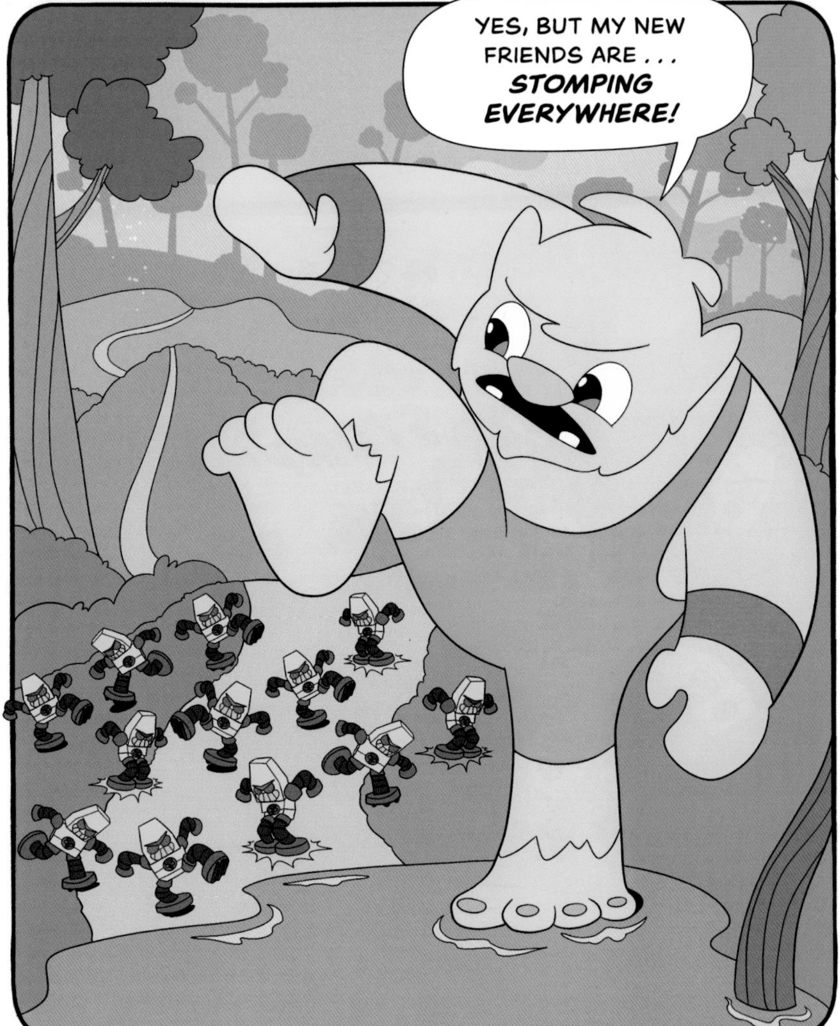
YES, BUT MY NEW FRIENDS ARE . . . *STOMPING EVERYWHERE!*

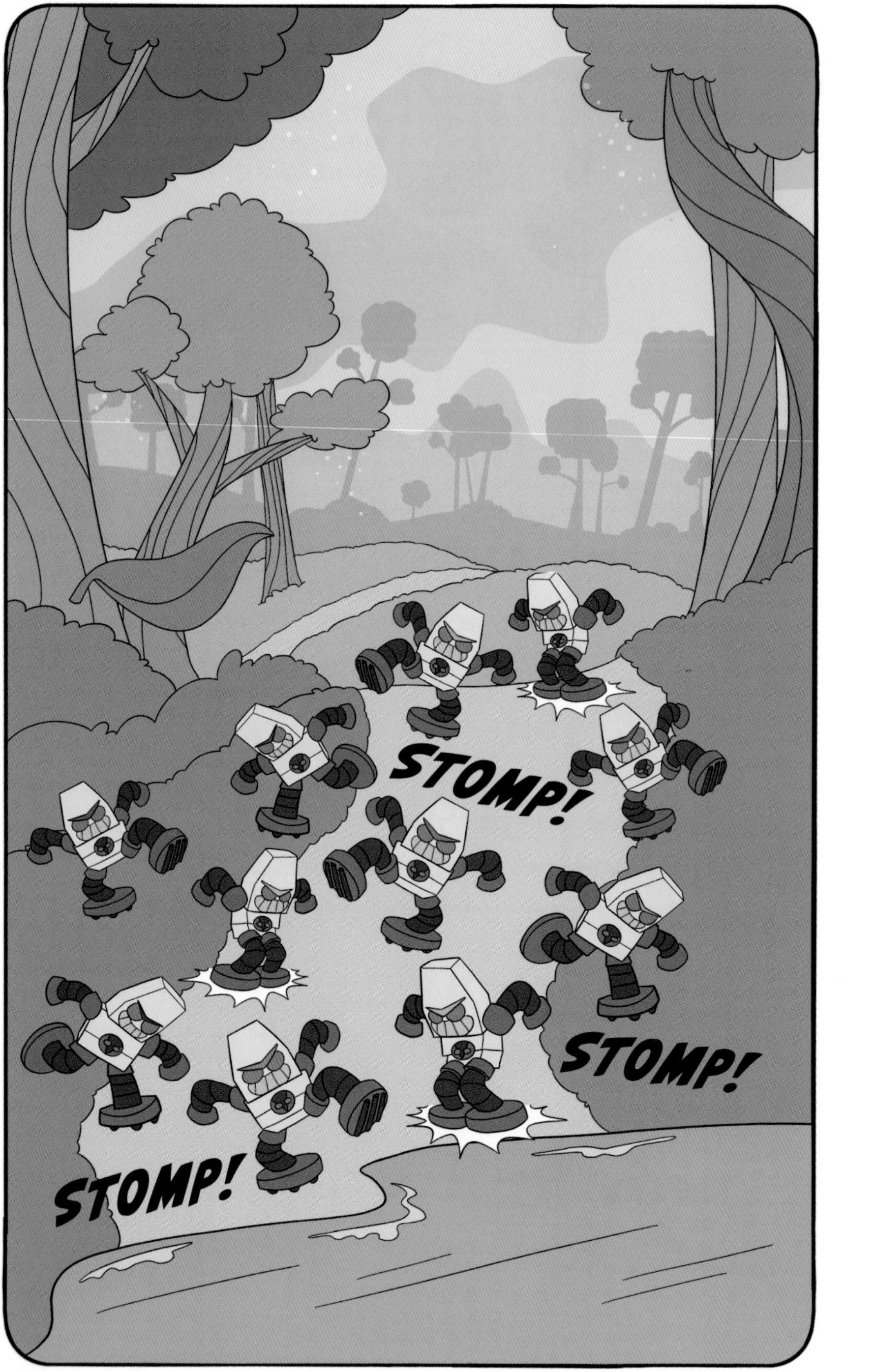
STOMP!
STOMP!
STOMP!

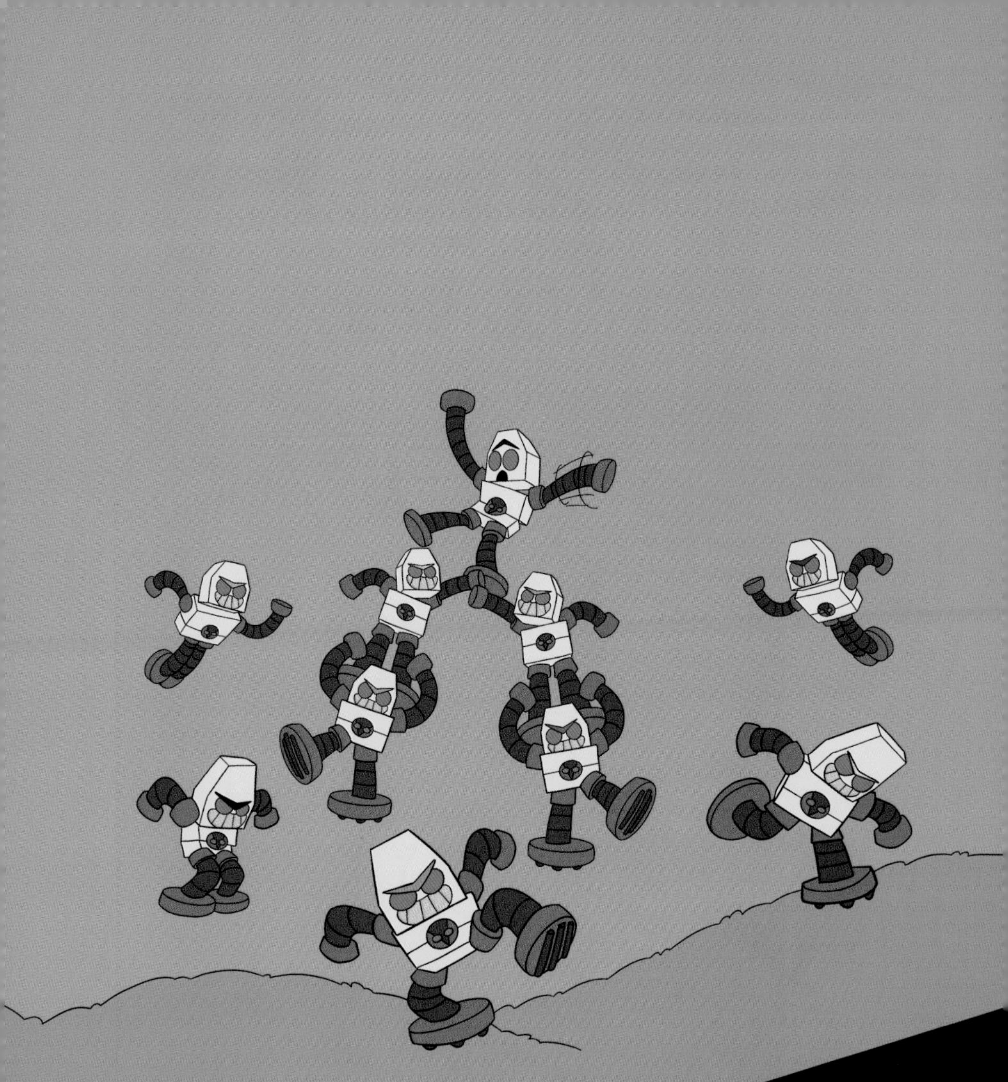

CHAPTER 9:
ROBO-OGRE DOOM!

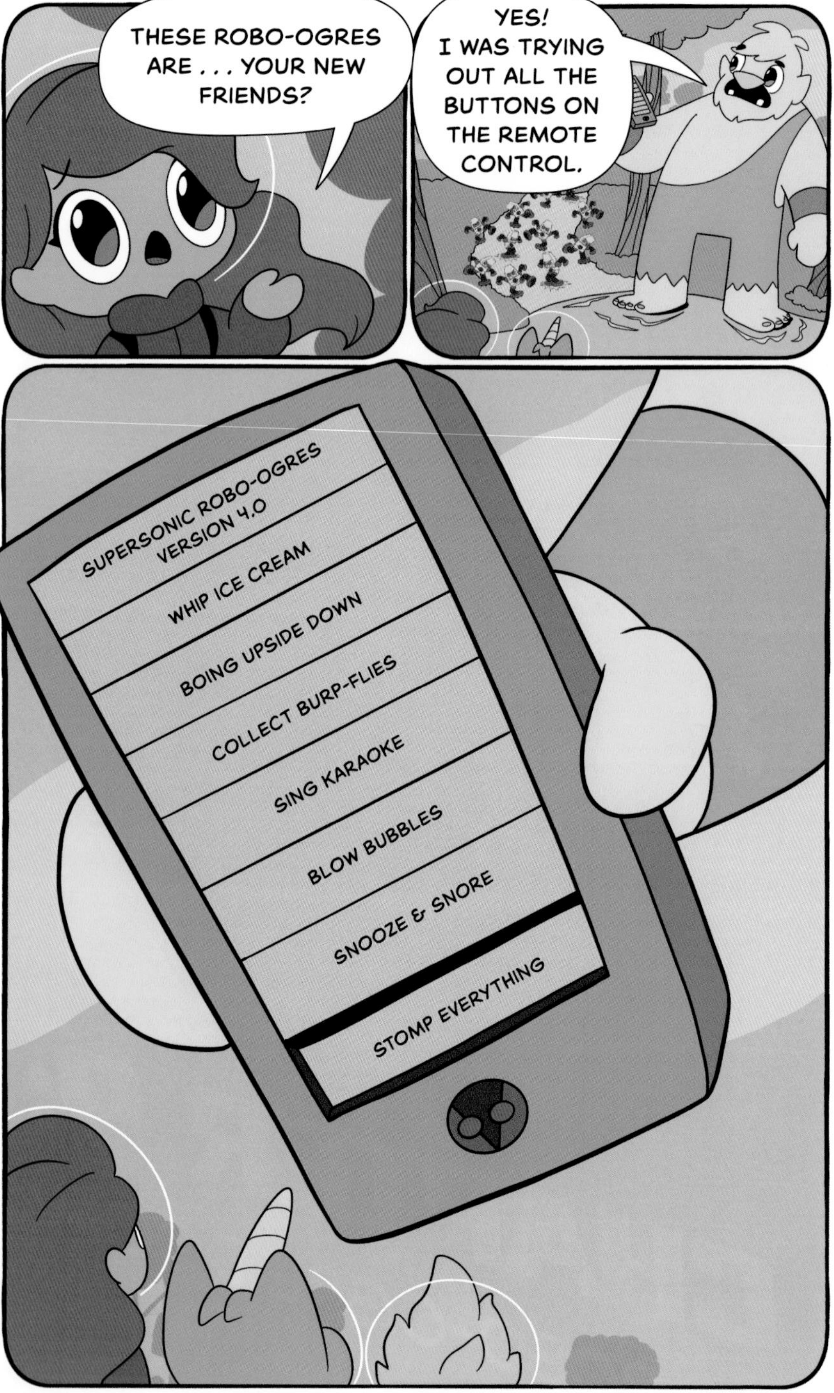
THESE ROBO-OGRES ARE . . . YOUR NEW FRIENDS?
YES! I WAS TRYING OUT ALL THE BUTTONS ON THE REMOTE CONTROL.
SUPERSONIC ROBO-OGRES VERSION 4.0
WHIP ICE CREAM
BOING UPSIDE DOWN
COLLECT BURP-FLIES
SING KARAOKE
BLOW BUBBLES
SNOOZE & SNORE
STOMP EVERYTHING

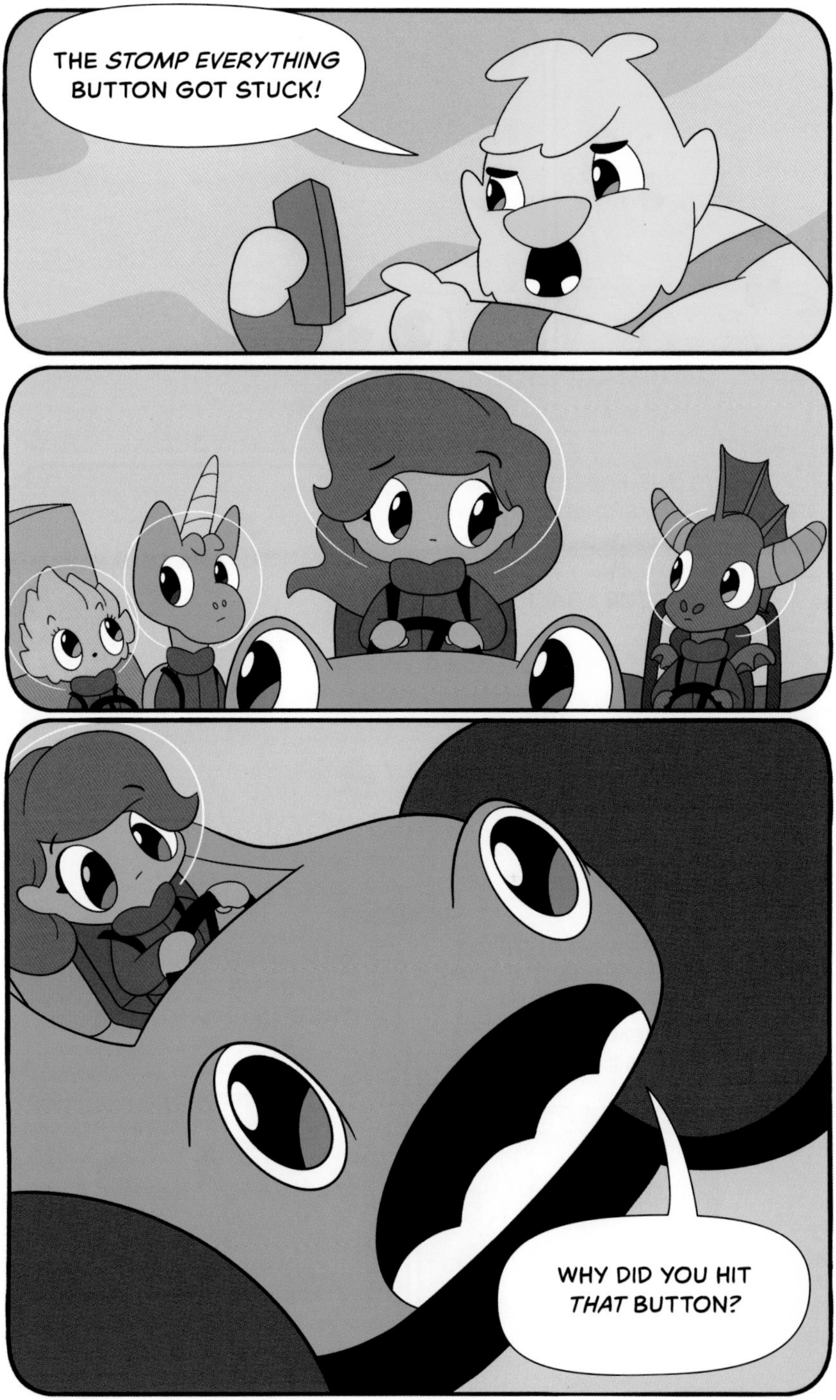
THE STOMP EVERYTHING BUTTON GOT STUCK!
WHY DID YOU HIT THAT BUTTON?

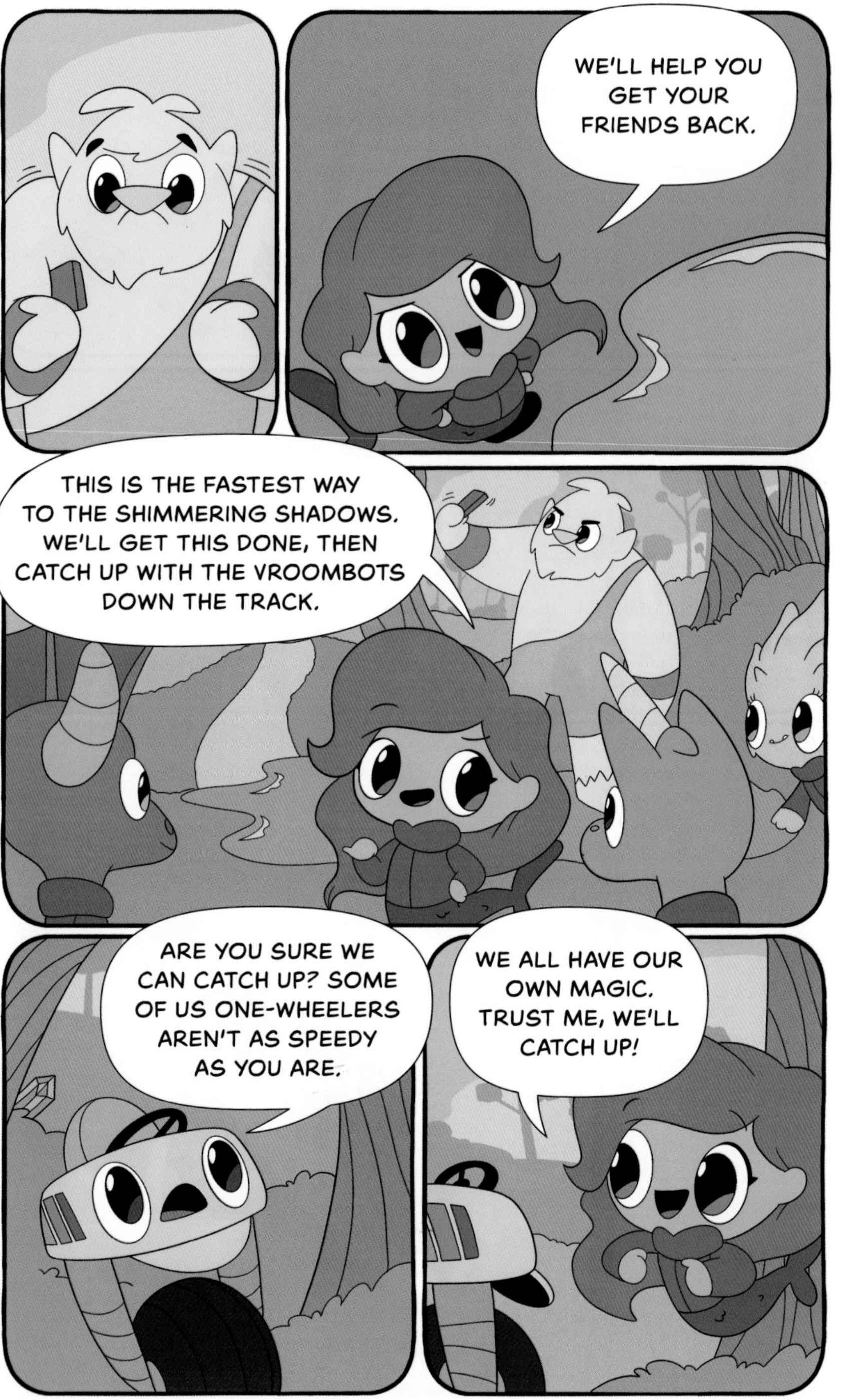
WE'LL HELP YOU GET YOUR FRIENDS BACK.
THIS IS THE FASTEST WAY TO THE SHIMMERING SHADOWS. WE'LL GET THIS DONE, THEN CATCH UP WITH THE VROOMBOTS DOWN THE TRACK.
ARE YOU SURE WE CAN CATCH UP? SOME OF US ONE-WHEELERS AREN'T AS SPEEDY AS YOU ARE.
WE ALL HAVE OUR OWN MAGIC. TRUST ME, WE'LL CATCH UP!

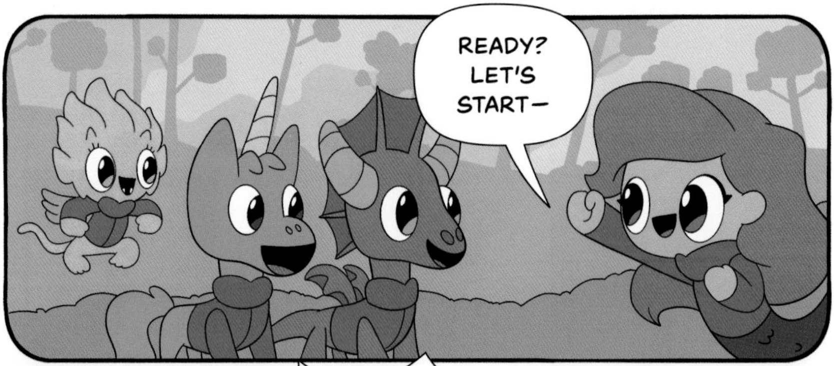
READY? LET'S START—

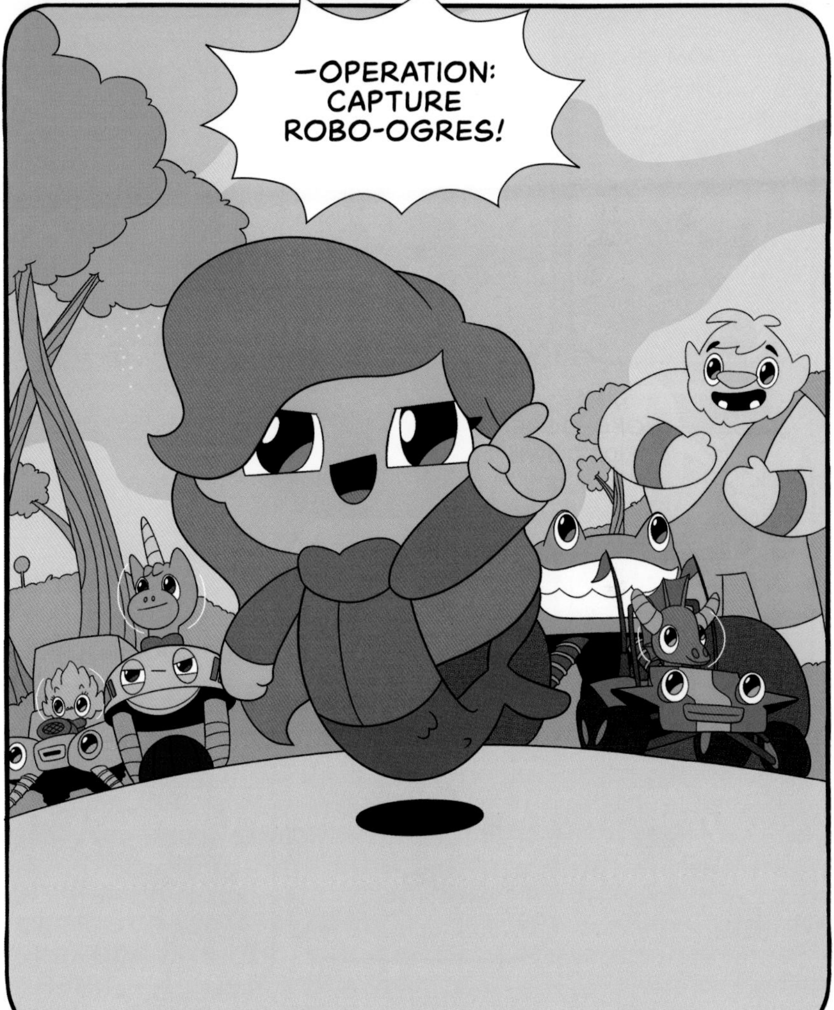
—OPERATION: CAPTURE ROBO-OGRES!

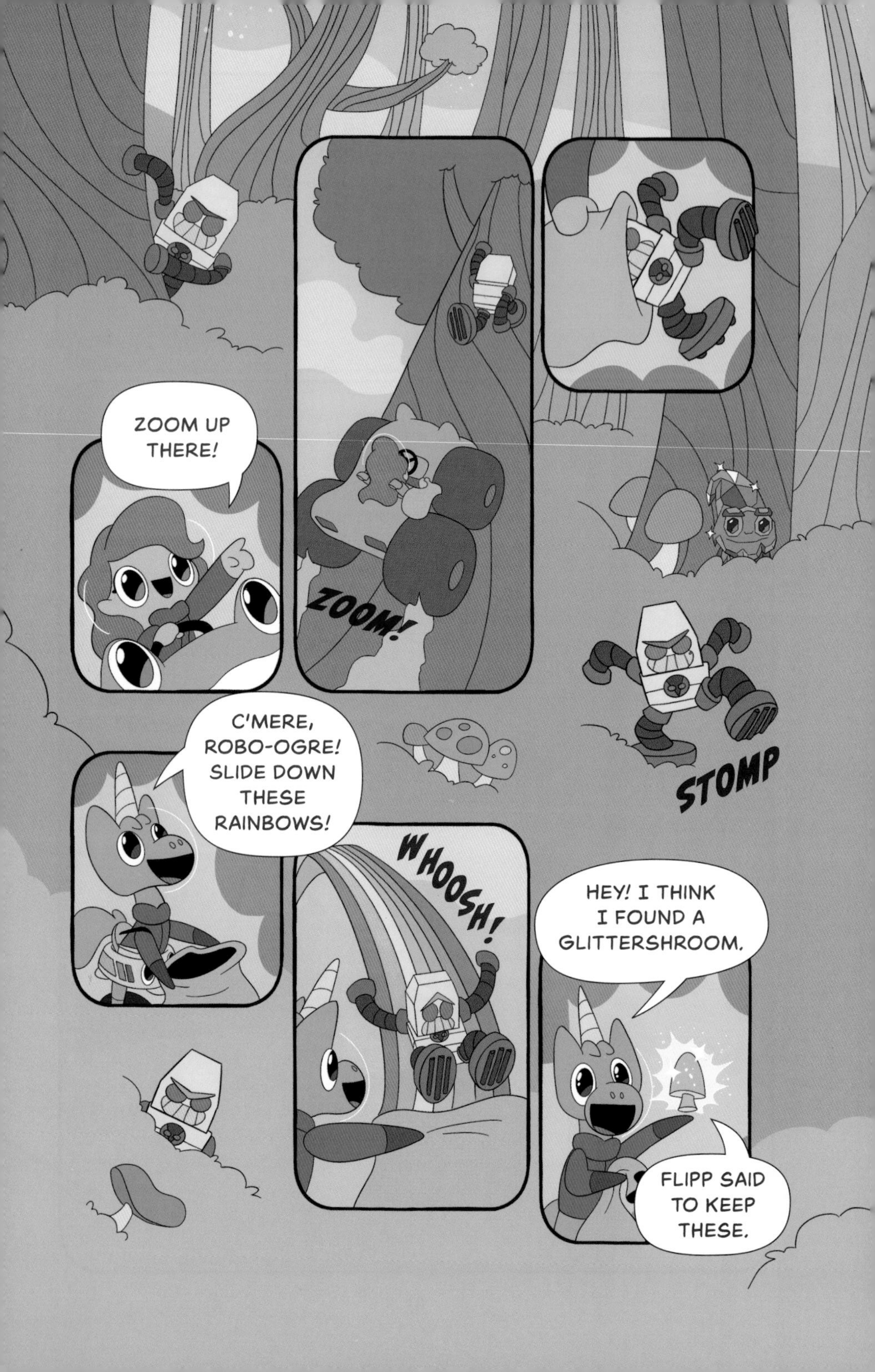
ZOOM UP THERE!
ZOOM!
STOMP
C'MERE, ROBO-OGRE! SLIDE DOWN THESE RAINBOWS!
WHOOSH!
HEY! I THINK I FOUND A GLITTERSHROOM.
FLIPP SAID TO KEEP THESE.

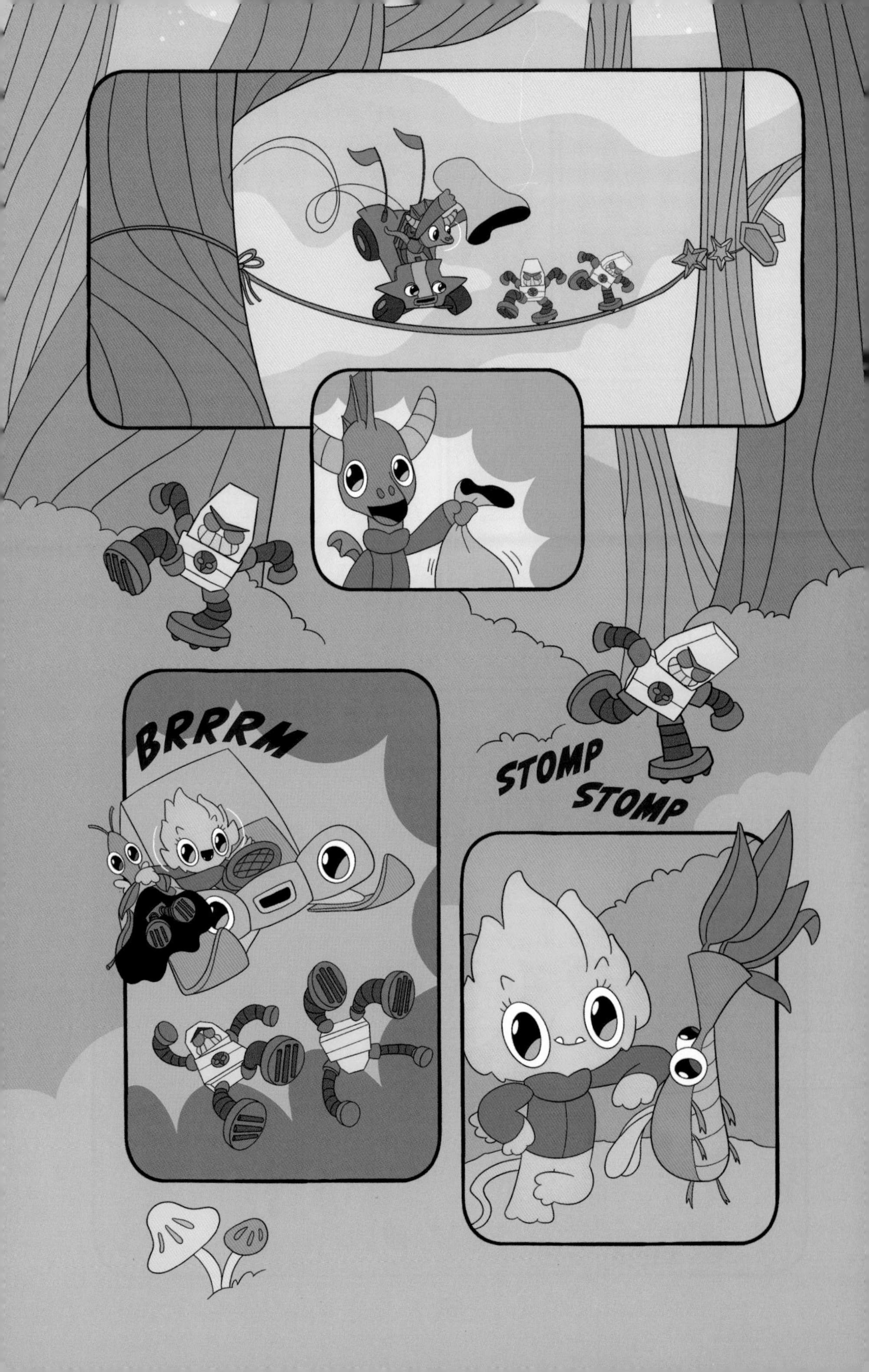
BRRRM
STOMP
STOMP

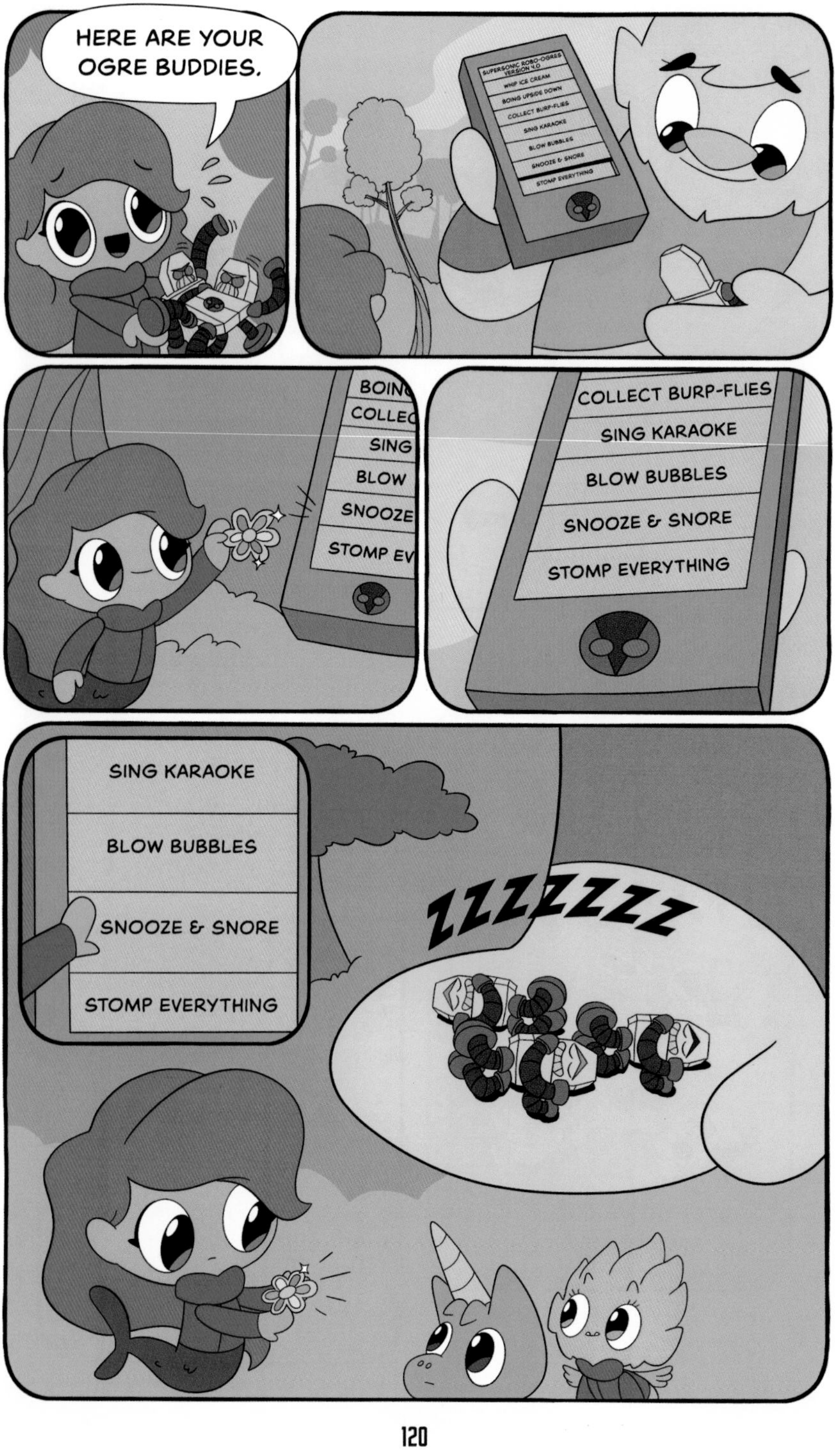

HERE ARE YOUR OGRE BUDDIES.
SUPERSONIC ROBO-OGRES VERSION 4.0
WHIP ICE CREAM
BOING UPSIDE DOWN
COLLECT BURP-FLIES
SING KARAOKE
BLOW BUBBLES
SNOOZE & SNORE
STOMP EVERYTHING
COLLECT BURP-FLIES
SING KARAOKE
BLOW BUBBLES
SNOOZE & SNORE
STOMP EVERYTHING
SING KARAOKE
BLOW BUBBLES
SNOOZE & SNORE
STOMP EVERYTHING
ZZZZZZZ

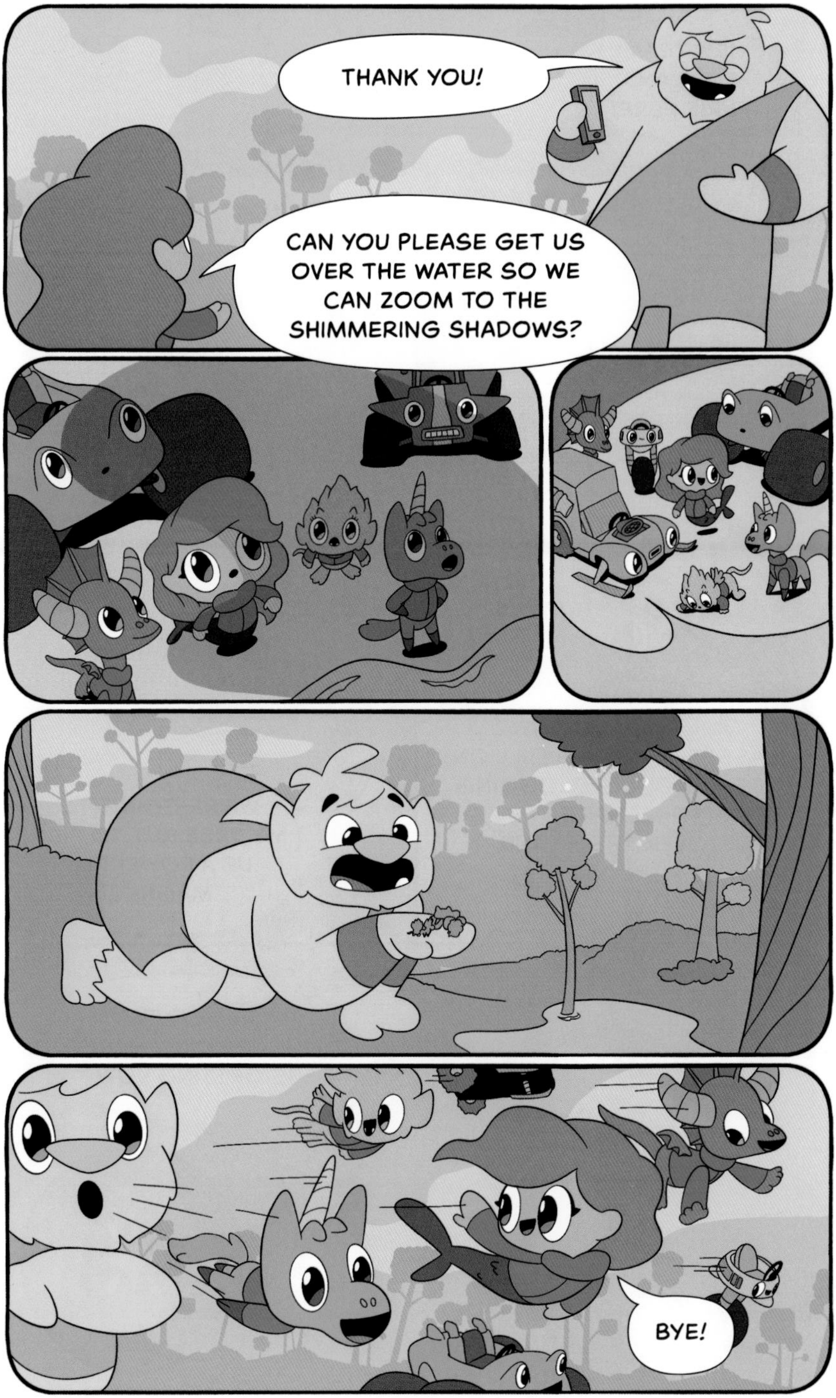
THANK YOU!
CAN YOU PLEASE GET US OVER THE WATER SO WE CAN ZOOM TO THE SHIMMERING SHADOWS?
BYE!

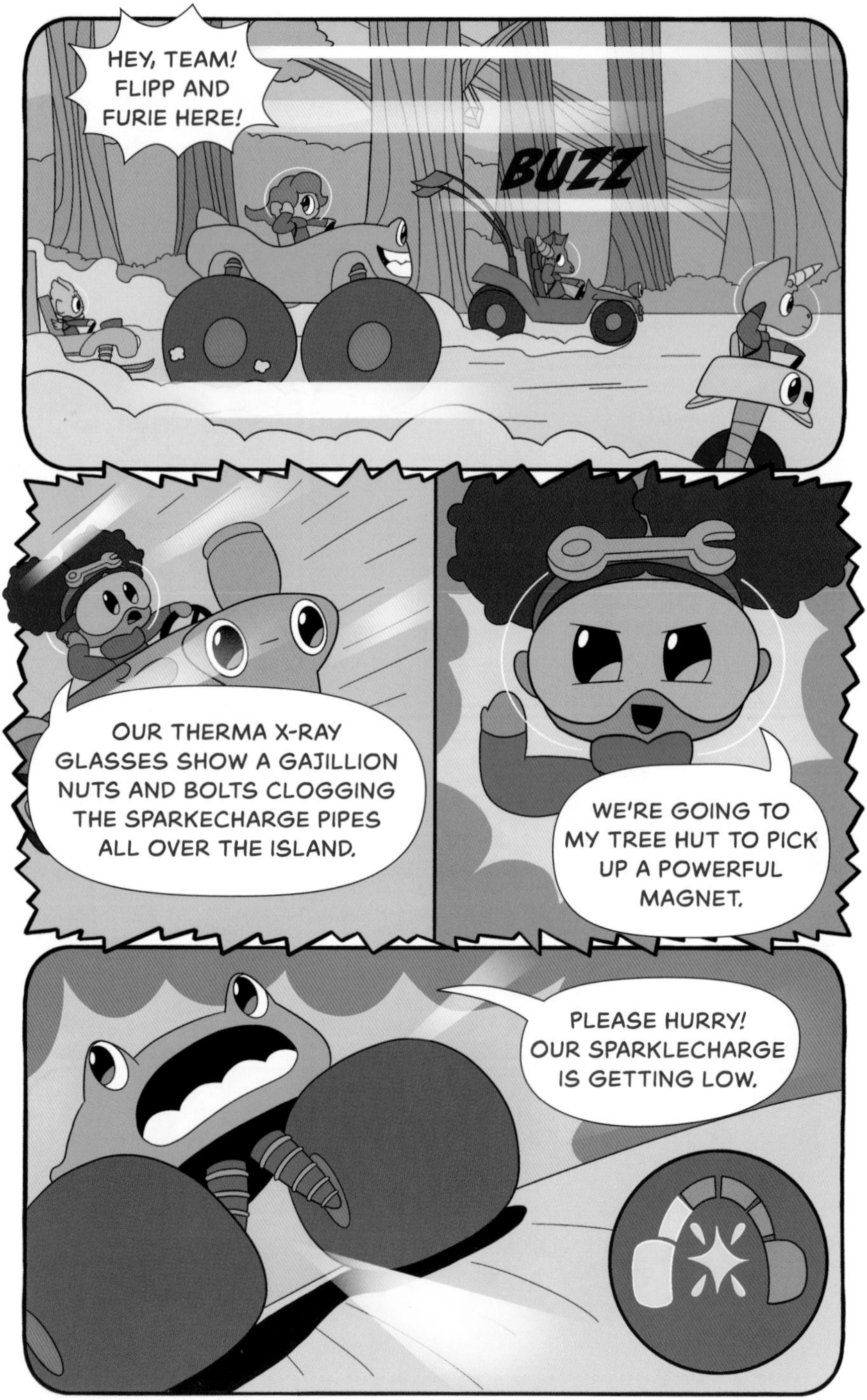
HEY, TEAM! FLIPP AND FURIE HERE!
BUZZ
OUR THERMA X-RAY GLASSES SHOW A GAJILLION NUTS AND BOLTS CLOGGING THE SPARKECHARGE PIPES ALL OVER THE ISLAND.
WE'RE GOING TO MY TREE HUT TO PICK UP A POWERFUL MAGNET.
PLEASE HURRY! OUR SPARKLECHARGE IS GETTING LOW.

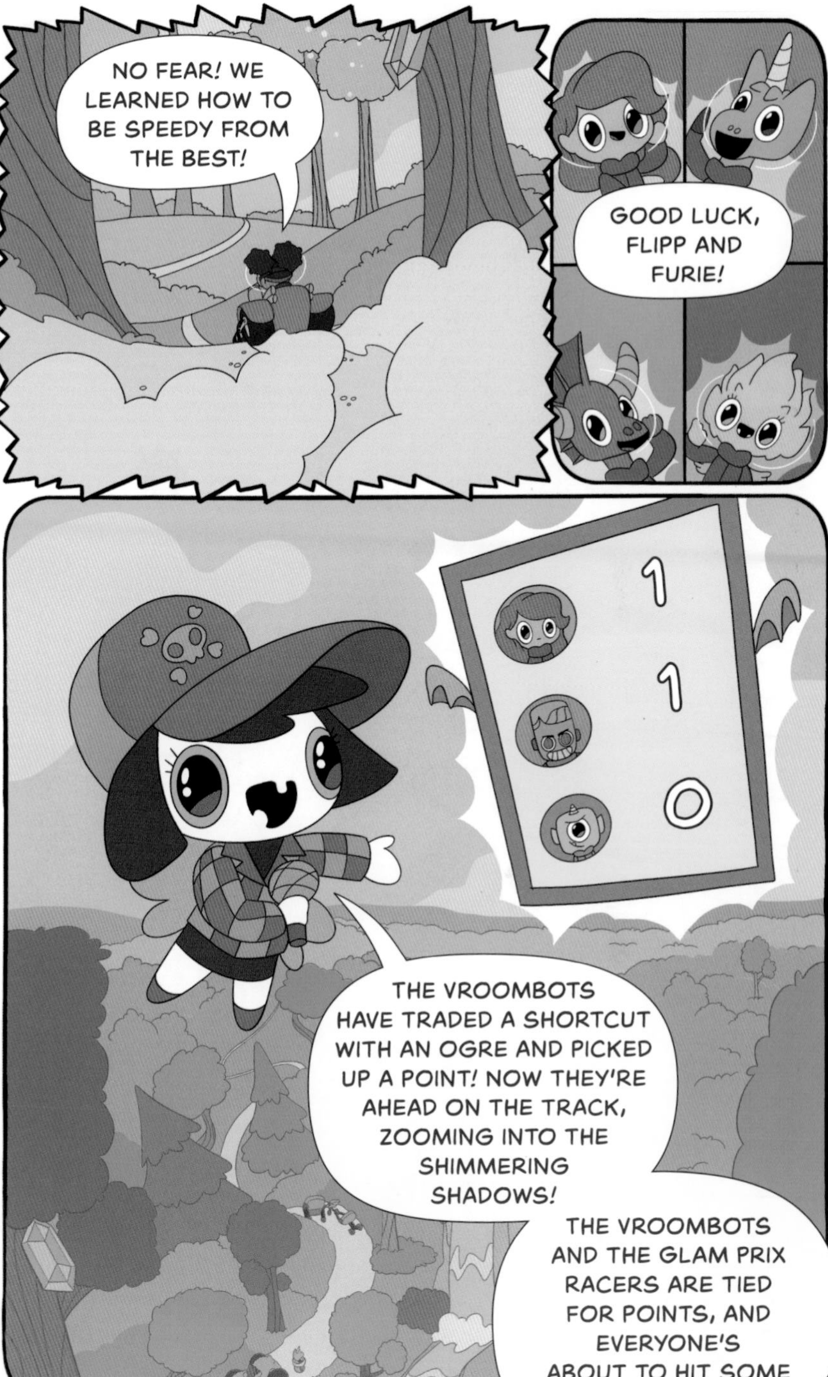
NO FEAR! WE LEARNED HOW TO BE SPEEDY FROM THE BEST!
GOOD LUCK, FLIPP AND FURIE!
1
1
0
THE VROOMBOTS HAVE TRADED A SHORTCUT WITH AN OGRE AND PICKED UP A POINT! NOW THEY'RE AHEAD ON THE TRACK, ZOOMING INTO THE SHIMMERING SHADOWS!
THE VROOMBOTS AND THE GLAM PRIX RACERS ARE TIED FOR POINTS, AND EVERYONE'S ABOUT TO HIT SOME DENSE FOREST . . .

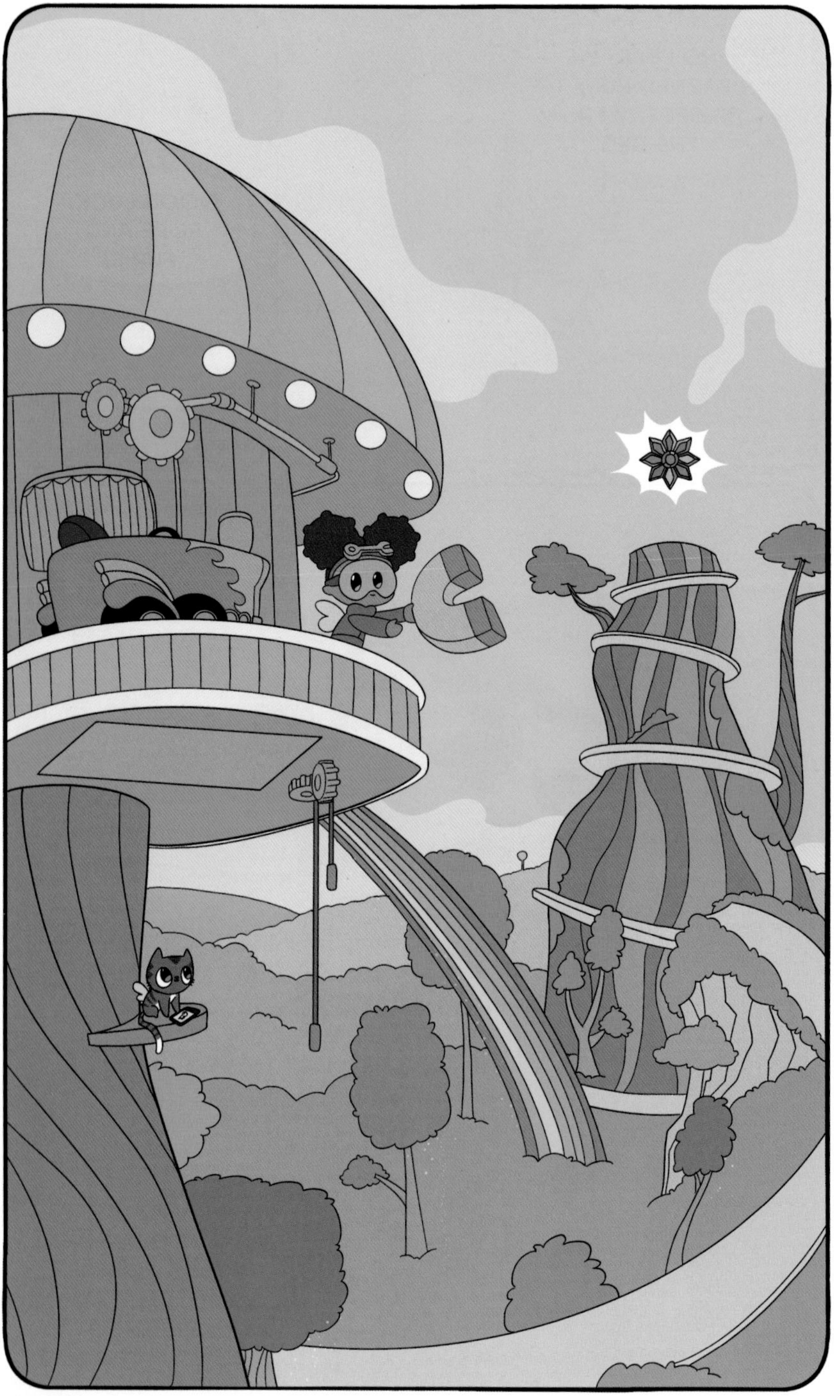

CHAPTER 10:
GLORIOUS GEM!

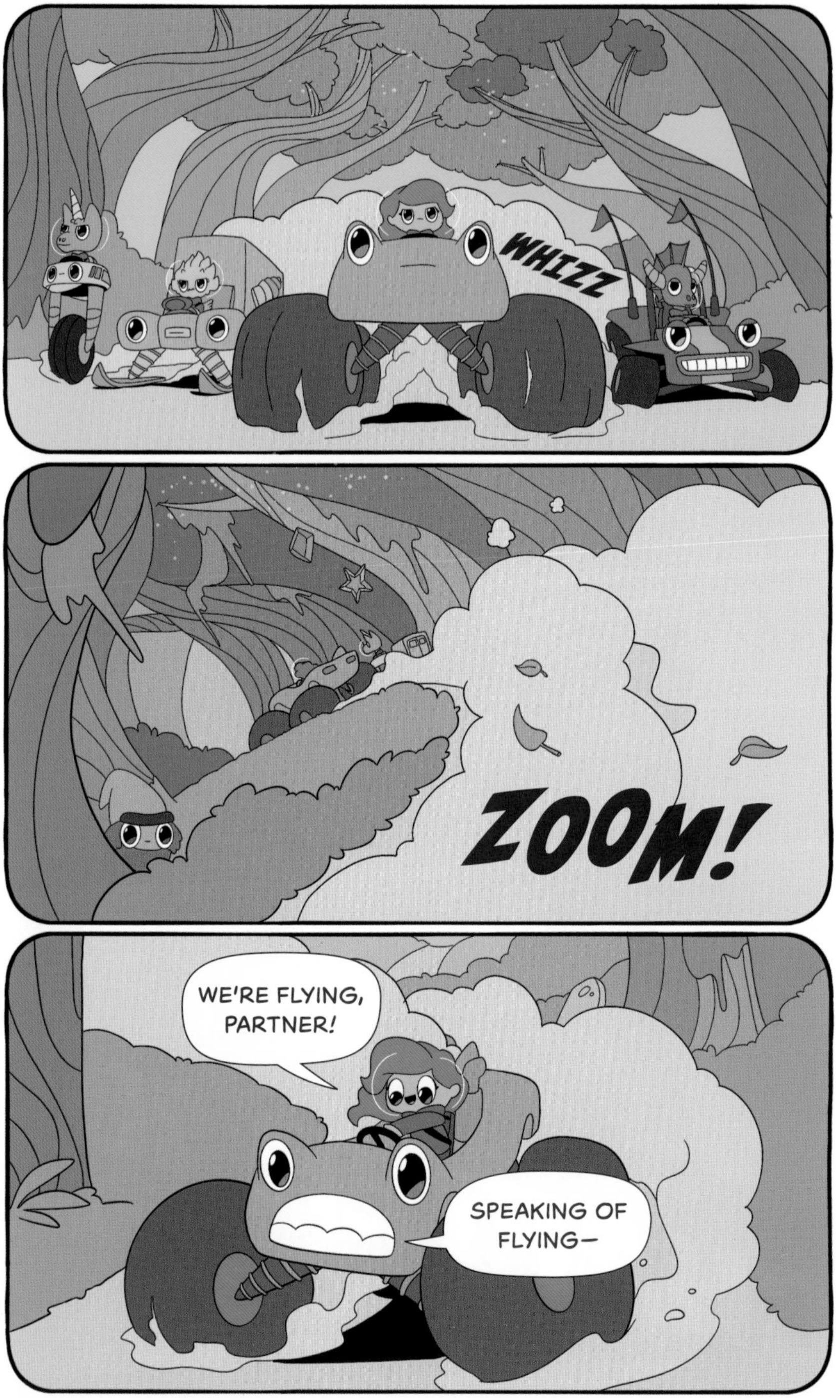
WHIZZ
ZOOM!
WE'RE FLYING, PARTNER!
SPEAKING OF FLYING—

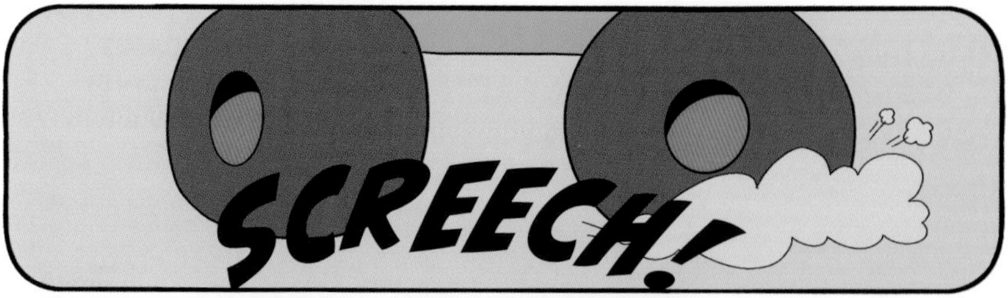
SCREECH!

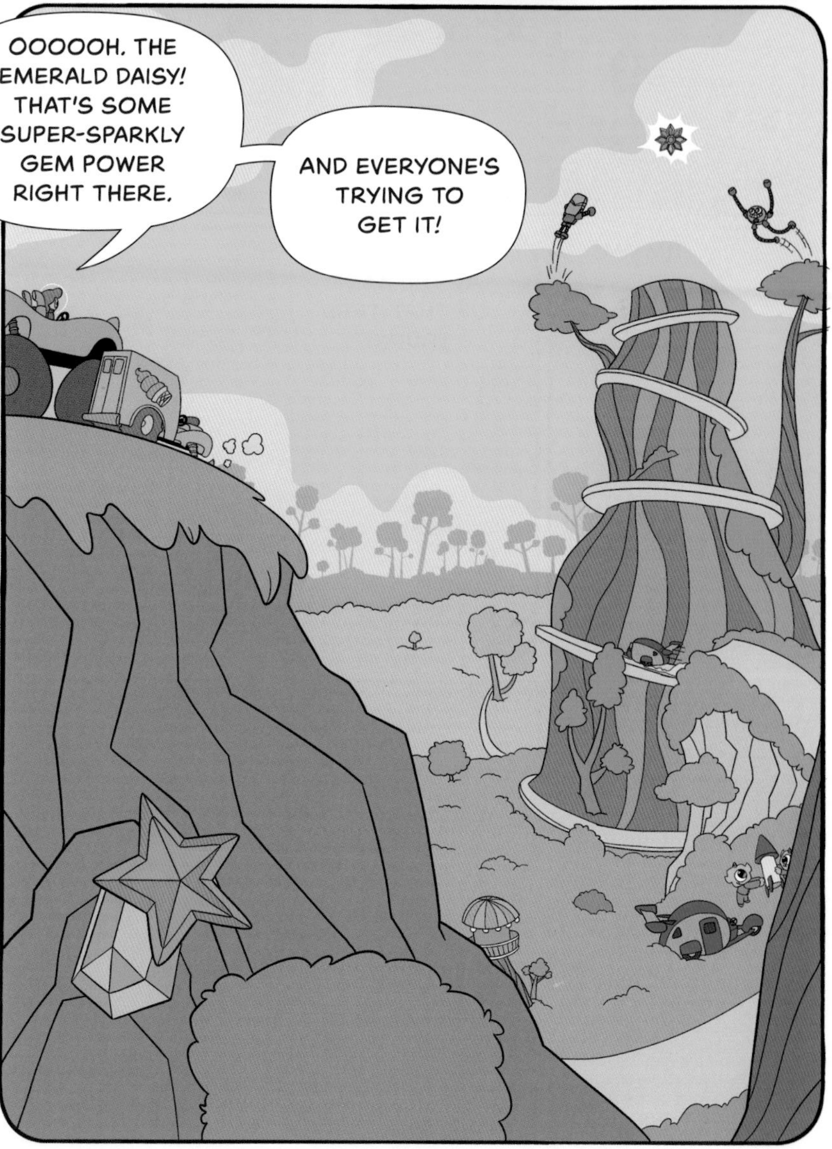
OOOOOH, THE EMERALD DAISY! THAT'S SOME SUPER-SPARKLY GEM POWER RIGHT THERE.
AND EVERYONE'S TRYING TO GET IT!

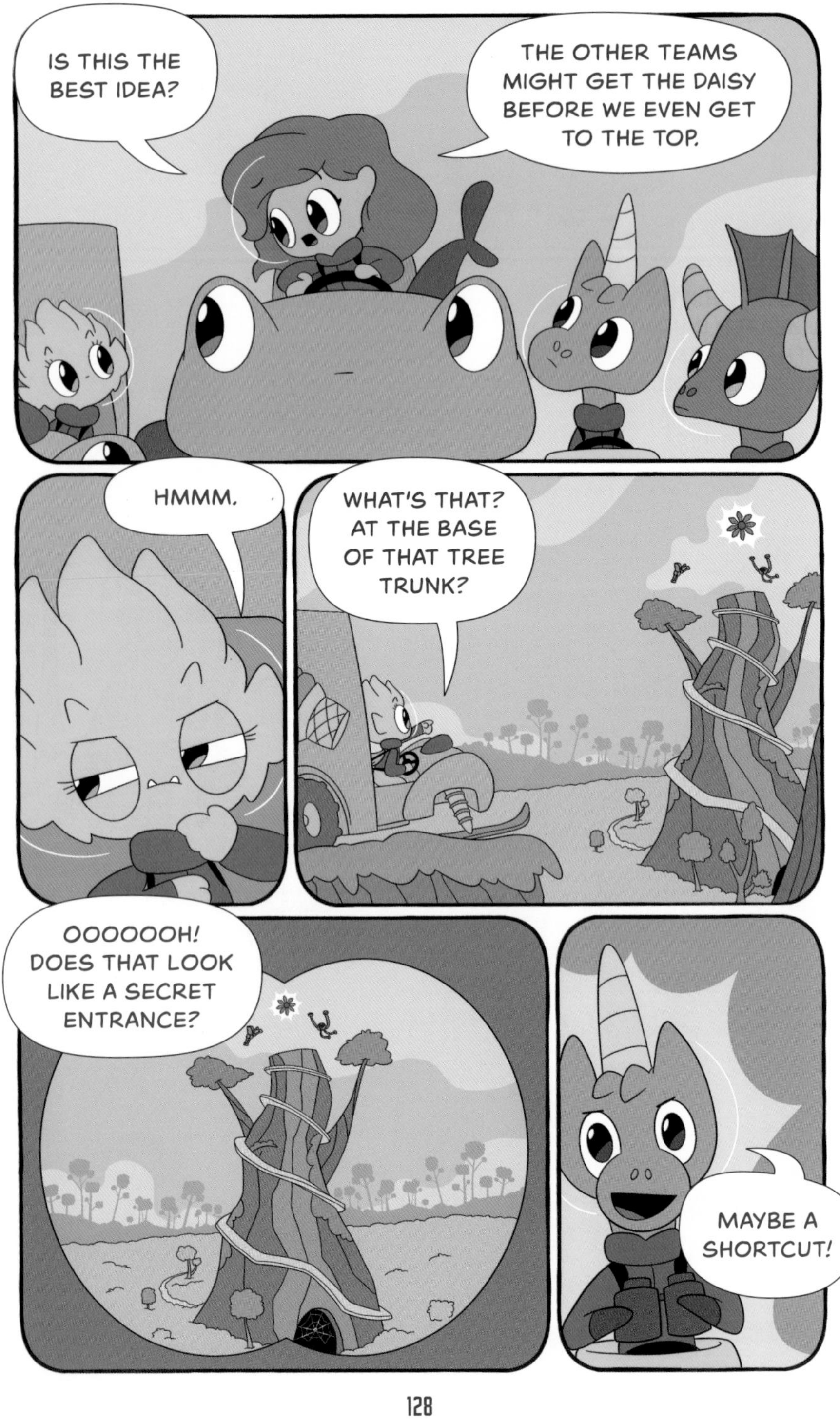
IS THIS THE BEST IDEA?
THE OTHER TEAMS MIGHT GET THE DAISY BEFORE WE EVEN GET TO THE TOP.
HMMM.
WHAT'S THAT? AT THE BASE OF THAT TREE TRUNK?
OOOOOOH! DOES THAT LOOK LIKE A SECRET ENTRANCE?
MAYBE A SHORTCUT!

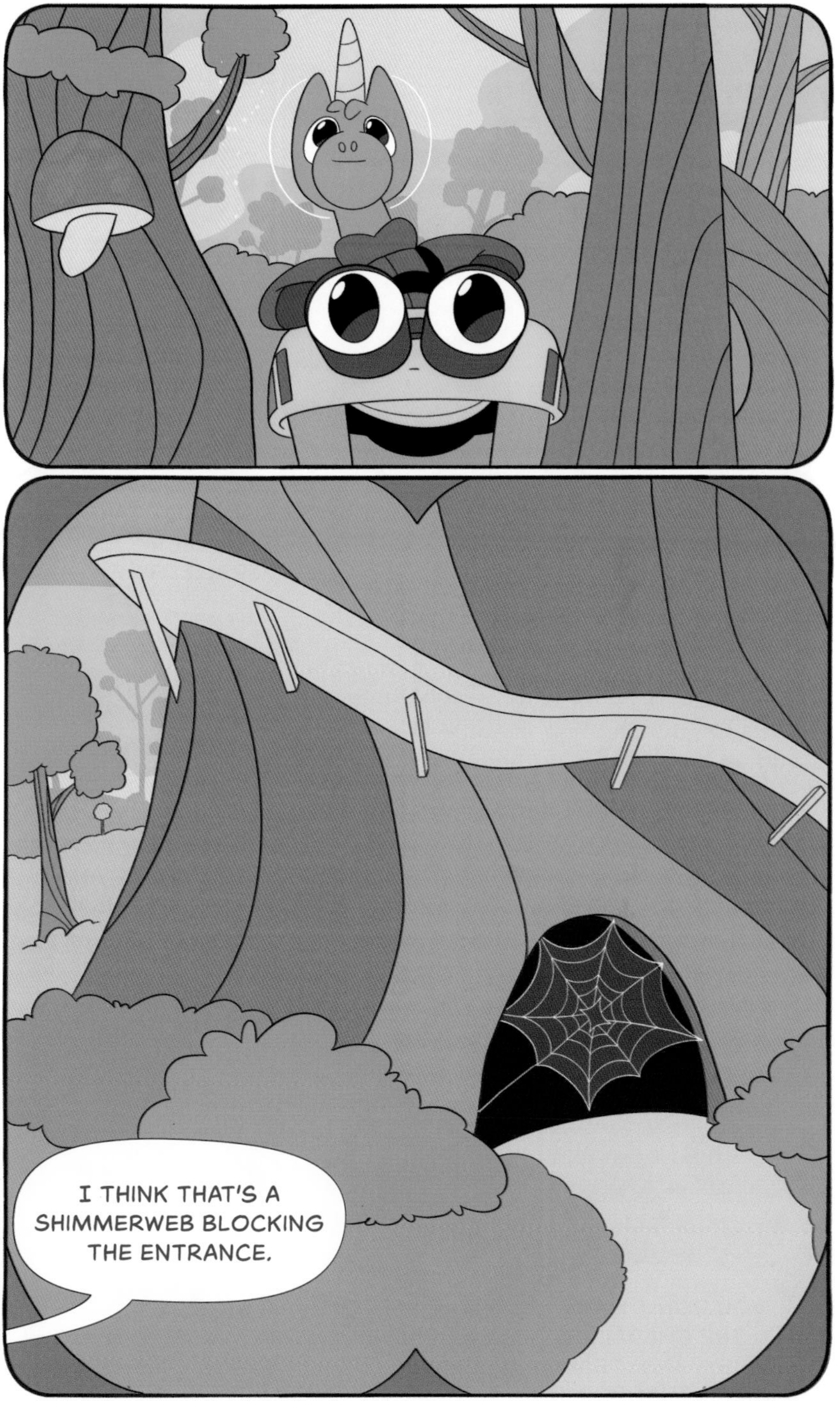
I THINK THAT'S A SHIMMERWEB BLOCKING THE ENTRANCE.

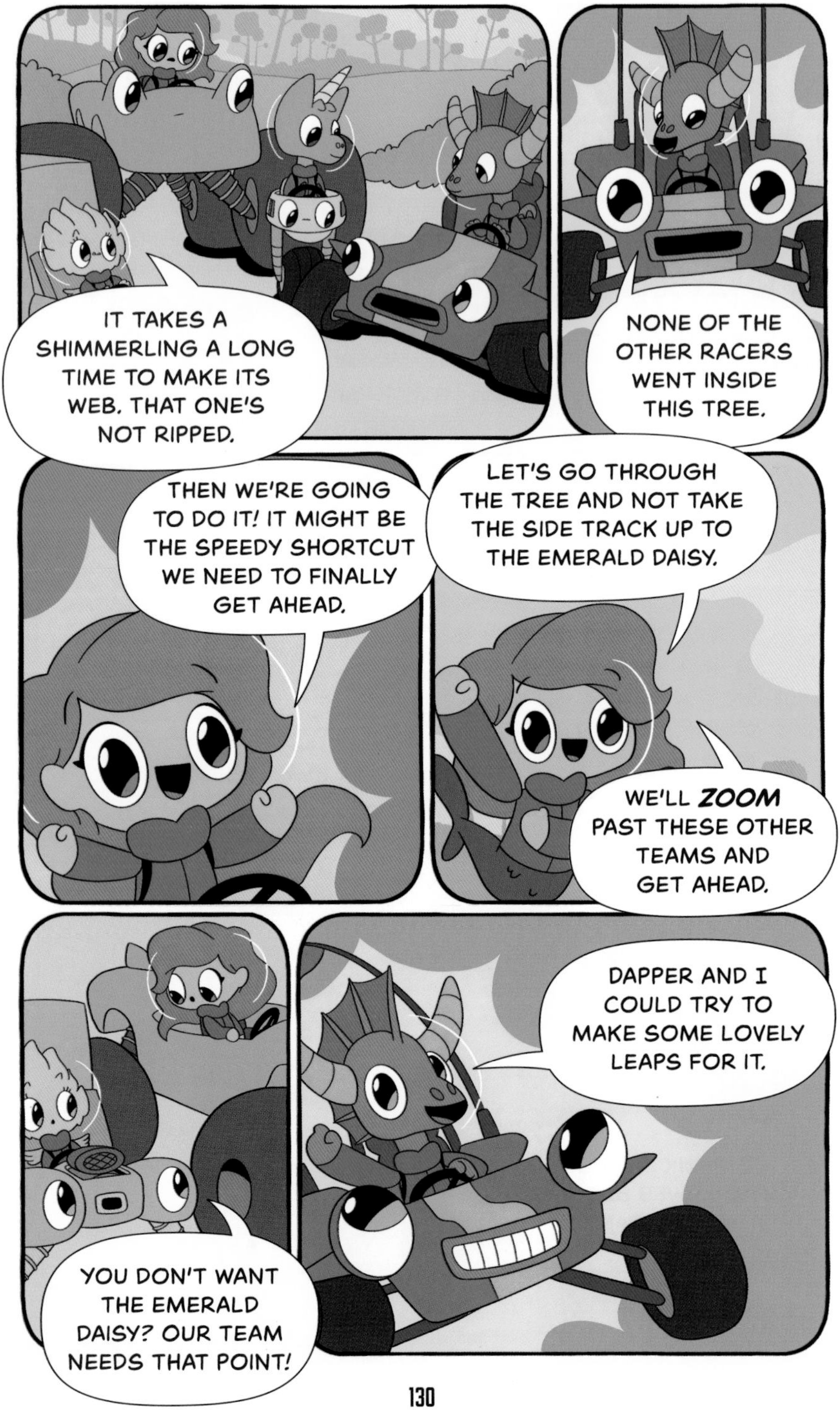
IT TAKES A SHIMMERLING A LONG TIME TO MAKE ITS WEB. THAT ONE'S NOT RIPPED.
NONE OF THE OTHER RACERS WENT INSIDE THIS TREE.
THEN WE'RE GOING TO DO IT! IT MIGHT BE THE SPEEDY SHORTCUT WE NEED TO FINALLY GET AHEAD.
LET'S GO THROUGH THE TREE AND NOT TAKE THE SIDE TRACK UP TO THE EMERALD DAISY.
WE'LL *ZOOM* PAST THESE OTHER TEAMS AND GET AHEAD.
DAPPER AND I COULD TRY TO MAKE SOME LOVELY LEAPS FOR IT.
YOU DON'T WANT THE EMERALD DAISY? OUR TEAM NEEDS THAT POINT!

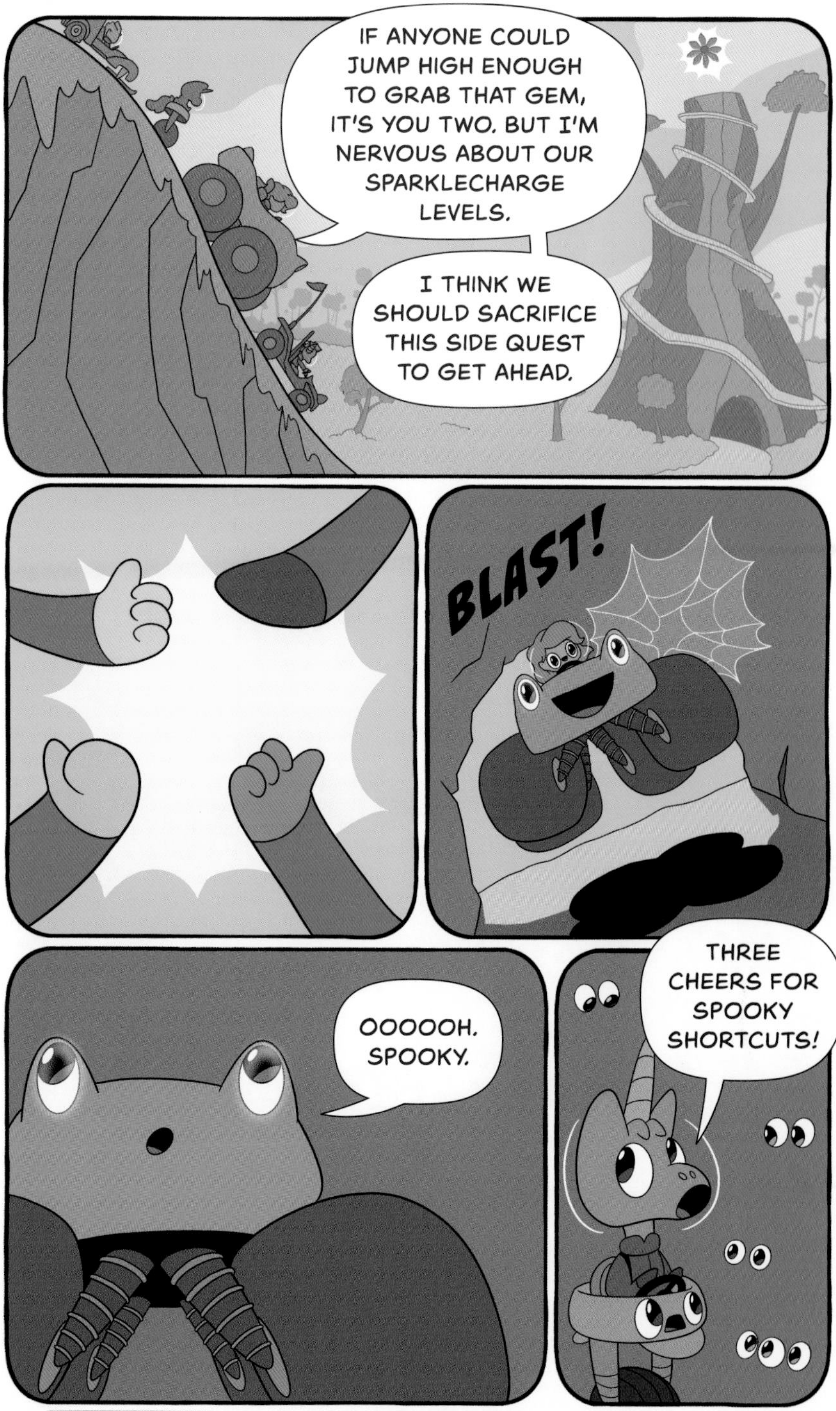
IF ANYONE COULD JUMP HIGH ENOUGH TO GRAB THAT GEM, IT'S YOU TWO. BUT I'M NERVOUS ABOUT OUR SPARKLECHARGE LEVELS.
I THINK WE SHOULD SACRIFICE THIS SIDE QUEST TO GET AHEAD.
BLAST!
OOOOOH. SPOOKY.
THREE CHEERS FOR SPOOKY SHORTCUTS!

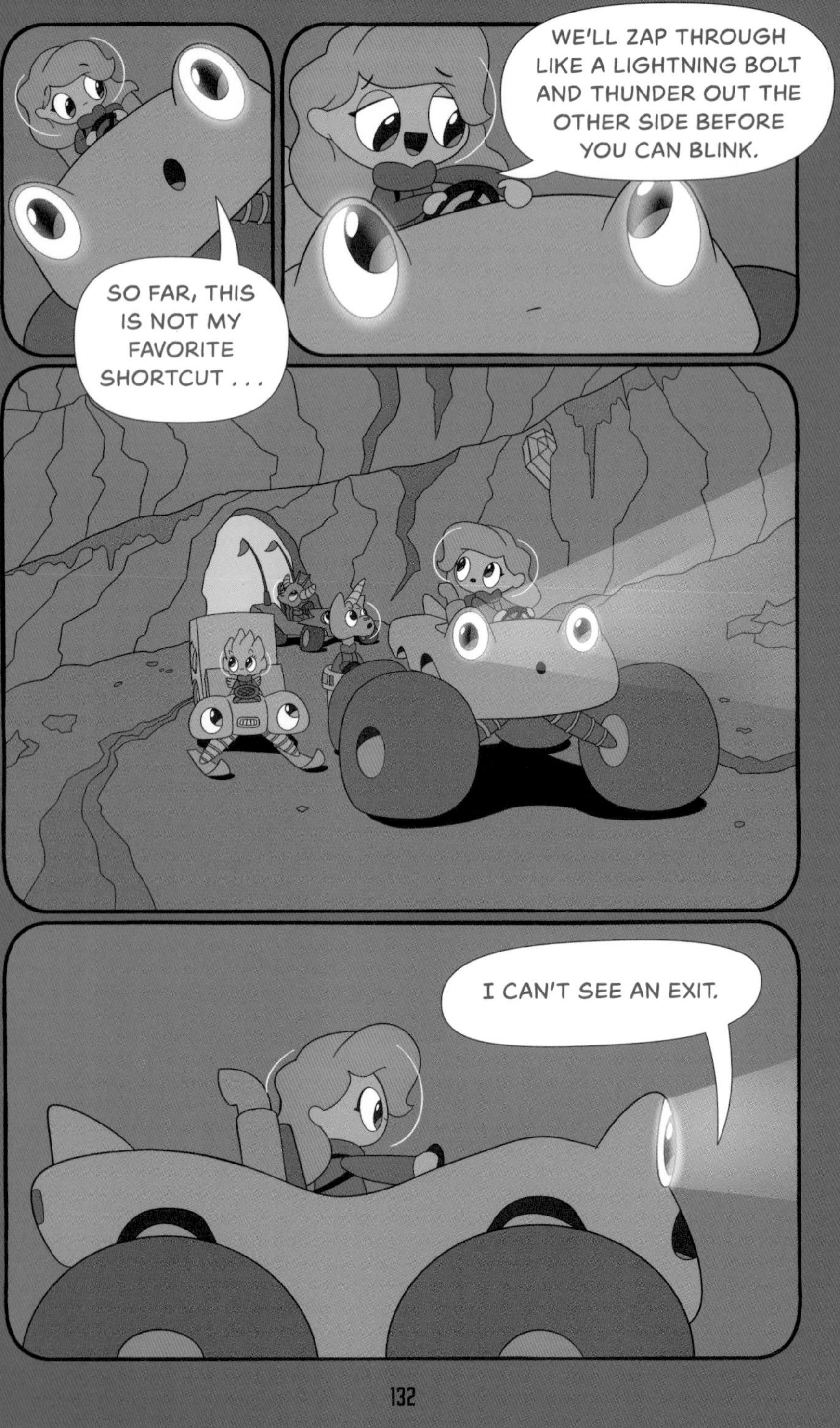
SO FAR, THIS IS NOT MY FAVORITE SHORTCUT . . .
WE'LL ZAP THROUGH LIKE A LIGHTNING BOLT AND THUNDER OUT THE OTHER SIDE BEFORE YOU CAN BLINK.
I CAN'T SEE AN EXIT.

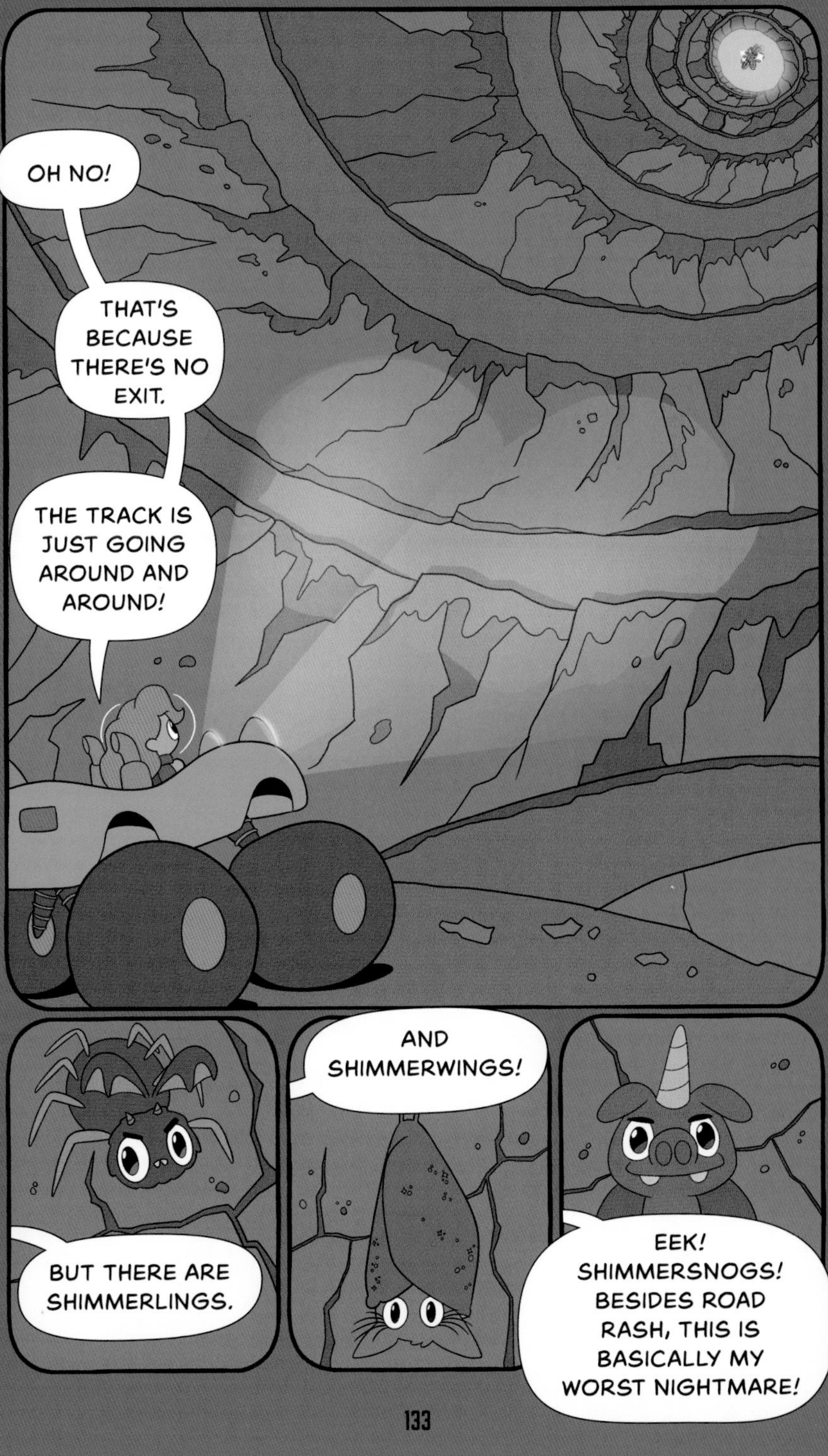
OH NO!
THAT'S BECAUSE THERE'S NO EXIT.
THE TRACK IS JUST GOING AROUND AND AROUND!
BUT THERE ARE SHIMMERLINGS.
AND SHIMMERWINGS!
EEK! SHIMMERSNOGS! BESIDES ROAD RASH, THIS IS BASICALLY MY WORST NIGHTMARE!

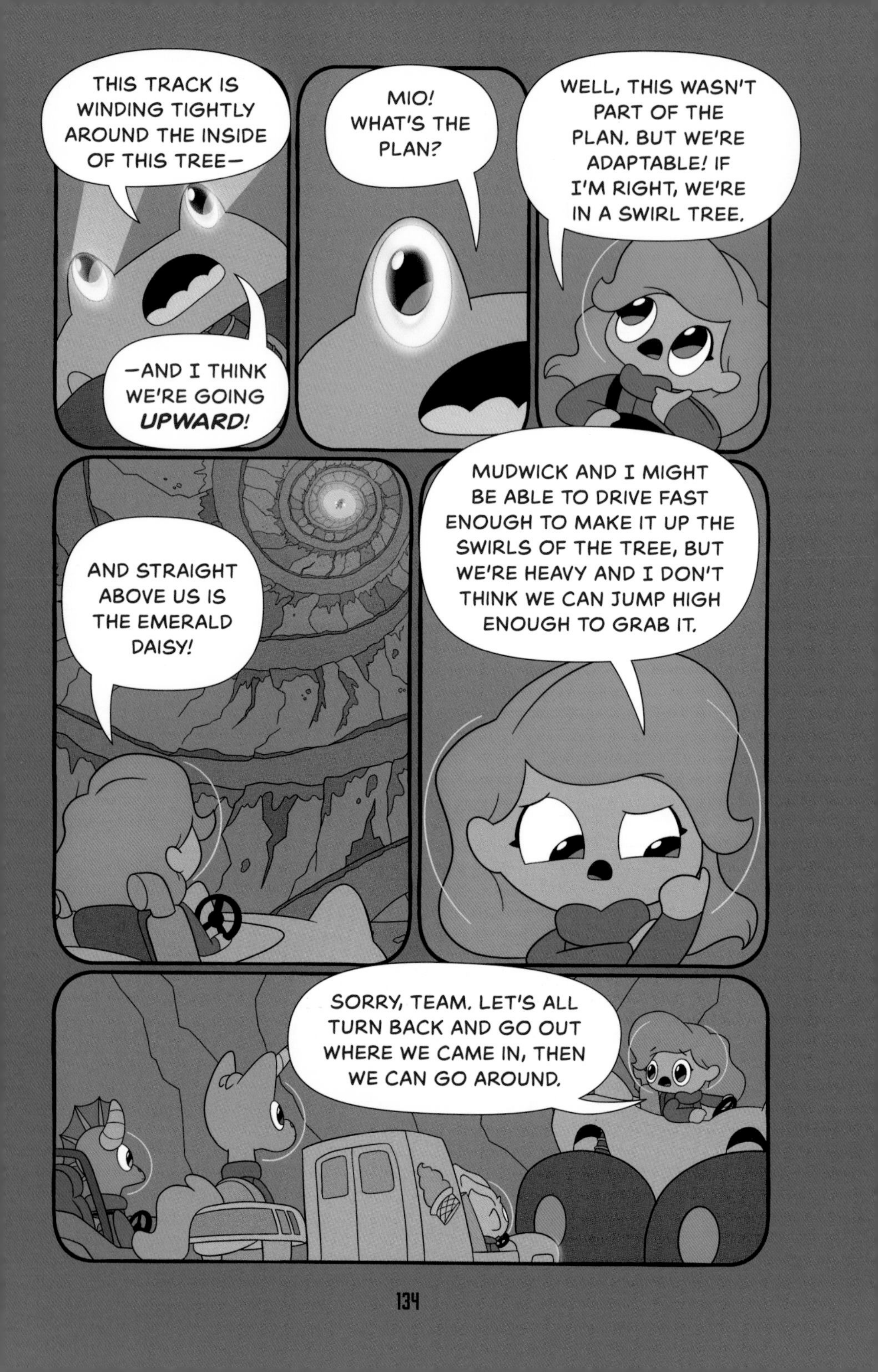

THIS TRACK IS WINDING TIGHTLY AROUND THE INSIDE OF THIS TREE—
—AND I THINK WE'RE GOING ***UPWARD***!
MIO! WHAT'S THE PLAN?
WELL, THIS WASN'T PART OF THE PLAN. BUT WE'RE ADAPTABLE! IF I'M RIGHT, WE'RE IN A SWIRL TREE.
AND STRAIGHT ABOVE US IS THE EMERALD DAISY!
MUDWICK AND I MIGHT BE ABLE TO DRIVE FAST ENOUGH TO MAKE IT UP THE SWIRLS OF THE TREE, BUT WE'RE HEAVY AND I DON'T THINK WE CAN JUMP HIGH ENOUGH TO GRAB IT.
SORRY, TEAM. LET'S ALL TURN BACK AND GO OUT WHERE WE CAME IN, THEN WE CAN GO AROUND.

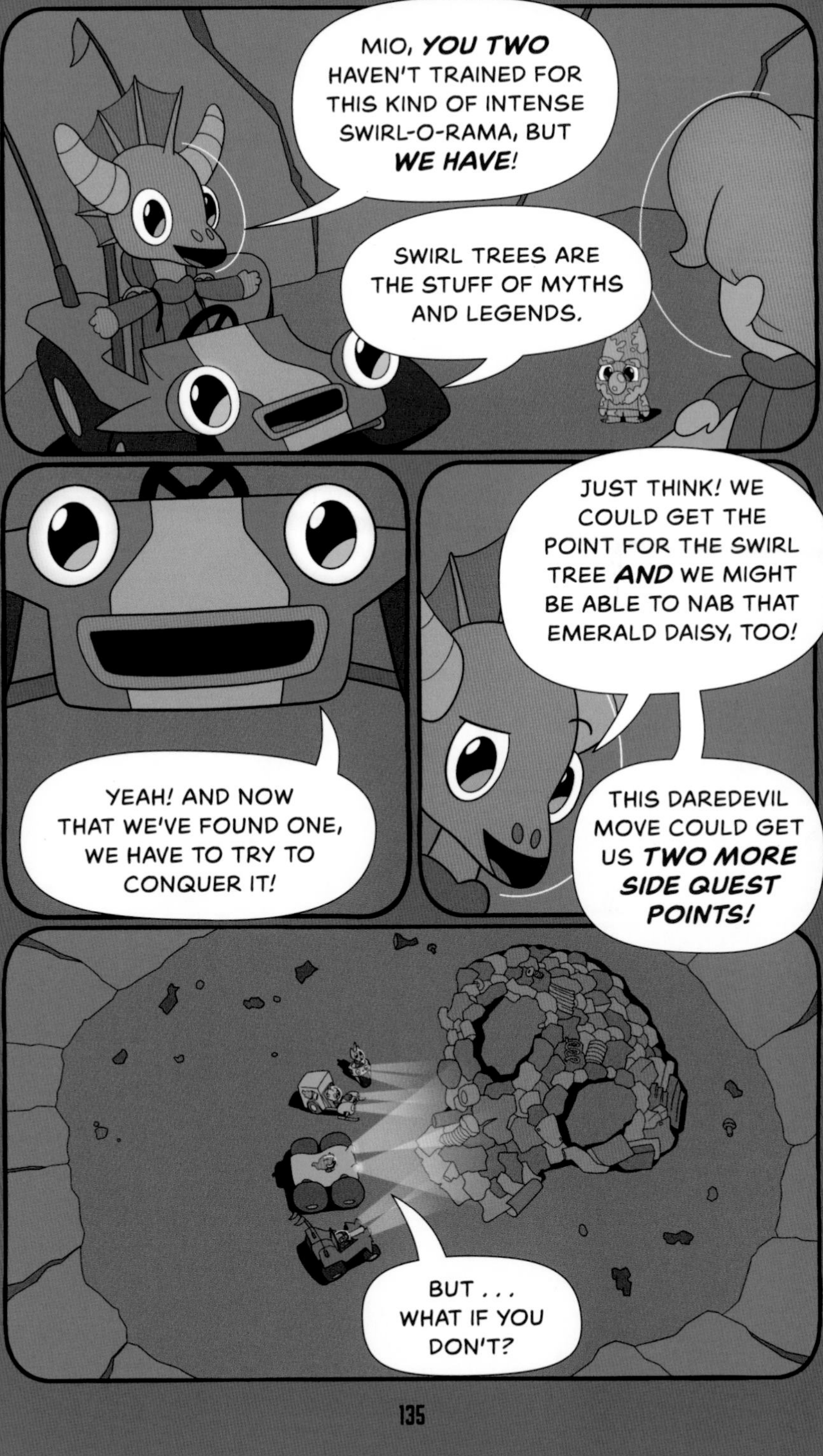
MIO, YOU TWO HAVEN'T TRAINED FOR THIS KIND OF INTENSE SWIRL-O-RAMA, BUT WE HAVE!
SWIRL TREES ARE THE STUFF OF MYTHS AND LEGENDS.
YEAH! AND NOW THAT WE'VE FOUND ONE, WE HAVE TO TRY TO CONQUER IT!
JUST THINK! WE COULD GET THE POINT FOR THE SWIRL TREE AND WE MIGHT BE ABLE TO NAB THAT EMERALD DAISY, TOO!
THIS DAREDEVIL MOVE COULD GET US TWO MORE SIDE QUEST POINTS!
BUT . . . WHAT IF YOU DON'T?

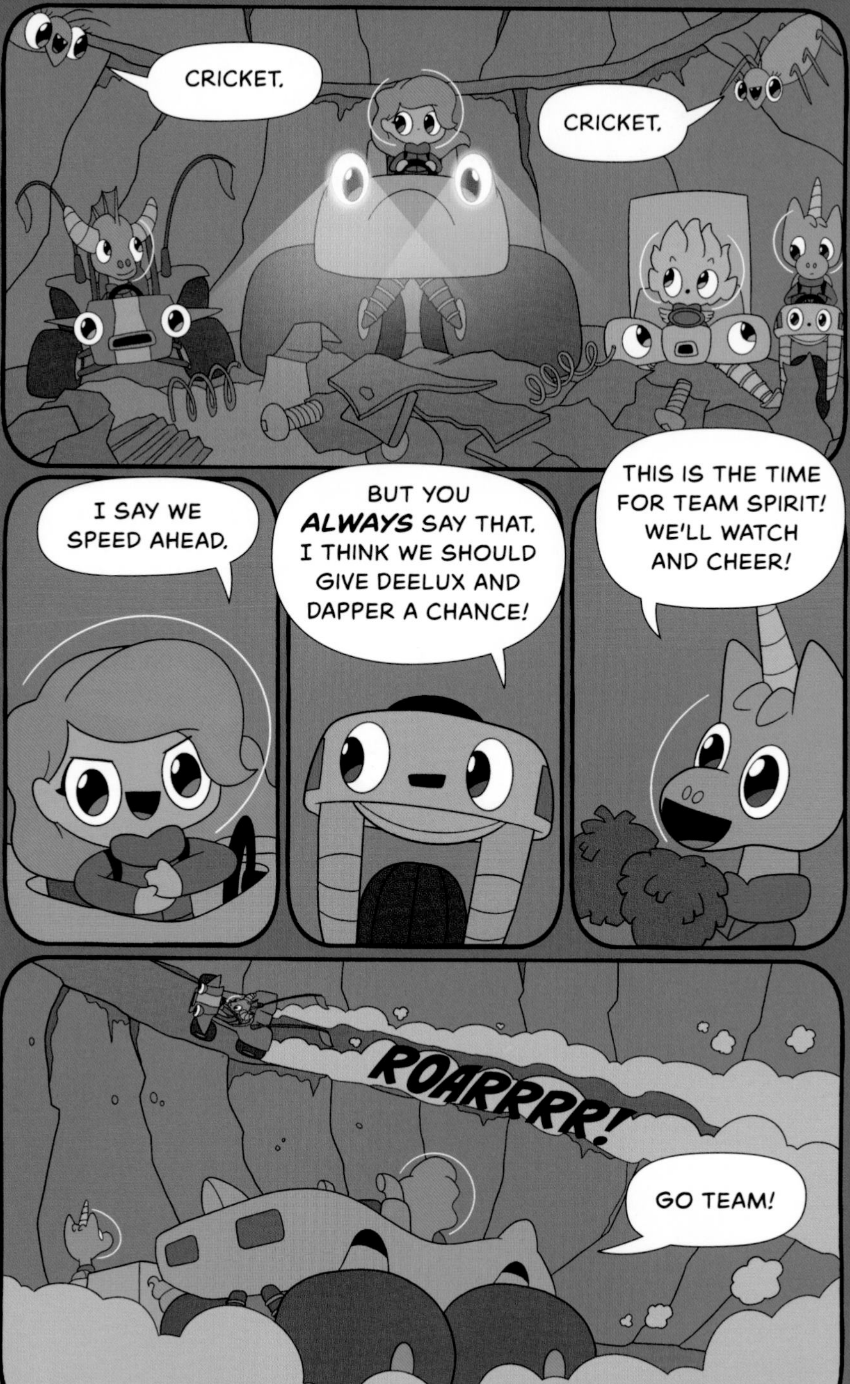
CRICKET.
CRICKET.
I SAY WE SPEED AHEAD.
BUT YOU ALWAYS SAY THAT. I THINK WE SHOULD GIVE DEELUX AND DAPPER A CHANCE!
THIS IS THE TIME FOR TEAM SPIRIT! WE'LL WATCH AND CHEER!
ROARRRRR!
GO TEAM!

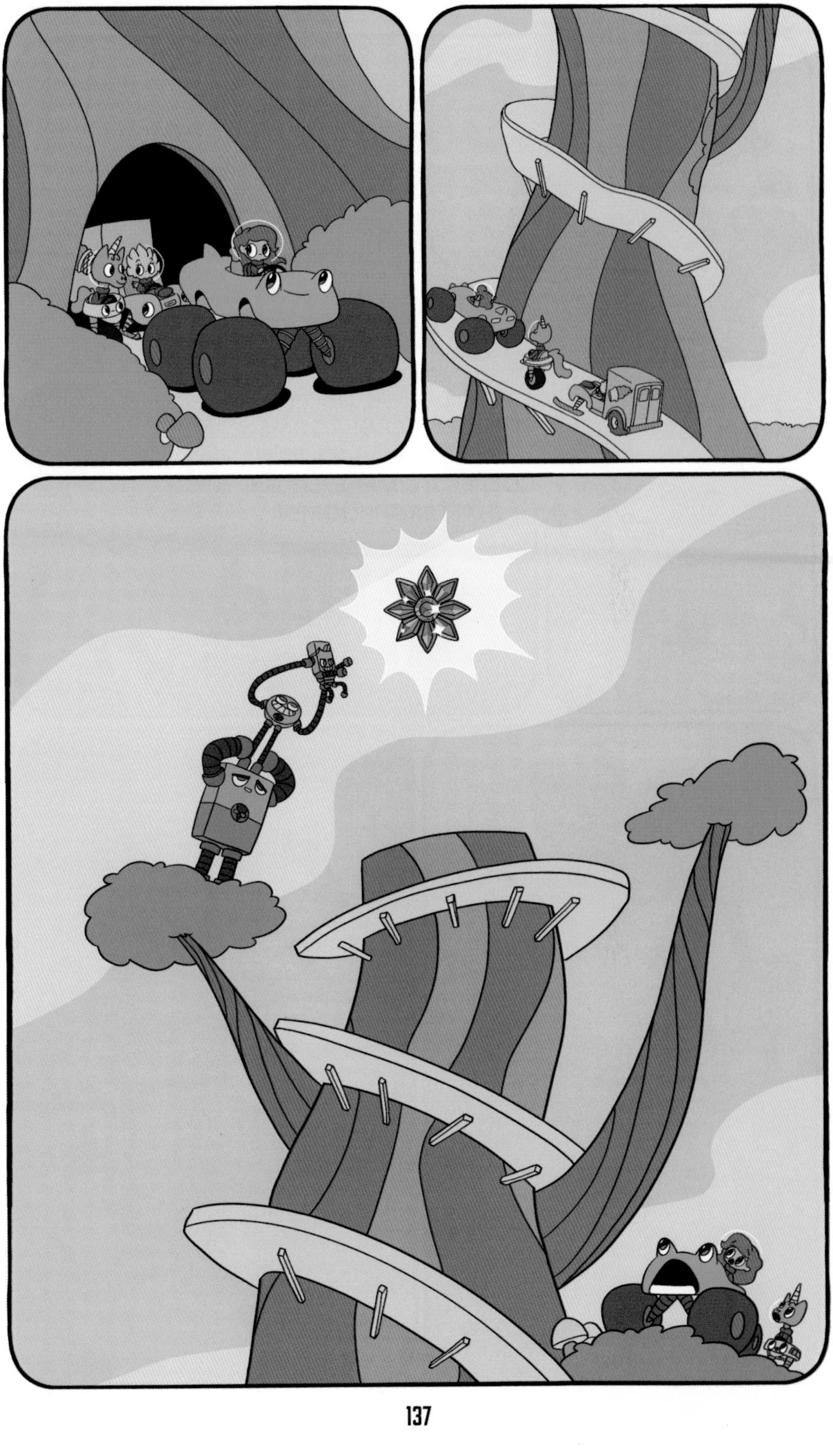

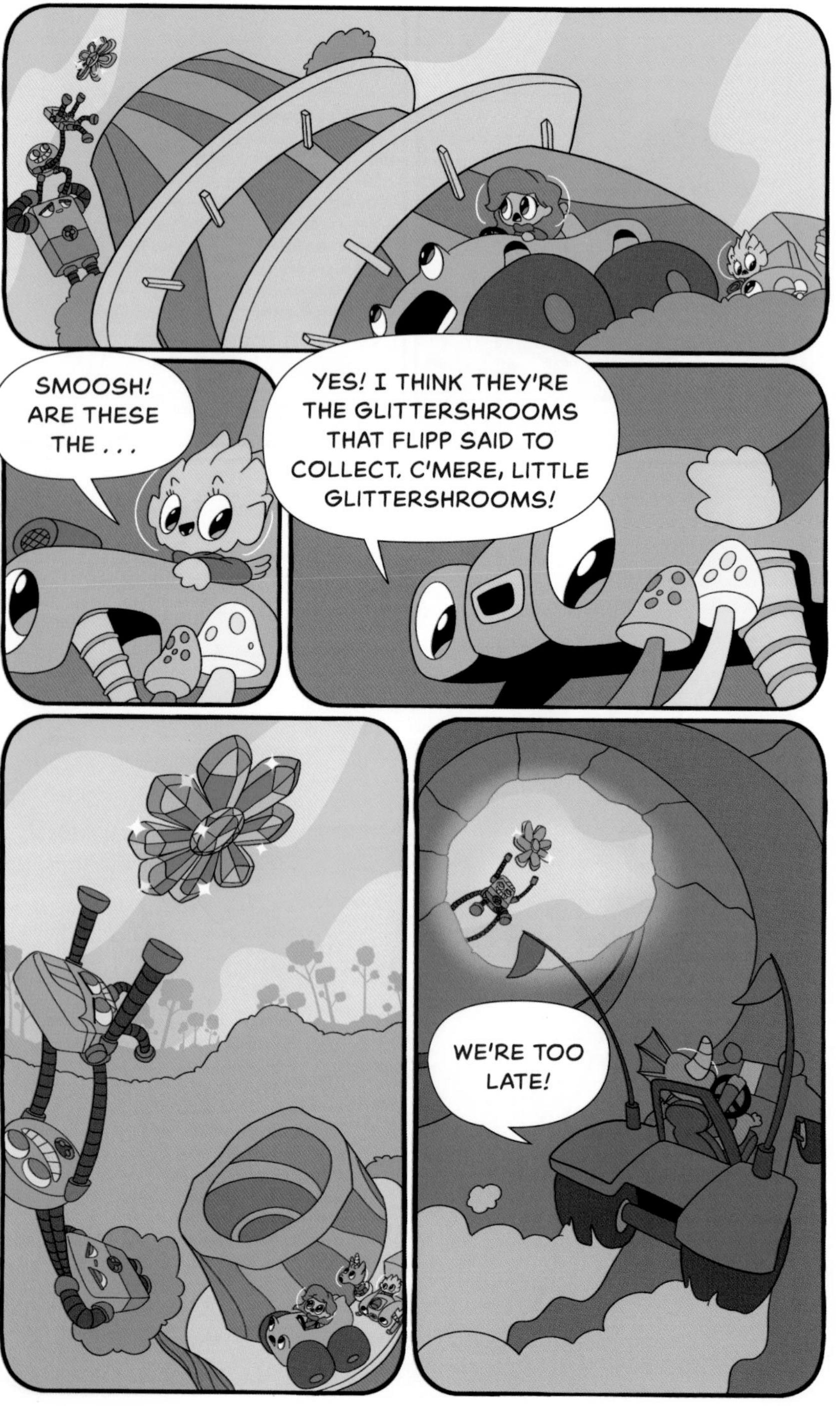
SMOOSH! ARE THESE THE . . .
YES! I THINK THEY'RE THE GLITTERSHROOMS THAT FLIPP SAID TO COLLECT. C'MERE, LITTLE GLITTERSHROOMS!
WE'RE TOO LATE!

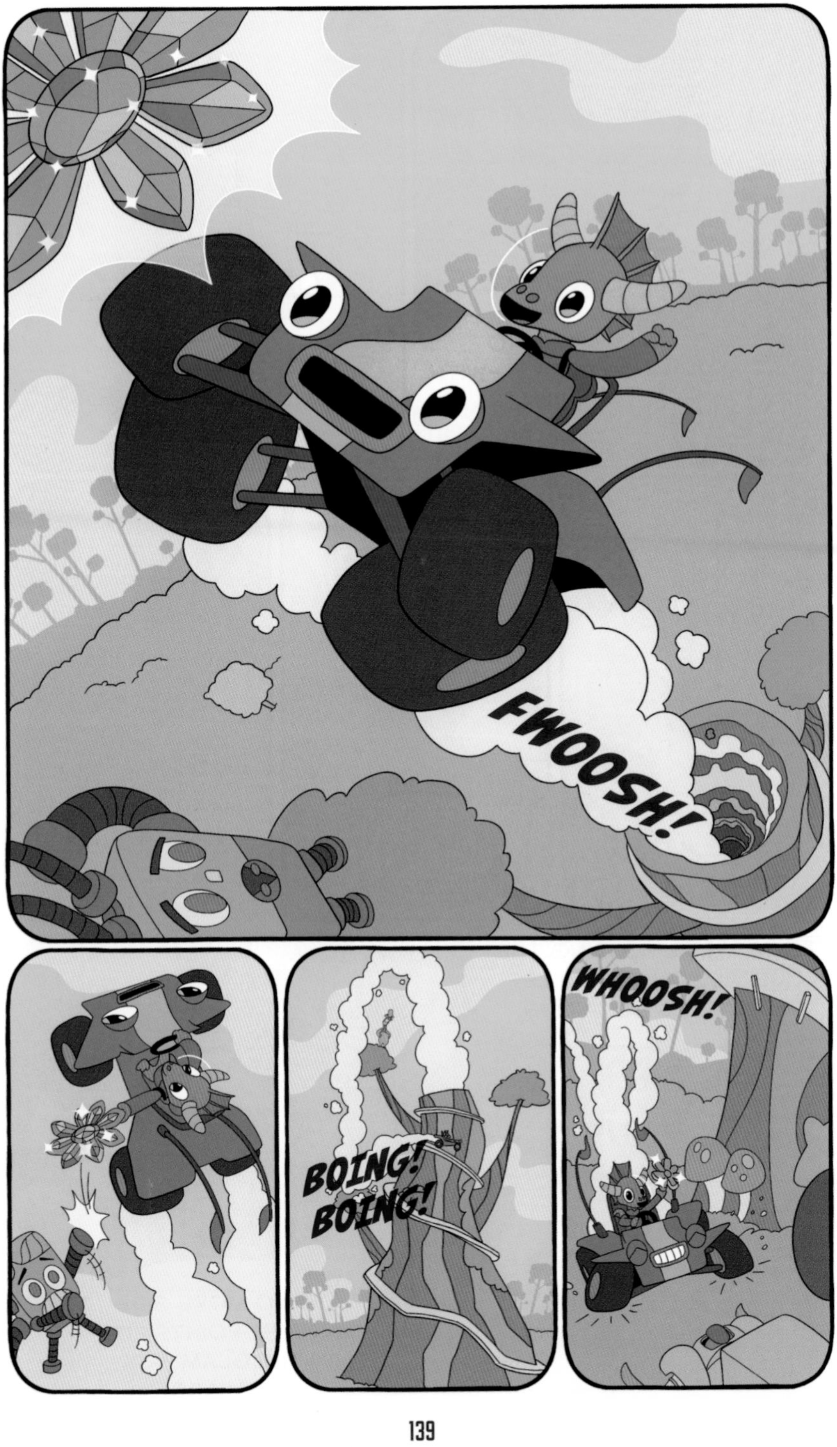
FWOOSH!
BOING!
BOING!
WHOOSH!

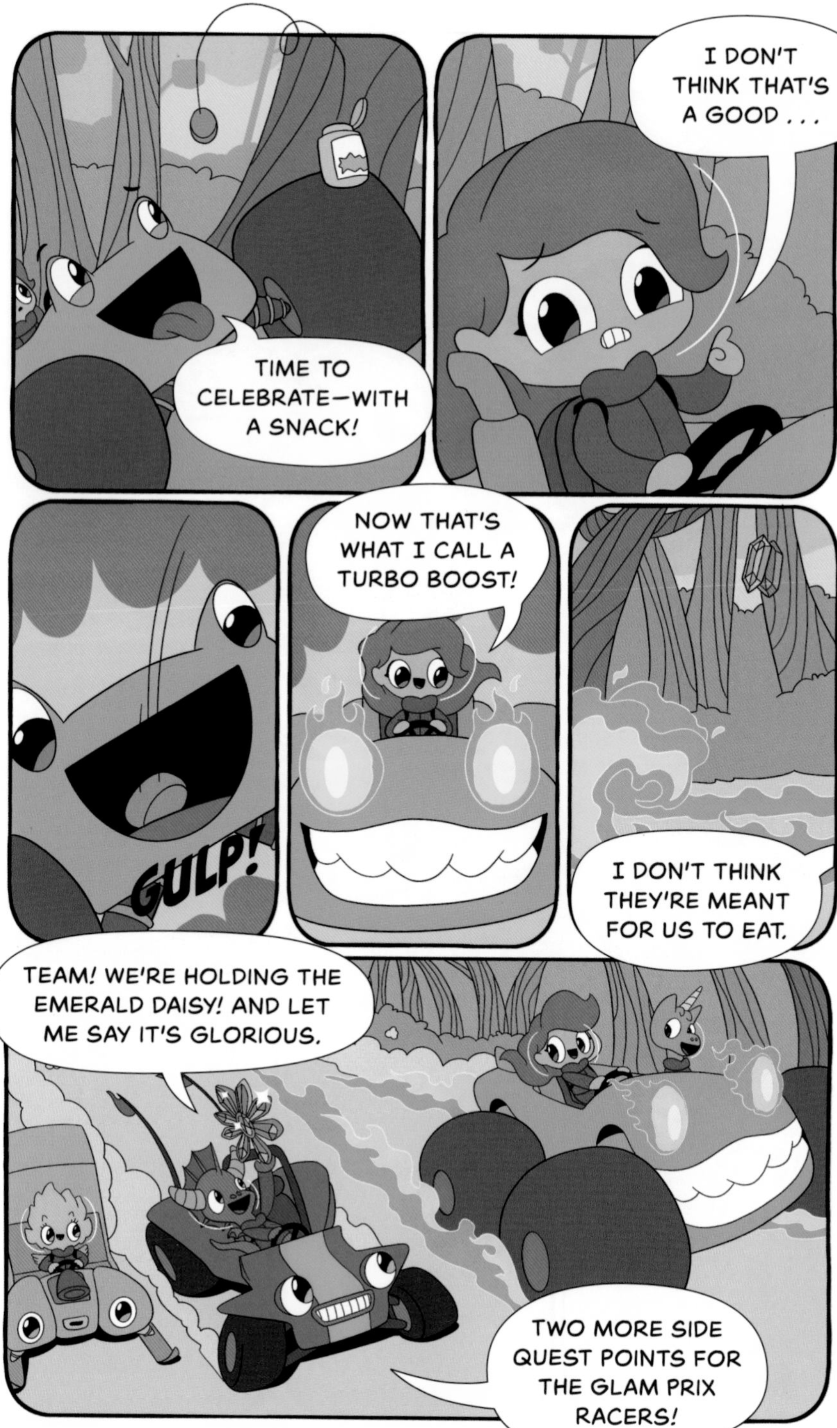
TIME TO CELEBRATE—WITH A SNACK!
I DON'T THINK THAT'S A GOOD . . .
GULP!
NOW THAT'S WHAT I CALL A TURBO BOOST!
I DON'T THINK THEY'RE MEANT FOR US TO EAT.
TEAM! WE'RE HOLDING THE EMERALD DAISY! AND LET ME SAY IT'S GLORIOUS.
TWO MORE SIDE QUEST POINTS FOR THE GLAM PRIX RACERS!

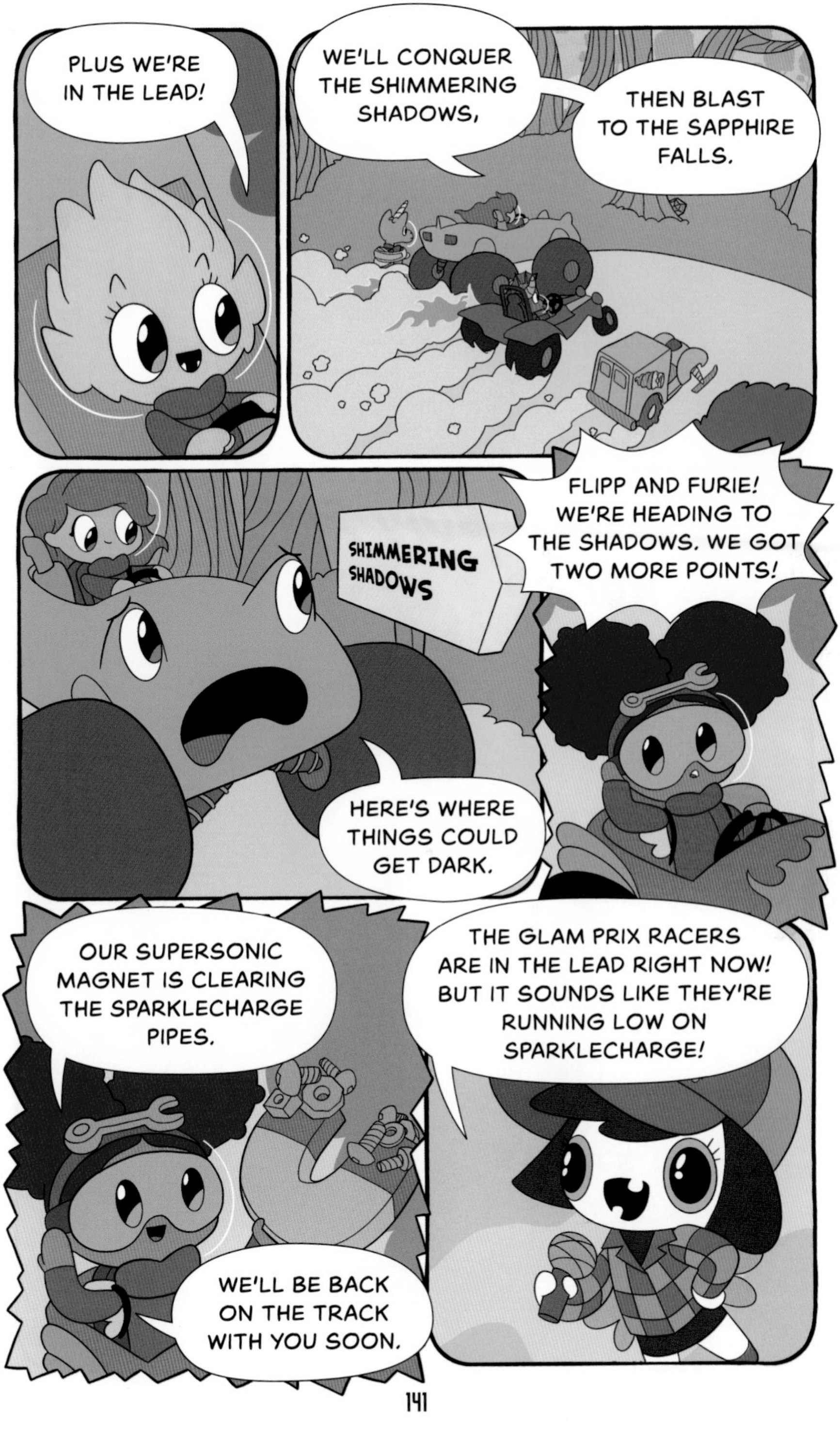
PLUS WE'RE IN THE LEAD!
WE'LL CONQUER THE SHIMMERING SHADOWS,
THEN BLAST TO THE SAPPHIRE FALLS.
SHIMMERING SHADOWS
FLIPP AND FURIE! WE'RE HEADING TO THE SHADOWS. WE GOT TWO MORE POINTS!
HERE'S WHERE THINGS COULD GET DARK.
OUR SUPERSONIC MAGNET IS CLEARING THE SPARKLECHARGE PIPES.
WE'LL BE BACK ON THE TRACK WITH YOU SOON.
THE GLAM PRIX RACERS ARE IN THE LEAD RIGHT NOW! BUT IT SOUNDS LIKE THEY'RE RUNNING LOW ON SPARKLECHARGE!

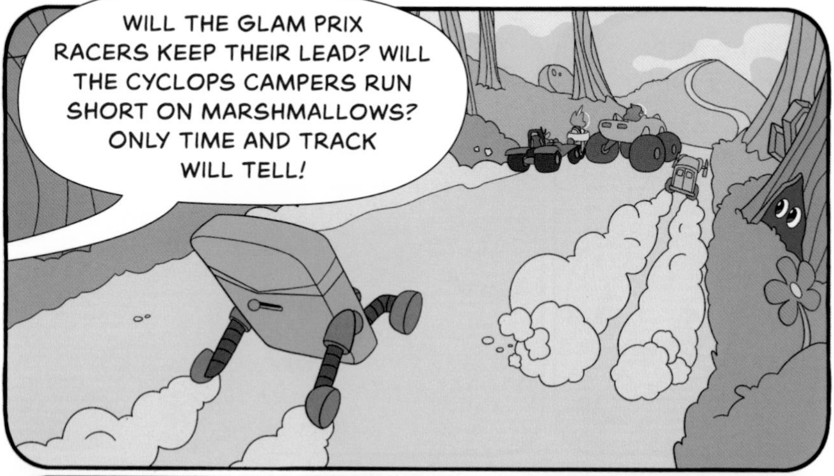
WILL THE GLAM PRIX RACERS KEEP THEIR LEAD? WILL THE CYCLOPS CAMPERS RUN SHORT ON MARSHMALLOWS? ONLY TIME AND TRACK WILL TELL!

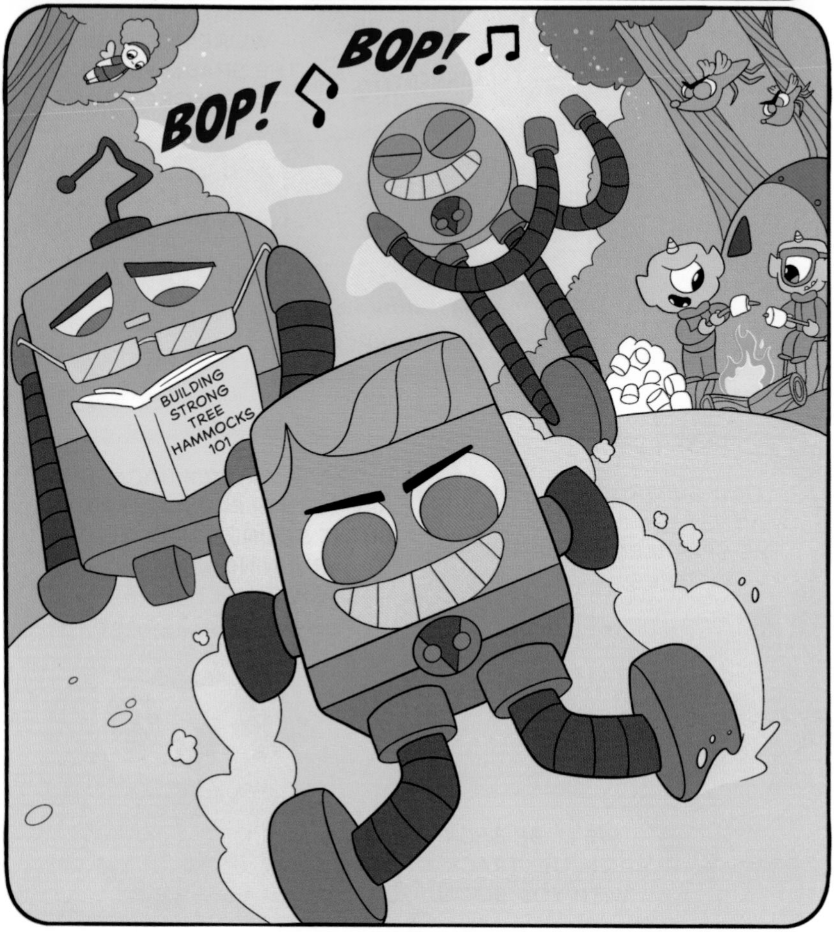
BOP!
BOP!
BUILDING STRONG TREE HAMMOCKS 101

CHAPTER 11:
FUN-GUY FRENZY!

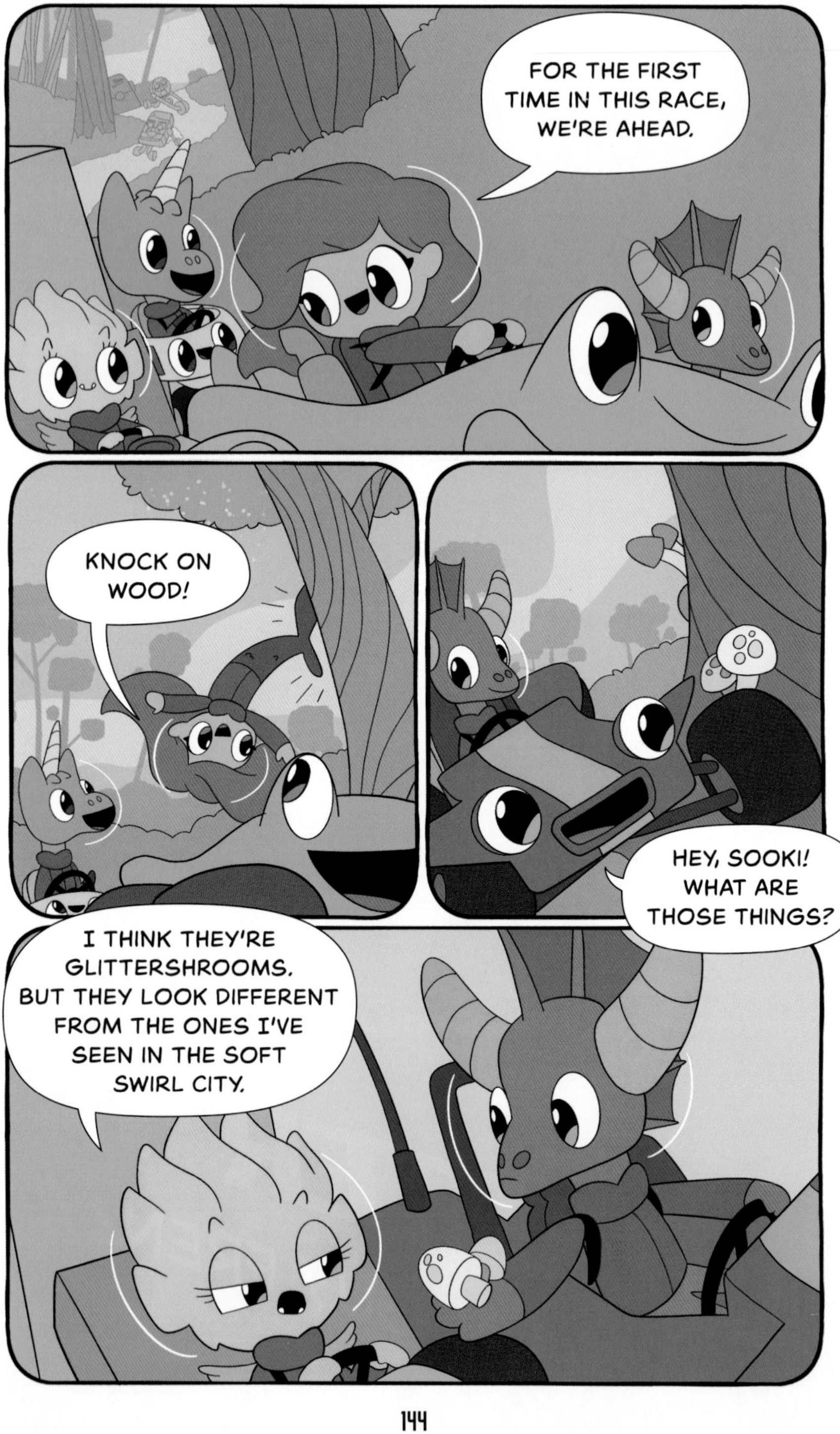
FOR THE FIRST TIME IN THIS RACE, WE'RE AHEAD.
KNOCK ON WOOD!
HEY, SOOKI! WHAT ARE THOSE THINGS?
I THINK THEY'RE GLITTERSHROOMS. BUT THEY LOOK DIFFERENT FROM THE ONES I'VE SEEN IN THE SOFT SWIRL CITY.

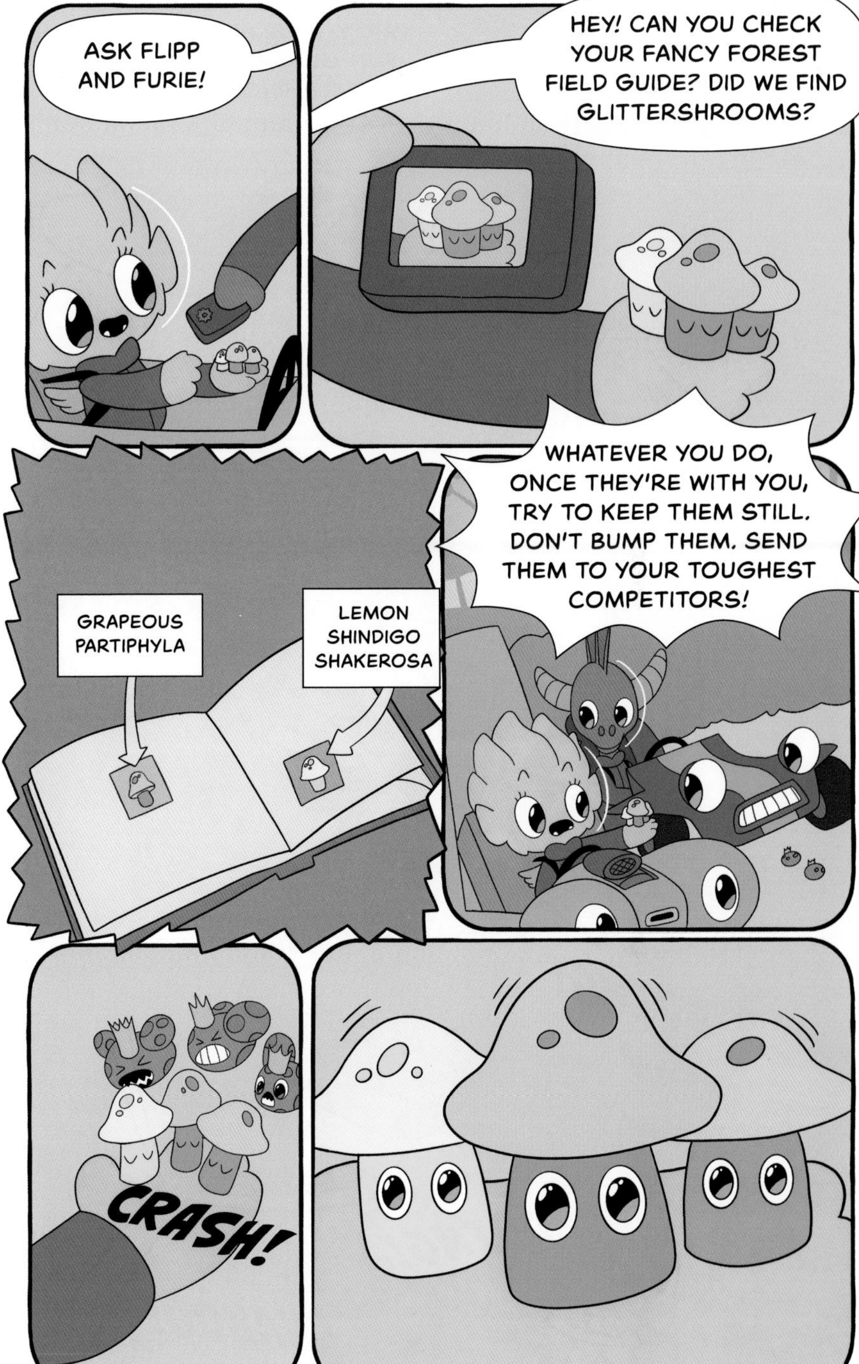
ASK FLIPP AND FURIE!
HEY! CAN YOU CHECK YOUR FANCY FOREST FIELD GUIDE? DID WE FIND GLITTERSHROOMS?
GRAPEOUS PARTIPHYLA
LEMON SHINDIGO SHAKEROSA
WHATEVER YOU DO, ONCE THEY'RE WITH YOU, TRY TO KEEP THEM STILL. DON'T BUMP THEM. SEND THEM TO YOUR TOUGHEST COMPETITORS!
CRASH!

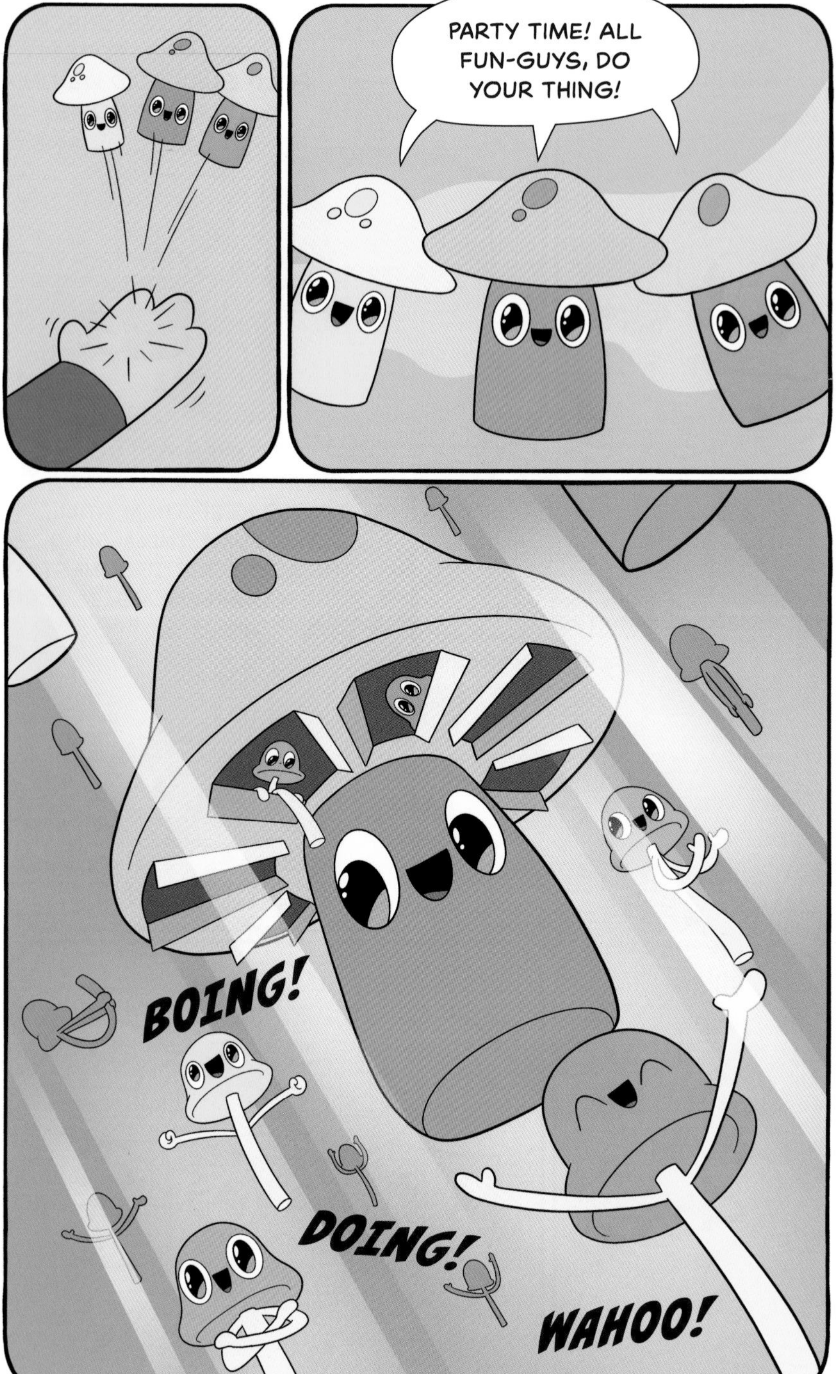
PARTY TIME! ALL FUN-GUYS, DO YOUR THING!
BOING!
DOING!
WAHOO!

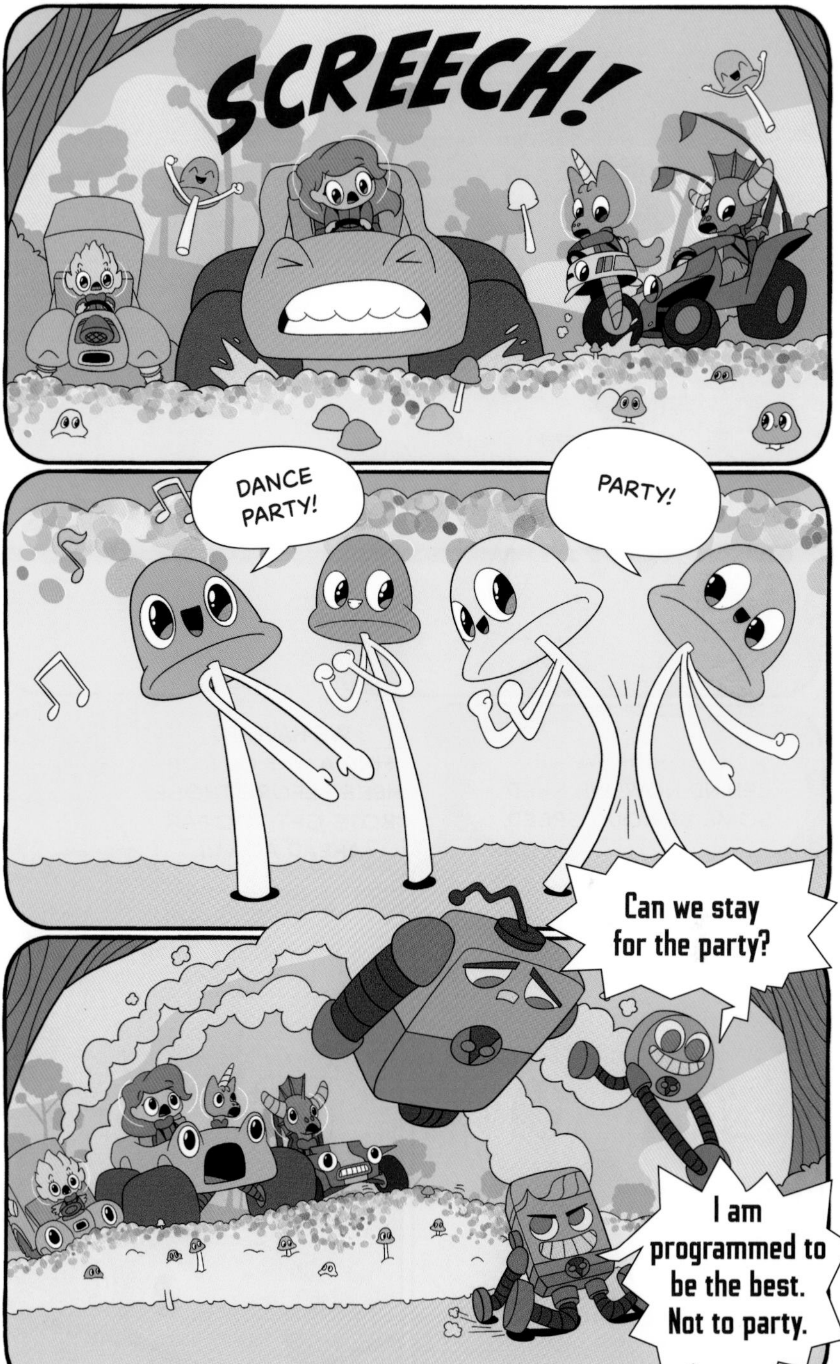
SCREECH!
DANCE PARTY!
PARTY!
Can we stay for the party?
I am programmed to be the best. Not to party.

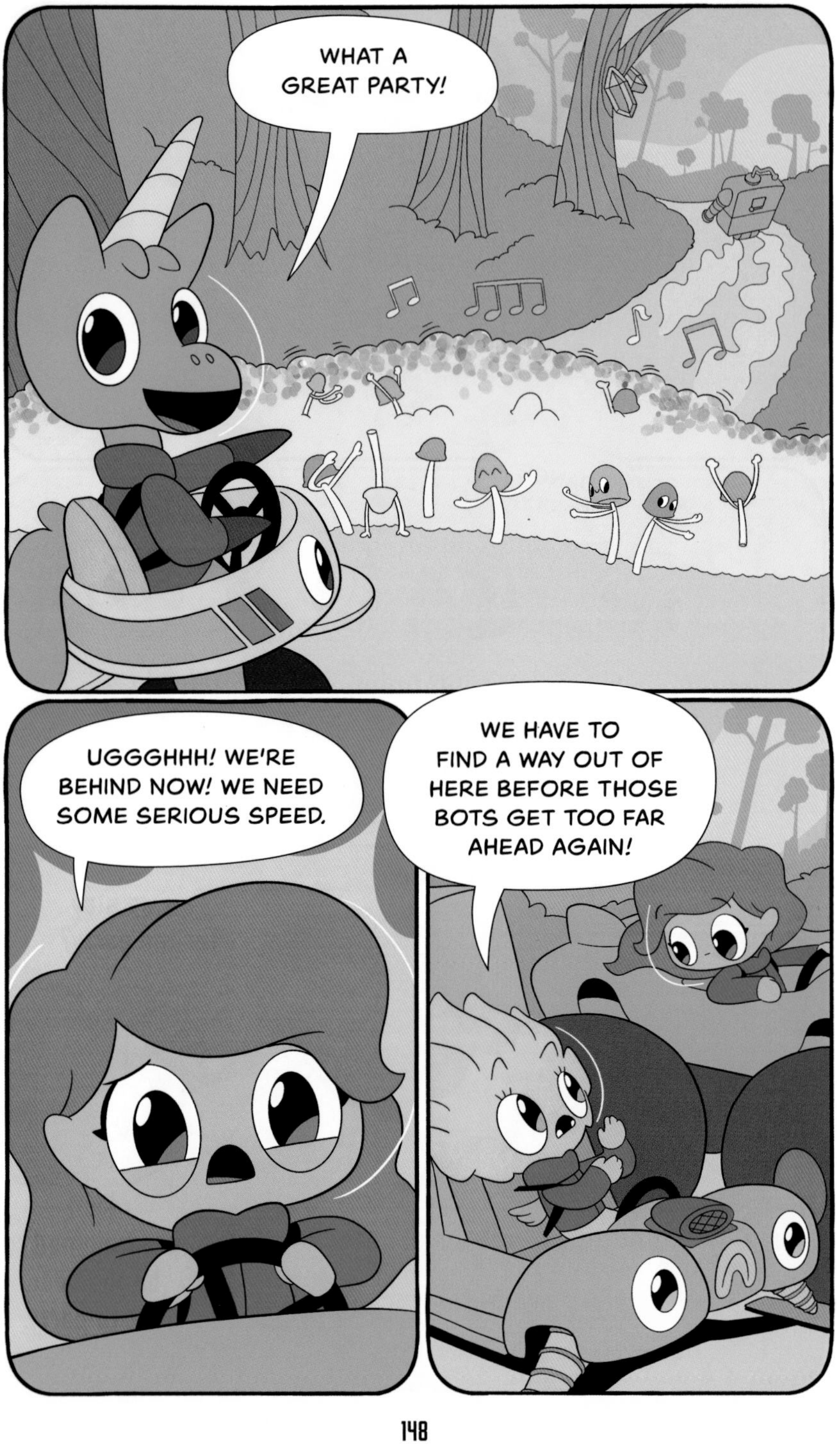
WHAT A GREAT PARTY!
UGGGHHH! WE'RE BEHIND NOW! WE NEED SOME SERIOUS SPEED.
WE HAVE TO FIND A WAY OUT OF HERE BEFORE THOSE BOTS GET TOO FAR AHEAD AGAIN!

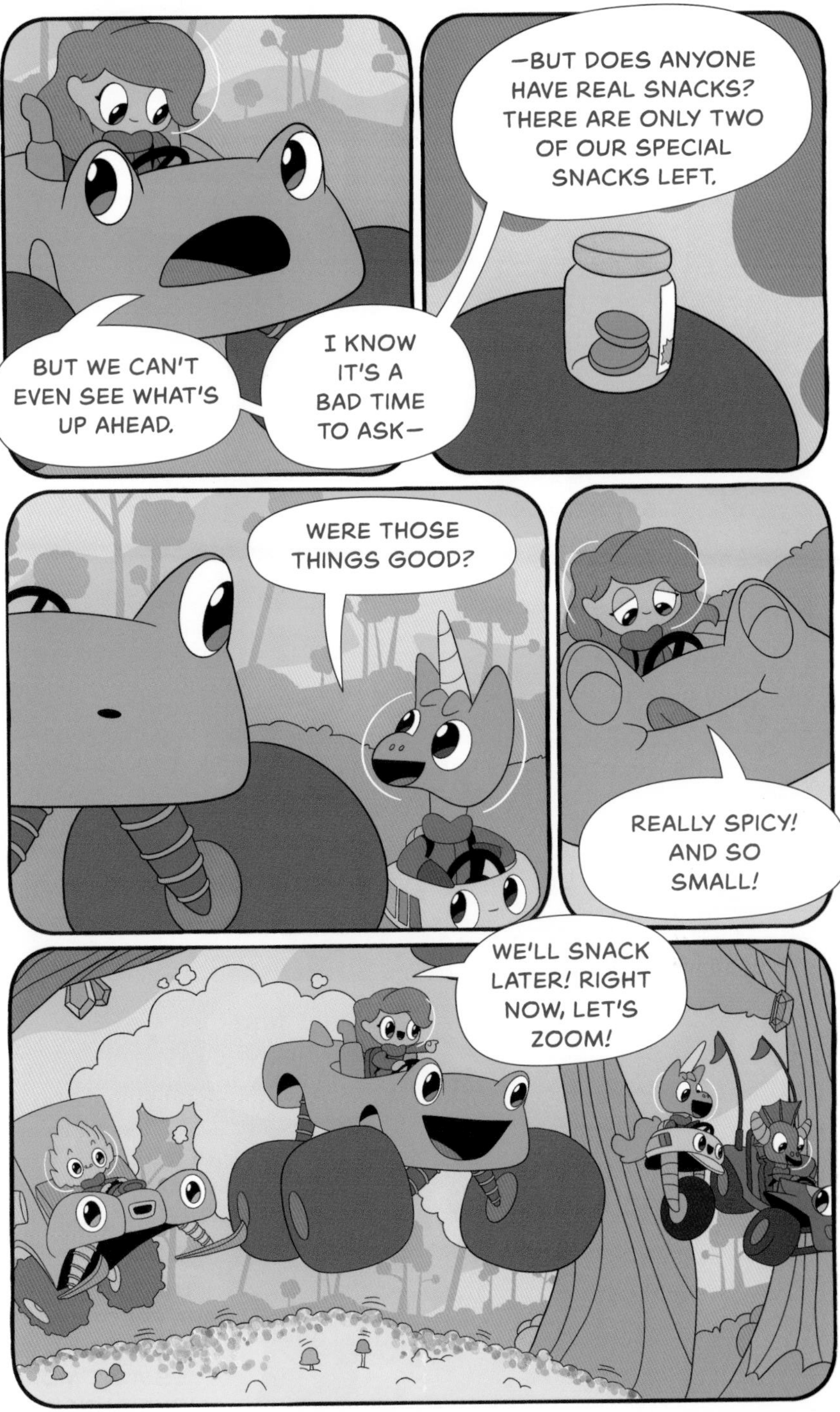
BUT WE CAN'T EVEN SEE WHAT'S UP AHEAD.
I KNOW IT'S A BAD TIME TO ASK—
—BUT DOES ANYONE HAVE REAL SNACKS? THERE ARE ONLY TWO OF OUR SPECIAL SNACKS LEFT.
WERE THOSE THINGS GOOD?
REALLY SPICY! AND SO SMALL!
WE'LL SNACK LATER! RIGHT NOW, LET'S ZOOM!

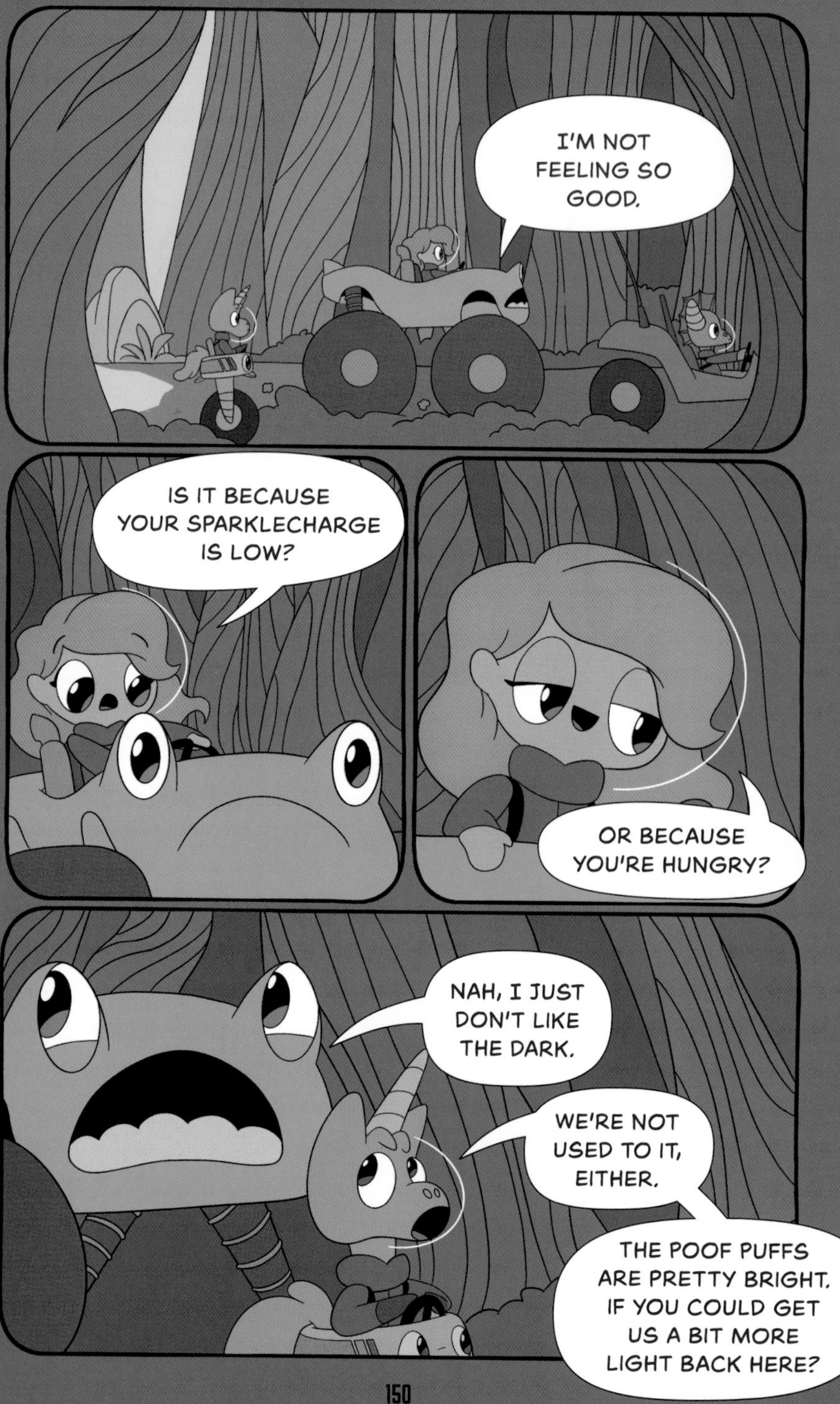
I'M NOT FEELING SO GOOD.
IS IT BECAUSE YOUR SPARKLECHARGE IS LOW?
OR BECAUSE YOU'RE HUNGRY?
NAH, I JUST DON'T LIKE THE DARK.
WE'RE NOT USED TO IT, EITHER.
THE POOF PUFFS ARE PRETTY BRIGHT. IF YOU COULD GET US A BIT MORE LIGHT BACK HERE?

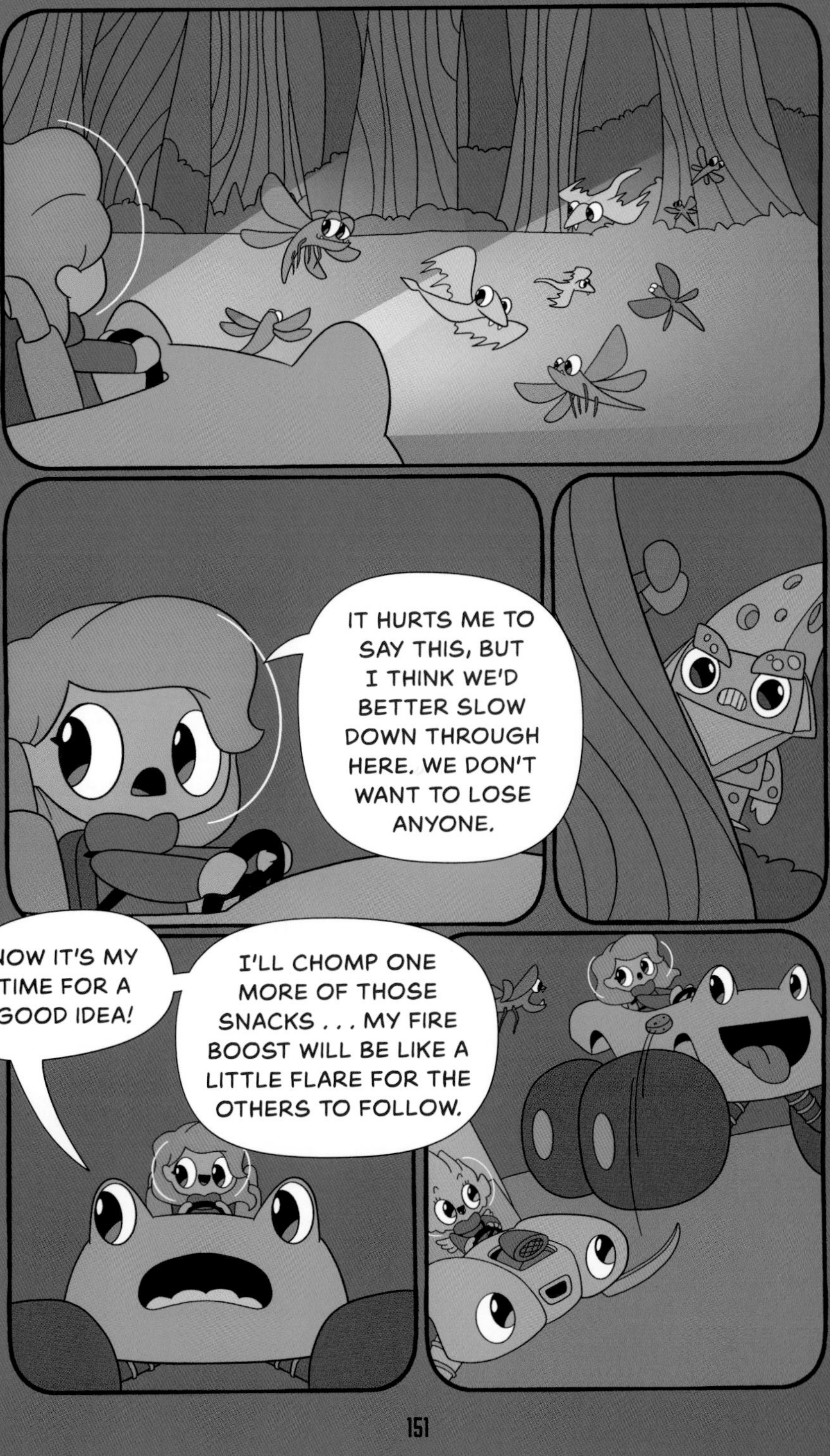
IT HURTS ME TO SAY THIS, BUT I THINK WE'D BETTER SLOW DOWN THROUGH HERE. WE DON'T WANT TO LOSE ANYONE.
NOW IT'S MY TIME FOR A GOOD IDEA!
I'LL CHOMP ONE MORE OF THOSE SNACKS . . . MY FIRE BOOST WILL BE LIKE A LITTLE FLARE FOR THE OTHERS TO FOLLOW.

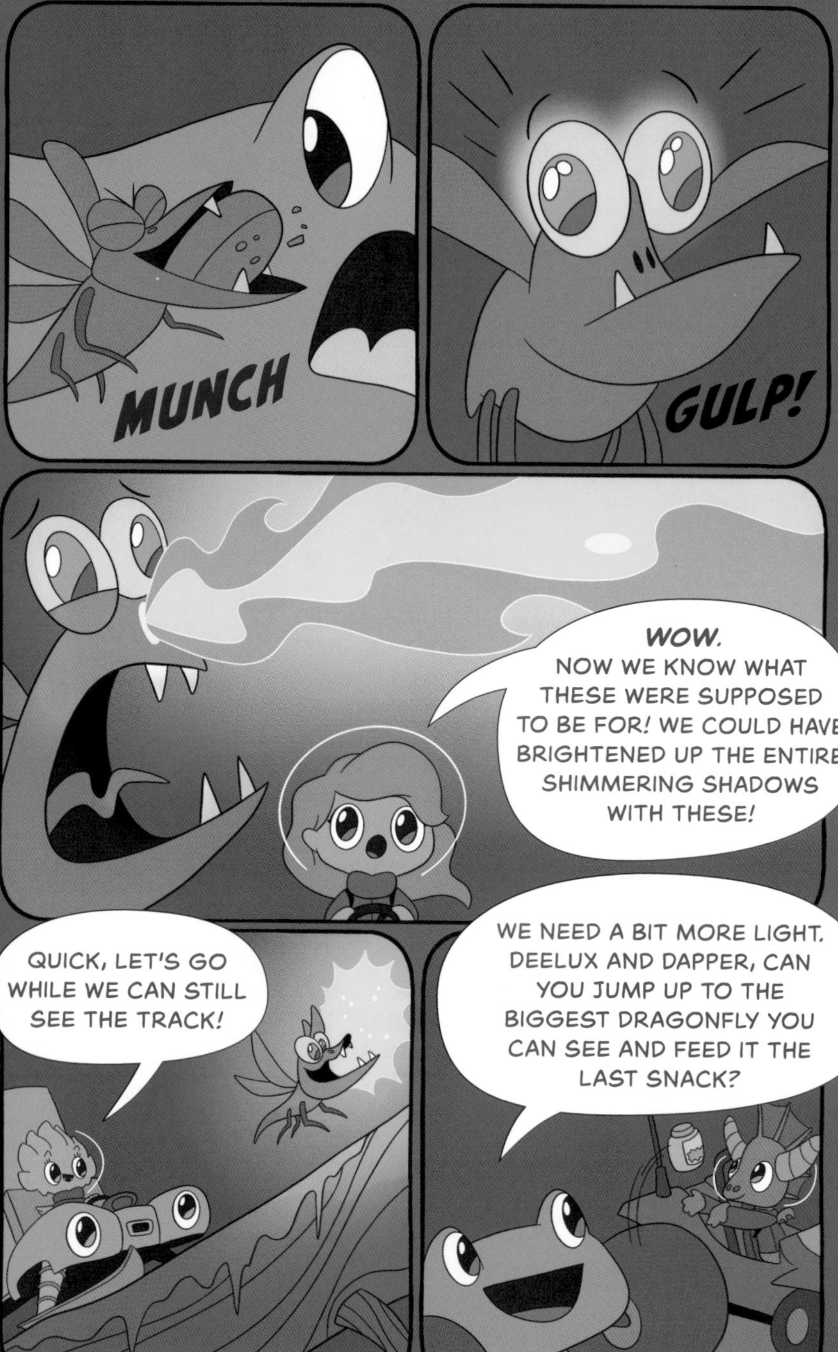
MUNCH
GULP!
WOW. NOW WE KNOW WHAT THESE WERE SUPPOSED TO BE FOR! WE COULD HAVE BRIGHTENED UP THE ENTIRE SHIMMERING SHADOWS WITH THESE!
QUICK, LET'S GO WHILE WE CAN STILL SEE THE TRACK!
WE NEED A BIT MORE LIGHT. DEELUX AND DAPPER, CAN YOU JUMP UP TO THE BIGGEST DRAGONFLY YOU CAN SEE AND FEED IT THE LAST SNACK?

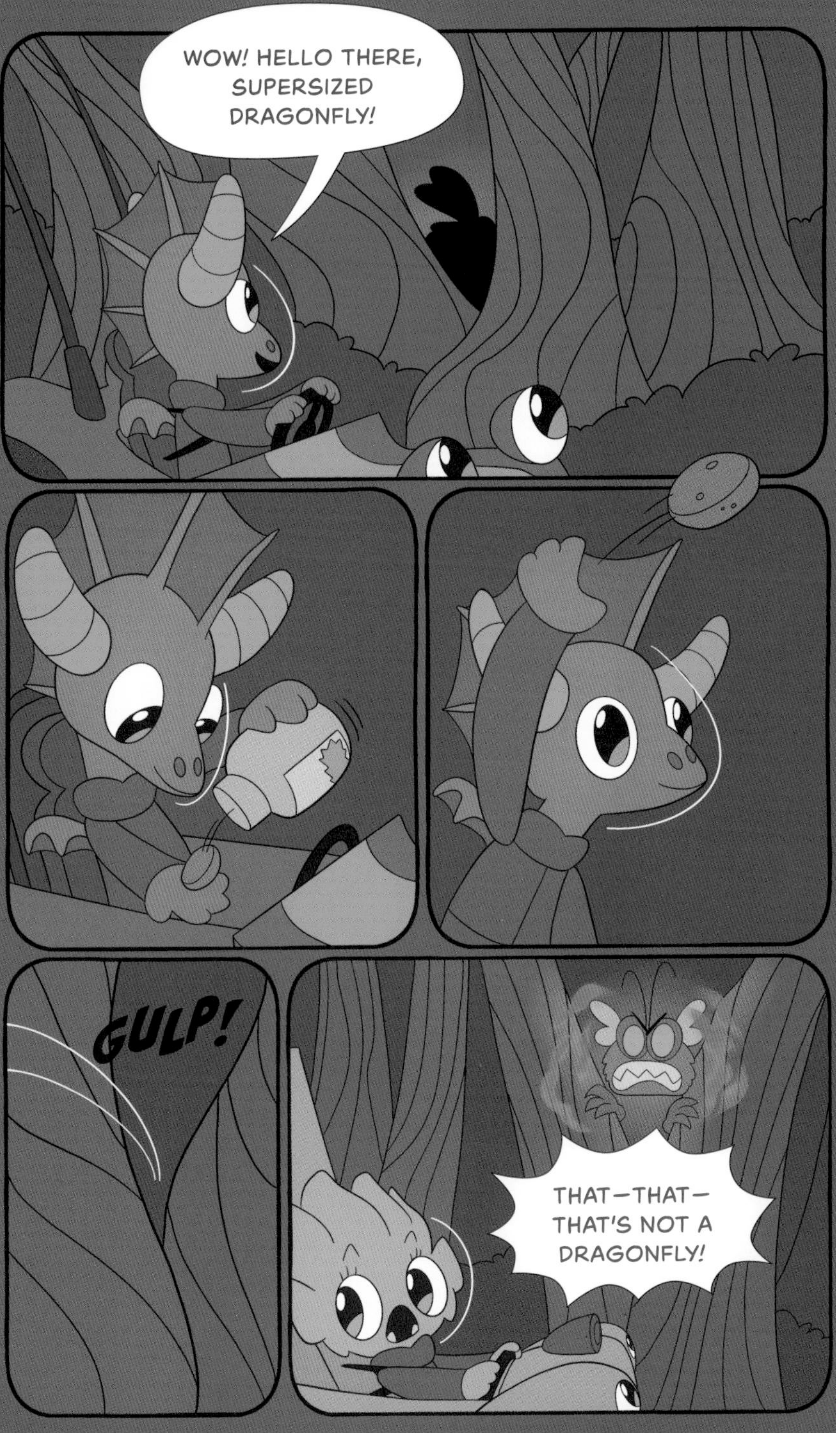
WOW! HELLO THERE, SUPERSIZED DRAGONFLY!
GULP!
THAT—THAT—THAT'S NOT A DRAGONFLY!

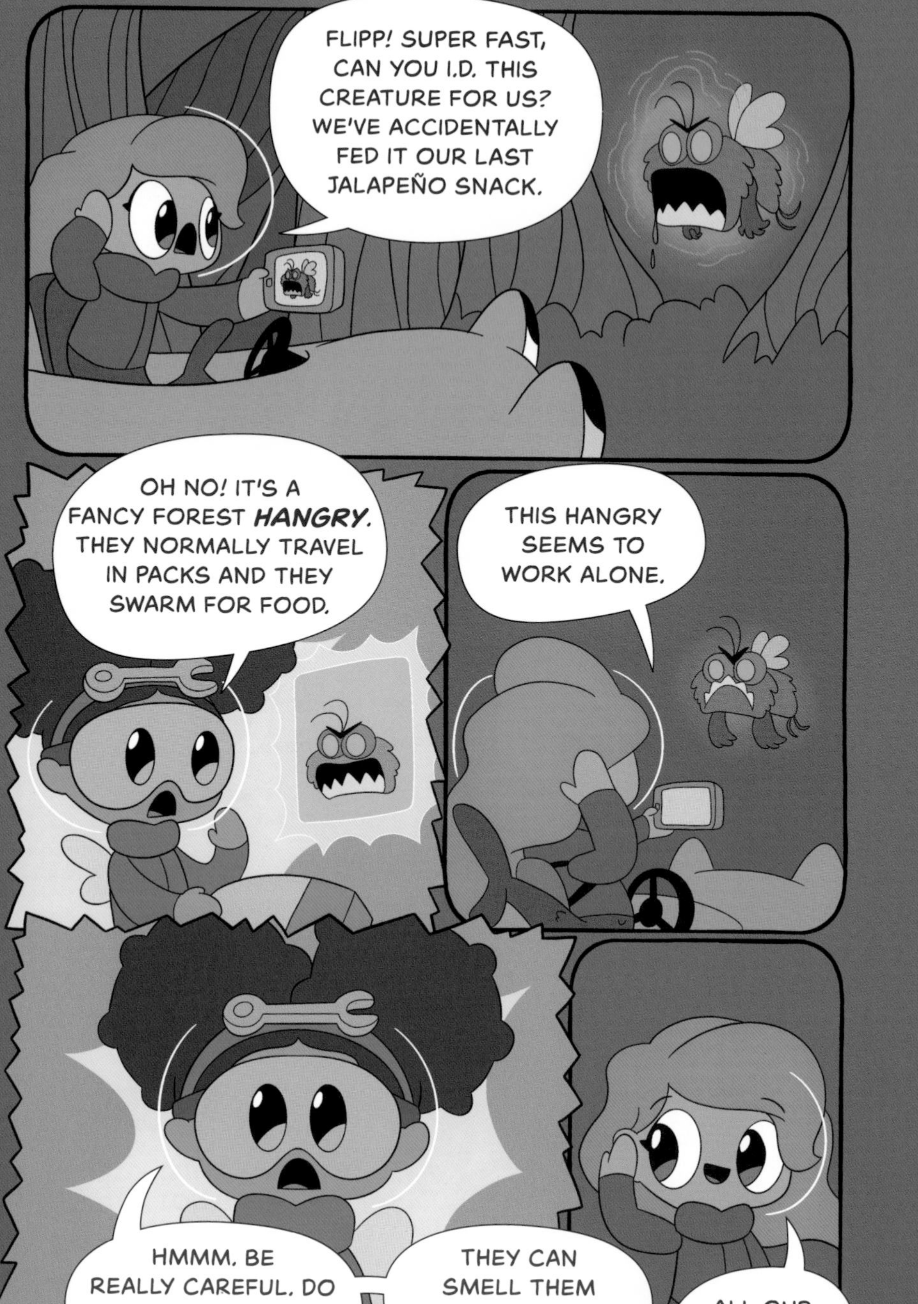
FLIPP! SUPER FAST, CAN YOU I.D. THIS CREATURE FOR US? WE'VE ACCIDENTALLY FED IT OUR LAST JALAPEÑO SNACK.
OH NO! IT'S A FANCY FOREST **HANGRY**. THEY NORMALLY TRAVEL IN PACKS AND THEY SWARM FOR FOOD.
THIS HANGRY SEEMS TO WORK ALONE.
HMMM. BE REALLY CAREFUL. DO YOU HAVE ANY MORE SNACKS LEFT?
THEY CAN SMELL THEM FROM A MILE AWAY.
ALL OUR SNACKS ARE GONE.

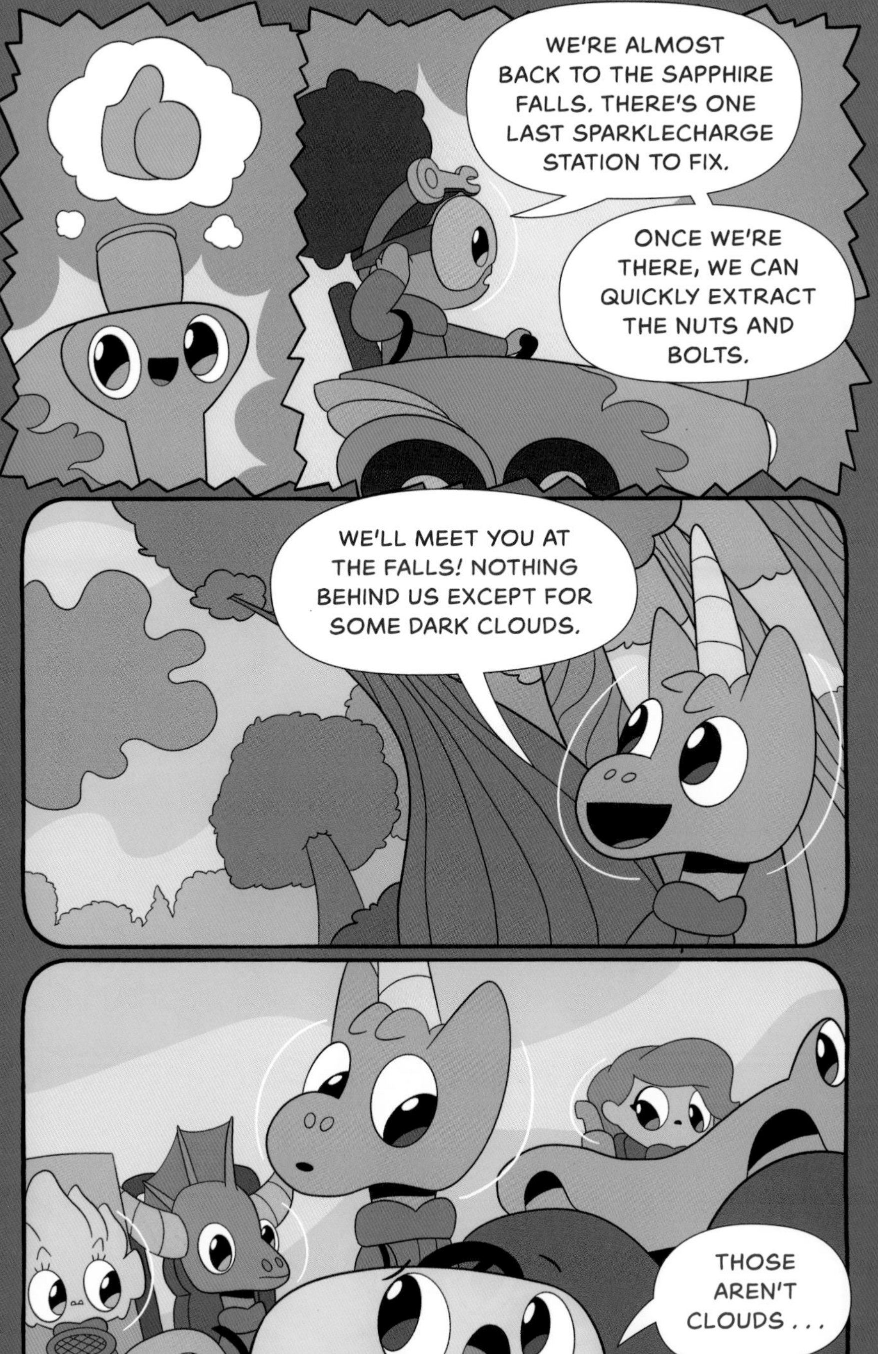
WE'RE ALMOST BACK TO THE SAPPHIRE FALLS. THERE'S ONE LAST SPARKLECHARGE STATION TO FIX.
ONCE WE'RE THERE, WE CAN QUICKLY EXTRACT THE NUTS AND BOLTS.
WE'LL MEET YOU AT THE FALLS! NOTHING BEHIND US EXCEPT FOR SOME DARK CLOUDS.
THOSE AREN'T CLOUDS . . .

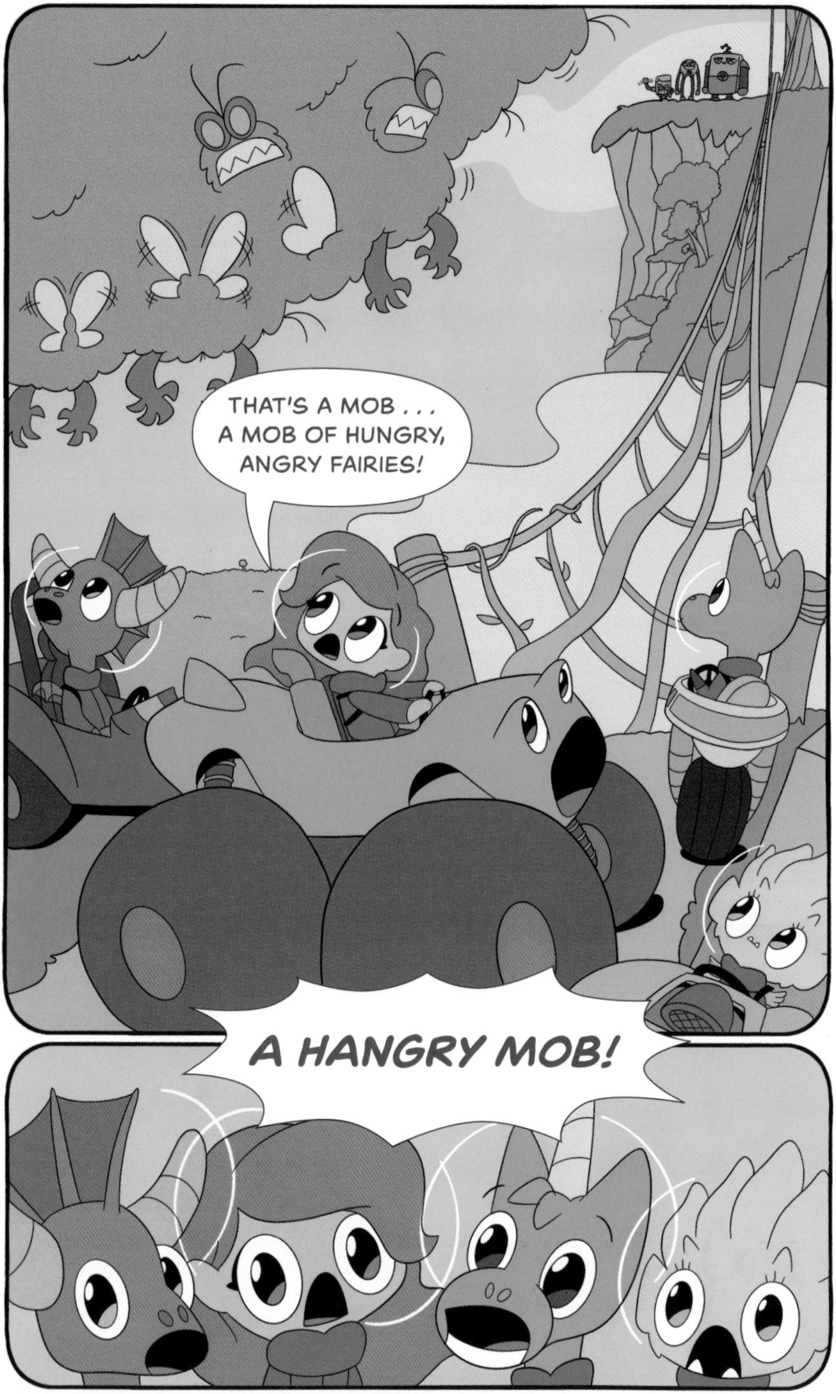
THAT'S A MOB . . .
A MOB OF HUNGRY,
ANGRY FAIRIES!
A HANGRY MOB!

CHAPTER 12:
HANGRIES!

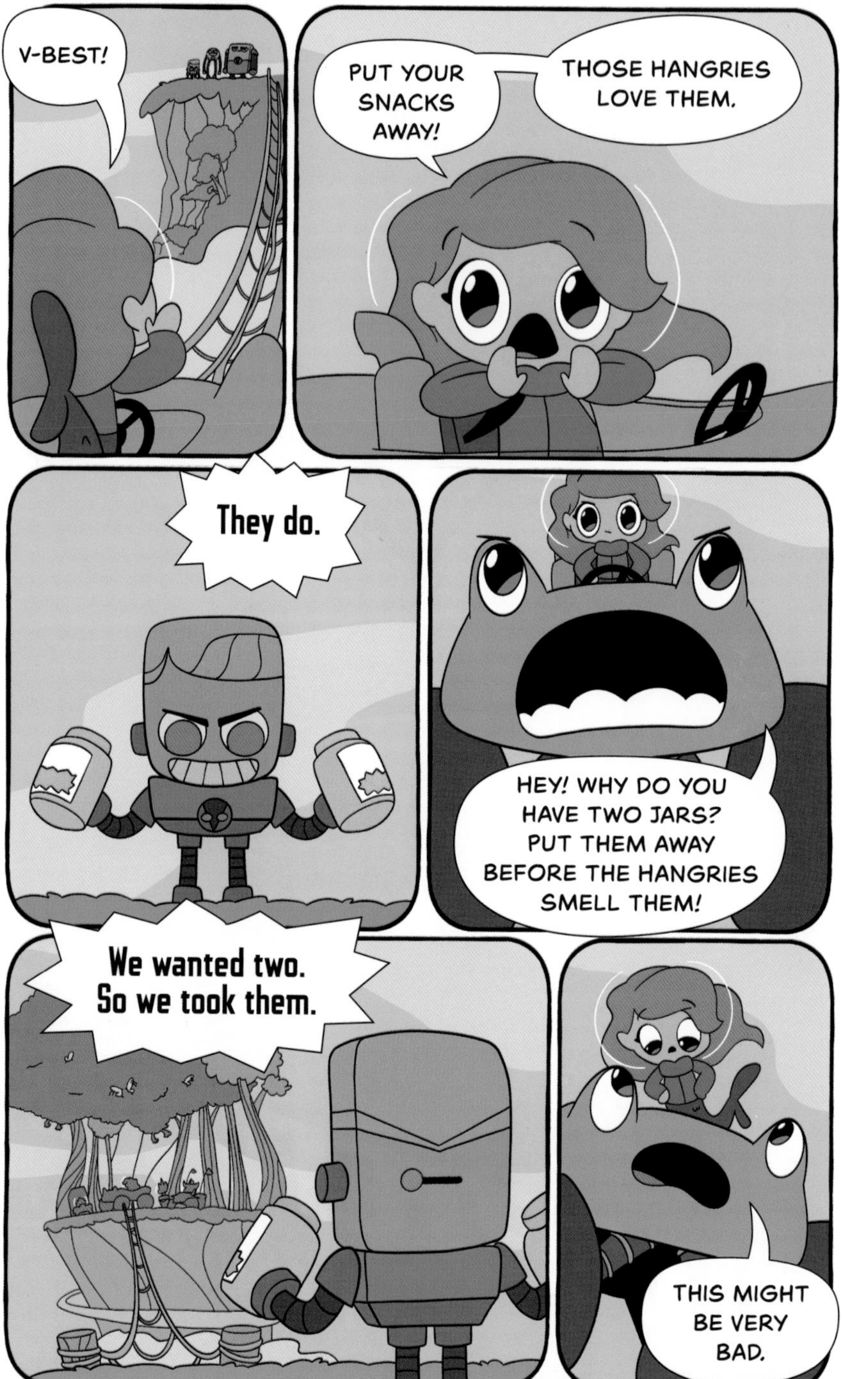
V-BEST!
PUT YOUR SNACKS AWAY!
THOSE HANGRIES LOVE THEM.
They do.
HEY! WHY DO YOU HAVE TWO JARS? PUT THEM AWAY BEFORE THE HANGRIES SMELL THEM!
We wanted two. So we took them.
THIS MIGHT BE VERY BAD.

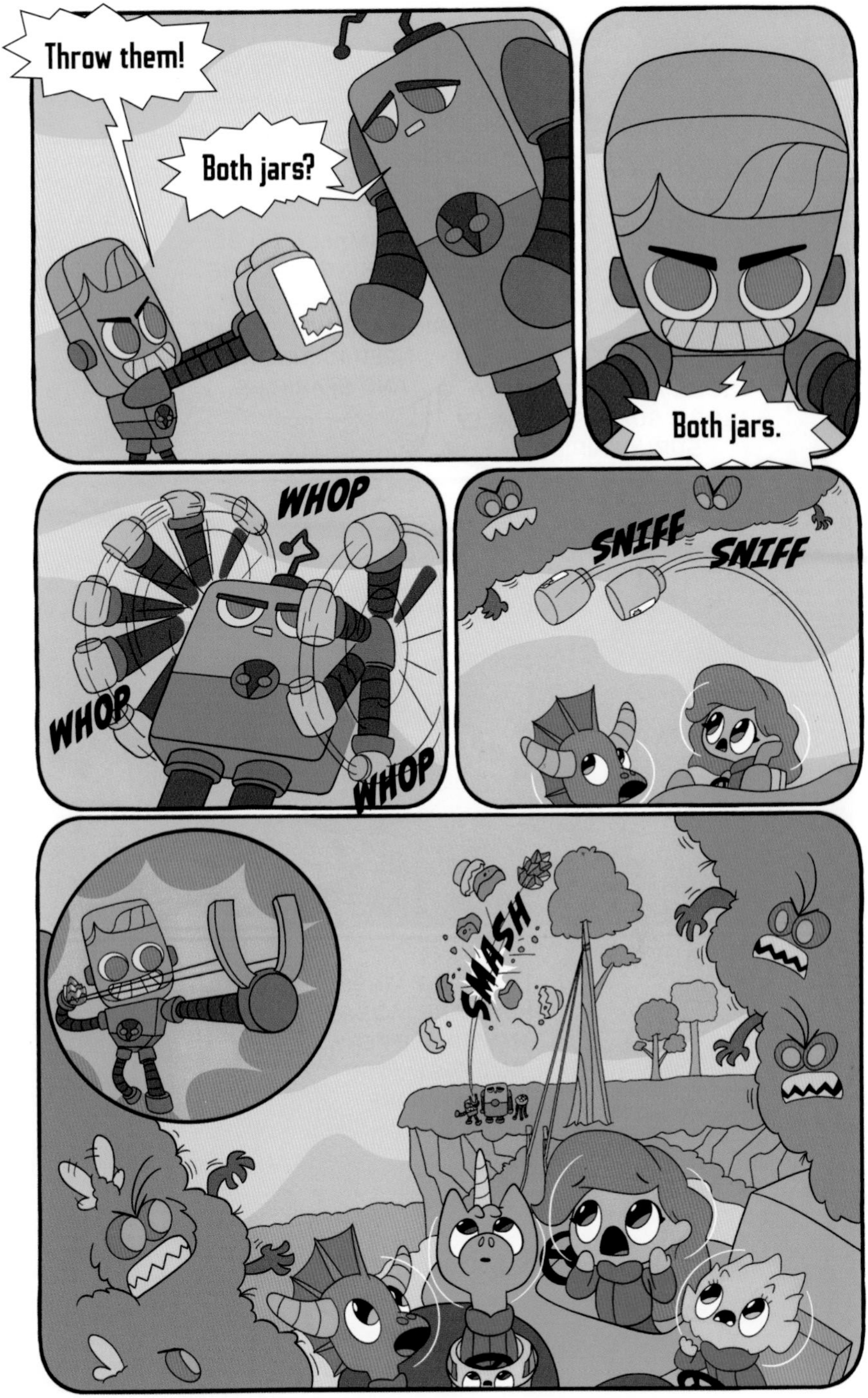
Throw them!
Both jars?
Both jars.
WHOP
WHOP
WHOP
SNIFF
SNIFF
SMASH

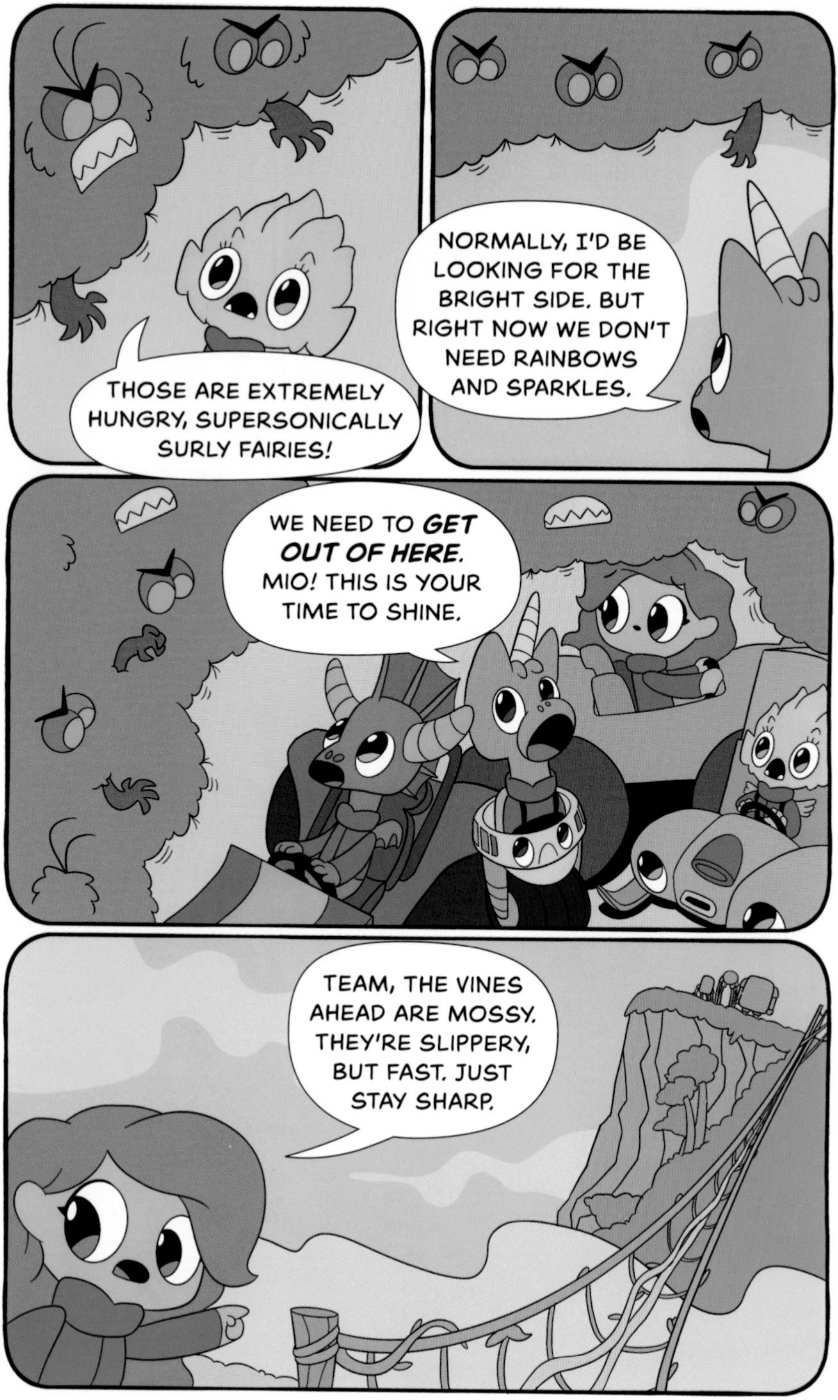
THOSE ARE EXTREMELY HUNGRY, SUPERSONICALLY SURLY FAIRIES!
NORMALLY, I'D BE LOOKING FOR THE BRIGHT SIDE. BUT RIGHT NOW WE DON'T NEED RAINBOWS AND SPARKLES.
WE NEED TO ***GET OUT OF HERE.*** MIO! THIS IS YOUR TIME TO SHINE.
TEAM, THE VINES AHEAD ARE MOSSY. THEY'RE SLIPPERY, BUT FAST. JUST STAY SHARP.

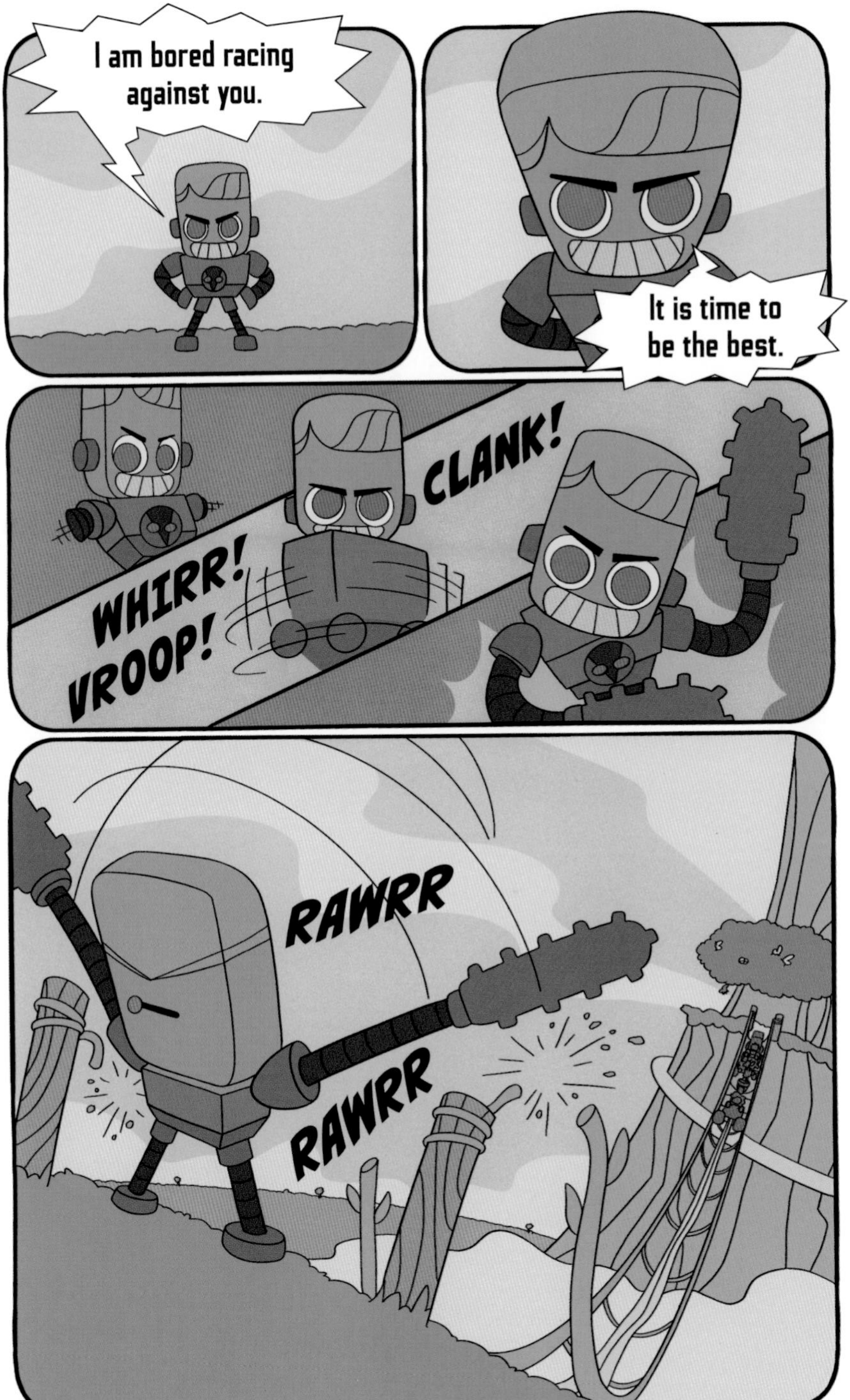
I am bored racing against you.
It is time to be the best.
CLANK!
WHIRR!
VROOP!
RAWRR
RAWRR

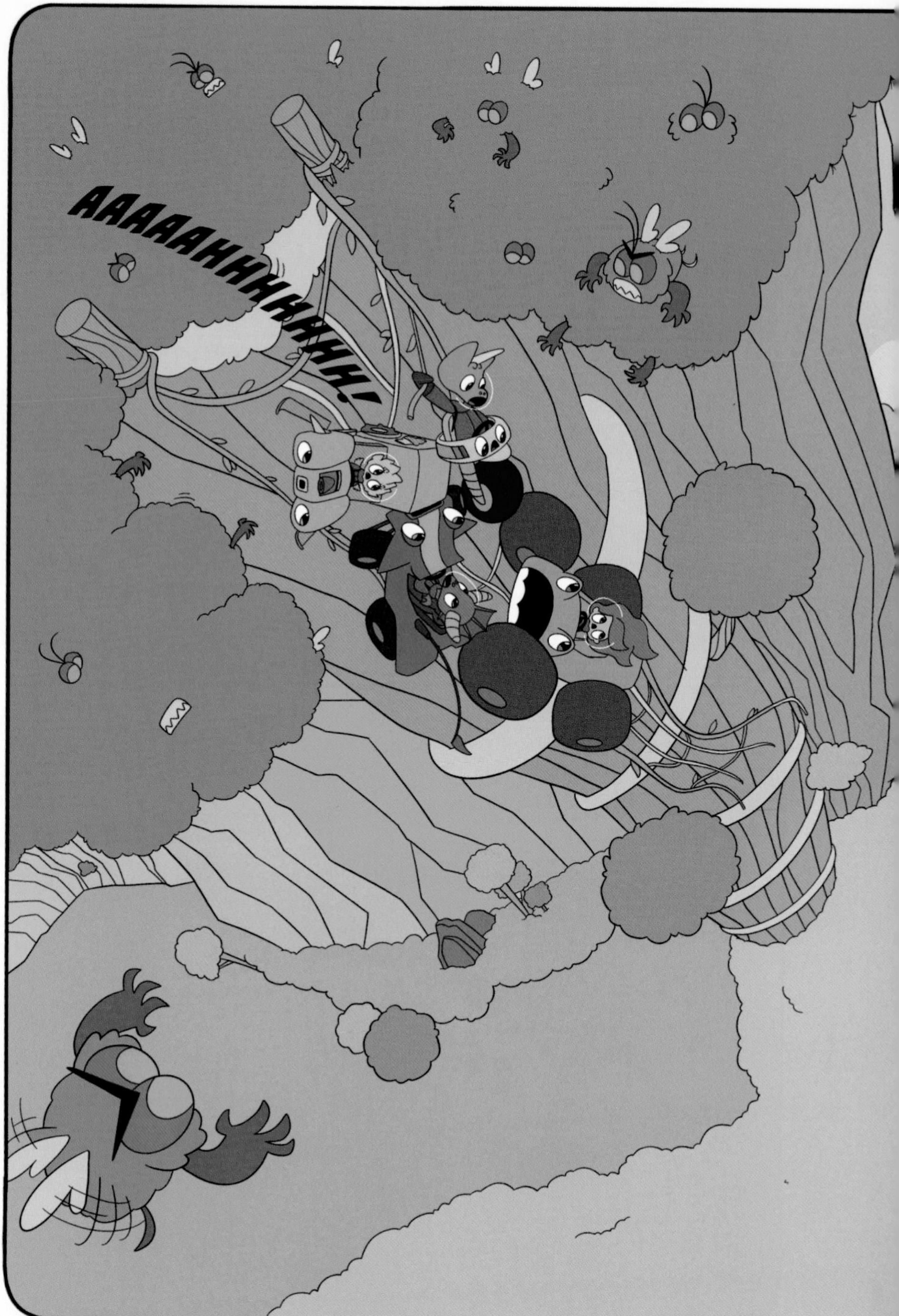
AAAAAHHHHHHHHH!

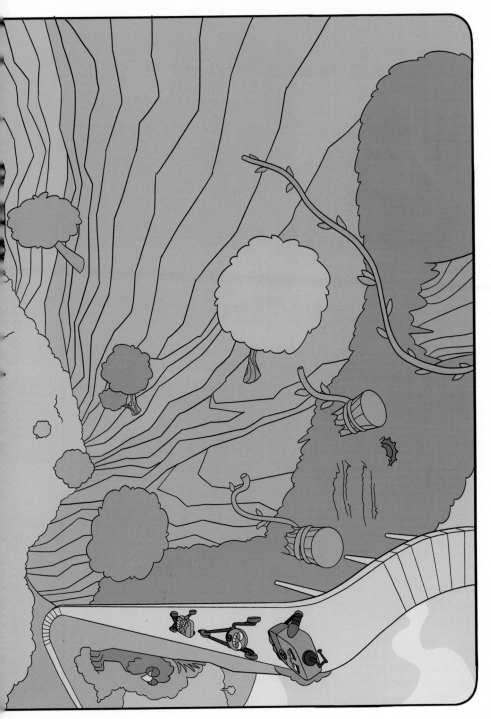

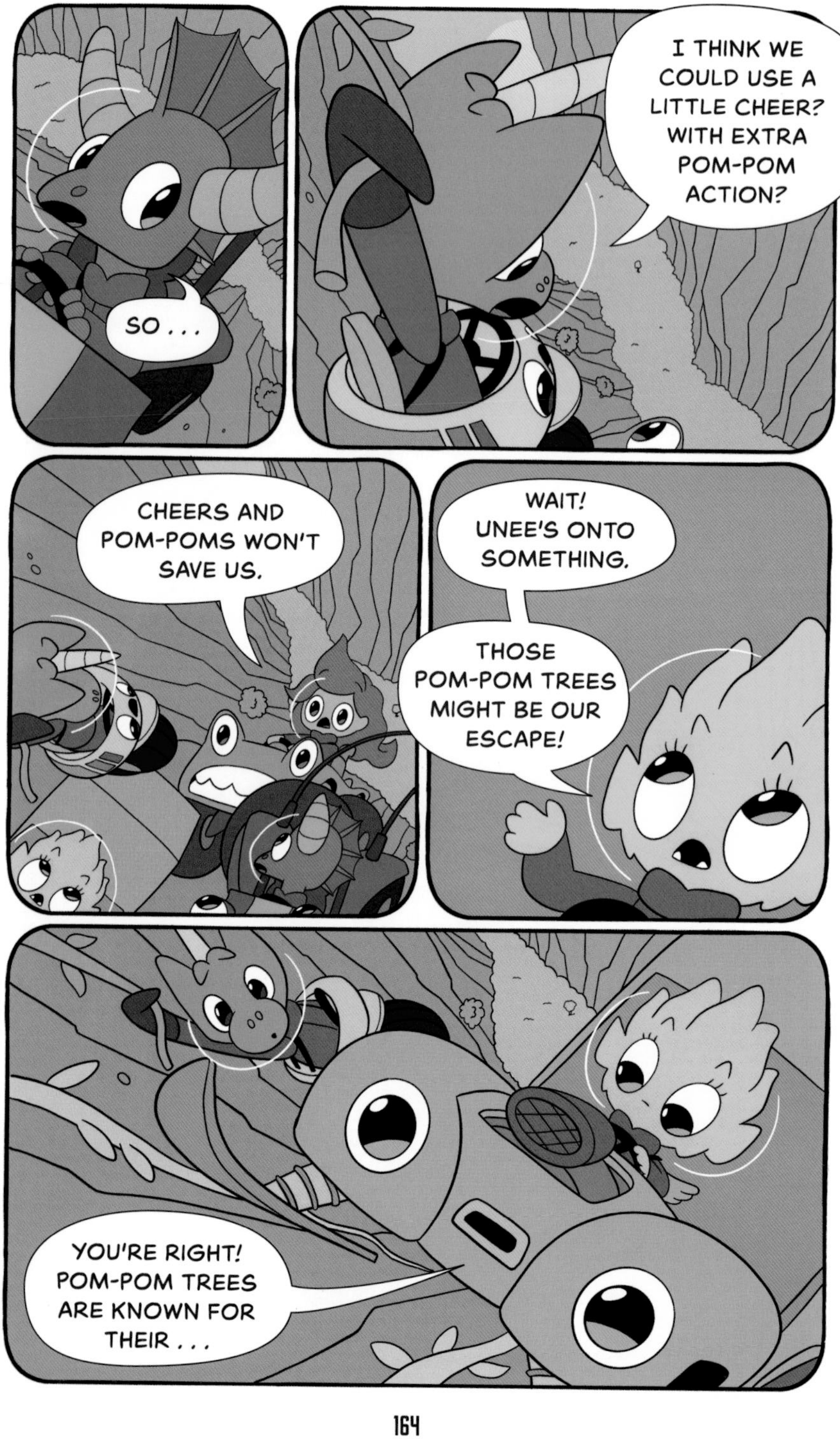
SO . . .
I THINK WE COULD USE A LITTLE CHEER? WITH EXTRA POM-POM ACTION?
CHEERS AND POM-POMS WON'T SAVE US.
WAIT! UNEE'S ONTO SOMETHING.
THOSE POM-POM TREES MIGHT BE OUR ESCAPE!
YOU'RE RIGHT! POM-POM TREES ARE KNOWN FOR THEIR . . .

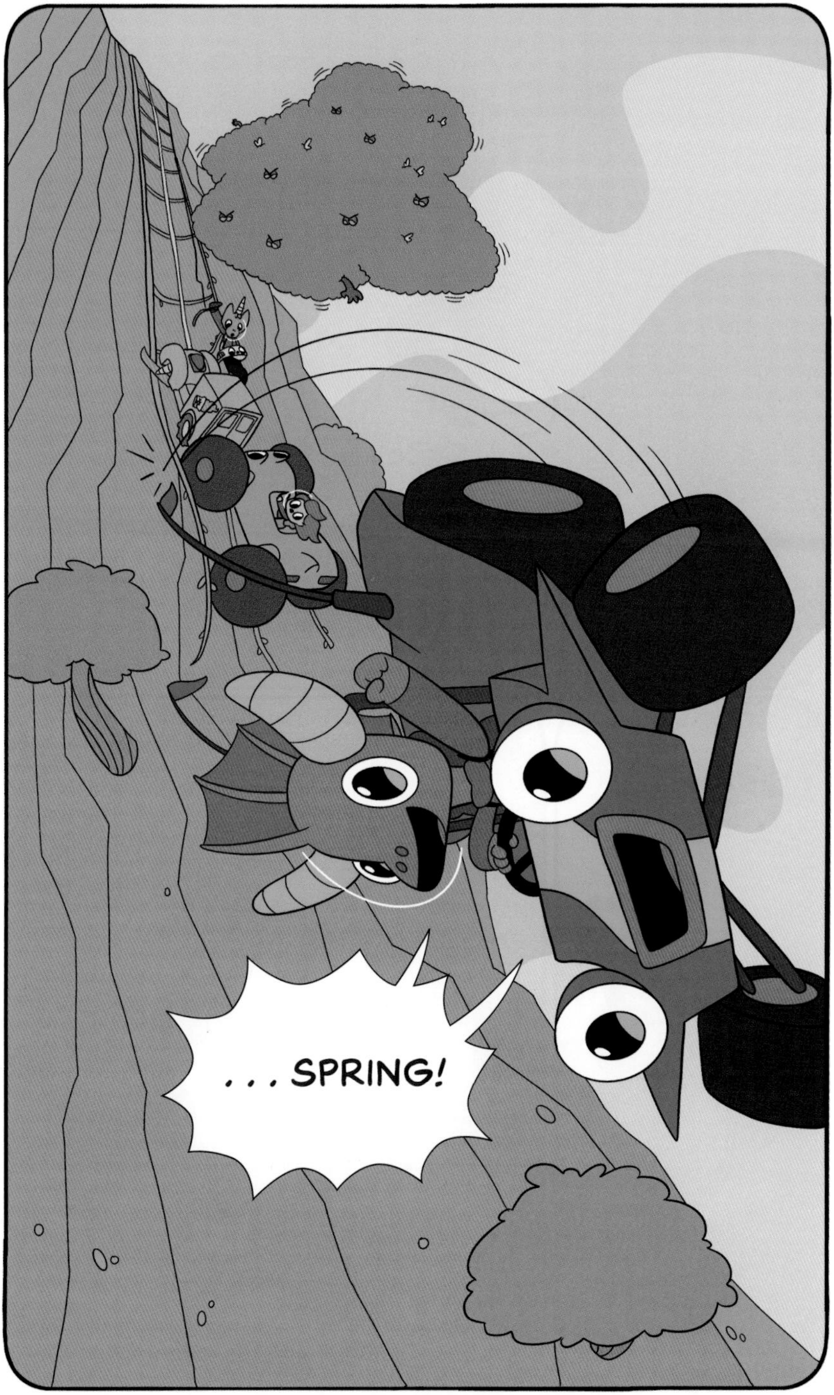
. . . SPRING!

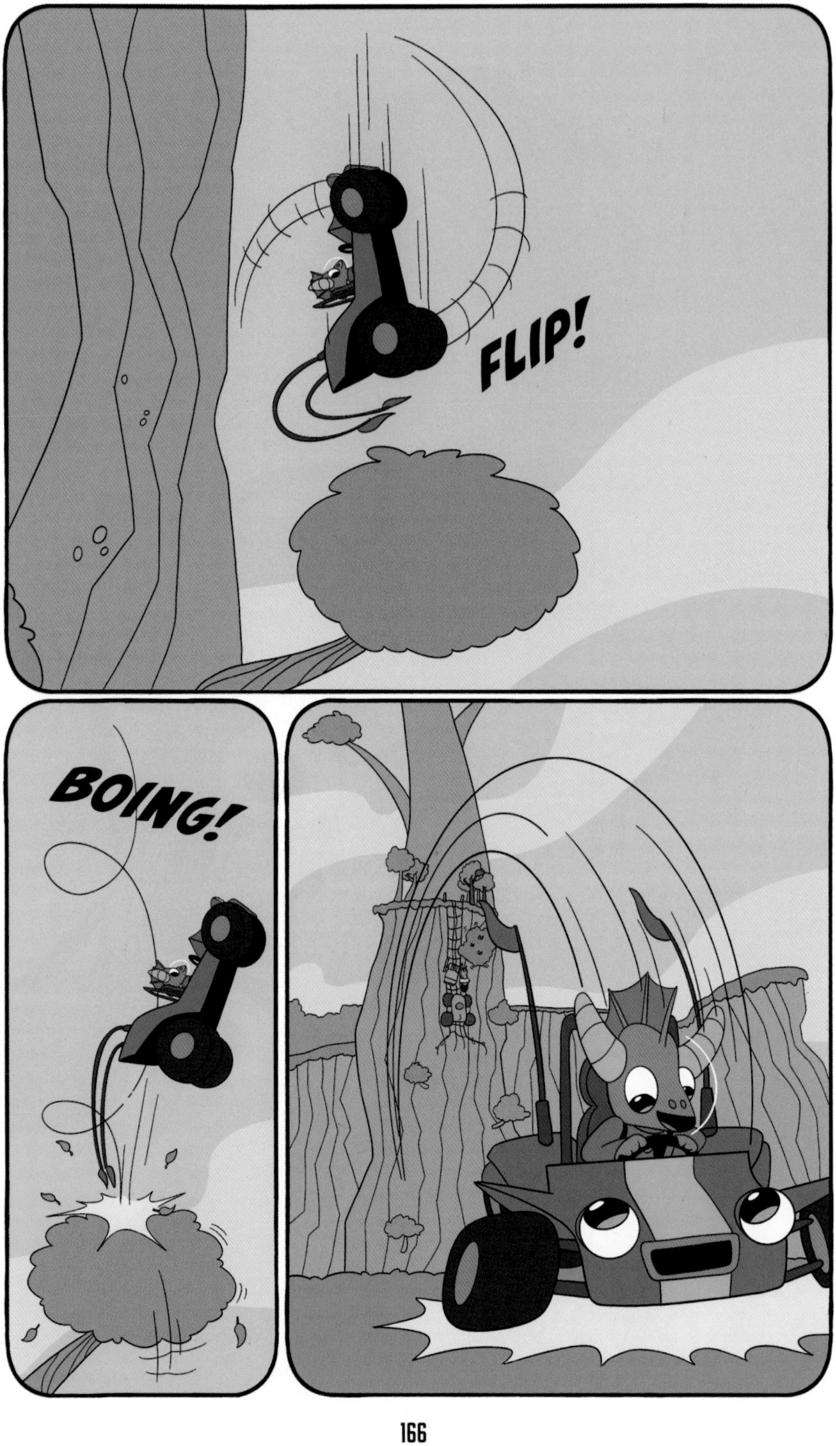
FLIP!
BOING!

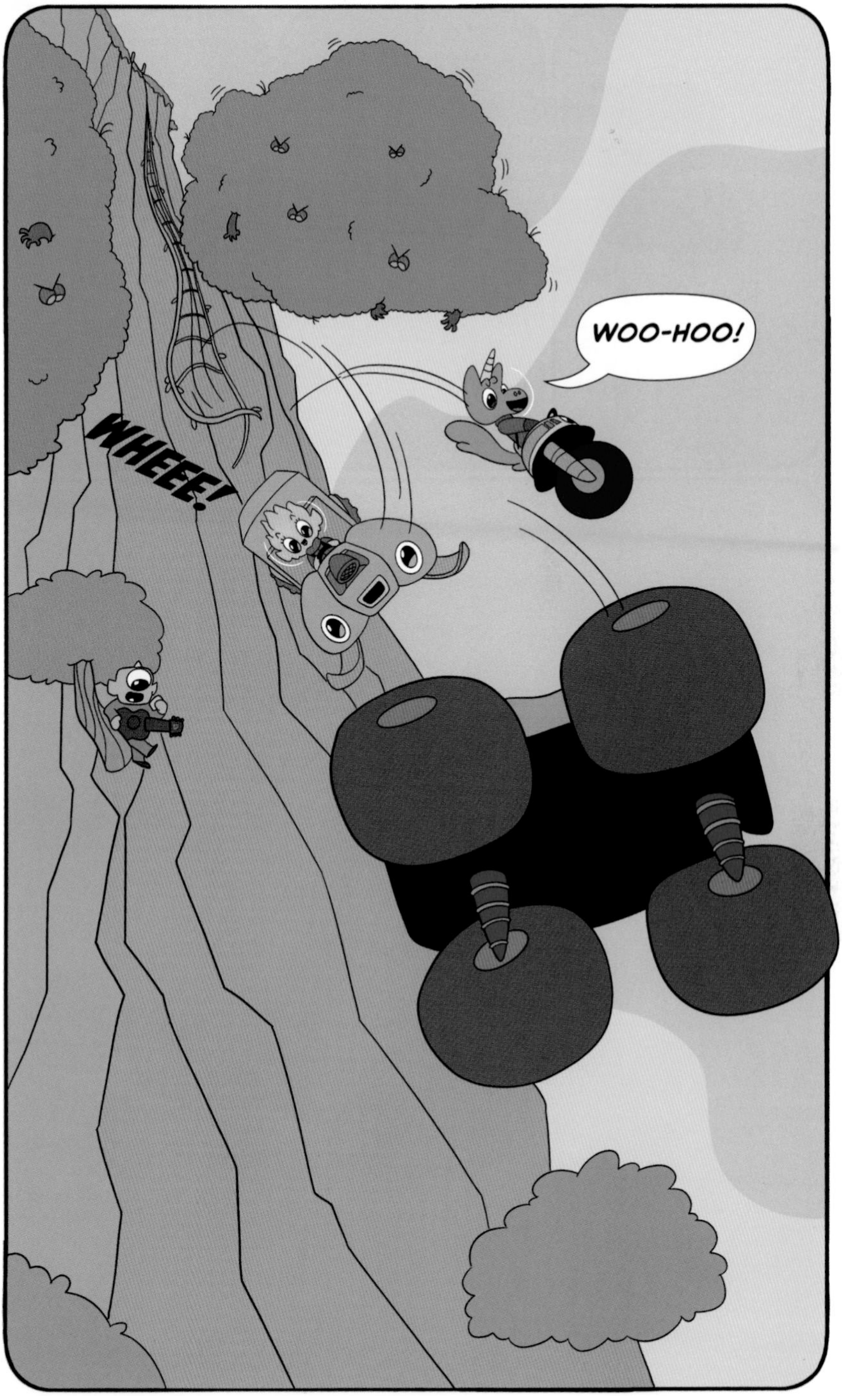
WOO-HOO!
WHEEE!

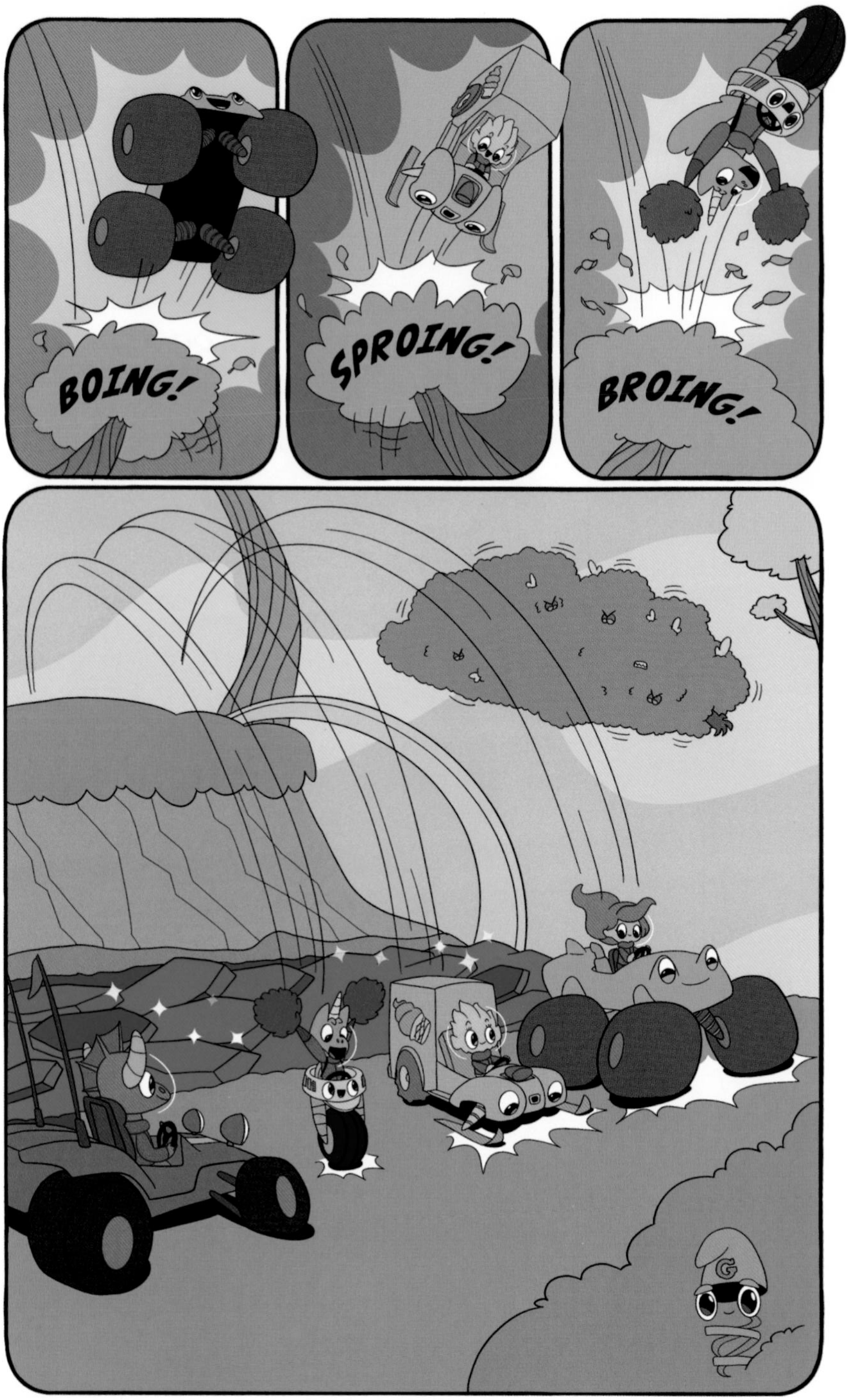
BOING!
SPROING!
BROING!

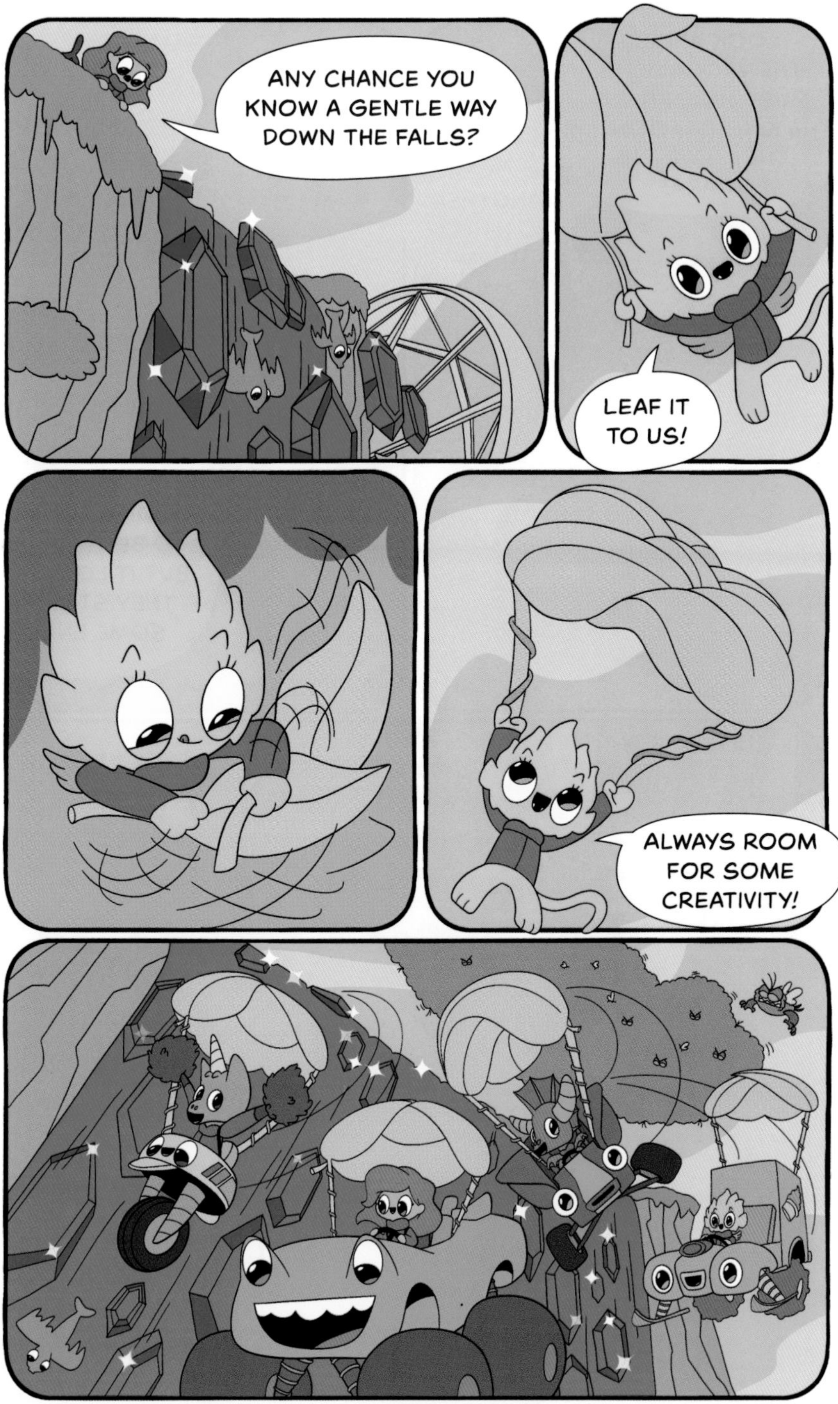
ANY CHANCE YOU KNOW A GENTLE WAY DOWN THE FALLS?
LEAF IT TO US!
ALWAYS ROOM FOR SOME CREATIVITY!

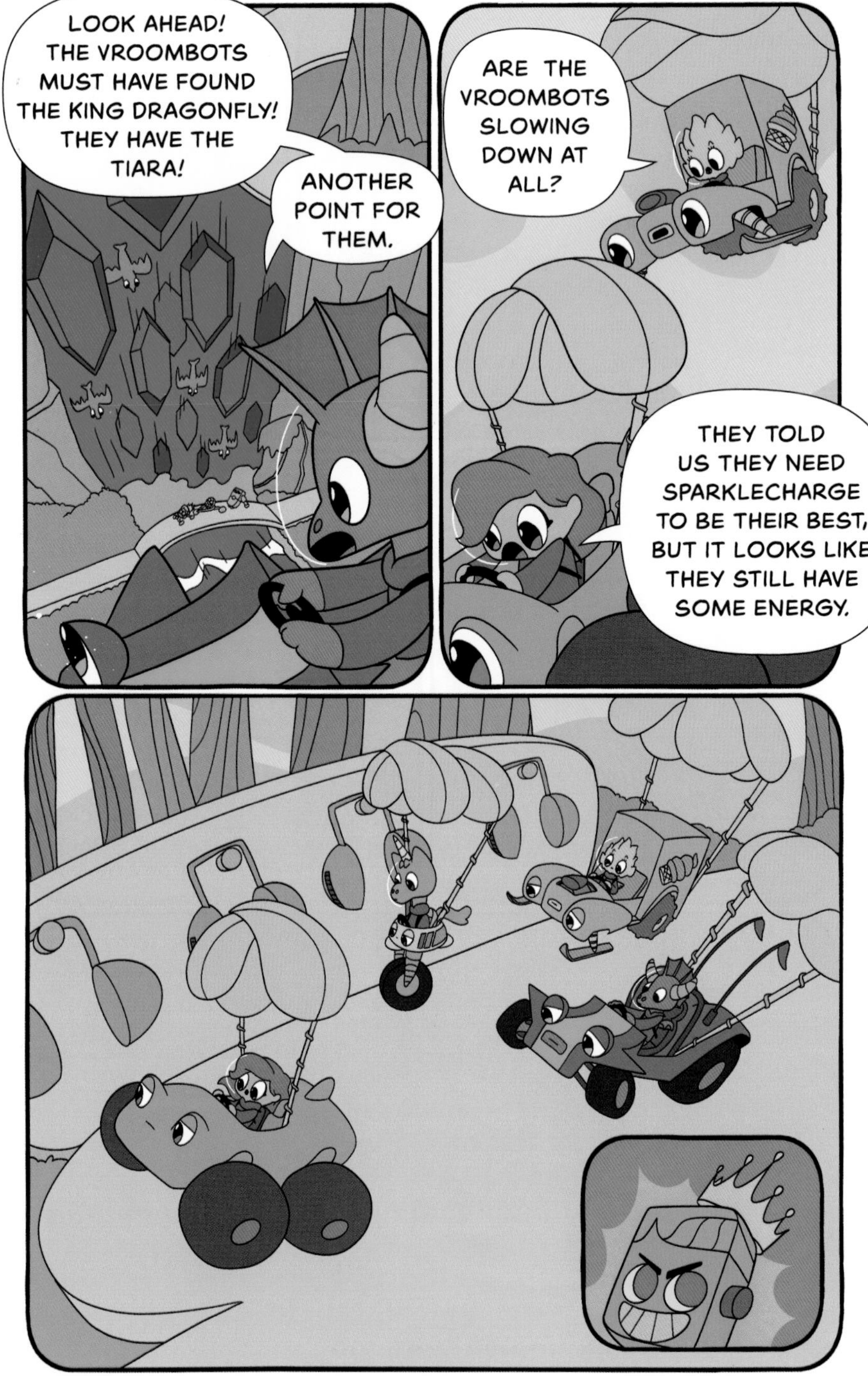
LOOK AHEAD! THE VROOMBOTS MUST HAVE FOUND THE KING DRAGONFLY! THEY HAVE THE TIARA!
ANOTHER POINT FOR THEM.
ARE THE VROOMBOTS SLOWING DOWN AT ALL?
THEY TOLD US THEY NEED SPARKLECHARGE TO BE THEIR BEST, BUT IT LOOKS LIKE THEY STILL HAVE SOME ENERGY.

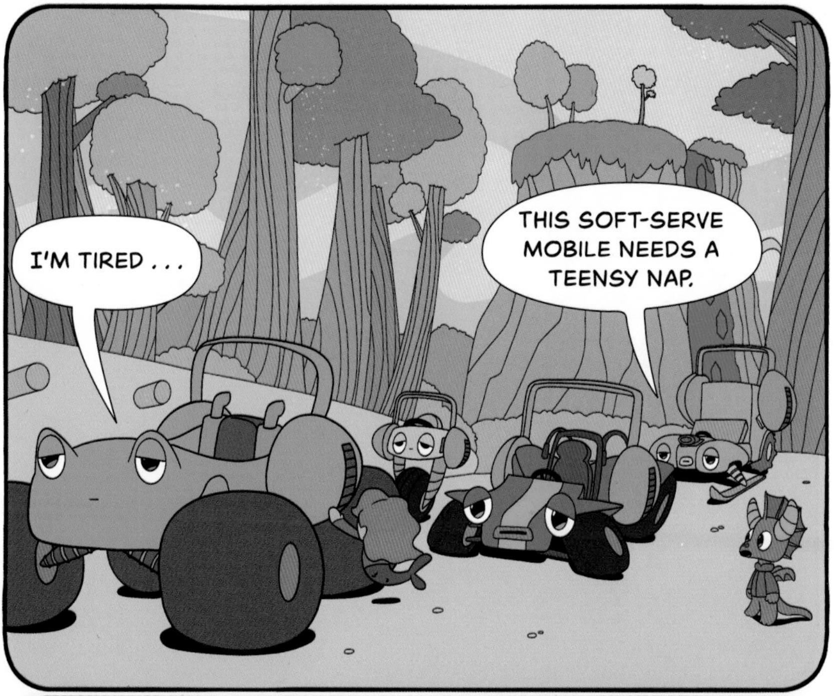
I'M TIRED . . .
THIS SOFT-SERVE MOBILE NEEDS A TEENSY NAP.

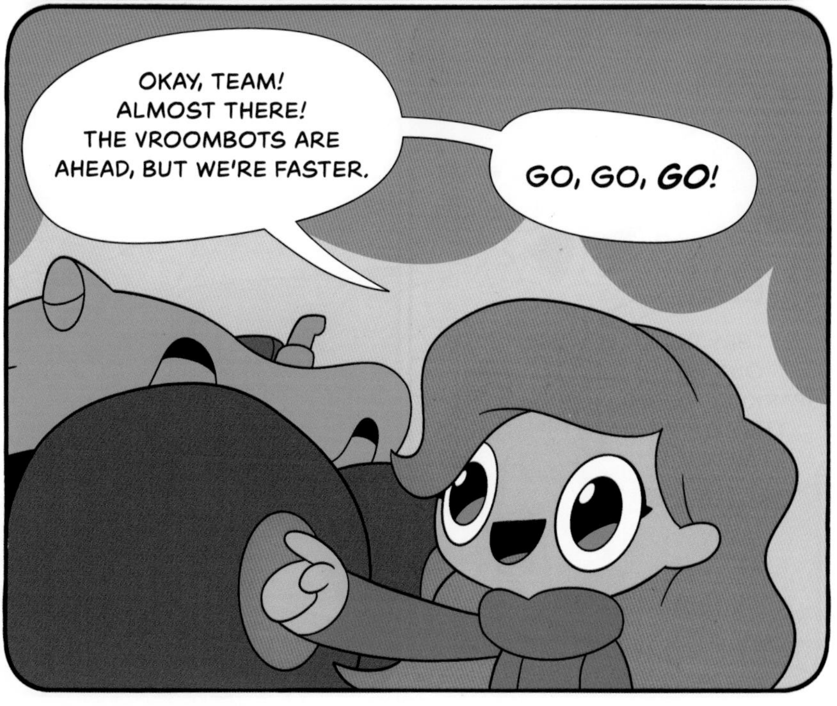
OKAY, TEAM! ALMOST THERE! THE VROOMBOTS ARE AHEAD, BUT WE'RE FASTER.
GO, GO, **GO**!

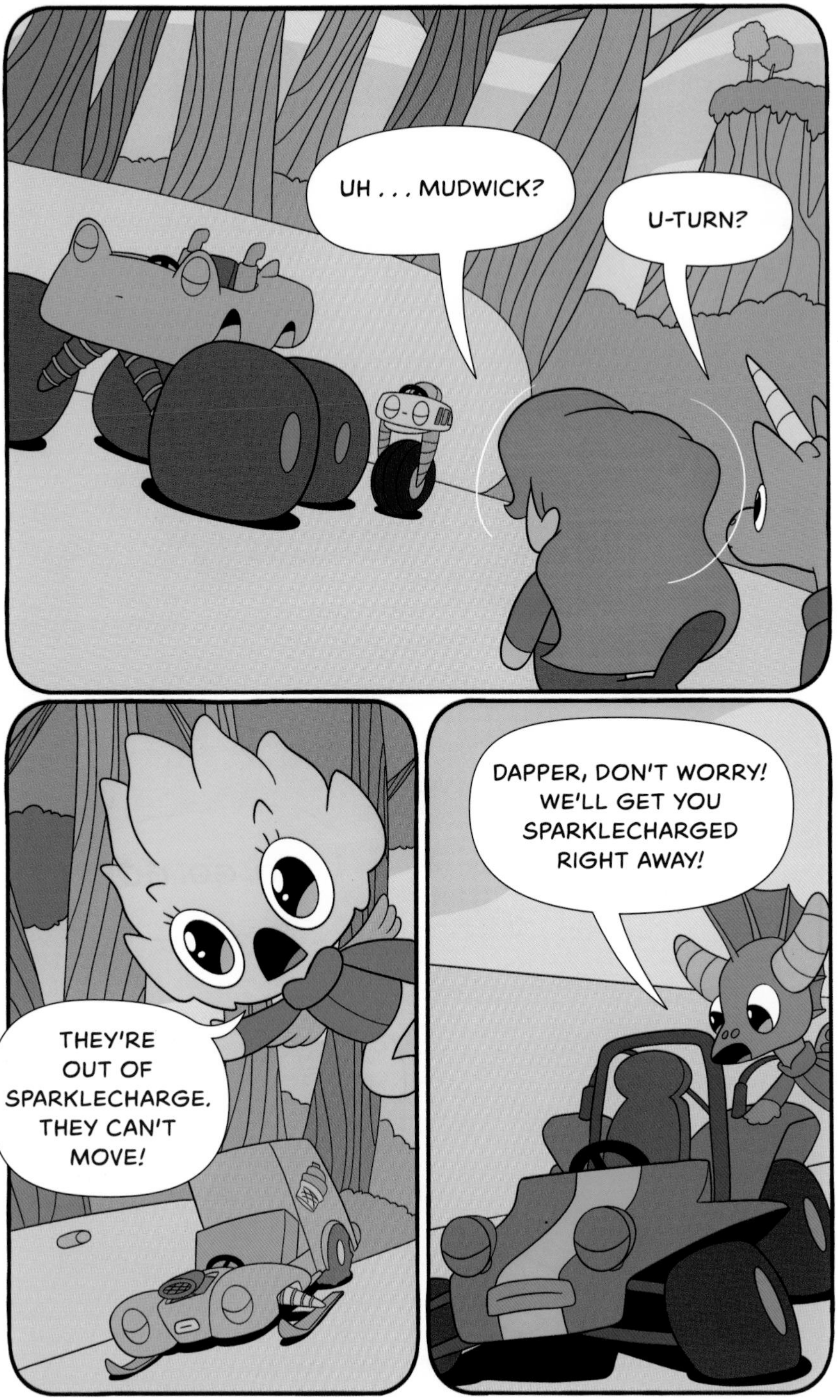
UH . . . MUDWICK?
U-TURN?
THEY'RE OUT OF SPARKLECHARGE. THEY CAN'T MOVE!
DAPPER, DON'T WORRY! WE'LL GET YOU SPARKLECHARGED RIGHT AWAY!

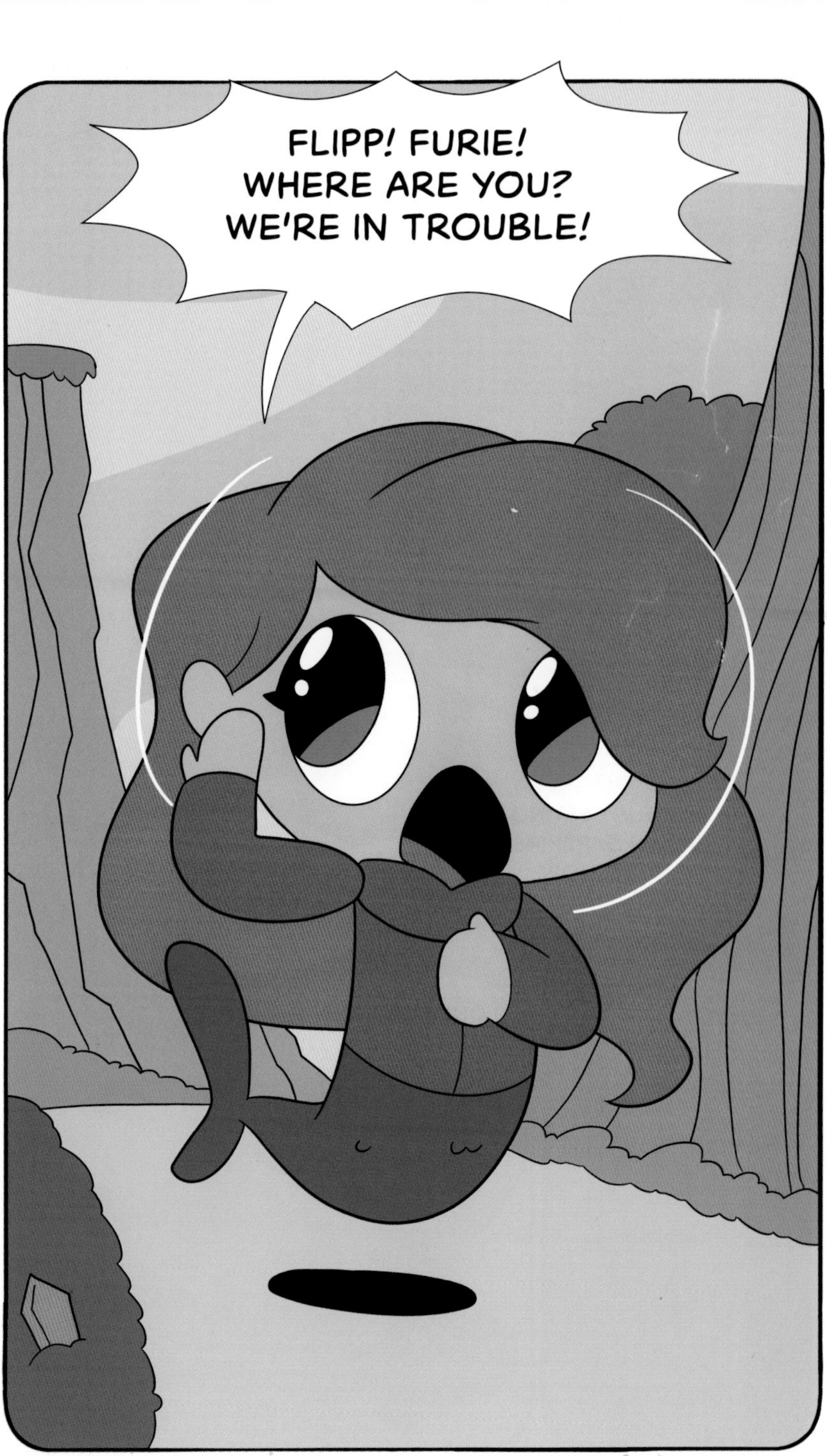
FLIPP! FURIE! WHERE ARE YOU? WE'RE IN TROUBLE!

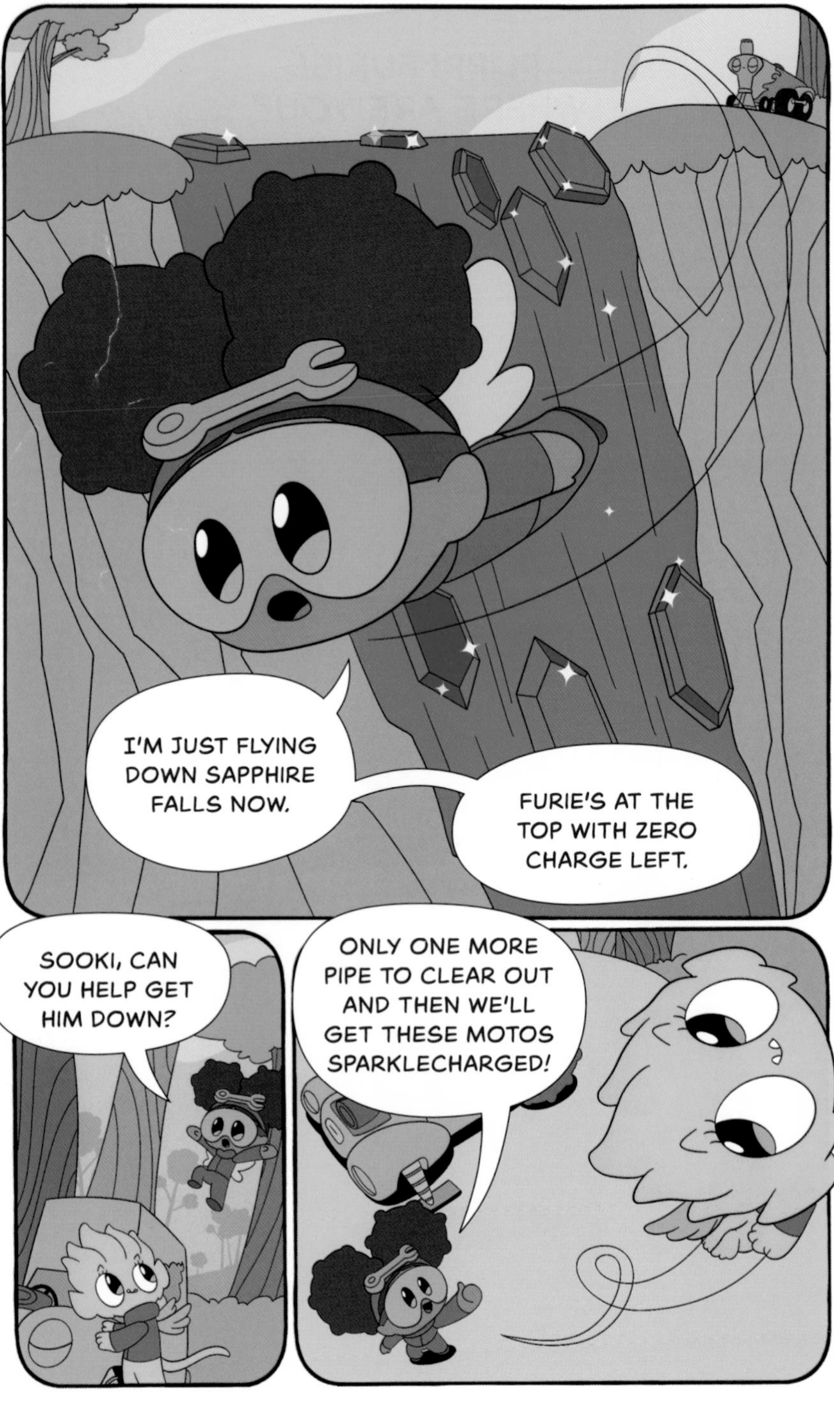
I'M JUST FLYING DOWN SAPPHIRE FALLS NOW.
FURIE'S AT THE TOP WITH ZERO CHARGE LEFT.
SOOKI, CAN YOU HELP GET HIM DOWN?
ONLY ONE MORE PIPE TO CLEAR OUT AND THEN WE'LL GET THESE MOTOS SPARKLECHARGED!

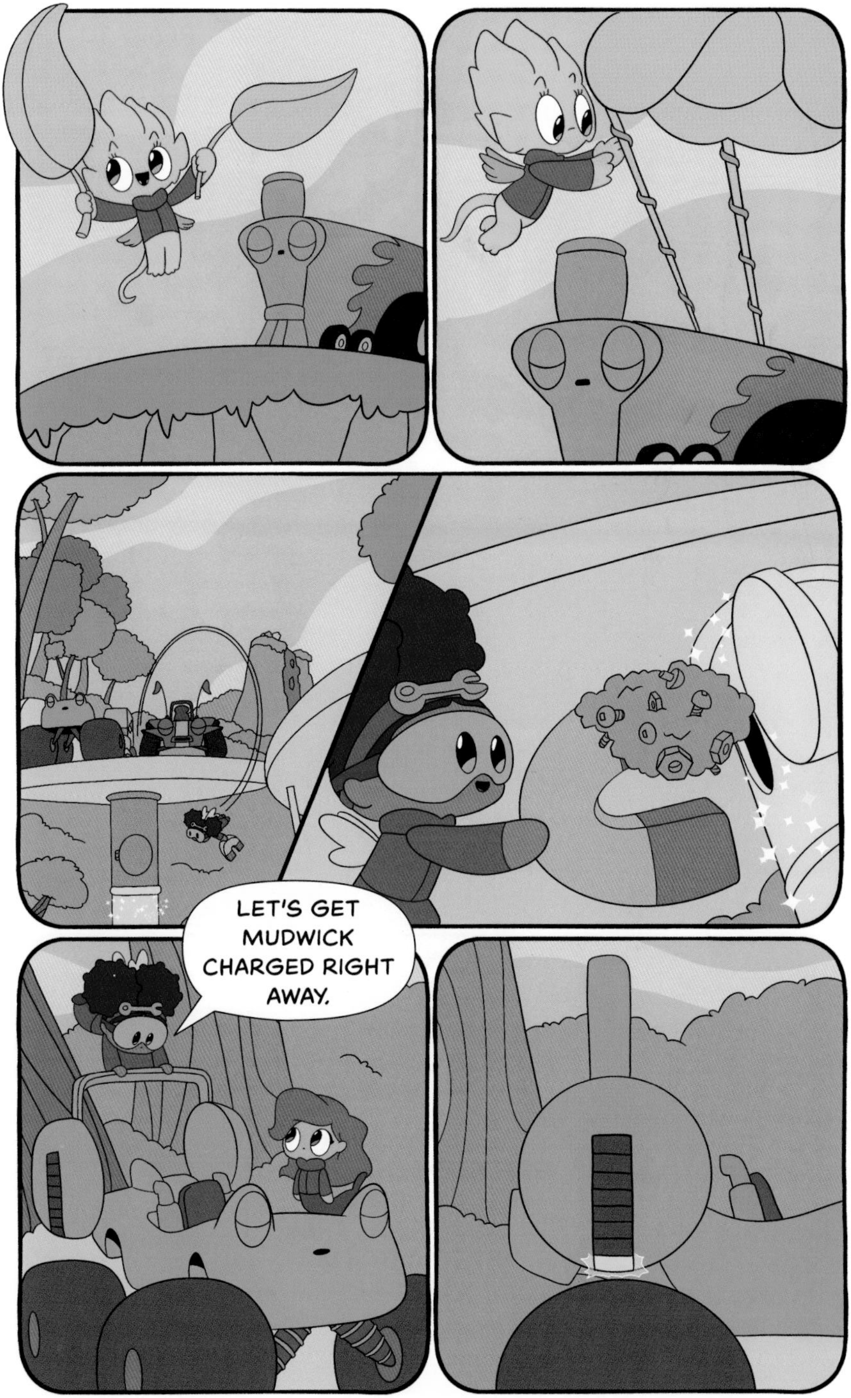
LET'S GET MUDWICK CHARGED RIGHT AWAY.

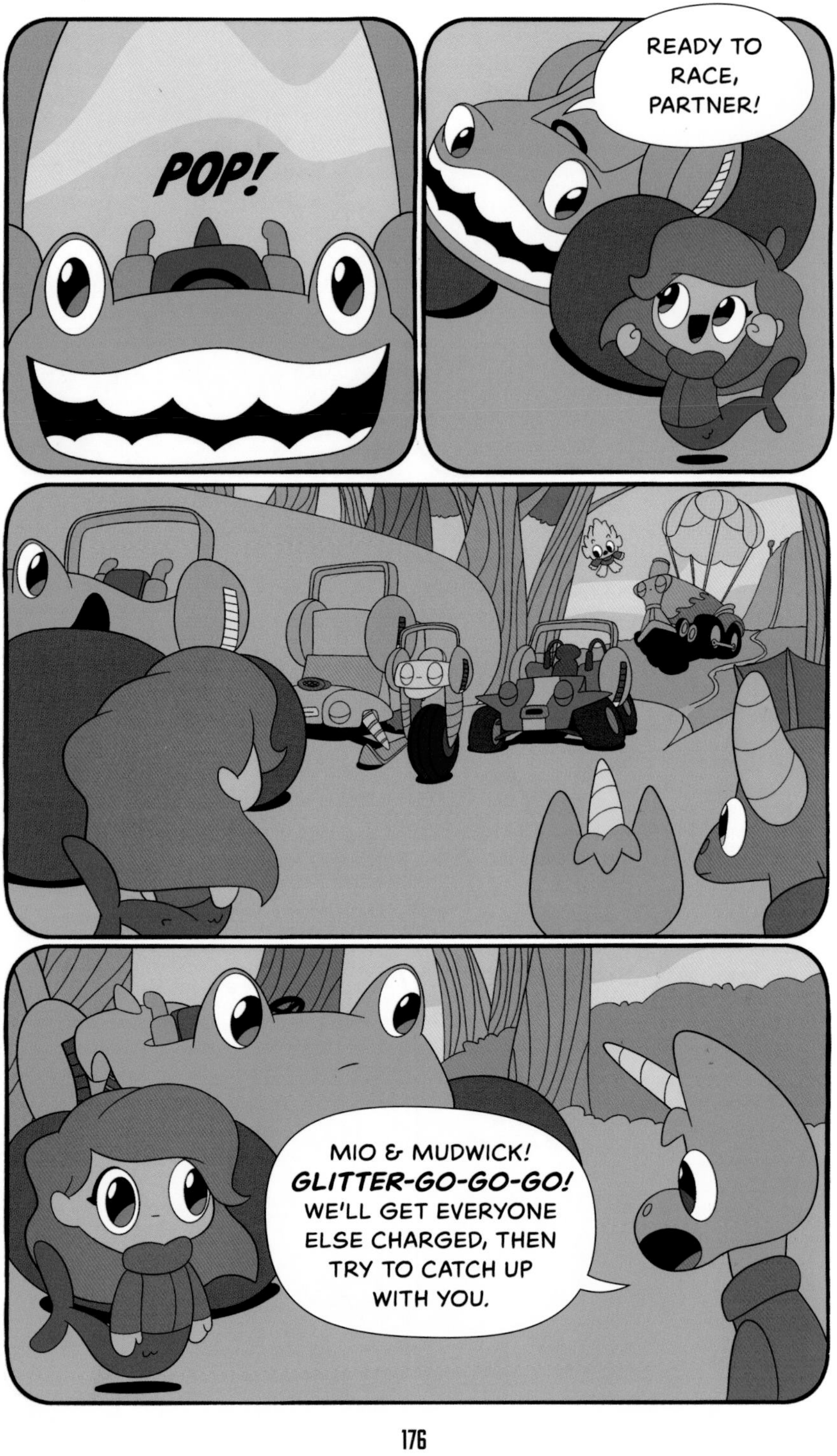
POP!
READY TO RACE, PARTNER!
MIO & MUDWICK! **GLITTER-GO-GO-GO!** WE'LL GET EVERYONE ELSE CHARGED, THEN TRY TO CATCH UP WITH YOU.

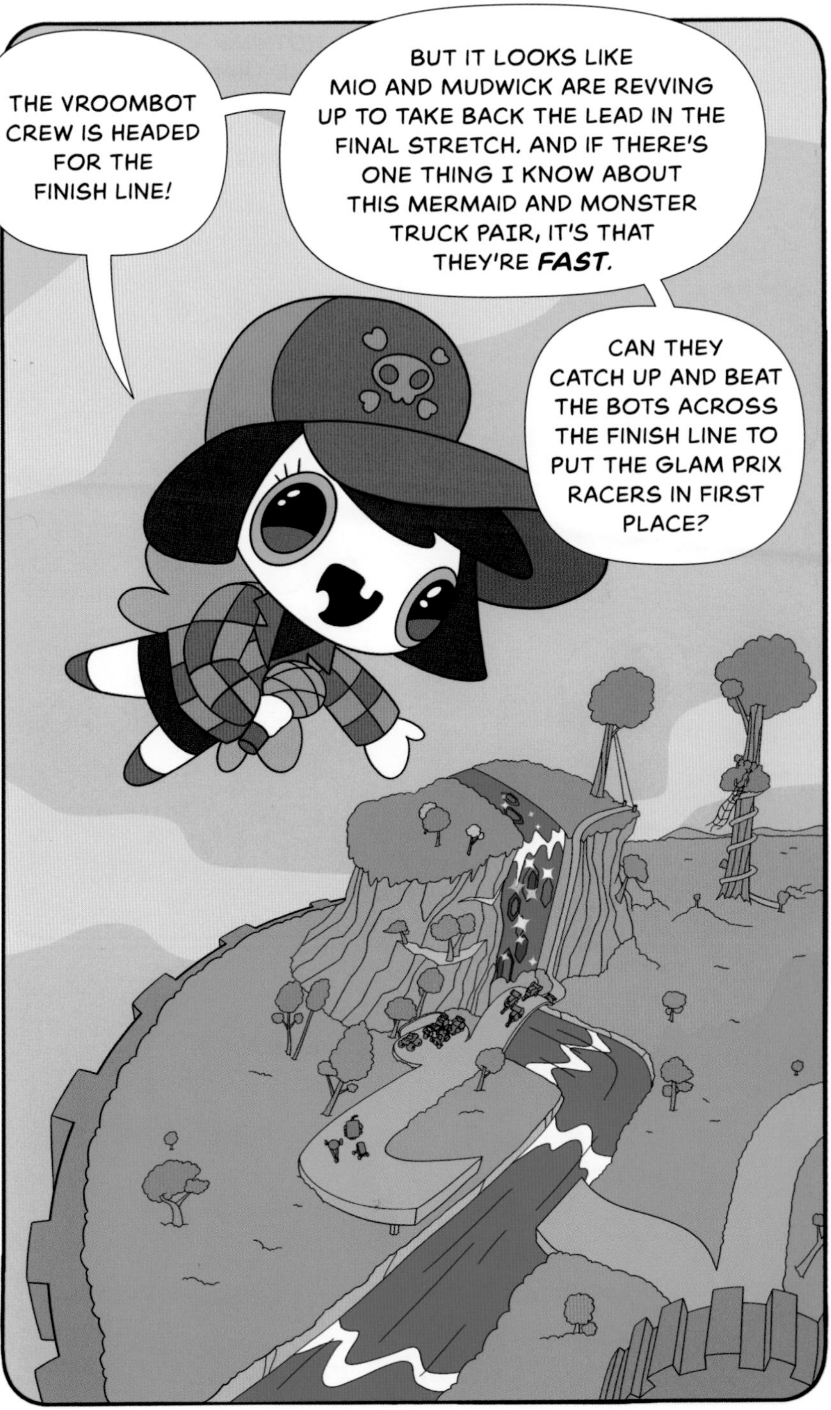
THE VROOMBOT CREW IS HEADED FOR THE FINISH LINE!
BUT IT LOOKS LIKE MIO AND MUDWICK ARE REVVING UP TO TAKE BACK THE LEAD IN THE FINAL STRETCH. AND IF THERE'S ONE THING I KNOW ABOUT THIS MERMAID AND MONSTER TRUCK PAIR, IT'S THAT THEY'RE ***FAST.***
CAN THEY CATCH UP AND BEAT THE BOTS ACROSS THE FINISH LINE TO PUT THE GLAM PRIX RACERS IN FIRST PLACE?

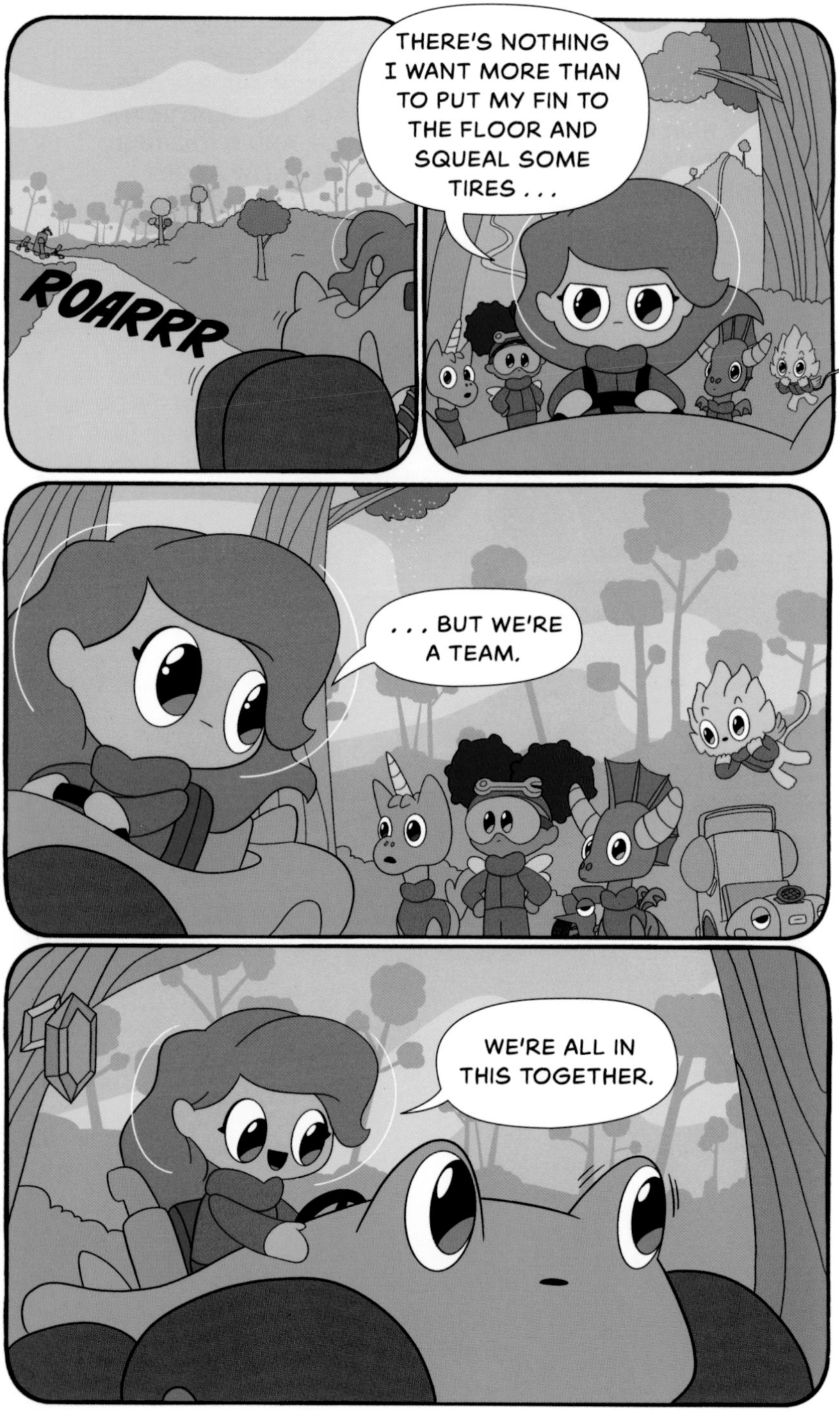
ROARRR
THERE'S NOTHING I WANT MORE THAN TO PUT MY FIN TO THE FLOOR AND SQUEAL SOME TIRES . . .
. . . BUT WE'RE A TEAM.
WE'RE ALL IN THIS TOGETHER.

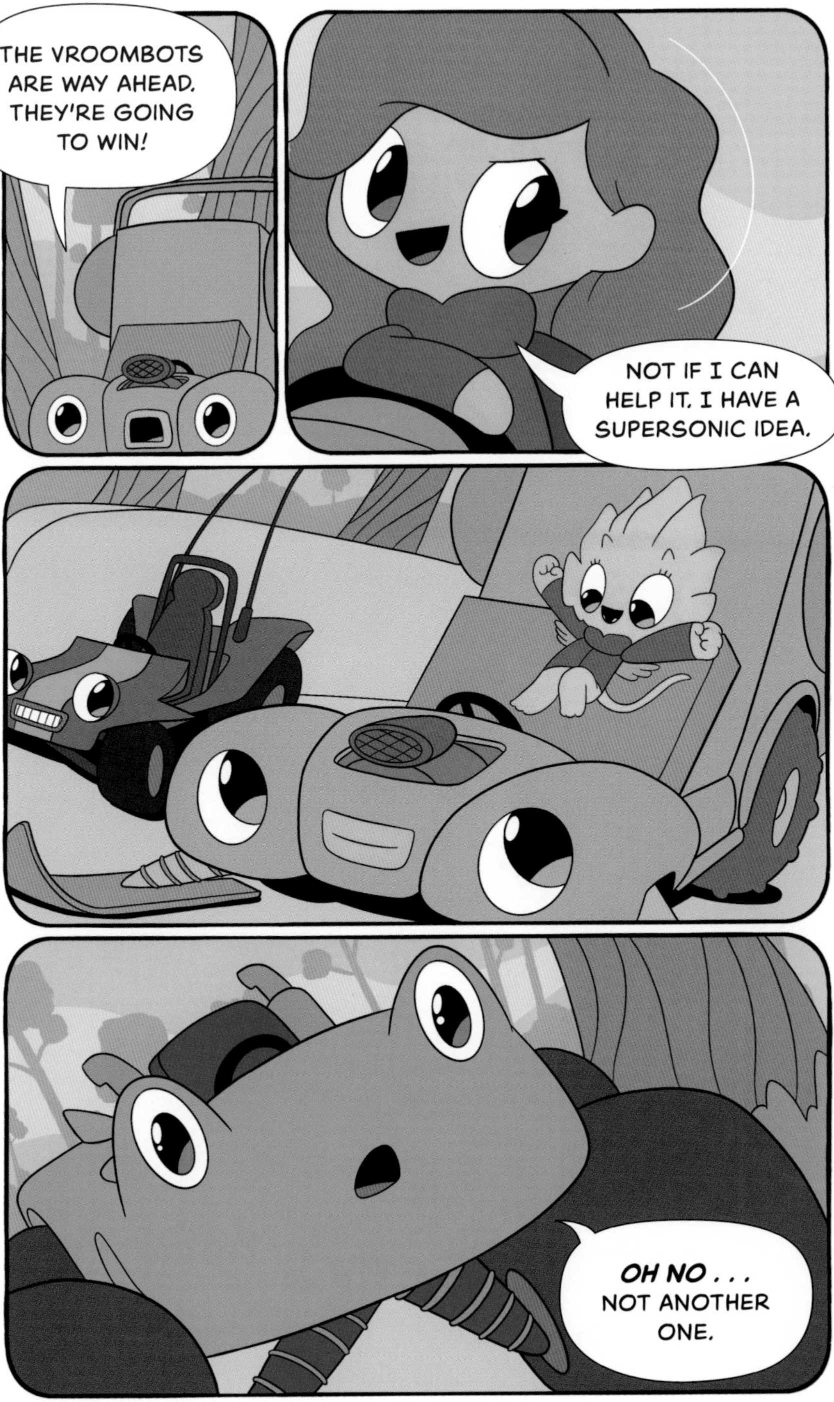
THE VROOMBOTS ARE WAY AHEAD. THEY'RE GOING TO WIN!
NOT IF I CAN HELP IT. I HAVE A SUPERSONIC IDEA.
OH NO . . . NOT ANOTHER ONE.

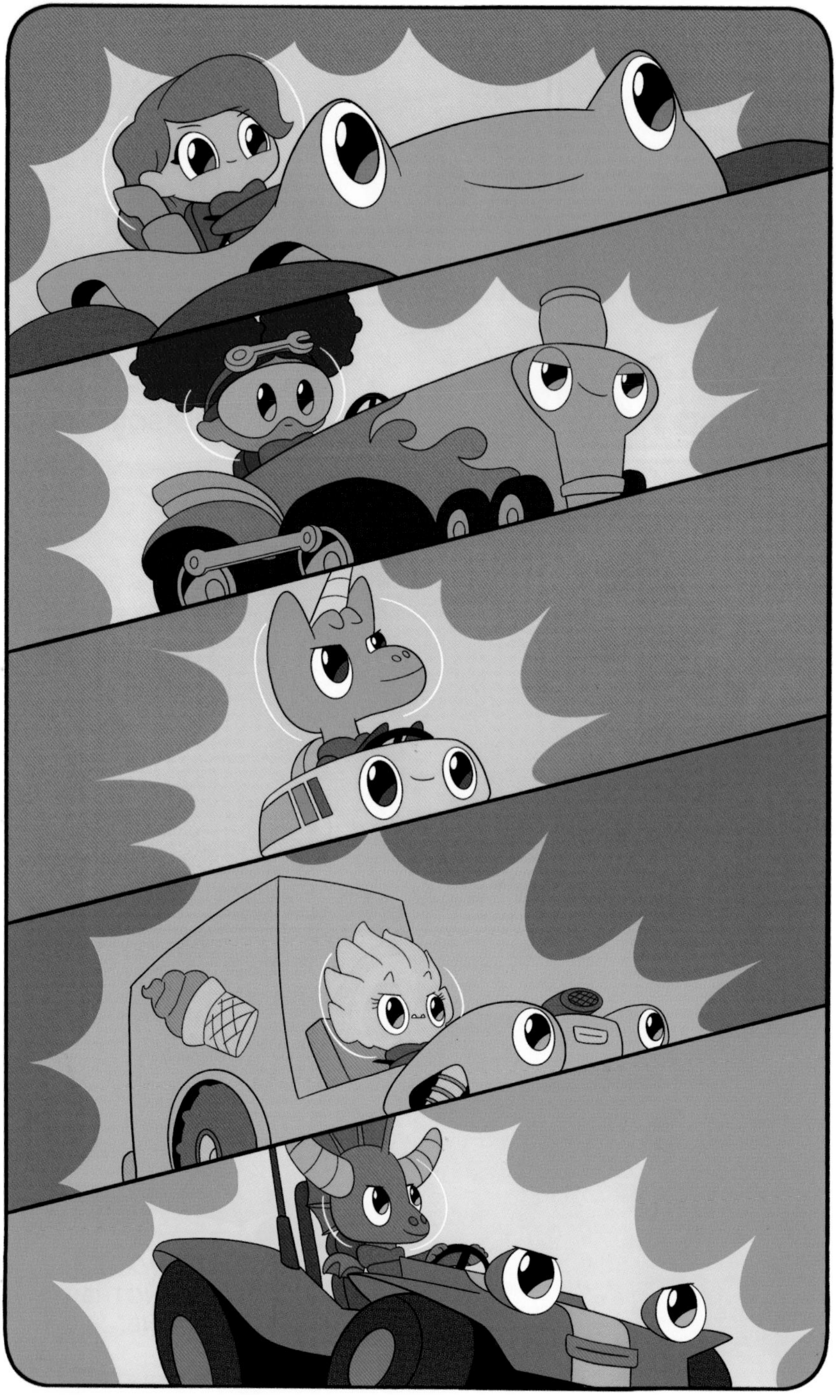

CHAPTER 13:
SPARKLY SACRIFICE

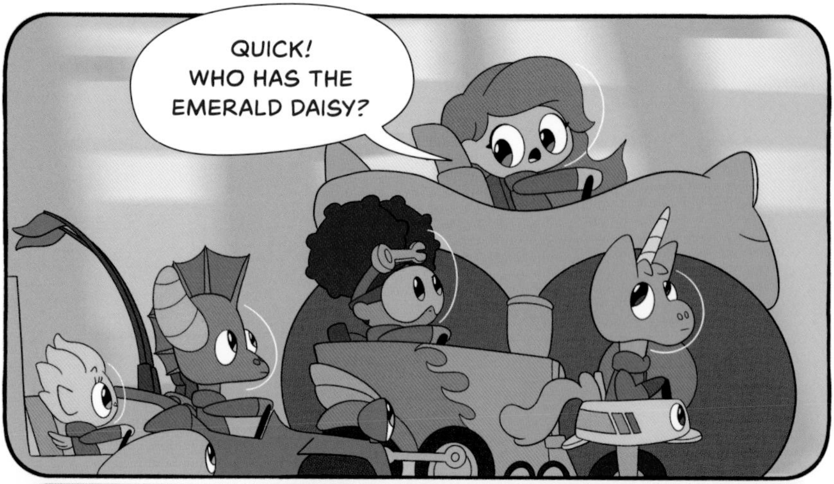
QUICK!
WHO HAS THE
EMERALD DAISY?

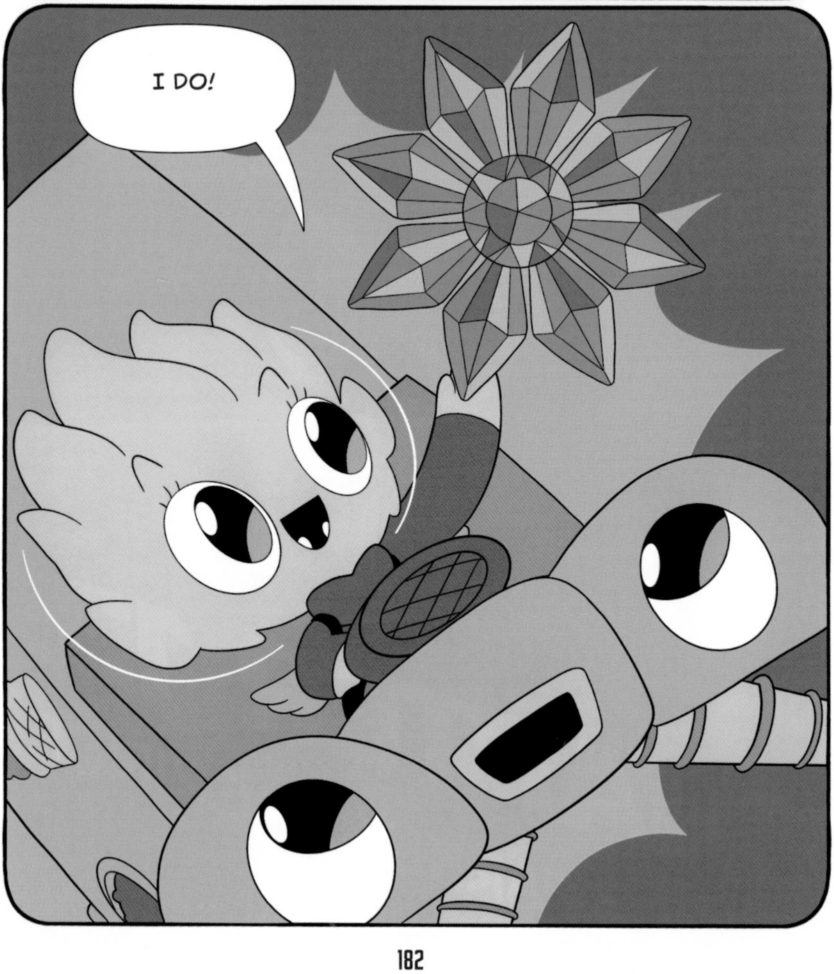
I DO!

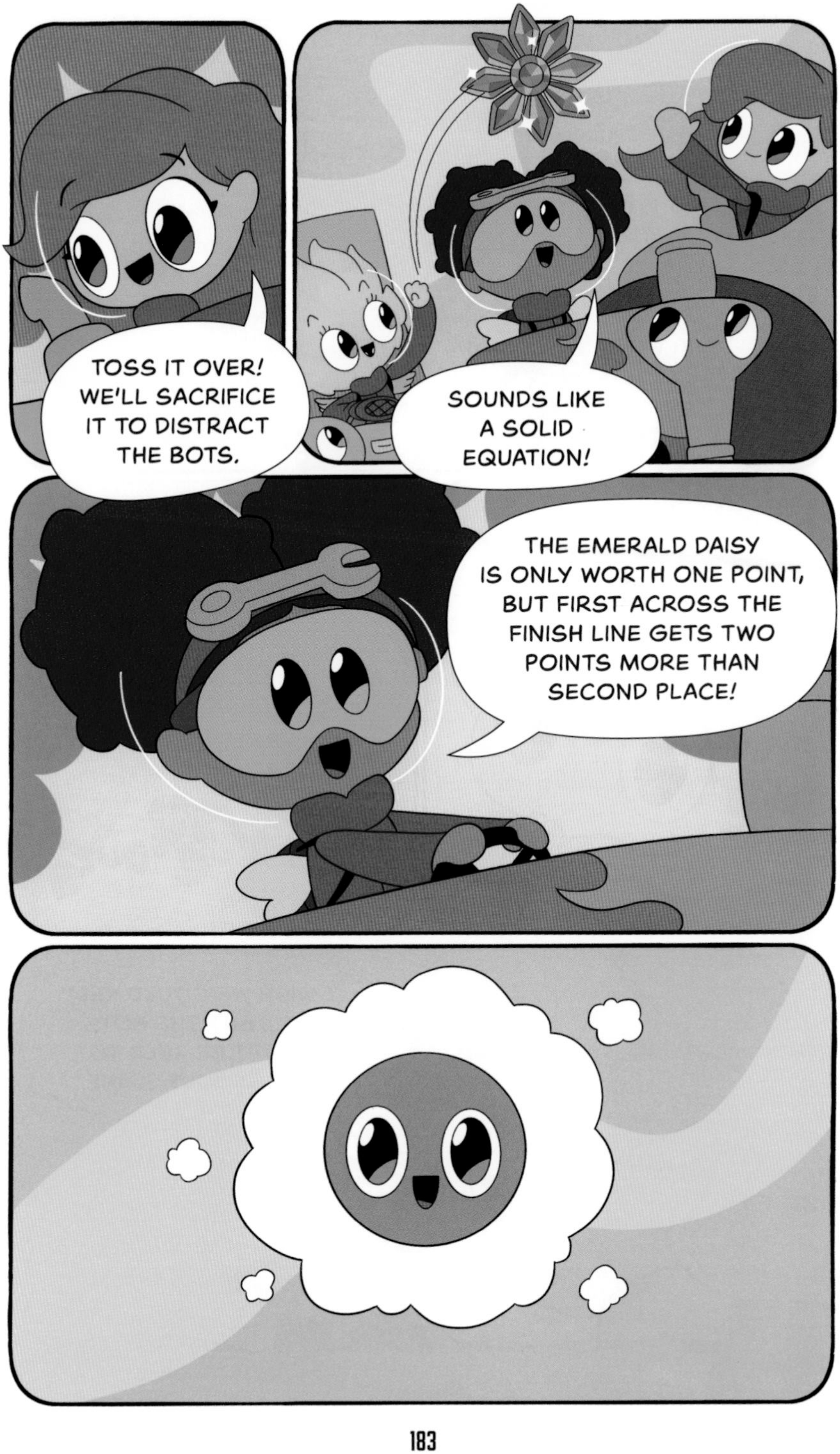
TOSS IT OVER! WE'LL SACRIFICE IT TO DISTRACT THE BOTS.
SOUNDS LIKE A SOLID EQUATION!
THE EMERALD DAISY IS ONLY WORTH ONE POINT, BUT FIRST ACROSS THE FINISH LINE GETS TWO POINTS MORE THAN SECOND PLACE!

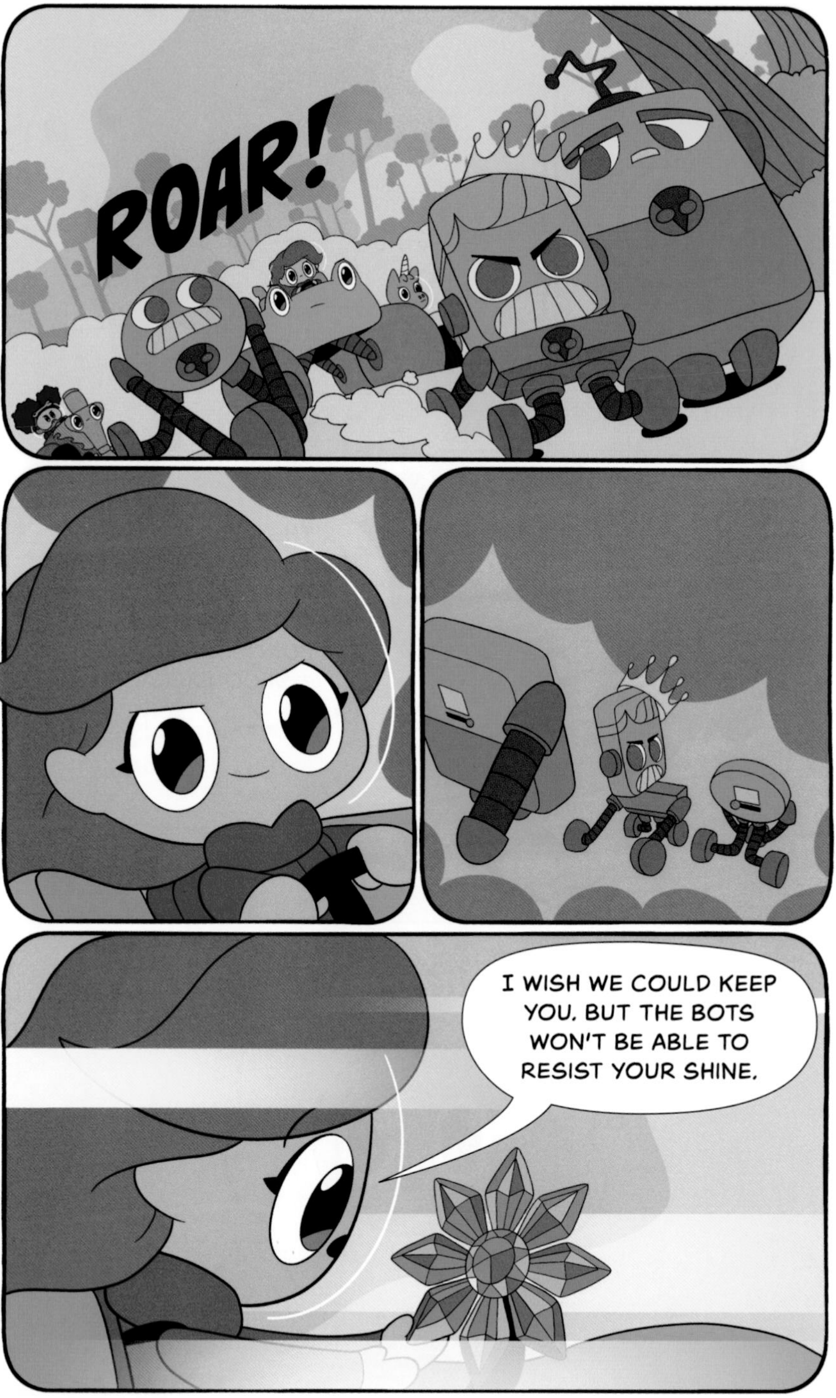
ROAR!
I WISH WE COULD KEEP YOU, BUT THE BOTS WON'T BE ABLE TO RESIST YOUR SHINE.

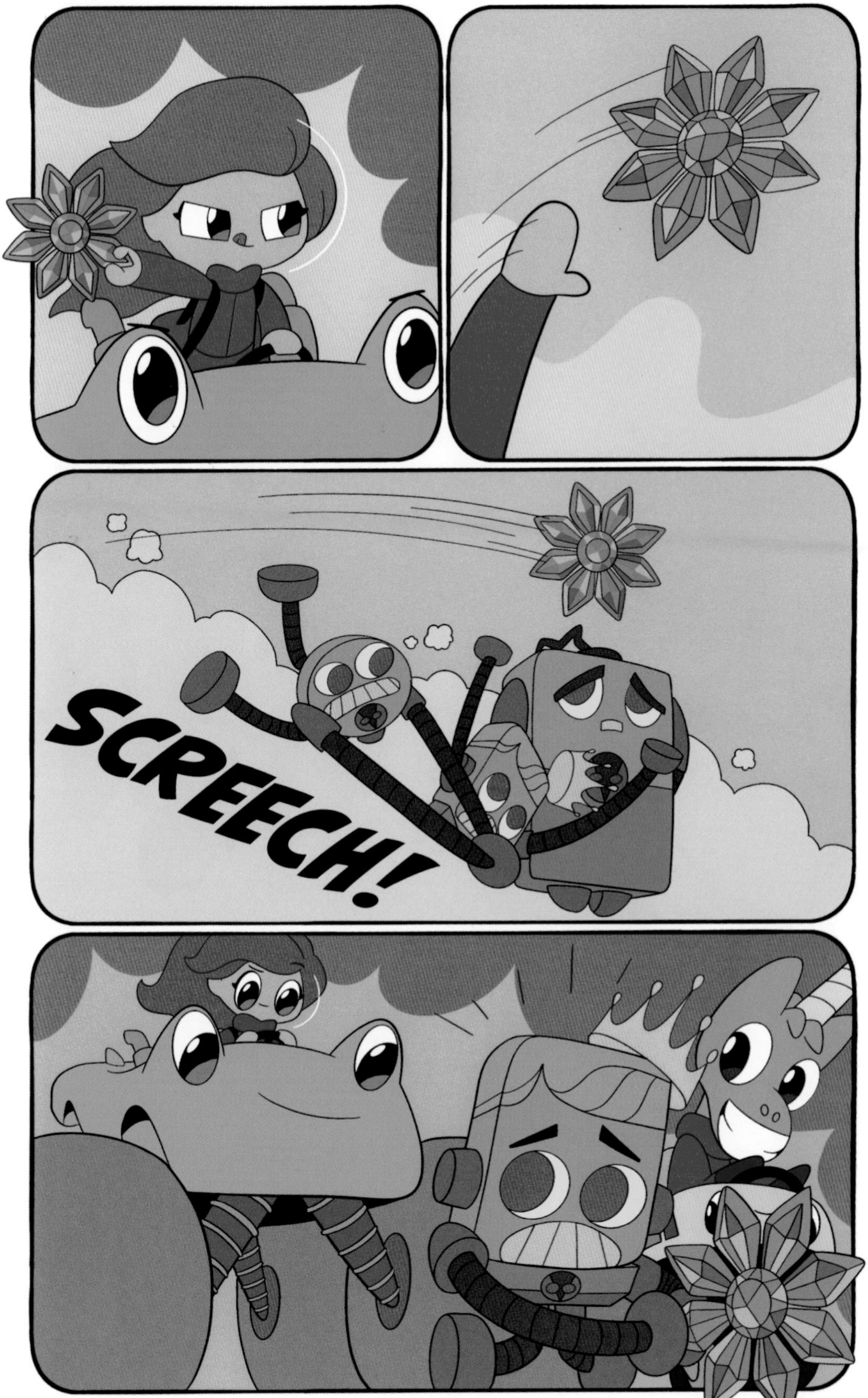
SCREECH!

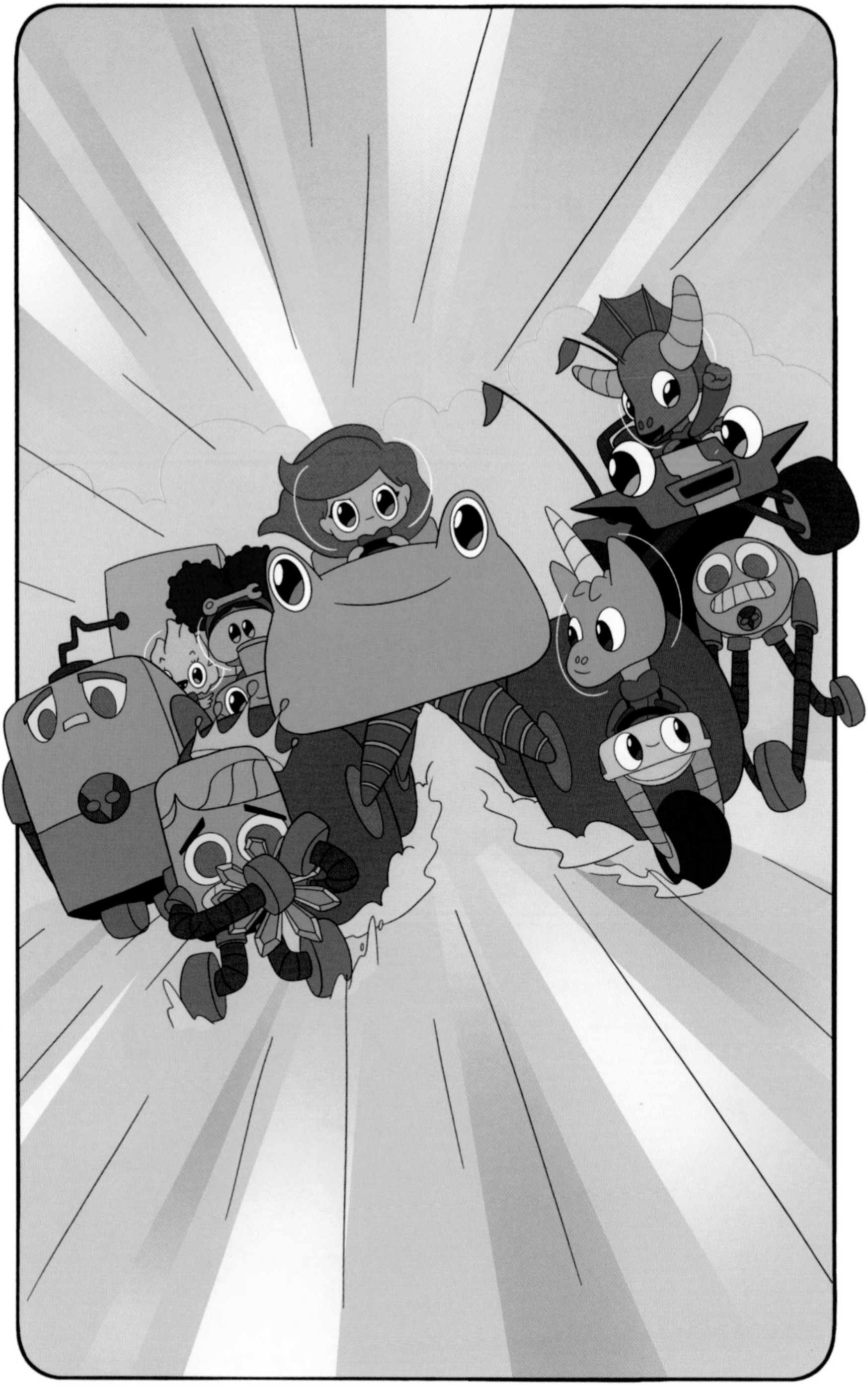

CHAPTER 14:
WINNER!

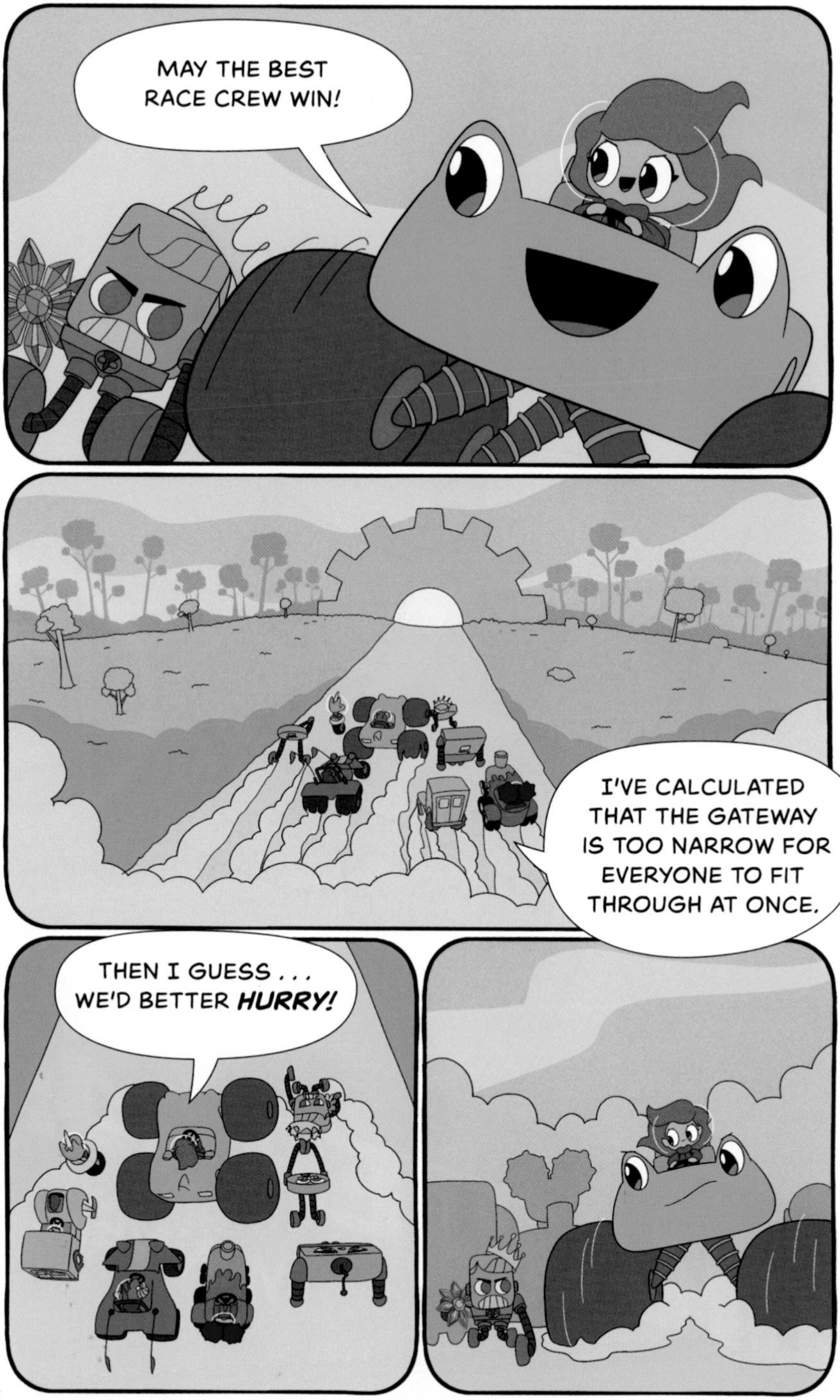
MAY THE BEST RACE CREW WIN!
I'VE CALCULATED THAT THE GATEWAY IS TOO NARROW FOR EVERYONE TO FIT THROUGH AT ONCE.
THEN I GUESS . . . WE'D BETTER **HURRY!**

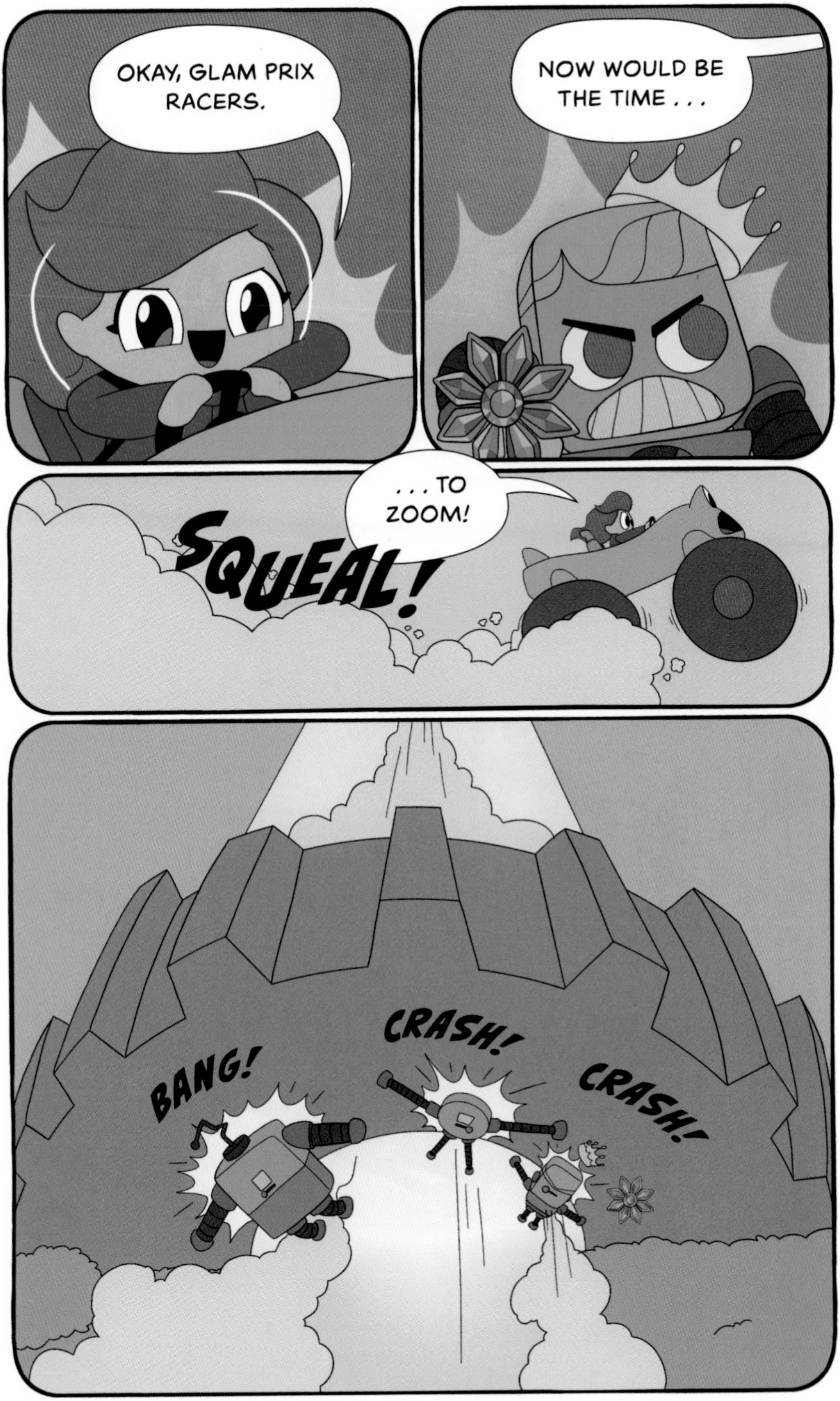
OKAY, GLAM PRIX RACERS.
NOW WOULD BE THE TIME . . .
. . . TO ZOOM!
SQUEAL!
CRASH!
BANG!
CRASH!

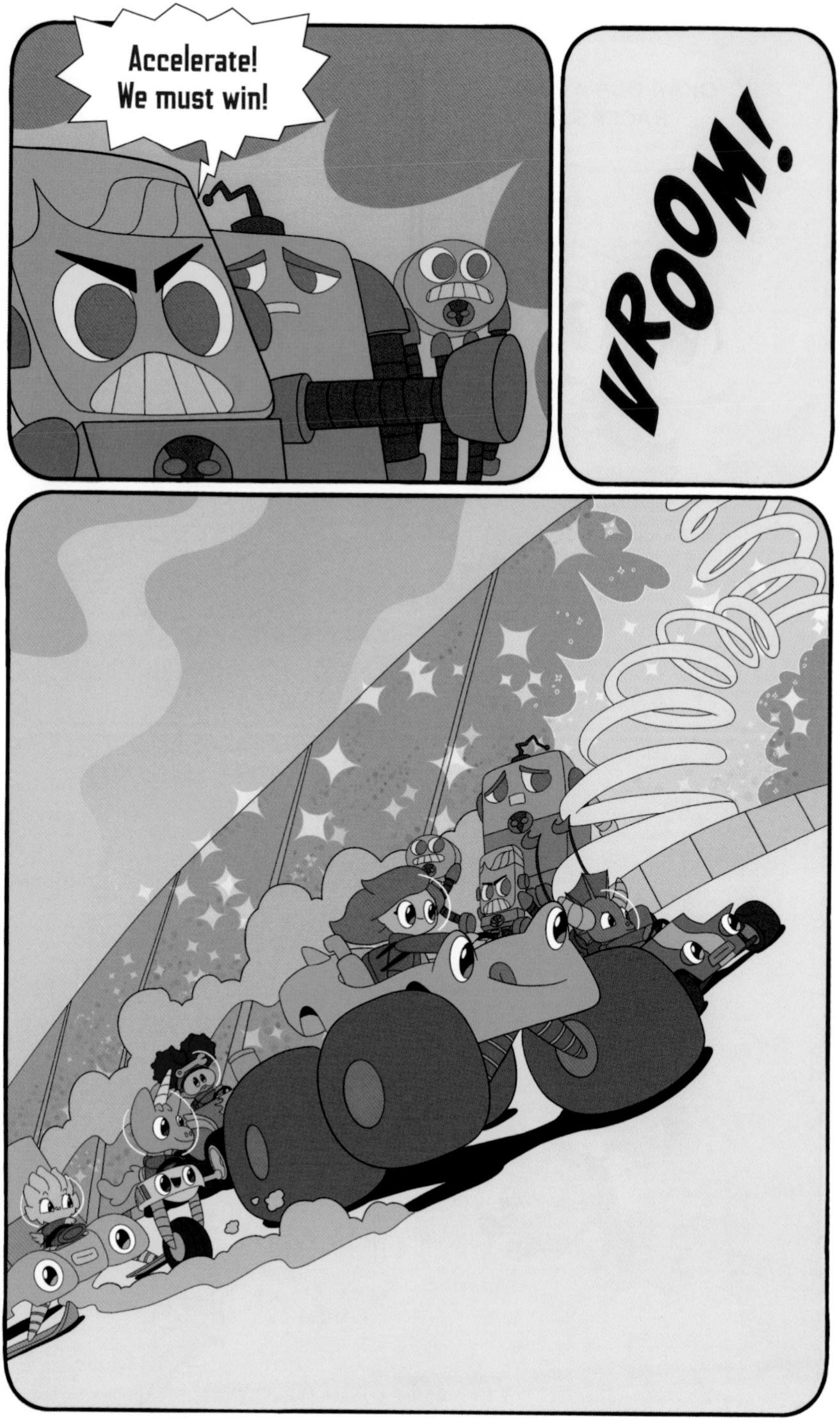
Accelerate!
We must win!
VROOM!

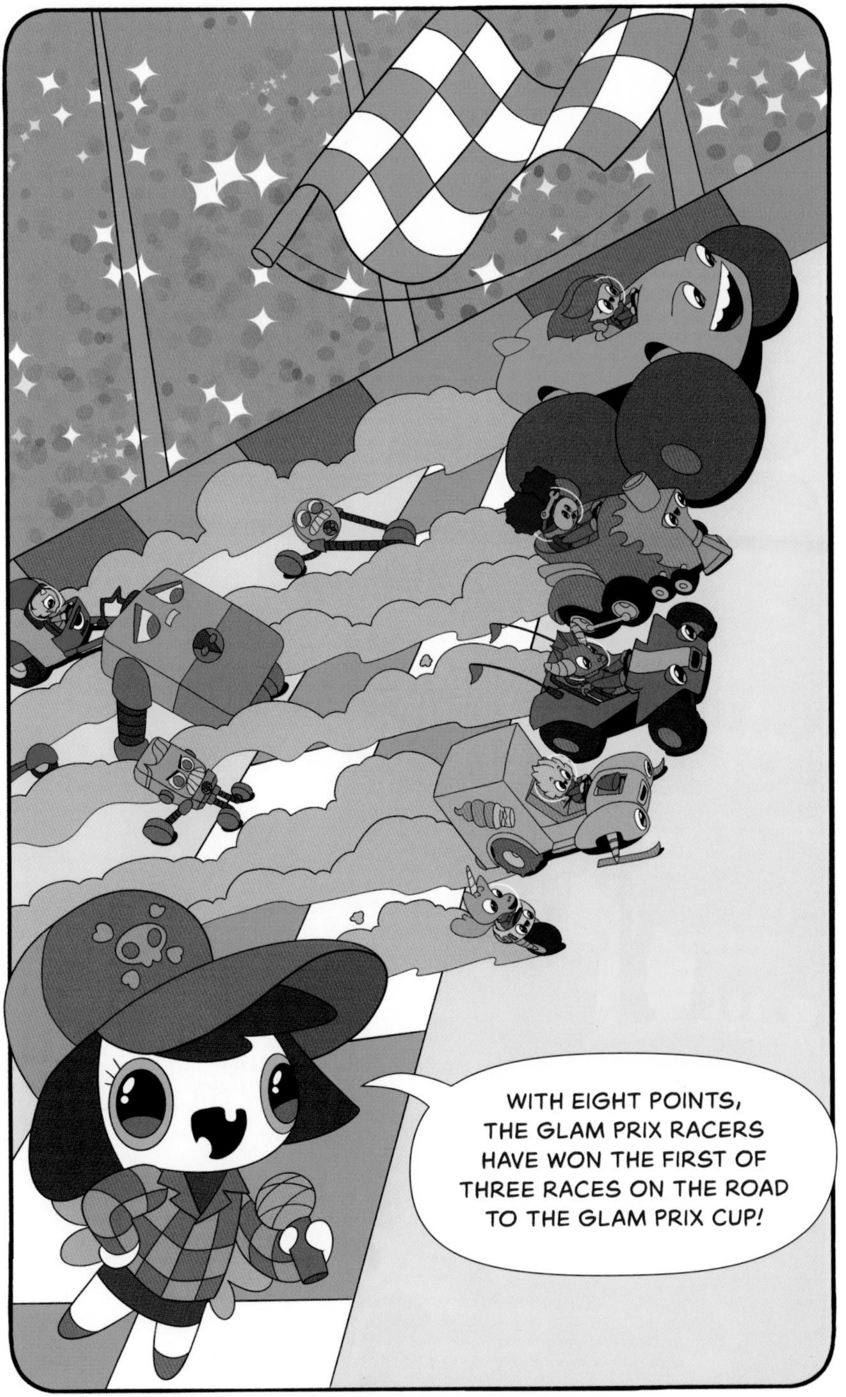
WITH EIGHT POINTS, THE GLAM PRIX RACERS HAVE WON THE FIRST OF THREE RACES ON THE ROAD TO THE GLAM PRIX CUP!

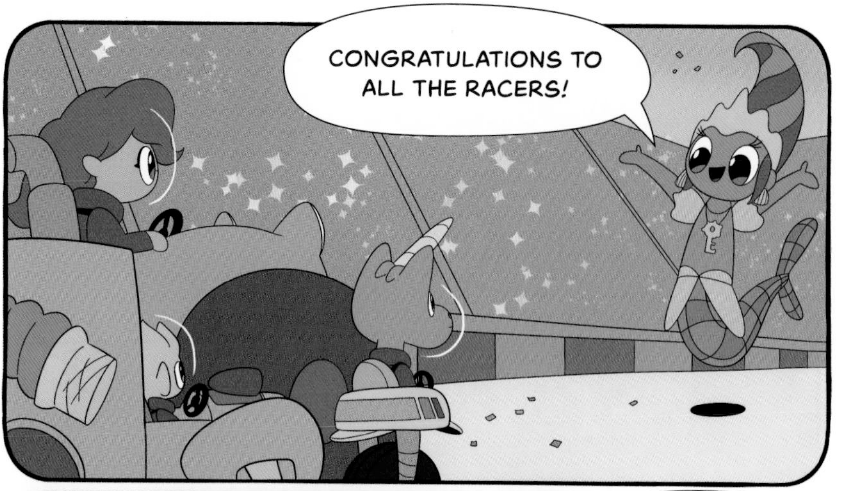
CONGRATULATIONS TO ALL THE RACERS!

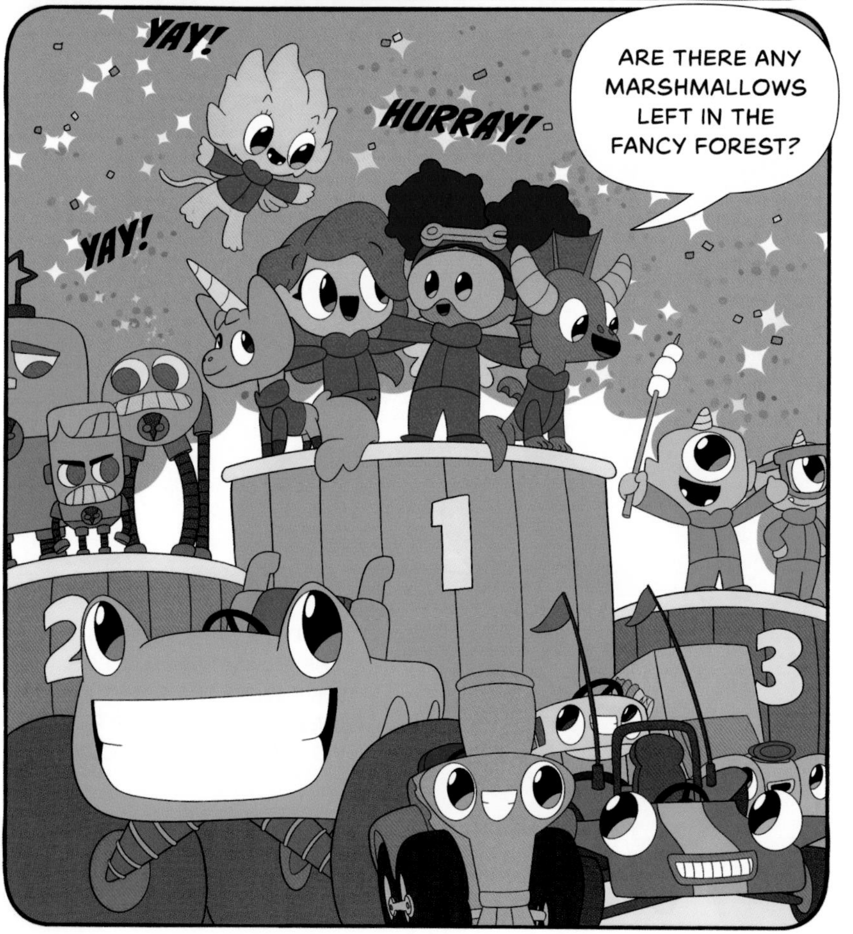
YAY!
HURRAY!
YAY!
ARE THERE ANY MARSHMALLOWS LEFT IN THE FANCY FOREST?
1
2
3

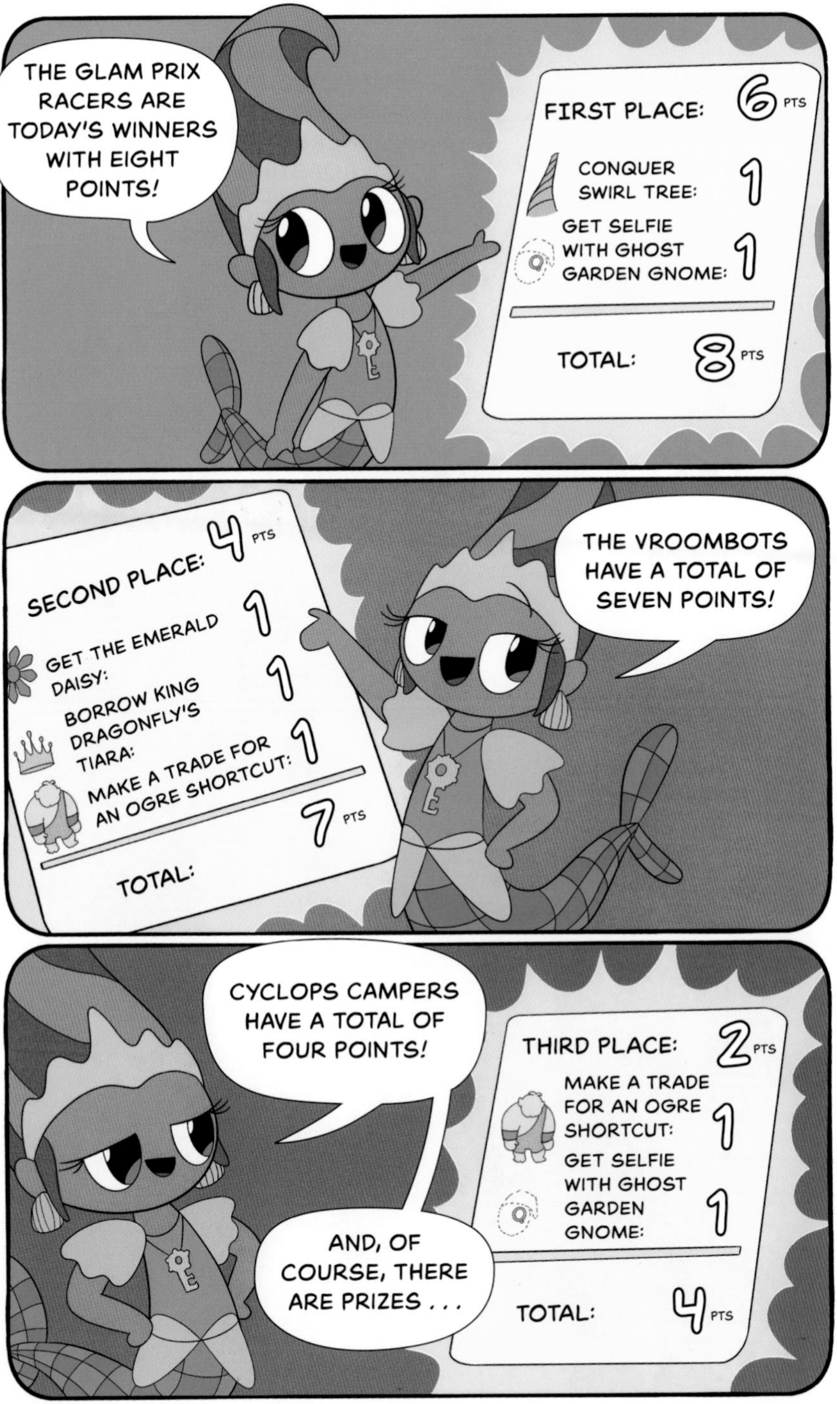
THE GLAM PRIX RACERS ARE TODAY'S WINNERS WITH EIGHT POINTS!
FIRST PLACE: 6 PTS
CONQUER SWIRL TREE: 1
GET SELFIE WITH GHOST GARDEN GNOME: 1
TOTAL: 8 PTS
THE VROOMBOTS HAVE A TOTAL OF SEVEN POINTS!
SECOND PLACE: 4 PTS
GET THE EMERALD DAISY: 1
BORROW KING DRAGONFLY'S TIARA: 1
MAKE A TRADE FOR AN OGRE SHORTCUT: 1
TOTAL: 7 PTS
CYCLOPS CAMPERS HAVE A TOTAL OF FOUR POINTS!
THIRD PLACE: 2 PTS
MAKE A TRADE FOR AN OGRE SHORTCUT: 1
GET SELFIE WITH GHOST GARDEN GNOME: 1
TOTAL: 4 PTS
AND, OF COURSE, THERE ARE PRIZES . . .

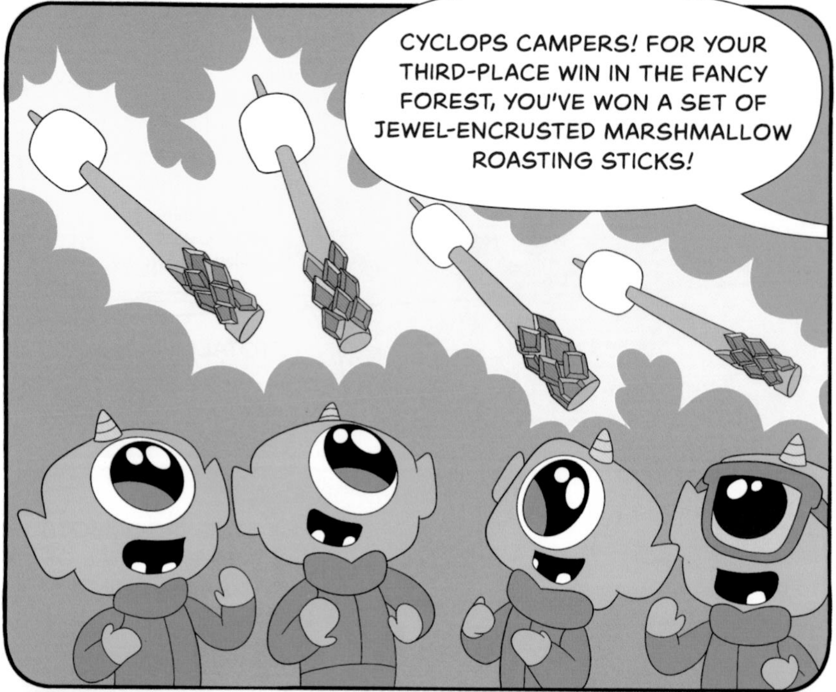
CYCLOPS CAMPERS! FOR YOUR THIRD-PLACE WIN IN THE FANCY FOREST, YOU'VE WON A SET OF JEWEL-ENCRUSTED MARSHMALLOW ROASTING STICKS!

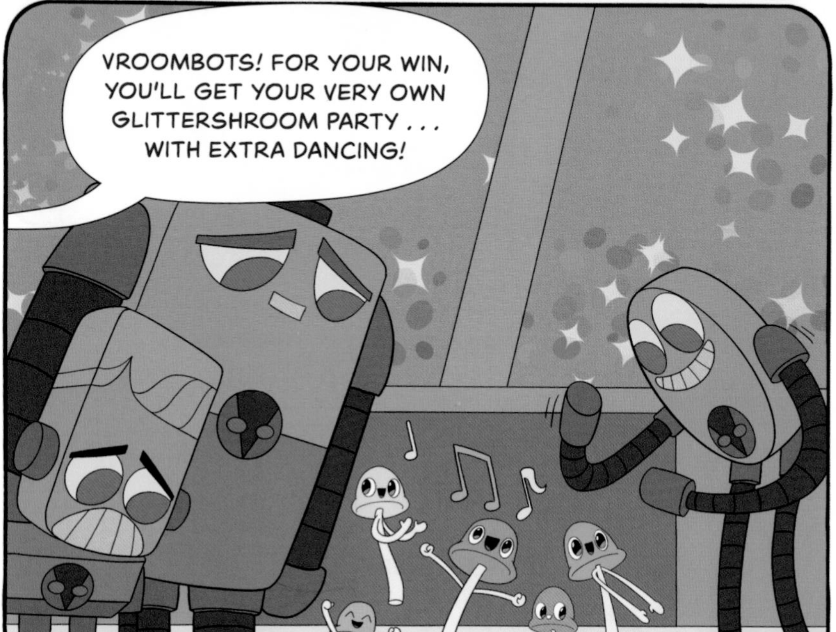
VROOMBOTS! FOR YOUR WIN, YOU'LL GET YOUR VERY OWN GLITTERSHROOM PARTY . . . WITH EXTRA DANCING!

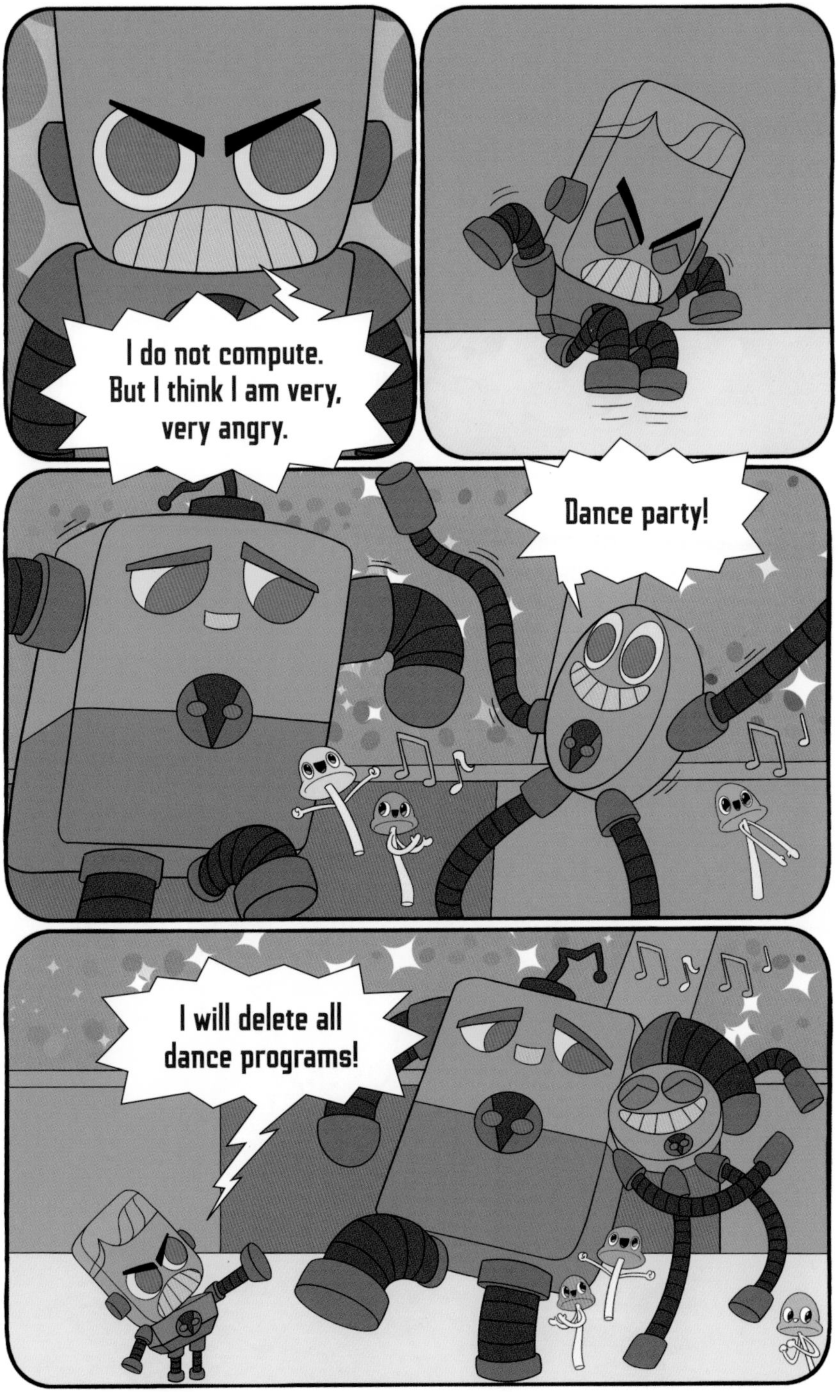
I do not compute. But I think I am very, very angry.
Dance party!
I will delete all dance programs!

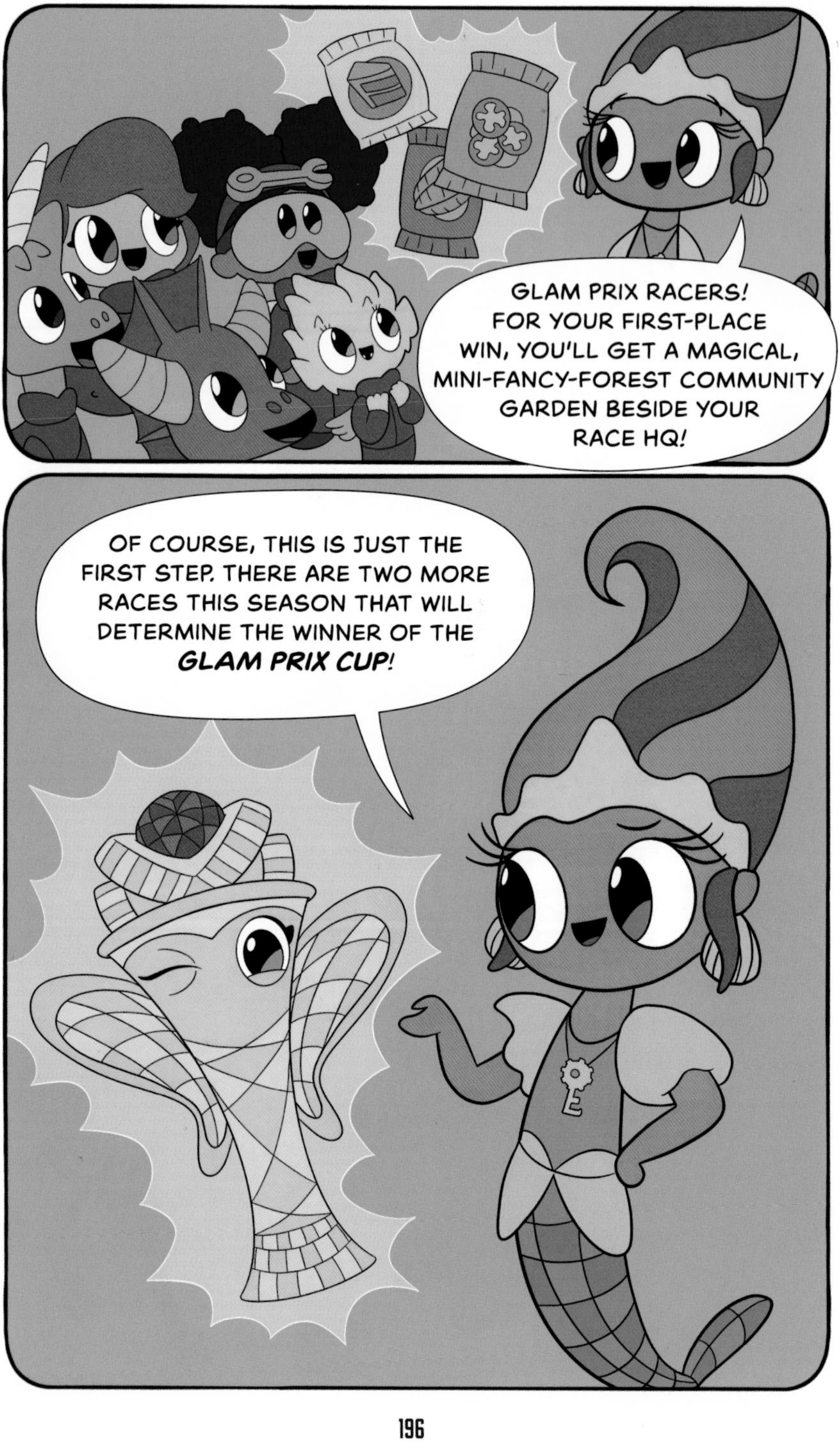
GLAM PRIX RACERS! FOR YOUR FIRST-PLACE WIN, YOU'LL GET A MAGICAL, MINI-FANCY-FOREST COMMUNITY GARDEN BESIDE YOUR RACE HQ!
OF COURSE, THIS IS JUST THE FIRST STEP. THERE ARE TWO MORE RACES THIS SEASON THAT WILL DETERMINE THE WINNER OF THE ***GLAM PRIX CUP***!

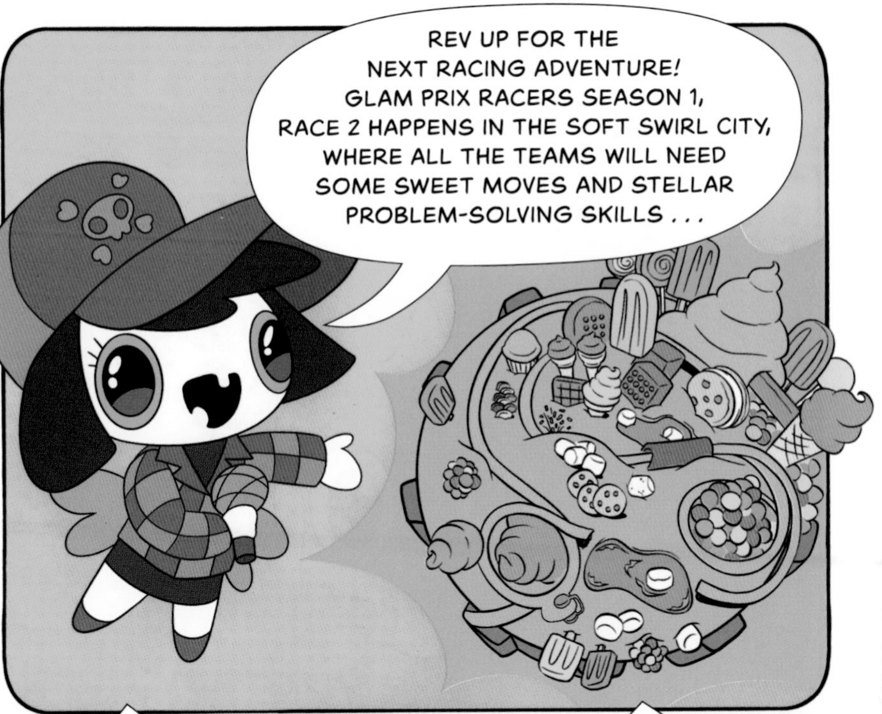
REV UP FOR THE NEXT RACING ADVENTURE! GLAM PRIX RACERS SEASON 1, RACE 2 HAPPENS IN THE SOFT SWIRL CITY, WHERE ALL THE TEAMS WILL NEED SOME SWEET MOVES AND STELLAR PROBLEM-SOLVING SKILLS . . .

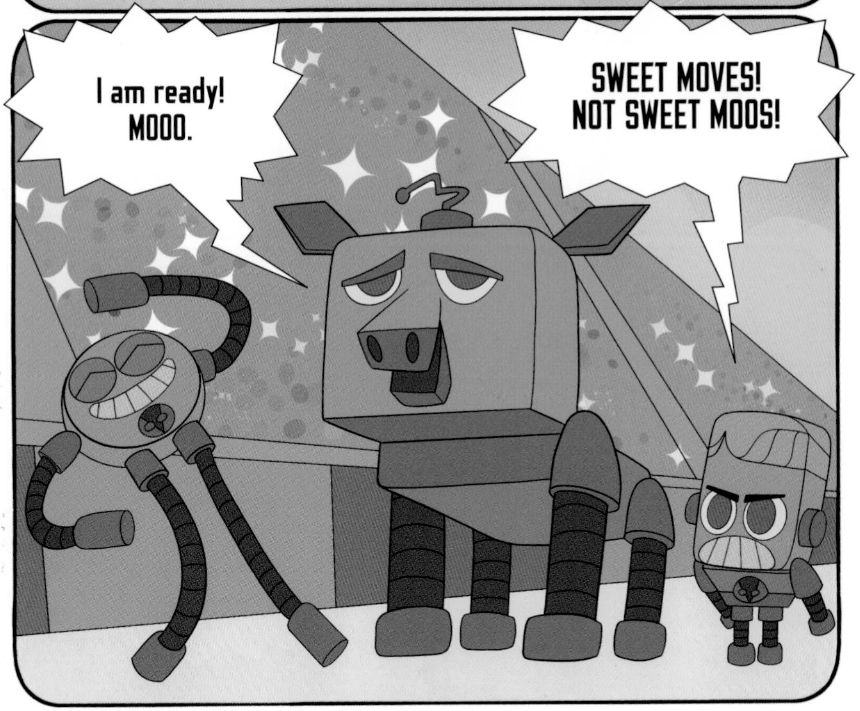
I am ready! MOOO.
SWEET MOVES! NOT SWEET MOOS!

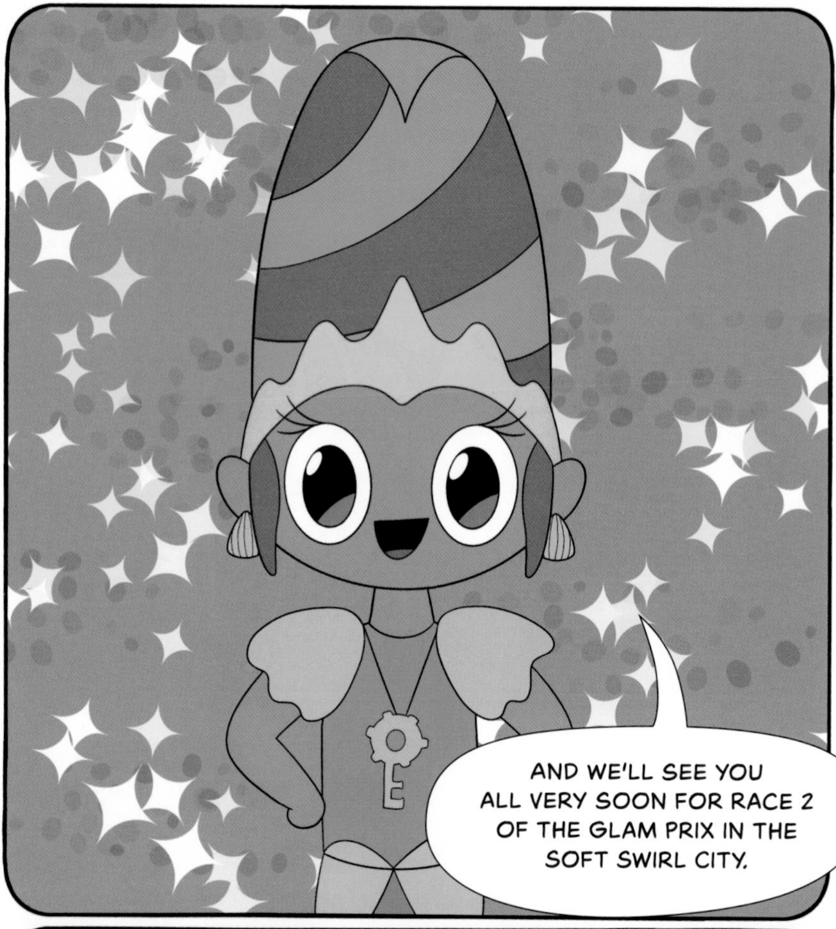
AND WE'LL SEE YOU ALL VERY SOON FOR RACE 2 OF THE GLAM PRIX IN THE SOFT SWIRL CITY.

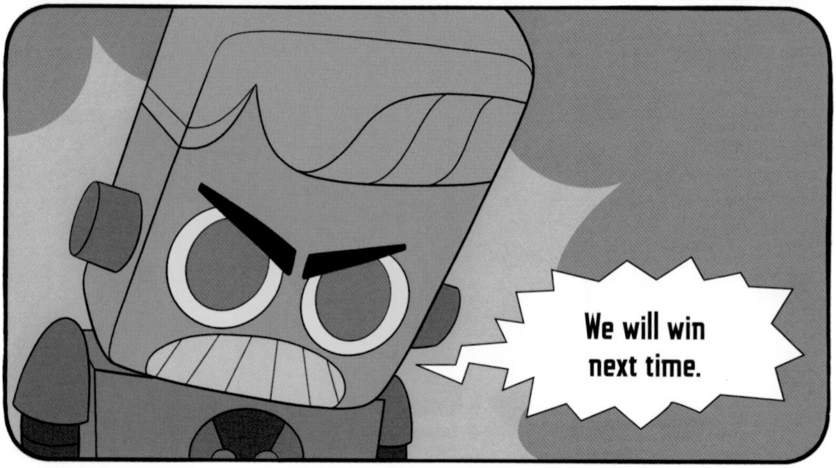
We will win next time.

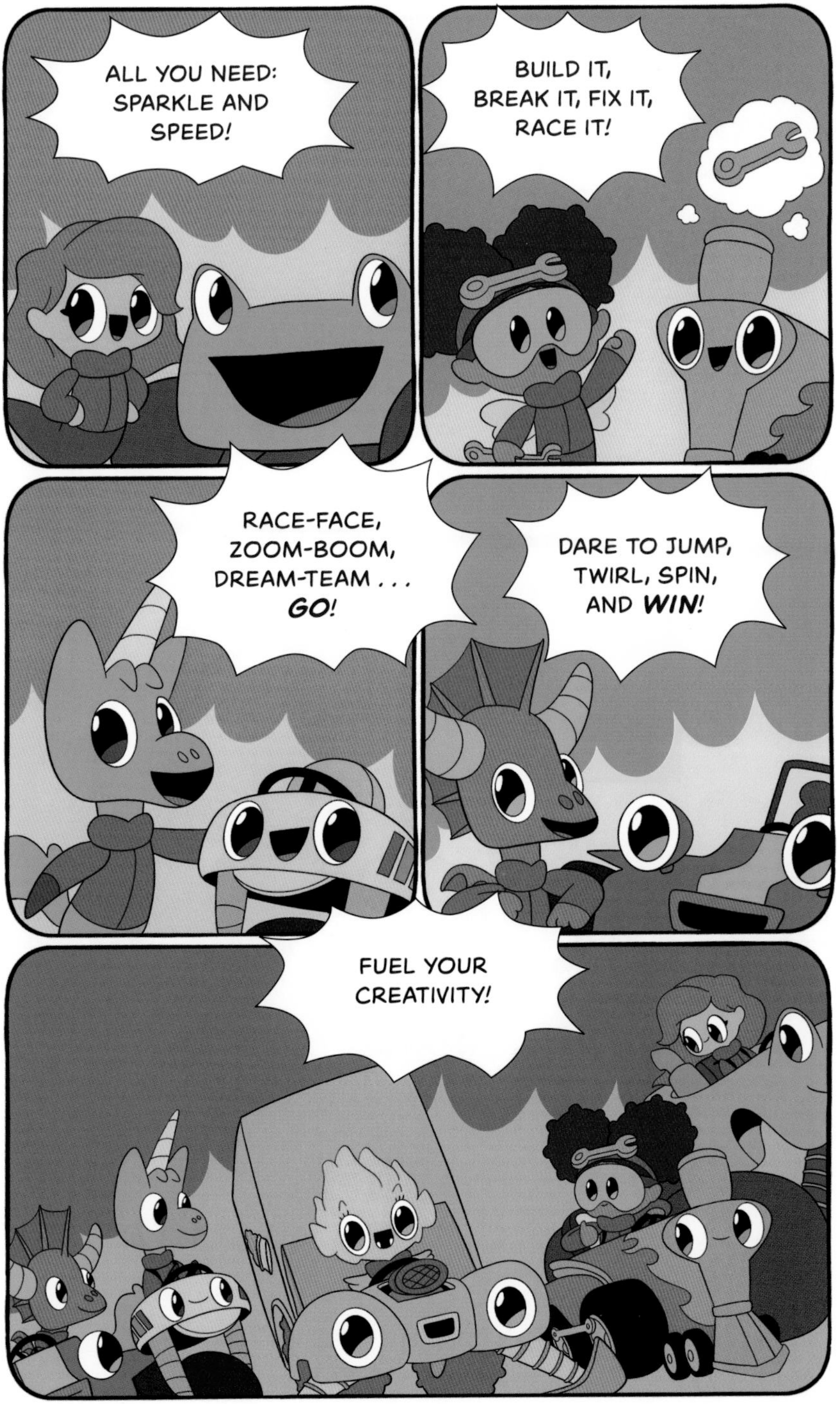
ALL YOU NEED: SPARKLE AND SPEED!
BUILD IT, BREAK IT, FIX IT, RACE IT!
RACE-FACE, ZOOM-BOOM, DREAM-TEAM . . . *GO*!
DARE TO JUMP, TWIRL, SPIN, AND *WIN*!
FUEL YOUR CREATIVITY!

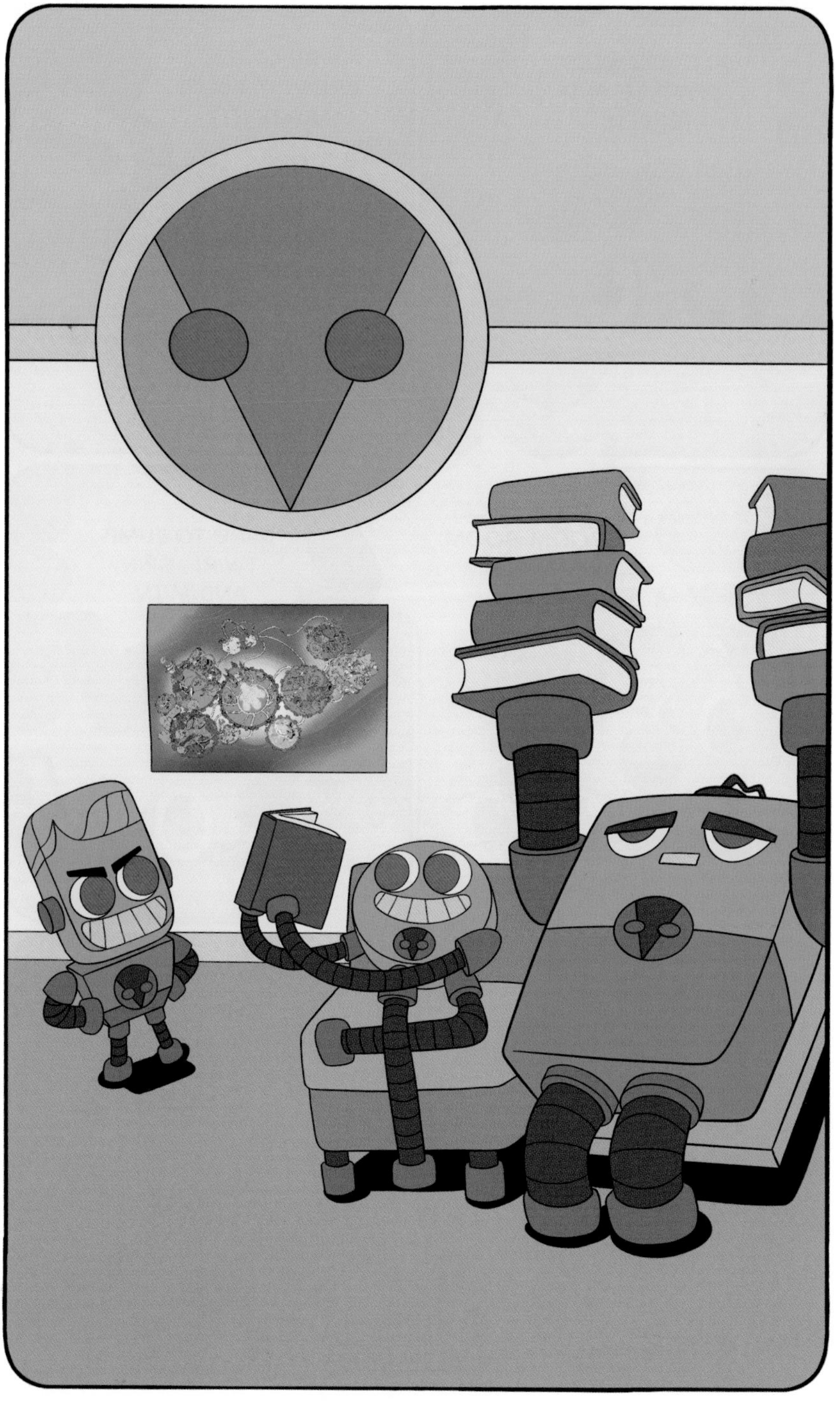

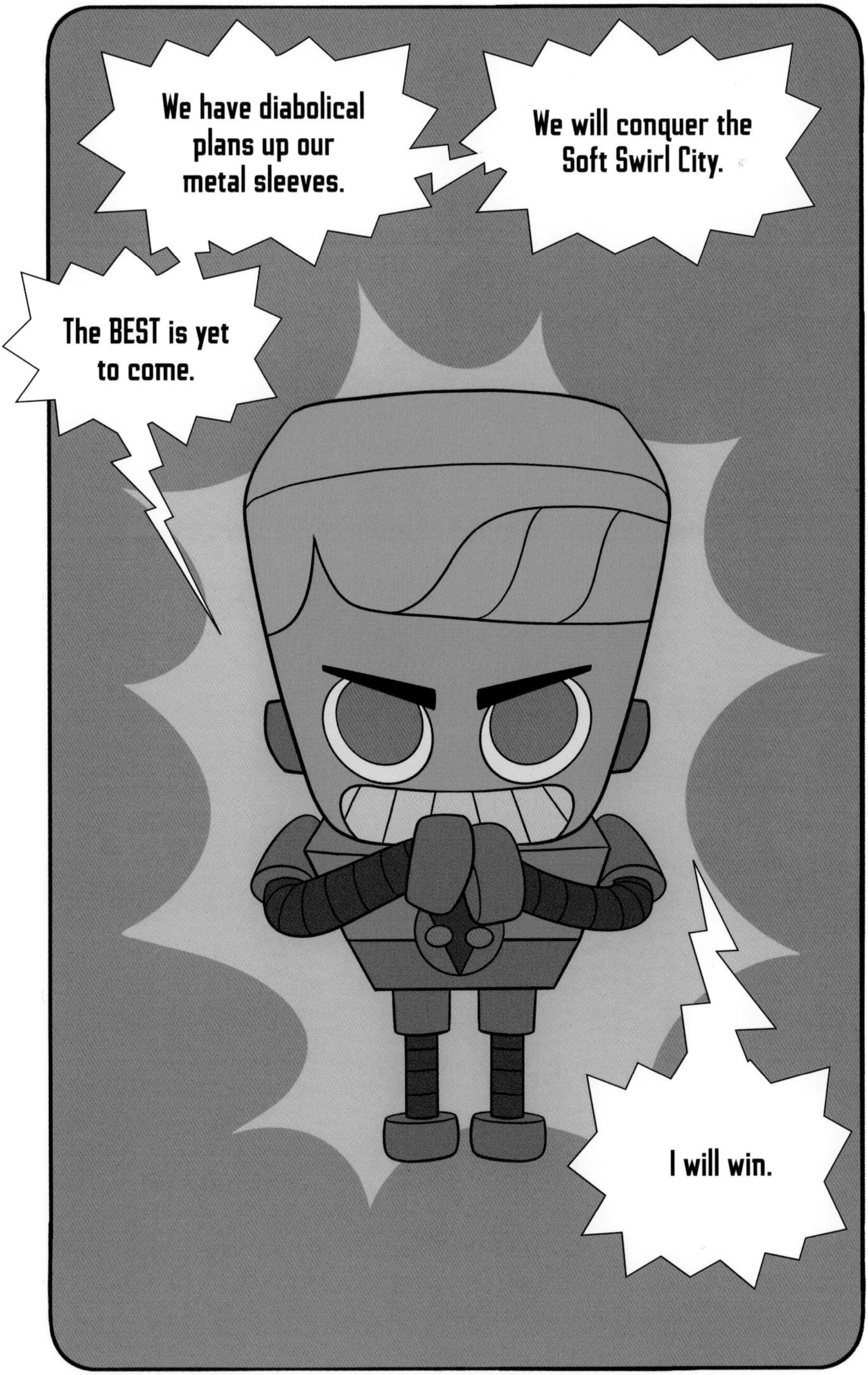
We have diabolical plans up our metal sleeves.
We will conquer the Soft Swirl City.
The BEST is yet to come.
I will win.

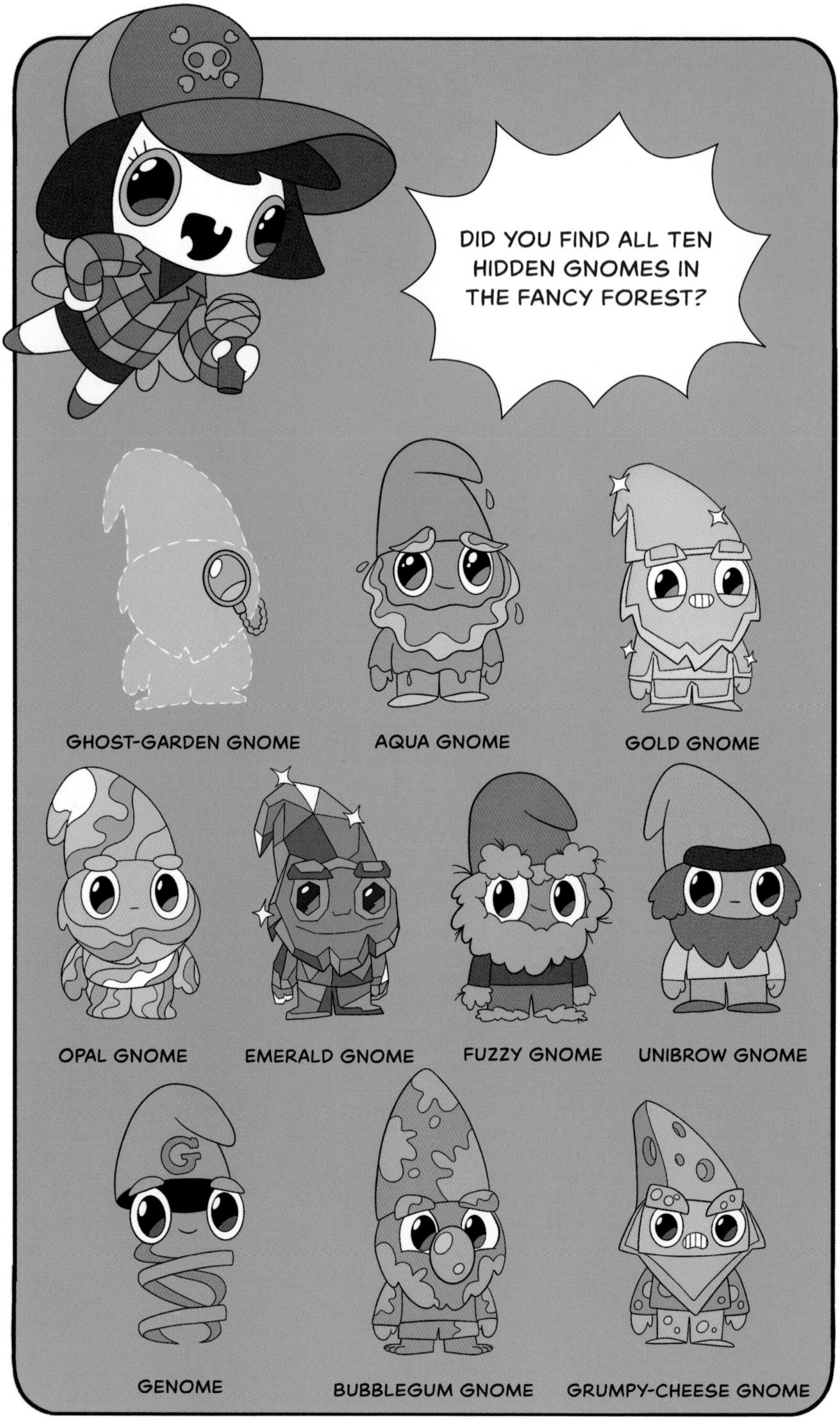
DID YOU FIND ALL TEN HIDDEN GNOMES IN THE FANCY FOREST?
GHOST-GARDEN GNOME
AQUA GNOME
GOLD GNOME
OPAL GNOME
EMERALD GNOME
FUZZY GNOME
UNIBROW GNOME
GENOME
BUBBLEGUM GNOME
GRUMPY-CHEESE GNOME

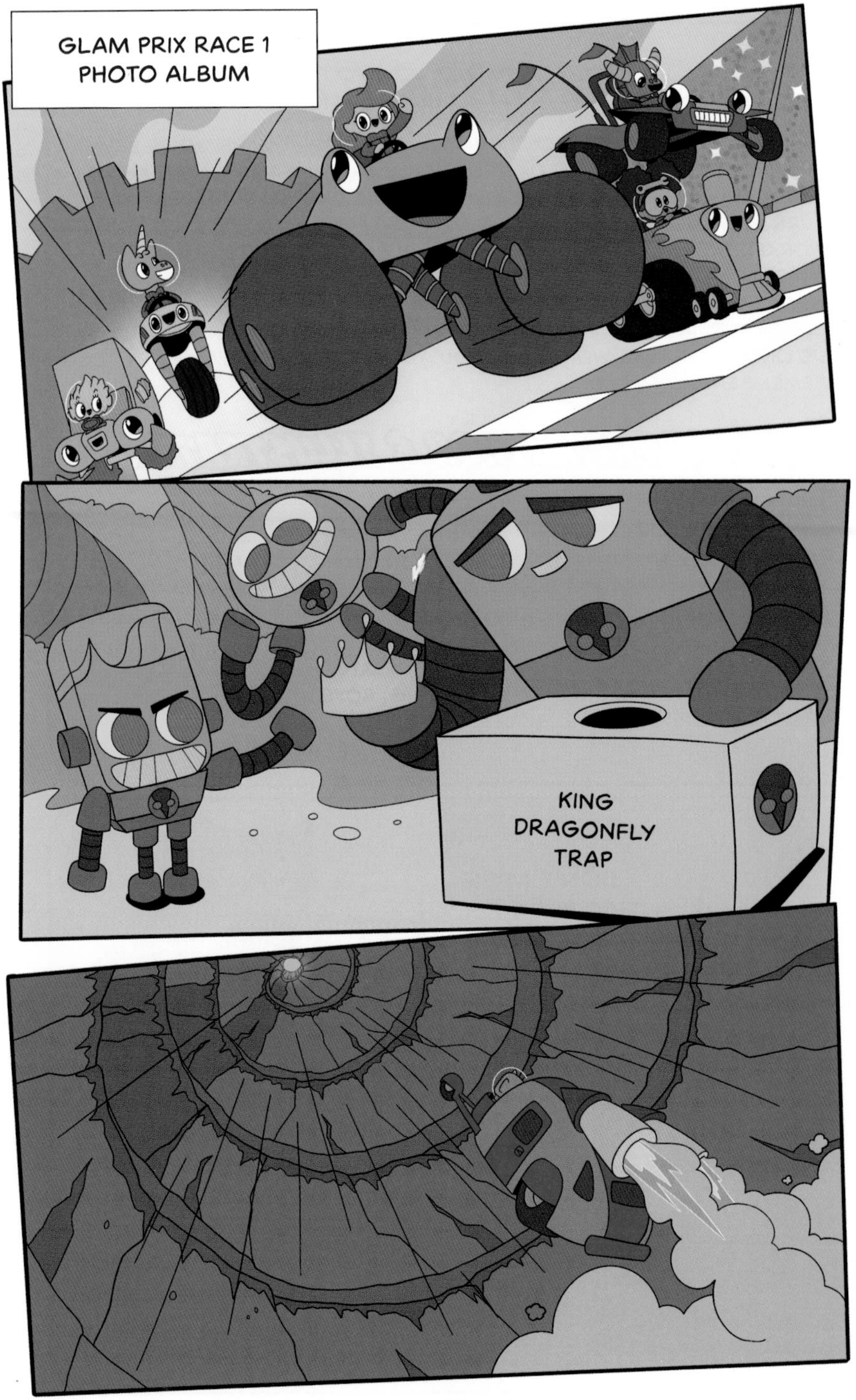
GLAM PRIX RACE 1
PHOTO ALBUM
KING
DRAGONFLY
TRAP

ACKNOWLEDGMENTS

WE BELIEVE IN THE POWER OF TEAMWORK. OVER THE YEARS, WE'VE BEEN LUCKY ENOUGH TO BE PART OF SOME TRULY GREAT TEAMS AND WE KNOW THAT COLLABORATING WITH INSPIRING PEOPLE ON A SHARED VISION CAN TURN INTO MAGICAL THINGS. TO ALL THE CREATIVE POWERHOUSES WE'VE WORKED WITH, LEARNED FROM, OR BEEN MENTORED BY, THANK YOU. SUPERSONIC, SPARKLY THANKS TO GEMMA COOPER, ERIN STEIN, THE WHOLE MACMILLAN IMPRINT TEAM, AND LIBRARIANS EVERYWHERE. AND BIG GRATITUDE TO OUR BRILLIANT FRIEND, KRISTENE TURNER, WHO TOLD US ONCE THAT, "LIFE WORKS FOR YOU. TRUST THE JOURNEY." WE TRY TO REMEMBER IT EVERY DAY.

ABOUT THE AUTHOR & ILLUSTRATOR

DEANNA KENT AND ***NEIL HOOSON*** HAVE WORKED ON BOOKS, BRAND AND MARKETING CAMPAIGNS, AND INTERACTIVE EXPERIENCES. DEANNA LOVES TWINKLE STRING LIGHTS, BLACK LICORICE, AND EDNA MODE, AND SHE MAY BE THE ONLY PERSON ON THE PLANET WHO SAYS "TEAMWORK MAKES THE DREAM WORK" WITHOUT A HINT OF SARCASM. NEIL IS KING OF A LES PAUL GUITAR, MAKES A KILLER SMOKED BRISKET, AND REALLY WANTS ALIENS TO LAND IN HIS BACKYARD. BY FAR, THEIR GREATEST CREATIVE CHALLENGE IS RAISING FOUR (VERY BUSY, VERY AMAZING) BOYS. GLAM PRIX RACERS IS THEIR FIRST GRAPHIC NOVEL SERIES.

DON'T MISS THIS PURR-FECT SERIES!
SNAZZY CAT CAPERS
DEANNA KENT
ILLUSTRATED BY NEIL HOOSON
SNAZZY CAT CAPERS
THE FAST AND THE FURRIEST
DEANNA KENT
ILLUSTRATED BY NEIL HOOSON
SNAZZY CAT CAPERS
MEOW OR NEVER
DEANNA KENT
ILLUSTRATED BY NEIL HOOSON

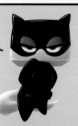

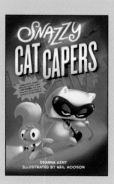

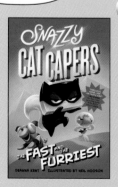

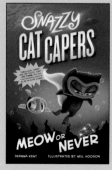